ACCIDENTAL ENCOUNTER

NOEL CARROLL

HOLLIS BOOKS

Alexandria, Va   Santa Cruz, CA   New York, NY

To Bob and Glad, the first to approve

and the last to criticize.

And to Maude who will not see the results.

ISBN:1-928781-23-3

Published by Hollis Books

Cover by Hollis Books

AUTHOR'S NOTE

The layout in Wyoming is pretty much as described in this book, although some liberties have been taken with respect to the little town of Kelly. It is indeed small, thirty residents in winter, rising to as many as one hundred in summer, but it is laid out differently than the book suggests.

To the best of our recollection, all else, on both Earth and Mantz, is correctly portrayed.

PROLOGUE

His body stretched in more directions than he thought possible as it metamorphosed from the sensible being he had been to the Earth form he was now required to assume. It hurt to move, but still he pushed on, his dislike of the mercurial environment—first one thing then quite another—a more powerful influence. There were times when it seemed the tunnel would never end. But wanting to keep moving did not make it easier to do so. With a body half one being and half another, muscles get confused and often work at cross purposes.

The problem was really the transporter tunnel itself, how it was set up; too much distance between points, forcing him and all those who came before him to spend hours when a well-spent microsecond or two could do the job. He longed for the day when a receiver could be set up at the Earth end, the day when reason would win over hysteria—the Council was terrified that some alien might stumble into it. Not there yet; not even close. First they have to feel comfortable with the idea of announcing themselves to this latest of new worlds, and who knew how long that would take.

The scene became surrealistic; he was in the middle of the warp, had to be. Soft images of lodge-pole pines and aspens were gently introducing themselves then as quickly fading out of view as if poorly-managed holographic projections. Fascinating when one got used to the oddity of it. Such vegetation would dominate at the other end, something he looked forward to seeing up close. Not that the point of insertion had been chosen with an eye toward pleasing him; it was mandated, he knew, by complicated mathematics. It was fortunate that a connection existed at all, that they were able to find that illusive spot that could be warped back to the lab. So far, one connection was all they had found, but in time, assuming the planet continued to be of interest, there would be others—no one seriously doubted that. In the interim a quiet exit into wilderness had distinct advantages, among which was no witnesses. And playing the role of a domesticated Earth animal, as was already proven by those who went before him, would make him virtually invisible.

He luxuriated in his new form. It was lighter by some fifty pounds, and what remained was distributed over four legs instead of two. It gave his spirits an upward bounce, and had his "costume" permitted such things, he would have whistled as he pressed through the last stage of the transporter and out into Wyoming's Bridger-Teton National Forest.

Hours later, as the rising sun began to soften the chill of an autumn morning, he arrived at his destination: the tiny, mountain community of Kelly, a town that for more than a year had unknowingly served as a rest stop for interplanetary explorers. When a quick glance told him there was little there to concern him, he walked without haste toward an old but still functioning post office then lowered his canine body to the ground. It was time for rejuvenation. None of Kelly's few residents were yet up, not that it mattered; there were many canines in that part of the country, and one more German shepherd, especially one whose unblemished fur testified to the love and care it must receive, would attract little attention. This and his ability to assimilate, even while asleep, the carelessly discarded thoughts of passing aliens, would insure him an undisturbed rest.

True sleep, however, was long in coming. A disturbing image kept replaying itself in his mind, and it would not be purged even as he recognized it to be beyond his control—someone else's problem. At that moment a human being, a member of Earth's dominant species, was trapped in the transporter and warping his way toward disaster.

Light years beyond the range of mountains in which the alien traveler rested, the scene was a desolate one. An atmosphere of utter hopelessness surrounded a badly confused young man as he huddled against a smokeless and oddly-glowing fire. Questions without answers, too many of them, collectively trapping his body within a constant state of shiver; this, even though the fire was not stingy in the heat it offered to those brave enough to ignore its eccentricities. His face, unshaven and lined with fatigue, accentuated the river of misery that flowed from hollow, red-lined eyes.

Misery for sure, and a touch of madness as well, the latter inevitable considering the creature off to his left, a creature who even now was leaning in a most uncanine way against a tree with an identity problem—smooth bark and blue-gray, perfectly round leaves, it had first appeared as a ghostly spirit then, as if reluctant to do so, inched its way into earthly form, nudging out an aspen in the process. Shortly before, the creature had been a copper-colored German shepherd, a common house pet and, at the time, a sorely needed companion. The young man expelled a mirthless chuckle at his naiveté—some companion! Allowing no time to prepare for the shock, it too had begun to change, at first giving the impression that it was bent on self destruction—its extremities withdrew and its fur began to dissolve. Like the forest, it wanted to be something else, something unnatural, something that did not exist in the real world. Worse was the way its eyes burned into his, and its misshapen face held to a look of anger combined with pity—it was the pity he feared most of all. It as much as said that, whatever it was to become, it had already written him off. He avoided the eyes, preferring even the fire's illogical glow to that. He shuffled closer, then closer still when the shivering failed to give up its hold on him.

Even the air was abnormal; it was heavy and odd smelling and had a red tint to it. He tried taking shallow breaths, but gave it up as he realized it would make no difference. He let his mind join his eyes in the glowing coals to give what remained of his sanity time to search for a reasonable explanation for so unreasonable a scene. In different circumstances he might have chuckled at the irony, how the intent had been to get away from it all—if nothing else, he had succeeded in that. He began to retrace the steps he had taken since marching off to what was supposed to be American wilderness—what had he done, or failed to do, that would bring him in such misery to such a god-forsaken place? In time the coals took on a new dimension, their pulsating glow assuming the role of orchestrated dancers undulating in smooth, even movements. The ghost of a smile appeared on his face as he surrendered his mind to whatever they would make of it.

C H A P T E R 1

"Give me a break, Sandy!"

"I am. 'Pain-in-the-ass,' is only a fraction of what I'm thinking!"

Mark Carter could see no trace of humor in his friend's words, which spoke of the depth of his frustration. Moping around like a mistreated puppy—and Mark knew that much of Sandy's argument was true—was getting to be more than the poor man could handle. Even so, he could thing of no better response than to stare at his accuser with listless eyes and a look of indifference. He watched as Sandy tried to shake off the anger that threatened to worm its way past his resolve.

The two of them had been partners for better than seven years, and friends for a lot longer than that, and in all this time they had not had a confrontation, at least not a serious one. Nor one so personal. Mark's eyes reflected the sadness he felt as Sandy adjusted his frame in the armless, wooden chair in which he sat then smiled to camouflage his feelings—the redness in his cheeks gave him away.

Sandy had a great sense of humor, and the way his bounced his head and his short, stocky frame as he made use of it made it easier to laugh along with him. He was four inches short of Mark's six-feet-one and a good fifty pounds heavier, and his reddish brown hair appeared to be receding in direct proportion to the expansion of his middle. He had once compared himself to Mark's athletic form and rich black hair and wondered what God had against him.

Mark began to wonder the same, only about himself rather than Sandy—what was wrong with him? For sure the problem was not business. Damnit, he was a first-rate photographer; he knew his business and knew how to please his clients. His work appeared with profitable frequency in respected magazines. Hell, there wasn't anyone he didn't like and who didn't like him.

"Is it Kathy? You two having problems? For Christ's sake, you can tell me about it. I'm the epitome of fairness and impartiality—although I feel compelled to tell you that that little lady is the best thing that ever happened to an aging pain-in-the-ass like you."

"Thanks, 'friend!'" Mark attempted a smile, even as he felt a vague hurt at the "aging" comment. Since turning thirty, he had developed a sensitivity to such things, the awareness of which only added to his discomfort.

"You're welcome! Is that it? Is it Kathy?"

Mark sigh was louder than it needed to be. "Hell, Sandy, I'm not sure I know. I know with her I'm getting a taste of my own medicine. I might want to get serious while she's still playing me the way I used to play others."

"'Might' want to get serious?"

"Well, maybe I do."

"'Maybe?'"

"Hey, cut me some slack, will you!? All right, I do want to get serious!" The words were a cut too loud and Sandy paused a moment to give the fog of animosity time to fade. He wanted to help, not cause a further separation from his friend.

"All right, we've decided Kathy is a part of this. Are you two ge...?"

Mark's interruption, and the way he handled it, turning away and not attempting to hide a cynical sneer, revealed more of his feelings, "It's not that simple, Sandy. If it were I'd sit the girl down and we'd have it out. This thing goes deeper than that."

"Well then, what?"

"Damnit, that's just it, I don't know!"

Mark began pacing the small, windowless room in which he and Sandy had retreated to talk it out. Confined by shelves that rose from floor to ceiling on three sides, his hands had no place to go, and, in anger he jammed them into his pockets, the move and the reason for it not lost on Sandy. When next Mark spoke, there was misery dripping from every word. "I feel restless. I feel itchy. I have bouts of depression and I can never nail down the reason."

"Hell, we all feel that; it's called aging."

"I'm serious, Sandy. What I feel is not in any way amusing!"

Sandy tried to assume an expression of understanding as he said, "Well, you've got to think it through, find out what's eating at you before there's nothing left for me to complain about."

"Easy to say, but less easy to do." He halted his pacing but held his eyes to the floor. "God, I feel like some kind of asshole talking like this."

"Let's just say that's a given. But even assholes can have their day in the sun."

Mark was forced to chuckle at Sandy's twisted metaphor, so typical of the man. "Well, this asshole should duck out of sight for awhile. His presence is making everybody sick."

Not knowing what Mark was leading up to, Sandy waited for more. Mark resumed his pacing, hands in pockets and eyes again glued to the floor, and when finally he spoke, his voice had a plea to it. "Hell, Sandy, I'm dumping on just about everyone I know." He hesitated for a moment before adding, "Maybe I even do it to Kathy, I don't know."

"I do. The answer is yes, you do dump on her."

Mark stared with suspicion at the still-seated figure, wondering what he and Kathy had discussed in regard to himself. Reluctant to press the issue, he focused instead on trying to release the tension in the back of his neck.

Kathy Montari was more of the problem than he cared to admit. He had never expected to be so captured by a woman, so in need of possessing her, so afraid of awakening one day and finding her gone. Kathy was easy to be with and impossible to be without. She was fascinating in a multitude of ways, some of which he had trouble defining. Her eyes were an enigma. Large and brushed with a hint of hazel, they flashed a private message beneath long, curving lashes, and even without knowing what that message was, it was enough to make conversation unnecessary. He never tired of looking into those eyes. She seldom used makeup, protesting that it made her "a slave to commercial opinion." (Finding amusement in the words and attracted by the challenge in her eyes as she spoke them, he had never asked her what that meant.) She had a natural beauty, and this extended to a petite body that offered unending promise regardless of what she wore. Her hair, which looked like something out of an Orphan Annie comic strip, and which he was not even sure he liked when they first met, was now so much a part of this woman that it was difficult to imagine her any other way. How pleasant the last year had been for the two of them; how easily they had come to flow in and out of each other's lives. So far it was from separate apartments, a left-over from a stubborn dedication to independence, but that was bound to change.

At least *he* wanted it to change. Mark smiled at the silent admission;

he of all people. But it was true; he wanted more of her, more of *us*. He shook his head. Kathy was not ready; maybe she never would be. "I wonder if I really know that woman," he said, the suddenness of his comment surprising Sandy who had seen promise in the smile. "I think she's happy with what we have going but..." He shrugged and fell silent.

About to reply, Sandy thought better of the idea. Mark needed time to work out his thoughts.

"Maybe I really should get away for a while." This time it was said with a hint of self pity, made even worse when Sandy's face lit up at the suggestion.

"You know, that's not such a bad idea. Take a vacation; go away some place; relax. Work all this crap out of your system." He pointedly ignored the hurt on Mark's face as he pushed on. "Take Kathy and dash off to the tropics or something. Better yet, you stay here and I'll dash off to the tropics with Kathy."

Mark smiled in spite of himself. Sandy Mellon was a friend to have at such times. He hoped he had not gone so far as to threaten that friendship. "Have you forgotten your wife—again?"

"I'll take her next time. For now, I have a duty to perform for a friend."

Having gained the desired momentum, Sandy fought to keep the conversation light, a task that was made easier as Mark began to take seriously the prospect of a getaway vacation. Why not indeed? He could sort things out without the pressure of well-meaning but accusing faces. Kathy would not appreciate being left behind, but she'd like what came back to her—at least he hoped she would.

"Bottom line, Mark: You can't go on the way you have for the last few weeks. It's hurting you and everyone around you. You've got to take the bull by the horn and turn him into hamburger."

Mark smiled but without much enthusiasm. "Thank you, *Doctor* Mellon."

"No problem. Just take two women and call me in the morning. Or better yet, call me after you find the two women."

Mark had little smile left in him as he stepped out of the suite of offices into the nearly empty hall then closed the door behind him. An unreasonable fear had begun to flood his gut, a fear that he was in the process of turning his world upside down, that running off to play hermit would change his life forever. The feeling did not lessen as he descended the stairs of Mellon and Carter and pushed his way out into the lonely afternoon.

CHAPTER 2

"This is ridiculous! They're all about German shepherds, and always the same size and color. And, if you believe the stories, they're all capable of leaping tall buildings in a single bound. I can't write crap like that; I'd never be taken seriously again!"

With a telephone pressed between one ear and her shoulder, Kathy Montari stabbed with two hands and a modicum of contempt at the assortment of news articles laid out on the desk in front of her, an early-morning present from her editor. She had lost more than an hour trying to decide what to make of them, then another staring out one of only two windows offered by her tiny apartment.

At the other end of the line, a snicker preceded her editor's reply. "Well, maybe you would and maybe you wouldn't, but if that's what's happening then that's what you've got to report. Besides, if you search a little further you'll know what the true story is." He paused a moment, then added, "You've got to admit, though, it makes good reading. A little way-out, but what the hell."

"Good reading? This is closer to tabloid than literature." But the protestations fooled no one and Kathy hesitated only momentarily before delivering the expected pitch. "Both of us are going to smell funny if this turns out to be nonsense. Will you guys spring for a trip to California to check it out? And for some kryptonite to protect me from the supermutts?"

Kathy smiled to herself as she put down the phone then leaned back in her chair. Even with the caveats and the not-so-subtle warnings the money man felt obligated to deliver, he had approved what amounted to a free vacation, something that did not often happen to a freelance writer.

In notable contrast to Mark, Kathy was content with her life. She enjoyed her freedom, she enjoyed the way she made her living and she enjoyed her current lover—arranging them in that order brought a momentary tinge of guilt. Most of what she wanted and needed out of a relationship Mark provided—he was different, independent like herself yet warm and close when she needed warm and close—but she was in no hurry to change, feeling comfortable in the assumption that it would all come in time. Still... She let her eyes roam the single room that was her apartment, seeing for the first time how really small it was. Here and there was clutter: a few magazines, breakfast dishes yet undone and one too many knickknacks on the breakfront which, although small, occupied a big chunk of her living space. Claiming the rest of the room was an old secretary desk, now used as a bar, a sofa and one stuffed chair, both dark brown, a kitchen table, which also doubled as a part-time workspace, and a bed normally tucked up into the wall but now demanding a place on the floor. There was evidence of Mark as well, something she once objected to but now found... comfortable.

With a sigh she had trouble understanding, she tucked the bottom of her light blue tee shirt into her jeans then reapplied herself to the literary effort still occupying the typewriter. It was about canines, anecdotal incidents meant to entertain dog lovers. Prior to the delivery of the articles, all that remained to be done was to make readable sense out of a jumble of notes. Now it was back to the drawing board.

She sorted through the articles, two of which were from California. They read as if collective imaginations had gone astray: German Shepherds performing feats that would make Lassie seem impotent. But there was enough of substance, especially considering the absence of a tie-in between sources, to warrant looking into. And, in truth, her story could use a touch of humor. She selected the most promising then decided the order in which each would be investigated. As she worked, she absently stroked the handsome animal that so often sat by her side. Although this dog was a mongrel, it was not unlike what she expected the story animals to be— medium sized, light colored and friendly. She called it "Me-too" because whatever she did it wanted to do as well, including, much to Mark's chagrin, joining them in the bedroom, sometimes on the bed itself. Let him work for it, she thought!

The opening of the apartment door and a short rap on the door— Mark's way of acknowledging her much-expressed desire for privacy— caused her to look up from her typewriter and acknowledge his presence with a smile and a silent kiss. The secretary-desk bar was sitting open and she watched as he accepted its unspoken invitation. "Care for one, babe?" he asked.

"I have mine, thanks." She turned back to her work, which, unknown to her at the moment, Mark found irritating. Despite the upbeat ending to his conversation with Sandy, he was in a mood to exaggerate anything that hinted of the negative. She listened as he wandered around the cramped apartment, dividing his attention between the window that opened onto the street and the faded avant-garde posters that he'd seen hundreds of times before. A sigh, louder than it should have been, announced his discontent.

It was impossible to ignore either the sigh or the mood. She had been looking forward to a pleasant evening, something that rarely occurred when it began in such a way. Bowing to the inevitable, she asked, "Bad day?"

Mark gave a light toss of his shoulders and said, "Just blue," but he was pleased that he had finally gotten her attention.

She stopped what she was doing and swung around to confront him, her expression now one of annoyance. She was growing weary of Mark's moodiness, the source of which escaped her, and this was as good a time as any to get it out on the table. "What is it, Mark?" she said not attempting to hide the exasperation she felt. "You seem to be 'blue' a lot lately."

Pausing to take a sip from his drink, Mark answered slowly and with thought, as if the question had been unexpected. "It's just this...emptiness I feel."

"Thanks!" But the word only brought a look of resentment to his face. He had something to say, and did not appreciate being diverted from it.

"I didn't mean it that way! It's...I'm restless, Kathy; I feel I should be out doing something, that life is passing me by—its hard to explain."

She did not appreciate being included in the contemptuous "emptiness" of his life, but this time she kept it to herself. "There's nothing wrong with your life," she offered instead, her voice and her expression both showing the hurt she was unable to hide.

"You don't understand. It's not that something identifiable is wrong with my life, it's more that...well, whatever *is* happening is not enough." He hesitated, his face a twisted plea and his hands spread wide as if to indicate the magnitude of the problem.

It was true, she did not understand, at least not entirely. She had a nagging feeling that Mark was beginning to tire of the chase. His next words did little to soothe her fears.

"I need a time-out, Kathy. Two weeks, three at the most."

The hurt turned to shock, even as she knew he would see this as further evidence of her lack of understanding.

"I made the reservations this afternoon. I'm going for...well, think of it as a long hike." He paused then, with a weak attempt at enthusiasm, added, "Wyoming." She failed to respond, and his hands moved expressively once again, this time to help him find the right words. "I need to get lost in the woods—real woods, not some adult playground." When she again failed to respond, he dropped his arms and raised his eyes to the ceiling, as if wondering what he was doing, not only to himself but to the one woman he'd ever felt serious about. In time he moved to the bar to add strength to an only half-consumed drink, spilling part of it on the wooden surface in the process—he contemptuously stabbed at the mess with his sleeve.

Kathy was waiting for the other shoe to drop. What Mark said didn't make sense. The two of them had camped together before in what was hardly an "adult playground," and she had been anything but a shrinking violet then. She had done whatever Mark did, willingly and without complaint. And what was it he wanted to escape, her?

"You'll be gone two weeks?" she asked softly.

"I'll call you if it gets to be longer than that."

"How can you call if you're 'lost in the woods'?" she added spitefully.

Mark's ire returned in both expression and voice. "I mean I'll call when I can. It's only two weeks, not forever."

"No?" she asked softly.

"Damnit, Kathy, I'm not doing this to hurt you! If you can't understand that then please just try to accept it!"

"But you're not qualified to travel in that kind of wilderness!" It was not the thing to say and she knew it immediately.

"Damnit, I know what the hell I'm doing!" He resumed his pacing and the exaggerated hand movements, and when next he spoke, he talked more to the floor than to her. "Damnit, you know what I've been like lately. Even Sandy says I should get away!"

She could no longer keep her voice level. "He didn't say you should lose yourself in some God-forsaken wilderness; he just said you should get your act together!"

"Well it's the same thing! And how do you know what he said? You two decide these things behind my back?"

Another mistake; the discussion was going from bad to worse. "Mark, Sandy is your friend. He's concerned about you; we all are. What's wrong with us talking about it?" By now she wanted to avoid saying anything at all, but this was proving increasingly difficult to manage. "Yes, I know how you've been, Mark, and I'm trying very hard to understand it. It hasn't done much for our relationship you know! Neither will this," she added softly.

"Damnit, don't do that, Kathy. I want us to succeed as much if not more than you do. That's not the problem...at least not the whole problem." As evidenced by the sharp rise of her head and the moisture that began filling her eyes, Mark knew he still had a tendency to hurt. He put a hand to his forehead, closed his eyes and began to rub.

Kathy wondered whether she had waited too long to respond to Mark's unspoken plea for a more formal relationship. Or whether it would have mattered in any case. She got up slowly, knowing that to say anything at that moment would compound mistakes already made. At the bar, after refilling her own drink, she subconsciously took a towel and rubbed the spot where Mark had spilled his, unaware of the nagging effect this had on him.

The rest of the evening was no better. Mark made one attempt to instill in Kathy an enthusiasm for the area in which he intended to travel, but she was in no mood to respond. Except to note that Kelly, the town in Wyoming from which this walk into isolation would begin, was mentioned in one of the reports of unusual dog behavior that sat on her desk, exactly in what context she felt no inclination to recall.

CHAPTER 3

Searching for a peace that was agonizingly slow in coming, Mark let his eyes roam the rugged Wyoming landscape, still some four miles below the aircraft. At the same time, and with an action more mechanical than deliberate, he took a sip from his third Martini since leaving Philadelphia. He told himself for the hundredth time that he was doing the right thing; no good would come of continuing on as he had been. A couple of weeks, away from all distractions, maybe then he would be fit to rejoin the human race. But he was anything but convinced as he leaned back in his seat and tipped the remainder of the drink into his mouth.

The initial view of Kelly helped evaporate the air of uncertainty. Surrounded by mountains, some already dusted with snow, it was a relic of another time. There were no more than a handful of buildings, all of them small and in need of maintenance, but collectively they presented a feeling of intimacy, of belonging. Although the day still had a few hours to play itself out, there was very little activity to be seen. Only a German shepherd sleeping on the lawn of an ancient post office and one old man rocking in quarter time on an ancient wooden porch—they could have been mannequins from a Disney World set. Having no idea where to go next, Mark headed for the man on the porch.

"Thompson's. Thisaway tuh thuh corner, then right. Tain't fer." The bewiskered old man was friendly enough as he answered Mark's inquiry of a place to stay, but his smile showed a trace of amusement, probably at the thought that anyone could have trouble finding anything in that town. Mark thanked him with a nod but held back a "much obliged" which he suspected might not be appreciated.

Thompson's was the local saloon which just happened to have "rooms to let," or so the sign implied. It also said, "with bath," which brought a smile to Mark's face as he wondered whether it was filled with buckets of water heated over a wood-burning stove. Nailing down a room was easy. As the desk clerk informed him, tourism, not a major industry in Kelly at any time of year, was in its off season. Mark accepted a key then headed up a flight of stairs that creaked so badly even a tiny rodent would have trouble keeping his presence from being known.

Like the town, the room turned out to be much to his liking, sparse but with a strong hint of the old west. It contained a single bed, an old wooden chair with no pads and a bureau and matching mirror, the latter supported by a combination of gravity and hope. The bath was a short walk down the hall, but it was functional—for the next two weeks, there would not even be that. Leaving his heavy backpack on the bed, Mark took the time to wash up before heading down to the bar for a drink. He had only one night in town, one night to absorb its ambiance. At first light he would be on his way.

It was not difficult to strike up a conversation with local residents, in part a reflection of Mark's willingness to buy. There were about a dozen people in the bar, including the bartender. Two were leaning against an ancient, unvarnished bar while the remainder sat in hard, wooden chairs arranged in a circle around a potbellied stove that had not been lit for months. After a few words to the bartender, which no one bothered to pretend not to hear, Mark was invited to join the larger group. He accepted without hesitation, his spirits at that moment higher than they had been for months.

Ninety minutes later, after enough alcohol was consumed to add meaning to any discussion, the conversation switched from copious and often conflicting advice on how to stay alive in the woods to the local mystery, the as-yet-unexplained appearance of German shepherds in Kelly. Seduced by the alcohol, Mark listened as if it were as much his problem as theirs. He vaguely recalled the shepherd seen on the way in, the one sleeping by the post office. A foggy voice to his left claimed the animals were studying the townspeople—not just watching but studying. "They jes sits there a'starin', not makin' no sounds a 'tall an not takin' they's eyes off'en us." Everyone (including Mark) nodded his head in agreement. "At fust we used tuh grab um. Yuh know, 'cause we thought they was lost. But we never could figger out who they belonged tuh. An after a piece they allas managed tuh git away. Don't know how, they just gits theyself loose an vanishes." He shook his head in appreciation of the gravity of his pronouncements. "They is strange goin's on in them woods!"

Most of the permanent residents of Kelly had seen at least one of these canine visitors, one claiming to have witnessed a vanishing act through a locked door—again the nodding of heads as if the truth of this could not be in doubt. But there was no atmosphere of concern. Curiosity, yes; concern, no. The animals were always well mannered—no one in town had ever been hurt or even threatened—so the feeling was to "let sleeping dogs lie"—Mark started to laugh at the pun, then, realizing it was unintended, quickly stopped.

As one after another of the bar's occupants offered his opinion, Mark learned that the dogs emerged from the woods generally one at a time and spaced days and sometimes weeks apart—there was no set pattern to their arrival. All were the same breed and color and each hung around only a short time before disappearing. To where, no one could say. The story had even reached the papers in Jackson. Mark began to suspect he was being given the treatment reserved for visiting city boys. It was more than a possibility that the "strange goin's on in them woods" was to give him something to think about while on the trail. He was amused but not offended.

First light was within shouting distance when finally Mark decided to pack it in. The night had been fun, a special kind of fun. For the first time in as long as he could remember, he was relaxed and doing what he really wanted to do. Negotiating the narrow stairs was not easy, but after a quick stop down the hall to relieve himself, he managed to make it to his room. Then, without bothering to remove his clothes, he fell onto the old feather bed and was instantly asleep. At precisely the same moment, a light-colored, medium sized German shepherd lifted itself from the post office lawn, took a brief look around, then began a slow walk down the road to Jackson.

CHAPTER 4

By nightfall, Kelly was miles away and little more than a memory. Mark was tired but finally free of the overpowering hangover that had gripped him so tenaciously during much of the day. Once out of sight of the last of the town's few buildings, he had set a demanding pace, and only when daylight threatened to give up its last hold on his new world of solace and isolation did he permit himself to stop for the night.

The day had passed quickly, and even the work of getting a fire going and preparing something appetizing from his store of dried food was accepted with grace. Getting it all down took no time at all, and afterward Mark tucked his tired body into his sleeping bag then settled back against a thick aspen tree to sip coffee and listen to the unique sounds of a wilderness at night.

It wasn't long before he began to appreciate how many creatures there were out there—odd that he hadn't noticed this before. And they sounded so...so agitated, as if unsure where they should be and what they should be doing. Curious but not more than that, Mark finished what remained of his coffee then lay back to rest.

The distant cry of a frightened animal caused him to bolt awake. Unsure of the time, or even where he was, Mark held his breath and waited for a repeat of whatever it was that had caused him to be so suddenly alert. But there was nothing, only the normal sounds of a forest at night. Exhaling slowly, he pulled the folds of his sleeping bag together to shut out the chill—the coals by now produced a glow but little else—then turned to find a more comfortable position. It took only a second to realize that the last thing he'd seen before turning over was a single eye faintly reflecting the fire's light from no more than twenty feet away.

Once again he was alert, this time jerking his head upward to scan the area where the apparition had shown itself. Eyes wide and heart racing, he strained to see what might be lingering just beyond the line of faintly-illuminated trees. It could not have been his imagination, nor could it have been a dream; something was really there. But all was as vacant as it had been earlier.

Then suddenly there it was, this time as a pair of floating eyes, eyes that only barely reflected the glow of a tired campfire. Propping himself up on one elbow, Mark struggled to make sense out of what he was seeing. He held his body ridged lest some involuntary motion provoke whatever it was into explosive action. With little to go on except those eyes, he judged the animal to be about the size of a wolf or a small mountain lion, in any case large enough to do harm. He searched anxiously for signs of aggressive intent, but the eyes, which still focused on him, were devoid of emotion as if their owner had already lost interest. They soon faded then disappeared altogether, this time for good—Mark searched the blackened forest for many minutes to be sure.

When finally he felt comfortable with the prospect of changing his position, he hastily added wood to the fire, then, pleased that its flames would provide hours of additional protection, brought his hunting knife to within easy reach. After that, he rolled back to where he could see the area where the invader last appeared then lowered his head to attempt sleep once again. It was many minutes and much opening and closing of his eyes before that sleep came.

He awoke in the morning with a start. A dream had preceded his consciousness; a dream involving eyes; large, penetrating eyes, smiling in sinister recognition of his capture. Unnerved by the experience, he sat up in his sleeping bag and looked around, his hands fumbling unsuccessfully for the zipper as he did so—having twisted around in his sleep, the opening was now in the back. He was propelled by a sense of urgency as he wrestled the bag to where his hands could engineer an escape.

There was no sign of whatever it was that had visited his camp during the night, and he was left with the feeling that it had not really happened, that it was part of the dream from which he had just emerged. Even so, he wasted little time moving through the motions of breakfast then breaking camp.

By mid morning, the incident forgotten, he found himself half-way up a mountain and heading for a rocky cut that reportedly led to a large valley. Gratefully, the map was not wrong. Tired from the climb, he paused at its entrance and looked out over some twenty miles of tightly packed trees and richly carpeted meadows. Perfect, exactly what he was hoping for. A smile of supreme satisfaction filled his face as he negotiated the rocks and gullies that led downward to the valley floor then pushed on toward what had appeared from the top to be a large stream some five miles away. There he intended to take the rest of the afternoon to bathe and relax.

It was early evening before, finally, he admitted to himself that he had lost his way. Not only was there no stream, but the scenery no longer matched what he remembered from his earlier scan of the valley. When exactly the change had begun, he wasn't sure, but by dusk it was too obvious to be ignored. The sky, previously a deep blue, was now infected with red, a red that was becoming more pronounced as the sun continued its decent. The vegetation was equally as unsettling—why hadn't he noticed this before? Pine and aspen had steadily given way to something he could not identify. The new trees, hazy and difficult to see in the dying light, had bark that was too smooth and leaves that were too thick and round, so round that they could have been constructed by a master craftsman using precision tools. And the color; the leaves had a hint of green but no more than that. Mostly they were blue, as if painted by a child who did not understand what color they were supposed to be. As if that weren't enough, the welcome aroma of pine had faded away, replaced by a scent that, although not unpleasant, was vaguely disturbing, almost chemical. Mark gave thought to examining one up close, but without knowing why, decided against it. Instead he gathered up what wood he could find and started a fire, building it higher than was necessary in a subconscious attempt to melt away his unsettled thoughts.

When the light disappeared altogether, Mark stared at the blackened woods and wondered what number of creatures were out there staring back at him. Nothing moved, at least nothing he could see, but the cacophony of animal sounds, unbroken the previous night, was conspicuously missing—wasn't that a sign that a large predator was near? The fire wasn't the same as before either. It provided heat and was easy enough to keep going, but it was not the right color and did not produce the right noise—indeed, it made no noise at all. And although there were flames of a sort, the fuel looked more like molten metal than burning wood. Further, it had begun glowing brightly from the start without the yellow flames associated with kindling and bark.

With so much to wonder about, the evening meal was more a trial than a pleasure, and after it was over, Mark felt a certain relief. He spent as little time as possible cleaning up then propped himself up against his backpack, wrapped his hands around a tepid cup of coffee and returned his thoughts to the vacant night.

Except for what was illuminated by the fire, there was nothing to see; no red sky, no odd-ball vegetation. Had it really been as strange as his tired mind recalled? Maybe, maybe not, but there was still the eerie silence. It was as if nature had elected to take the night off, sweeping all her creatures along with her. All except himself.

He turned again to the fire, taking comfort in its warmth while trying to ignore its alien composition and unnatural behavior. What did it all mean? This was unlike anything he had ever seen before; certainly it was not what he expected to find in Wyoming. *Well, whatever it is, it can be dealt with in the morning.* He moved his sleeping bag as close to the fire as he dared, poured himself into it then tried to concentrate on aspens and pines and friendly mountain communities.

His sleep was sound, so sound that the animal that found its way into his camp went unnoticed. About a foot tall, it was similar in color and appearance to a rodent, except it had flat teeth that curved upward from a broad lower jaw—at first glance, one would think it had lost the upper half of its dentures. Also unlike a rodent, it walked upright and had short forelegs that clung to its side as if atrophied. A short claw, which disappeared into its fur, appeared to lock the forelegs to the animal's body.

Its visit to the camp was short. It sniffed once at Mark's packet of dried food, shot a quick glance at the backpack lying off to one side then turned and walked back into the night.

Mark awoke to a sky so awash in red that it coated earth, water and vegetation alike—to describe anything one had to begin with the color red. Not convinced he was yet awake, it took a moment to accept the reality of what his eyes told him was there. Bathed in a red glow but still there were the blue/green trees, the symmetry of their round leaves as perfect as he remembered. They were everywhere, and they stood too straight to be real. And too smooth; they looked more like plastic poles than trees. Certainly no answers could be found in the fire; although not refreshed since early evening, it was still giving off penetrating heat— whatever the composition of that smooth material, it certainly was built to last.

The frown etched so deeply into Mark's forehead seemed destined to last forever as he left his sleeping bag for the cool morning air then grabbed his clothes and moved to the fire to dress. There he let his body soak in the warmth, while his mind retraced the steps of the previous day in search of that illusive point where he'd gone astray. It had to be after he left the mountain for the valley, maybe a bad turn once he became enveloped by trees. He extracted the map from his backpack then compared it to what he could see of the surrounding countryside.

What the hell! Although there were ample gaps in the blue/green trees, he could not even find the mountain that led to the valley. Nor the mountains on the other side. As far as the eye could see, there was only flat land.

Not possible! But it left him with a critical question: whether to backtrack or keep going and hope the familiar would return. The map showed a highway not far to the north; if things got bad he could always head in that direction and pick up a mile marker. Or some other way of reorienting himself. The thought was a reassuring one, enough so that the frown gave up some of its grip.

After a quick breakfast, followed by unexpected difficulty getting the tireless fire extinguished, Mark was back on his way. Inexplicably, he felt lighter and more springy, although with this came a perceptible tightening in his chest. He dismissed it all as the effects of high altitude. More difficult to dismiss was the alien forest that methodically closed in on him as he walked. It was enough to get him to pick up the pace, then pick it up again as time passed and the world stubbornly refused to return to normal. He ignored the fatigue that assailed his body, his mind needing the solace of the familiar: a bush, blue sky, an animal, something to prove the end of this was near.

When hunger joined his misery, he knew he had to stop. Besides, he was going nowhere. In deepening despair, he threw some dried stew into a canteen cup, poured enough water in to give it a chance of turning into something palatable, then began to force it down. Bad enough at any time, now it included a taste that had not been there a day earlier and was not welcome now, the taste of red—red vinegar more than red strawberries. He put aside what he could not finish then sat on a fallen log to ponder his next move. Perhaps it was time to admit defeat and head north toward the highway. Why not? Once properly oriented, he could pick out a new trail. And this time he would make damn sure he stuck to it! He rose to his feet then turned to retrieve his backpack, coming all the way around before noticing the a light-colored, medium-sized German shepherd that was observing him with cool detachment from a few yards away.

The cry of surprise that escaped Mark's lips was loud and sharp, and even before it ended, he was stumbling backward toward the fire as if pushed by an invisible hand—he tripped over the unconsumed coals but arrived on the other side still on his feet. The dog jumped slightly and a slight haze appeared to momentarily engulf its body, but it continued with its passive observation.

For a time thereafter, neither man nor beast moved. Frozen into a defensive crouch, Mark could only stare with bulging eyes at this latest offense to his senses. A shepherd; *another* shepherd! *What the hell is going on?!* Reminding himself that the Kelly animals were said to represent no threat to anyone helped. As did the dog's behavior; it made no hostile movements. It appeared peaceful, even friendly, and its being here at this time could just as easily be taken as a positive. Here was something that could lead him out of this mess.

Its head cocked to one side, the dog seemed to be enjoying his reaction, and encouraged by this, Mark ventured his first tentative comment. "Where the hell did you come from, boy?" He was surprised at his own voice; it was hoarse and the words were strained and forced.

The dog picked up his ears at the sound but otherwise did not move. Mark wondered whether it was waiting for some kind of command. "Hey, Spot, come here, boy." With mixed emotions, he watched as the dog got to its feet then moved without haste to Mark's side. There, with its body barely touching his, it lowered its head to be petted as if trained to behave in such a way.

Stroking the animal's well-kept fur pleased Mark as much as it did the animal. It was a familiar sight in an unfamiliar world. Perhaps recognizing the service it was performing by permitting the man's touch, it made no attempt to move. Mark thought about its owner and wondered if he were equally as friendly.

"Go home, boy!" Mark's hope was he could follow, and when the animal gave no indication that it understood, he tried again, this time adding a gentle push. But the shepherd continued to stare up at him with that same vague look of amusement. "Hell, with my luck, you're probably lost too."

Mark wondered what he should do next. He could not pin his hopes, and possibly his survival, on one reluctant animal. Better to stick with what he'd already decided. He rose to his feet, grabbed his pack and started off in the direction of the promised highway, only as an afterthought turning around to the still-sitting animal and saying, "Well what's it going to be, my friend?" As if finally getting the idea, the animal stood and began to follow. Mark's smile was both external and internal. Whatever else he was, he was no longer alone.

The unusual scenery did not change as man and dog plodded onward through woods that appeared devoid of life. An occasional bird could be seen, but when it appeared it would ignore the role nature intended for it. Instead it acted the part of a sentinel, watching in silence from high in a tree until the travelers moved away. The dog appeared not to notice.

Mark, however, was finding it hard to take anything in stride. Rather than improving his plight he was marching further and further into the unknown. He knew he had gone far enough to reach the highway, but it had not yet been found and there was nothing to indicate he was even heading toward one. His shoulders began to sag as time went on and the oppression of phony birds, red-tinted air and silent, alien woods continued to eat away at his confidence.

Movement nearby! It caught enough of Mark's eye to make him spin around in something close to panic—although by now desperate for company, he had no illusion that this was what he was about to see. His concern proved justified as there, not ten yards away, stood an animal that simply did not exist in the real world. It was the size of a coyote but a long way from looking like one. It had long ears that shot upward from a bovine head and its body was thick with soft gray fur. Supporting this body but not sharing the fur were six stubby legs each ending in a three-toed hoof—Mark focused on the legs, willing the six to dissolve into four. After a moment of mutual staring, the animal reared up as might a bear when confronted by an enemy, accomplishing this by first lifting its two front legs then the two in the middle of its body. Then time stood still, with neither man nor creature daring to move, each rendered impotent by the sight of the other.

Mark felt the beginning tug of a mind backing away from itself. An unreasonable fear was growing within him, fear that this impossible creature would soon show itself to be a devil in disguise, fear that he was spiraling toward disaster, an unwilling participant in an all-too-realistic nightmare. In helpless fascination, he watched as the creature tired of the game then lowered itself to the ground and took the first tentative steps in the opposite direction, its furry head twisted just enough to keep tabs on the alien it now sought to escape. The perfect synchronization of its six legs was a final stab at Mark's sanity, a cleverly arranged torment designed to remind him that normalcy must now be considered a thing of the past. Suffering the unlikely combination of wracking chills and heavy perspiration, he sank to his knees and watched in silence as the creature vanished into the trees.

CHAPTER 5

"Damn! I didn't mean to cry on your shoulder," Kathy said, "at least not in a literal sense."

She and Sandy Mellon were having a quiet drink together just down the street from the Mellon and Carter studio. Kathy had arrived in late afternoon and Sandy joined her there as soon as he was able to break away from work—not easy with Mark gone. Sandy was beginning to prefer a grouchy Mark to no Mark at all.

Kathy was well into her drink by the time Sandy arrived, which gave him an indication of how upset she was. The smile she tossed him as he sat himself down lacked her usual warmth. "What is it, Honey?" The cocktail lounge was small and nearly empty, forcing the lowering of their voices to conspiratorial levels.

A few awkward minutes later, Sandy had his answer. It was as he'd expected; Kathy was afraid she was going to lose Mark, the admission of which brought her to tears. Oddly relieved, he offered as gently as he could, "He loves you, Kathy. That's not what this is all about. He has no intention of leaving you; he just needs to get away for awhile, that's all."

"Yeah, away from me!" she sobbed bitterly.

"No not away from you. More away from himself than anything else, if that makes sense. He's just having his mid-life crisis a little early, that's all. The symptoms are all there; I've seen it before...although I'm too young to have gone through it myself, of course."

"But why Wyoming, and why do such a dumb, dangerous thing?"

Sandy paused to think. "Well, maybe that's it. It's exciting and offers something new. The danger, however much danger there is, might fit."

Kathy gave her friend an accusatory look. "Sandy, I don't see how you can even hint that it isn't dangerous! Those woods are wild. There are bears and God-knows-what-else in there!"

"Which I suspect will avoid Mark as much as I know he'll avoid them."

"It's not always that easy," Kathy retorted. "Don't you think people who get attacked by bears would rather avoid them?"

"I can't imagine anyone who would disappear faster than our boy if so much as a teddy bear came into view," answered Sandy. "Besides, he knows his way around woods."

"Not woods like that! Don't forget I've been with him on camping trips. He might know how to make a fire and chase women through the woods, but Daniel Boone he ain't!"

Sandy tilted his head as if thinking. "You'll have to let my wife know more about that chasing women through the woods stuff," he mused. "You might get her interested; except she might want to be chased by someone other than me."

"Sandy, you're trying to change the subject."

"Only partially; that subject does interest me at times, you know. Besides, what could we possibly do about it now? Mark's already left and there's no way I know of to get in touch with him."

"Tell me about it," Kathy admitted softly. "I don't even know if we'll be able to do anything when the two weeks are up. And I think the problem *will* arise." Her voice rose as she continued with, "How will we even know? Somehow I don't think Mark's too worried about a schedule, and that means we won't be able to tell when he's really lost."

"I don't agree with the assumption that he *will* be lost."

"Well, how will we know if he is or not?"

"Kathy, the only thing we can do now is wait. In the meantime I think you should stop trying to punish yourself. You're taking this too personally."

They paused while the waiter served another round of drinks; too slowly, or so it seemed to Kathy. As her vodka gimlet was lowered to the table, she averted her face, suddenly aware of how much her emotions were etched on it. Only when the waiter was out of earshot did she continue. "Do you think I'm being unfair, I mean about not wanting to live together or...get married?

"Have you and Mark talked about that?" Sandy asked cautiously.

"Have you?" Her voice was low and tentative.

"I asked you first."

"Well," Kathy began again. "Not in so many words, but I think it's on his mind."

"And you're afraid he feels rejected, and that's why he ran away?"

"Is it true?"

"Kathy, I'm not going to bullshit you with reassuring comments. As you know better than I, that is on his mind. In all honesty, however, I don't think it's the whole problem. I think it's more along the lines of what I said earlier."

Kathy paused again. "Do you think we should get married?" she asked hesitatingly.

"I'd love to, Kathy, but I already have a wife."

Kathy laughed in spite of herself, "I mean Mark and I, you idiot!"

"No way I'm going to be put in that position. I'd get blamed for everything that goes wrong from day one."

"Well then, do you think I'll lose him if we don't?"

"Same question," he responded, "just worded differently."

Kathy stared at her drink for a number of seconds, obviously having something more to say but not knowing how to say it. "I have been thinking about marriage," she said, clearing her throat in a vain attempt to add strength to a fading voice. "Actually its more than just thinking about it. I might want to do it—and it's not just because I'm afraid of losing the jerk!" As was his habit, Sandy remained silent, preferring to let Kathy work it out by herself. "Ever since he started his not-so-subtle hinting, I've been giving it thought. I guess my first reaction was a little negative, but then it's always been negative on that subject. And I figured: why disrupt the status quo if it's working." Her eyes looked to his for approval, but the only thing she got in return was a sympathetic nod. After a deep sigh, she pushed on, "Well, maybe Mark's the reason why. He wants to get married and I don't think he'll be satisfied with anything less. When I finally realized this I started questioning myself, what I was doing, not only to Mark, but to me. My tilting at windmills was putting our relationship in jeopardy. I could lose someone I really like...love. Someone I couldn't stand to be without."

She shook her head, afraid she was not making sense. Sandy held his tongue, knowing it was still her moment. As before she picked up the slack, now in a breaking voice. "The problem is, I never let Mark know. And that I chalk off to being too sure of myself; too sure that I had control of things." The tears began to flow as she ended with, "Now I'm afraid I might have waited too long."

Sandy waited until he was sure Kathy had nothing further to say, then reached over and took her hand. "I understand, Honey, and for what it's worth, I don't think you have anything to worry about. The guy's nuts about you, and as long as you don't tell him to get lost, he's not going to leave. Give him his time alone. When he gets home he'll have gotten the bugs out of his system and be more in a mood to listen. Then you can tell him what you just told me—I can tell you, that'll settle him down some." He let go of her hand then leaned back in his chair. "If that doesn't work, I'll give in to your demands and take you on as my second wife."

In the morning, her heart and mind still battling it out, Kathy set about trying to discover when Mark was due to return. She tried the airlines first, where a reluctant but sympathetic clerk, stating policy, turned down her request for specifics. All he could bring himself to do was pass on the name of the travel agency that had booked Mark's tickets. There, however, she got more than she wanted, at least more than she wanted to hear: Mark had left his return reservation open.

"Sandy, he's not coming back!" she cried over the telephone.

Sandy would have been amused had he not known how deeply Kathy was feeling this. "Calm down," he replied, "he paid for it so he intends to use it. All this means is he can't predict when he'll arrive back in Jackson—which could just as easily mean he might return early."

"You don't really believe that, Sandy."

"Maybe not, but I honestly don't see anything odd about what he's done. Remember, he's not staying at a hotel where he can just check out on a certain day."

"Somehow that doesn't make me feel better," Kathy said.

"Well look to the bright side. Right now our boy is doing what he really wants to do, what he felt he had to do. He'll come back tired and sore and look at us as if we were sent by the gods."

"And maybe he'll get hurt."

"And more probably he won't. There are rangers in those woods; guys well up on weekend mountain men like Mark. I've got to believe there's nothing Mark could do that they couldn't undo."

"Except if he's been eaten by a bear," Kathy offered sullenly.

"Maybe they even have a way around that, a quick C-section and zip, out he comes."

Once again Sandy had her laughing in spite of herself. "C-section?" she said.

"Well whatever section makes sense. Our boy would be reborn and all would be well, except the bear might want to mother him for awhile."

Sandy had sensed the elevation in Kathy's spirits and was pleased. Now if only he could do the same for himself. Regardless of what he'd said to her during their now completed conversation, he was truly worried and had difficulty keeping the worst of the unpleasant possibilities from flooding his mind. His friend and partner was going through an exaggerated personal crisis that could, the way he was going about it, do considerable harm to himself and to the people who cared for him. It was not so much the camping thing—in that, Mark could take care of himself. It was his destructive mood. Rather than avoid trouble, he might, consciously or unconsciously, seek it out.

It was not news to Sandy that Mark had decided not to make return reservations. Two days ago he had gone through the same investigative process as Kathy and had been equally as shaken by the disquieting results. Rationalizing to himself as he had to her, he had come close to accepting his own arguments. Now that was impossible.

He wondered whether anyone knew the direction Mark intended to take. In the mood to be difficult, he had revealed only that the town of Kelly was to be his jumping-off point. *Hell with him!* Ignoring the possibility that it would later be resented by his touchy partner, he decided to put in a call to Wyoming. It took three tries, but finally he was connected to the Teton County Sheriff's Office and explaining to a patient officer the concern he felt for his friend.

"No problem. We appreciate being alerted," the officer stated, his voice a slow western drawl that Sandy found calming. "We like to keep track of how many people are out there and when they're expected to return. It's big country, but we run a number of ranger stations, some in areas where even the locals hesitate to go. I'll put out the word all along the line to keep an eye out for your friend. From what you've told me, though, I don't see any cause to worry. It's true that people get lost from time to time, but mostly they just come back tired, dirty, hungry and embarrassed. Those who do get...confused...are not too difficult to find."

Sandy decided not to let Kathy know of his call to Wyoming, telling himself it would only set her off. Reality was he didn't want her to know how much *he* was "set off." He wondered what he would do if the worst happened, if Mark got himself lost and all those rangers with all their strategically-placed stations couldn't find him in time. It was not a good thought on which to end the day.

C H A P T E R   6

The six-legged creature was long gone, but Mark remained on his knees, struck by more fright than he'd ever experienced before, even as a child. Gone was any thought of continuing his solitary venture into the wilds. Gone was the confidence that flowed with such abundance only a day earlier. All he could manage was a slow rock of his raised head, as if beseeching the trees for a way out. He was sure he was losing it, sure his mind was as frozen as his body, frozen by the questions without answers that bounced noiselessly off its bruised walls.

When finally he remember the dog, he agonized his head to where he could confirm that it, at least was real. And that it had not left him. But neither did it appear moved by either the unlikely visitor or Mark's response to it. It just lay in silence on the ground, its eyes examining those of the man it had attached itself too. What looked like an expression of sympathy decked its expressive face.

"This isn't at all unusual to you, is it, Boy?" Mark whispered, his voice scratchy and broken as if it had suffered along with his emotions. The animal made no response, but the calm it continued to exude helped. So was the realization that it was well groomed and in good health—whatever was happening here, it was not life threatening.

It was not easy to regain his feet, and even after he did so he could only stand in place and wonder where to go from there. The trees with no names appeared closer than ever, and thick blades of blue grass, which he hadn't even noticed before, were everywhere. That he could not stay where he was, was a given, but would moving on be any better? Wobbly at first, he pushed off on one foot then the other, the direction of travel not as important as the need to be doing something. Every few steps he checked behind him to prove the dog was still following. It might be a part of this horror, but there was no way he wanted to suffer its absence.

With all sense of direction gone, his maps useless and his mind unable to tell him whether he was moving into the arms of safety or the clutches of insanity, he pushed on. Each step was a touch faster than the last, as if this would allow him to outpace the panic he knew was not far away. He moved at a grueling pace until lack of light and deep fatigue made it impossible to go further. Even then it was with the greatest reluctance that he slowed then slowed again then finally stopped altogether and let his body fall to the ground. For a long while thereafter he lay with his face barely above the dirt, held there by the weight of unsettled thoughts. Fear of enveloping darkness brought him back to his feet and encouraged him first toward a flashlight, then to scrounge enough wood to make a fire. As before, it lit quickly—too quickly—but its warmth helped even as its strange glow only emphasized how trapped he was in what he had little hope of understanding. The dog, silent and still during all of this, made no attempt to approach the fire, content to lie to one side and continue his study of his adopted companion.

It was warm for this time of year yet Mark felt a chill, a chill fed by the helplessness growing within him. Although not hungry, he knew he had to eat something; he had long since burned up what he'd eaten at...when was it, exactly? Then he realized he had neglected to fill his canteen. He did not even have enough water to make something edible out of his dehydrated food—on a day like this, what did he expect? Disgust mixed in with everything else he was feeling as he jammed a handful of dried food into his mouth and attempted to swallow it. It was a mistake, and he knew it immediately. Besides being all but unpalatable in that form, it seemed only to increase his thirst.

It was then that he realized his canine companion had had nothing to eat or drink since their introduction yet was showing no interest in the food. Inexplicably, this made Mark angry. "Why don't you find us some water, you dumb mutt!" But the animal held to its calm stare, oblivious or uncaring of the man's comments. Mark grunted then turned back to the fire, by now wanting only to retreat into sleep. He knew it would not be easy. He feared what he'd miss if he closed his eyes, and he feared what he'd see if he kept them opened. He even feared his dreams. With a sigh that spoke of a waning confidence, he lowered himself to the ground then arranged his body to where he could stare into the fire. Perhaps he would fall victim to its hypnotizing glow.

Hours went by, hours that changed nothing; sleep would not come. Twice he raised himself to where he could check on the dog, each time seeing it resting comfortably in a natural canine position, the slow movement of its sides indicating it was breathing its way through deep slumber. Dawn was within easy reach before fatigue finally won out and he fell into a fitful rest.

There were no dreams this time, but he woke with a start just the same. Something was moving within the camp. It was the dog; he was leaving. Startled into full consciousness, Mark felt an unreasonable fear shoot through him, fear that this unlikely pet was his last link to sanity and he would suffocate in a vacuum of despair if it were to leave. "Where are you going!" he shouted, his voice bouncing off the heavy atmosphere of red-tinted morning air. The animal gave no sign that it heard, and soon there was only a faint rustle in the brush to indicate where it had entered the woods.

"No!" He struggled to his feet, ripping apart his sleeping bag in the process. Then, pausing only long enough to grab his shoes, he ran after it, catching up to it wide-eyed and breathless even though the effort lasted less than a minute. The animal kept moving, its manner suggesting it cared little about who might follow. His feet bare and already suffering from contact with forest debris, Mark dutifully fell in behind.

The pace continued at a prodigious rate for hours, but Mark barely noticed. He'd had no food for almost a day, and his feet were beginning to bleed, but inside he was content. Here was direction; here was purpose. Then, without warning, the animal came to an abrupt stop, the action bringing on a near collision with a closely-following Mark. Its muzzle came up and jutted out to the front as if to sniff the air ahead. Mark imitated the move, sensing then hearing what had alerted his canine guide. Something was coming toward them, a large animal, a two-legged animal.

"A man!" Mark felt instant elation, even as a part of him whispered of the uncertainly of encountering another traveler in this nightmare world. But even if he were inclined to run, the footsteps were coming too fast; there was no time to hide. He shot a glance at the dog and was encouraged at the calm it continued to show—it was the last positive feeling he was to experience for some time.

It was upon them in a flash, bursting through the underbrush a scant ten yards away and pushing without pause in their direction. Within seconds, if it did not slow, it would mow them down. Its form was impossible. It was, as expected, two legged, but this gave Mark no comfort at all. What those two legs supported was grotesque, part one thing and part another, and as it agonized its way through the knee-high underbrush, its head stretched, first in one direction, then another as if unable to decide what it wanted to be. In like fashion, its body shifted constantly, shrinking in some areas and expanding in others. Muscles appeared out of nowhere, while limbs rearranged themselves in unnatural directions becoming more like those of an animal than a human. But no part of this thing could be thought of as human.

Then it hit him. "God, no!" Mark's cry was a whisper on the outside but a scream on the inside. Whatever this thing had once been, it was now trying to become a German shepherd—like his German shepherd, and like the many other German shepherds that moved unopposed through Kelly to unknown places beyond. His nightmare had reached a new plateau.

At the sight of Mark, the creature bolted to a stop and enveloped itself in a faint haze. Through it Mark could see shock and surprise explode onto its semi-converted face, not at seeing Mark's companion, which it ignored, but at discovering a human being. Mark, unable to move his eyes away, could only return the stare and wonder what the gods had in store for him next. Not that it mattered. A circuit-breaker had tripped in his mind, this to permit his over-shocked system time to drain itself of what it could no longer manage. He actually felt it happen, the snap and the welcome numbness that spread through limbs and torso alike, everything except his mind. In the unkindest cut of all, that was left to record what took place next.

Without halting or even slowing down the transformation, the creature turned toward Mark's traveling companion and fixed it with a hard stare, a stare that was returned with another of those amused looks. For a while nothing else happened; neither party moved or made a noise; even the expressions remained the same. Then the newcomer turned its distorted face back to Mark and awarded him a look that now had anger attached to it.

Mark watched all this as from a dream until, without warning, the creature began moving again. As before it was in his direction, but now it was accelerating as it moved as if intent on running him down...or worse. Mark wanted to get out of the way but was unable to get his muscles to respond. It was like the ending of so many bad dreams as a child, where the unspeakable approached at an ever-faster rate, the time when all respectable nightmares were supposed to end. Somehow he knew, however, that this time the monster would get him, this time the dream would not end. And he could not even collect himself to brace for the impact.

But it never came. One moment the creature was in his face and the next it was behind him. There was no sense of contact and no feeling of presence other than what was seen and heard. Mark stood with mouth open in a silent scream, his mind rebelling against this latest assault on it. The creature must have veered off at the last moment; maybe it hadn't been there at all. Unable to turn his head, he could only listen to the footsteps moving away, footsteps that now sounded as if the creature were walking on four legs instead of two.

After a time silence returned to the woods, silence undisturbed by Mark and the uncertainty that sat by his side, its expression now one of regret. Mark studied its face, even as he was unable to form an expression of his own—his facial muscles would not let go of the horror he felt, horror at what he now knew this animal to be. It had not reacted at all to whatever that thing was. It had not been surprised and it had not shown fear or even doubt. And this was because it was one of them.

One of them. What did "one of them" mean?

The question rapidly became irrelevant as his companion began moving away, as before, at an uncompromising pace. Fearing its absence more than its presence, Mark was moved to follow. But his muscles were still not his to command; he could only watch in horror as the animal made for the brush, uncaring of one human being's desperate need to follow. "Wait! You can't leave me here! Please!"

Echoes of the plea reverberated through the forest, followed by a return to the eerie quiet of before. But it had its effect; the dog stopped then turned to face its helpless companion. For a long moment, it searched his face in stony silence, but then, with a sigh that had no business coming out of a dog, it retraced its steps. Mark watched with pathetic gratitude as it moved to a nearby tree then lay down on the ground to wait.

Overcome with relief but still suffering paralyzing shock, Mark collapsed to his knees then fixed affectionate eyes on what would, for a moment longer, be a companion. After a while, his gaze vacant and glossy, he sank the remaining distance to the ground and retreated into welcome unconsciousness.

The dog was still there when he awoke but it did not look the same. Mark's eyes poked through the glow of a fire he did not remember building and tried to make a lethargic mind understand what it was seeing. The animal now sat upright like a man, its legs bent casually in front of it, legs that were longer than he remembered. Its neck was longer as well and its muzzle shorter, and its previously long ears were only half their former size. Forearms, now more human in shape, crossed over its chest.

And it was staring at Mark with a frown.

Past the point of caring, Mark turned his gaze to the fire. Wherever he was, whatever was being imposed upon him—the supernatural, metaphysical abstractions, the afterworld, or simply emotional illness— his position was hopeless. He was incapable of defending himself against any of it. His withdrawal was such that even if the thick vegetation had permitted it, he would not have noticed a second sun appearing in the eastern sky. Further away than the first, it was still close enough to make its presence known. It added substantially to the warmth of the day, warmth that also went unnoticed as Mark looked back with an odd sense of calm at the ridiculous sight the transforming creature presented.

"Why did you keep coming?"

The comment brought an instant end to Mark's lethargy, although confusion reigned in its place—he could not see the source of the voice. His head darted from side to side; his eyes did the same. *Damnit, that was real!* But there was only himself and the thing he stubbornly clung to for protection. Not wanting whoever it was to leave, he forced out a belated reply. "What? What did you say?" The words were tentative and his voice cracked as he offered them.

"I did not 'say' anything in the sense that you refer to sounds and speaking, I merely asked why you kept coming. What is your intent?"

It appeared to come from the area surrounding the creature. Or from the creature itself. Mark stared, his skepticism obvious. The unlikely animal had made no movement whatsoever, not even its muzzle or mouth or whatever that opening might now be called. Leaning forward, eyes squinting and feeling foolish on top of everything else, Mark asked, "Did you speak, Spot?"

The response was immediate. "I believe I have already answered that question."

Mark jumped to his feet, wanting to run but not knowing whether his muscles would cooperate even if he figured out which way to go. He had been staring directly at the creature's mouth when the answer came and had seen no movement. Yet the sound—if it really were a sound—had come from that area. "What...are...you?" he stammered.

"I would prefer you addressed my question first."

"Oh God, I don't understand any of this!" Mark cried, once again on the verge of hysteria.

"So it seems! However, far more pertinent at the present time is that I do not either."

"You...can't...be real!"

"In a purely abstract sense you might be right, but for the moment do you suppose you could imagine that I am?"

Mark's mind became a loaner in the process of being recalled; the situation, once only impossible, was now ridiculous. *I'm having a nervous breakdown*, he thought. *The symptoms were there even before I started this trip.* His shoulders sagged in self pity and despair, and his face took on the lines of an older man.

The creature, as if sharing Mark's thoughts, showed confusion. Then, after a moment of uncertain staring, pity began to compete with the annoyance which had, to that point, dominated its expression. "Come with me," it summarily ordered. With that it rose to its hind legs then turned to continue the trip. Mark was powerless to refuse. Still clutching his shoes, he stumbled along behind, noting as he did so that the creature had taken on a more humanoid form—except for its fur, which remained the same color and texture as before, it no longer resembled a canine. Its head now looked more like that of a human child, except no teeth were visible and its nose was almost non existent. The eyes, two of them and located about where human eyes are located, were small and round. There was no evidence of eyelids although logic suggested some such protection must be there. The ears, or what Mark assumed to be ears, were small disks, the lower portion of which disappeared into facial flesh. Fur circled most of the face, permitting only enough clear area for eyes, ears, nose and mouth. The same fur reached downward, covering much of the remainder of its body—Mark could identify no breaks for zippers or buttons. Two fingers and a thumb-like appendage broke through the fur at the end of long arms. Not so the legs; covered by the same ubiquitous fur and giving the appearance of a pair of bedroom slippers, the feet remained a mystery.

A short time later, the creature stopped by a pool of what appeared to be water and ordered Mark to drink. It made no attempt to do so itself. Mark hesitated, seeing the same unappetizing fluid that had caused him to forsake the filling of his canteens a day earlier. But his body demanded water; he would not survive unless he surrendered his doubts and drank. Slowly and with little enthusiasm, he lowered his head toward the red-tinted fluid.

It did not taste as he knew water should taste, yet it was not repulsive— and it was satisfying. And the red color did not give the aftertaste of rust that he thought would be the case. The process, however, was not without price. Cramps and a warning of nausea to come followed the liquid down his throat, both becoming more pronounced as it settled into his stomach. But the effect was only temporary and did not discourage further drinking.

Afterward he sat on the ground catching his breath and waiting out the aftereffects of whatever it was he had drank. From time to time, he shot a glance at the strange creature that was now in virtual control of his life. All the time he was drinking it had shown no interest in grabbing some for itself, this even though it had gone without water equally as long as he. It just stood nearby and observed him with that disturbing look of pity—why pity? What was it intending to do?

"Am I crazy?" whispered Mark hoarsely.

The creature ignored the rhetorical nature of the question in his prompt response. "I would suggest that the question has no value when directed at me since, in any event, you would be unsure of the answer. I am either unreal, in which case my response is merely an additional figment of your imagination, or I am real, which undoubtedly would be equally as unacceptable to you at this point."

Mark shook his head. "How can I get out of this madness?" he cried, his voice now a plea.

"Frankly, I have not yet made up my mind about that."

Deciding that enough time had been spent in rest and useless banter, the creature turned and began to walk away, confident that his adopted charge would be close behind. It was not wrong. Mark rose to follow what was now as important to him as a parent is to a small child. Anything would be better than being left alone, even playing rodent to this supernatural pied piper.

They walked through the red-tinted landscape for hours, creature leading and human stumbling along as close as strength and courage would permit. The second sun continued to add warmth to the day and intensity to the alien landscape, and in different circumstances, Mark would have been comforted, even awed, by the sight. Now he saw it as just another nail in the coffin that engulfed him. His strength and spirits continued to sag as the forced march continued at a brisk pace, even after darkness made it difficult to see where he was going. The creature to his front appeared to have the eyes of a cat; Mark could sense no hesitation in its step.

Then, in the distance, a glow appeared, faint at first but becoming more pronounced as darkness replaced the last rays of a descending pair of suns. Mark's tormented mind stared at it with longing; it was life; it was hope. And the creature was leading them directly toward it.

CHAPTER 7

"Oh great!" Kathy exclaimed aloud, "Canine with a 'K'!" A sleeping Me-too twitched his ears at the sound but otherwise did not move. "Damn you, Mark!" The irrationality of the words was pointedly ignored as she pounded her word processor as if it shared the blame with her missing lover.

Sandy's patient reassurances had not been enough to erase a lingering apprehension laced with guilt. She was being bombarded with replays of the last half hour before Mark retreated to his male-only bastion, and each incidence ended with a sense of having lost more than just an argument. She was loosing him. And whether or not she cared to admit it, fear of this changed everything. It made her realize how impossible life would be without him.

"Jerk!"

The article was now past the outline stage, and an idea of how to work in the additional information, still only partially investigated, had been formed. She would stick to what could readily be believed by her readers and add the unexplained mysteries as comic relief. Some of these mysteries, however, were leaving an emotional after-taste. Like the one involving an animal locked in a library overnight. It was discovered in the morning by an early-arriving librarian who caught it staring at an open book lying on the floor, as if expecting something to jump out. There were other books as well, also open and also nearby on the floor. That of itself was interesting, but not earthshaking, and if there were nothing more to it than that, it would have made an amusing photograph—assuming someone had been prepared at that moment to take it. What made it more than that was that after a few seconds the animal actually turned a page with an oddly-shaped paw then rotated its head toward the top of the new page as if continuing to read. So unexpected was this that the librarian let out an explosive gasp, which, of course, the animal picked up—it jumped and made what the librarian insisted was not the kind of sound one expects to hear from a dog. And as if this weren't enough, the poor woman had to watch as canine eyes widened to maniacal proportions and a funny haze spread around its body. Kathy chuckled as she imagined the scene: for an extended moment the dog and the librarian, each with bulging eyes, staring at one another in shock.

It was the animal who brought them out of it. It abruptly sat down on the floor and began to pant—the hazy light now gone and it's paw, whatever the librarian thought of it before, now perfectly normal—she was left staring in disbelief and self-doubt.

Local papers had playfully reported the story, and the subsequent disappearance of the animal from the pound after an unsuccessful attempt to find its owner. In this they had given inference to an overactive imagination on the part of a lonely librarian, although Kathy had found the woman to be outgoing, conscientious and very bright, not the type to be inclined toward exaggeration. In any event, the incident would be treated as interesting and amusing, not as something supernatural, which Kathy was certain it was not.

She was, however, vaguely disturbed. The librarian had confirmed the species and color—she'd had no doubt about that, nor had the pound officials whom Kathy had also interviewed. It was a shepherd and it had a light tan hue, supposedly the same species and color as in the cases yet to be investigated. Coincidence? So far as she was able to discover, there was nothing that would make that particular combination unique.

Another curious incident had not yet been looked into but Kathy was interested in doing so quickly, and for less than professional reasons. This was the one that got her a free trip to California. What made it so irresistible was that she had a business reason for stopping in Wyoming on the way back—she could be there when Mark emerged from the woods. With a smile of self satisfaction, she picked up the Jackson, Wyoming news article about a curious infestation of German shepherds in the small town of Kelly, the very place where Mark had begun his hermit thing. She regretted not mentioning this to him the night he left, although, considering his mood at the time, he might have thrown her out a window.

"Jerk!"

Her editor, thinking this report to be exaggerated mountain lore, had refused to pay for the diversion, but that concerned her very little; the difference in cost would be little. A more serious worry was how Mark would react. Would he be pleased or get angry? *I guess it depends on what he's decided*, she thought sadly, remembering that one of the purposes of the trip was to sort out the details of his life—she was one of those details.

The California story involved a dog that had befriended a computer-room night crew working for a Sunnyvale, California microchip manufacturer. It would greet them nightly, apparently more for affection than food since it spurned all of the latter that was offered. It was a very curious animal, interested in anything electronic. It would spend hours checking out the computer room, sometimes making a nuisance of itself in the process. It would stand behind the printer and appear to examine the printed pages as they poured out of the machine, giving the operator a fear that it might snap at the sheets as they dropped to a neat stack on the floor—he'd have a tough time explaining teeth marks to his superiors. This had been going on for weeks, finally evolving into a scandal when the animal was discovered early one morning still inside what should have been an empty office. The computer was on and printed reports were all over the place, some containing sensitive material. The responsible operator and his colleagues all swore the machine had been turned off after their shift ended at midnight.

As with the case of the librarian, this also appeared in the local papers, but here the slant was toward the lighter side—"Shepherd Takes the Graveyard Shift...," the story had said. Kathy agreed with this approach.

It was difficult to keep focused on the California incident considering the promised layover in Wyoming—Kathy smiled at the unintended pun. From San Francisco it should be easy to get to Kelly, although what exactly she would do then was as uncertain as was Mark's reaction. All she had in mind so far was to be there when he emerged from the woods. After he got through defending his male pride, they could talk.

"Mistake, Kathy!" Sandy said over the telephone. "The guy wants a little breathing room. This is exactly the wrong time to bug him."

"But if I'm in the area, why shouldn't I drop in?"

"I wouldn't exactly call that 'in the area.' How many hours out of your way is it? How much money are you spending on this casual fly by?"

"But I really have a reason for being there; there's a legitimate story in Kelly."

"Which your editor thought so much of he refused to pay for the cost of getting you there."

Kathy was disappointed that her arguments were so transparent. "But damnit, I feel responsible somehow."

"Responsible for what?" Sandy replied. "The guy's having a ball. He's running around the woods free of responsibility and cares and, perhaps most important right now, human beings."

"All I want to do is be there when he comes out. I want him to know I care that much for him. Right now I don't think he knows that."

"He knows, Kathy. Believe me, he knows. Don't you think he and I have talked about you in the past; I know it all, some of which makes me blush."

"Don't try to make me laugh, Sandy, I'm serious."

"I know you are, honey, but you've got to give him time to get over whatever's bugging him. Don't worry, he's not going to run away; he's reached the stage where he really wants to settle down. He's getting tired of having fun all the time."

"So he needs me to help end the party," she added sarcastically.

"Who else? You're perfect for it. Look, he knows you're not ready yet but there's no way he's not going to wait; there's no way you're going to lose him."

"Then what's wrong with surprising him with an innocent little visit?"

"Yeah, sure, just happened to be in the neighborhood."

"Something like that."

Sandy paused, "Sounds like you're really going to go," he said softly.

"Yes, Sandy, I am," she replied.

The trip across country was pleasant but agonizingly slow. What she really wanted to do was get to California, conduct the interview then, the same day if possible, head for Wyoming. At the San Francisco airport she rented a car then began the relatively short jog to Sunnyvale—short in distance, not in time; traffic was horrendous and it took an hour and a half to go the thirty-some miles. Even so, she arrived too early to catch the night crew and had to wait in a small, almost empty cafeteria for their arrival, something she found doubly distasteful: the waiting added to a growing apprehension about Mark, and the stale odors left over from what must have been a busy day, were threatening to give her nausea. Adding to the latter, the night supervisor arrived early in anticipation of the interview and immediately began demonstrating over coffee how little knowledge he had of the incident. Kathy was relieved when the true objects of her investigation finally arrived and the supervisor excused himself, promising to come back as soon as he saw to his duties. May all your problems be giant ones, she thought, hoping to have seen the last of him.

The night crew were pleasant to talk to, and Kathy could easily see how they could chance bending company rules to permit a dog into the building.

"Actually we were trying to keep him hidden in the computer room," one of them said. "If he'd gotten out into the building proper, he would've been spotted by the guard. Then we all would have been in deep shit."

"Aren't you in deep shit anyway?" Kathy asked. "Surely they aren't wild about what happened."

"Well I can tell you they definitely weren't pleased," the man replied. "What saved us was the fact that it ain't exactly easy to find night-shift computer operators nowadays."

"Plus," another man offered, "they got a kick out of the publicity. They pretended not to like it, but you could see the trouble they had hiding their smiles. We had our wrists slapped but not much more than that."

"You said the dog appeared to be interested in everything you did?" asked Kathy. "What did you mean by that?"

"The damn thing followed us everywhere we went—except the john!

We went to the tape room, he went to the tape room. We stared at the console, he stared at the console. We watched the reports come off the printer, he did the same. The mutt was fascinated by the machine."

"Nobody else agrees with me," interrupted a man who had to this point remained silent, "but there's more to that animal than meets the eye."

"Oh crap, Charlie. She doesn't want to hear that bullshit!"

"No, please," Kathy pleaded. "Let him speak. Sometimes bullshit makes good reading."

Encouraged, the man continued, "That animal knew how to get around this building. He knew how to get through closed doors—sometimes even locked doors." He frowned at the remembered reaction of his friends; even now they were rolling their eyes upward. "I myself saw him in the parking lot one night, when he was supposed to be in the computer room. I know I didn't let him out but somehow he was there. Later he reappeared back in the building."

"It was a different dog, dummy," one of his friends interjected.

"I told you a million times, that was our goddamn dog! Don't you think I can tell the difference?"

"Obviously not," offered the friend.

"Well how about the time we found him in the engineering room? We had to pick the lock to get him out. You still can't explain how he got in there."

"I admit that's a toughie, but it doesn't mean he's a frigging ghost. He found a way in, that's all; a hole nobody knows about."

In spite of herself, Kathy was being carried away by the story. The man seemed certain of what he was saying and, perhaps more importantly, he was willing to say it even with universal disapproval from his peers. The librarian had been much the same way. She too had stuck to her story despite all the jokes and snide remarks it generated. What were these animals? Why were they causing seemingly sane and responsible people to report unlikely events? She shook her head in disgust, recognizing the direction in which her thoughts were leading. If she started viewing these mutts as supernatural beings, the story would be a complete loss.

"How about your attempts to feed him," she asked, changing the subject.

"Somebody else must've been feeding that dog," the man replied. "He just didn't seem interested in anything we gave him. Sometimes he'd take a small bite or two, like he wanted to be polite or something, but never more than that. Not exactly your average dog."

Kathy hesitated before asking the next question, vaguely disturbed over what she knew the answer would be. "Are you sure it was light colored?"

"Yeah, a shepherd; got one of my own, although he's darker. You don't see many that light, and that's what makes it so easy to remember. Other than that it was just your average dog, about medium sized." He held up his hand to lend emphasis to his estimate of the animal's height.

The interview went on for longer than Kathy had intended. The men were fun to talk to and, except for the discomforting mysteries, the encounter was a pleasant experience. She was also pleased by their obvious attempts at flirtation, something she needed just then.

Spirits high in anticipation of finally being on the way to Wyoming and Mark, Kathy moved onto highway 101 and headed for San Francisco's airport. After saying her good-byes less than fifteen minutes before, she had hurried to the rental car, climbed in and thrown her briefcase over the front seat into the back. It had narrowly missed striking the light-colored shepherd that lay quietly on the floor.

With all thoughts focused on the next phase of the trip, she failed to detect the slight click that signaled the opening of the briefcase. Nor was she aware of the rustling of papers as a three-fingered hand carefully adjusted each sheet for inspection. She drove relentlessly on until finally reaching the rental lot where she was guided into a "Returning Cars" lane by a bored attendant.

"Grab your mileage and leave the keys in the car," he said in a practiced monotone.

Eager to comply and be on her way, Kathy reached behind and grabbed the briefcase. One clasp had become undone, and she absently snapped it shut before leaving the car. She left the door open for the attendant then moved to the trunk, opened the lid and retrieved her small suitcase. The lid was almost down before she spotted the dog.

Its canine eyes burned into hers from the other side of the back window. It did not look friendly. *Christ! It was there all along, right behind me!* She took a quick step backward and her mind filled with unreasonable thoughts of the supernatural. The horn of an arriving car made her stop, but it also made her feel that she was being attacked from all sides. She spun around to face the new danger, by now no danger at all; the vehicle, not traveling that fast to begin with, had come to a stop.

"Lady, your dog's getting away." The voice of the bored attendant spun her around once again. The animal was leaving the area without haste or alarm. Not wanting to be asked to assist in its recovery, the attendant turned away and headed down the line of parked cars.

Kathy stared at the vanishing animal, not knowing what to do or say. *How did it get in?* she thought. *What was it doing there?* The realization that this was the same kind of animal as the ones she'd been investigating gave her chills. She wondered whether it was the same animal that was seen in the Sunnyvale computer room. *Would that make matters better or worse?* She hurried into the rental office, suddenly anxious to surround herself with people.

On the flight to Jackson, Kathy forced herself to concentrate on sorting out interview notes, this to counter a lingering anxiety over the rental car incident. It was not easy, but it helped to know that each passing minute brought her closer to Mark. As the plane touched down, she tucked her papers away then prepared herself for a rapid exit. The flight had not been crowded thus the anxiety which a sluggish deplaning might have caused was avoided. Hurrying into the terminal, she raced through the small lobby to the lonely road that serviced the airport then searched for a means of getting to Kelly. Fifteen minutes later, she was in a cab and asking herself what she was doing here.

She got a good feel for the town as she walked bag and briefcase in hand down the quiet street to the saloon understood to be the only hope of finding a room. It was a pleasant enough community, and even in darkness presented itself well. The night was cool, a coolness more appreciated than resented as her body warmed to the exercise being demanded of it. She was tired, but it felt good to finally be able to stretch her legs.

She signed for a room, smiling but not otherwise reacting to the announcement of a shared bath down the hall. Then she dropped off her bags and went down to the lounge where, unbeknown to her, Mark had celebrated his arrival in Wyoming a little more than a week before. Not really hungry, she sat at the bar wondering what to do next.

A burly but friendly bartender lifted his eyes in question and Kathy ordered a vodka gimlet, settling for a vodka and ginger ale when the former proved to be too much of a challenge. As it arrived she considered whether the man might also have served Mark—it was likely that Mark had sought out the only watering hole in town. "Maybe the jerk did something to get himself noticed," she mumbled.

"You say somethin' ma'am?" the bartender asked.

"Oh, sorry. I was just thinking out loud." Impulsively, she added, "I'm trying to find a friend of mine who was in here last week."

"What's he look like?"

Although not sure why she felt that way, Kathy was annoyed that the bartender had made the assumption that her "friend" was a male. Pushing the thought aside, she described Mark to the man and explained why he had come to Kelly. She omitted the part about his wanting to think things out.

"Yeah, I seen him," the bartender said, bringing a look of surprise to Kathy's face. "That ain't so unusual, there ain't that many people coming through here this time of year. We're done the summer season and ain't yet started on the huntin' season. Your boyfriend tied one on with a few locals and I ain't seen him since."

"Were those boy locals or girl locals?" Kathy asked more sullen than she had intended. She raised the drink to her mouth as she waited for the answer.

The bartender laughed. "Don't worry, these was some of the ugliest guys I ever seen. And if that ain't enough there weren't no way your man could'a done nothing with no girl by the time he finished drinkin'."

After learning the names of two of the men Mark had met during his big night in town, Kathy left the bar and went up to her room. The men were not around and hadn't been all evening, and it was too late to search further. She would attempt to contact them in the morning.

With thoughts of fleeing lovers and strange dogs beginning to wear thin, Kathy stripped off her clothes and flopped on the bed. Cocktails and fatigue then combined to give her one of the best sleeps she'd had in some time.

CHAPTER 8

Half the day was gone by the time Kathy awoke, but what was left was filled with blue sky, sunshine and air so clear that mountains, trees and even the buildings within the town stood out as if outlined by a master artist. While dressing she stood by the bedroom window taking it all in and lamenting again Mark's refusal to invite her along. She imagined being with him now, sharing whatever level of hardship he had chosen for himself in his masochistic pilgrimage. After a while she turned from the window, grabbed a small handbag then left the hotel.

Lured by an appetite that grew rapidly in the cool, sweet smelling air, she headed down the street to a cafeteria where the decision of what meal to eat, breakfast or lunch, could be left to the individual. There she consumed volumes of hotcakes and sausage, savoring each mouthful as if it were the last she would ever get. *I'll make it up by skipping lunch*, she thought.

Afterward, she checked in at the hotel bar, only to learn that neither the bartender nor the two men who had reportedly seen Mark were there. No matter, it was not difficult to find something to occupy her time. She walked the town, then the surrounding woods, involving herself for hours in the reverie of private thoughts. Later, after a chilly bath down the hall, she dressed at leisure then headed once again for the bar. Her appetite restored by the walk, she would eat dinner there, this to give her a better chance of being around when and if her quarry appeared.

She was sitting at a table sipping a cocktail when the bartender shot a meaningful glance her way. His hand was on the shoulder of a rough looking, heavily bearded man in well worked coveralls, and he was whispering something in his ear. The bearded man was facing Kathy, but she could tell nothing from the blank expression on his face. Then he began walking toward her table, a move which brought on a momentary fear that he might have the wrong idea about her motives. She tried to remember exactly what she had said to the bartender the previous night.

"Yew wanna see me, ma'am?" the bearded man asked politely, his hesitant tone helping to drain Kathy's apprehension. "Am Cal Simmons."

"Yes, please," she said quickly, extending her arm at the same time as an invitation to sit. "May I buy you a drink?"

"Don't mind if'n ah dew. Whiskey."

"Bartender, a whiskey, please," Kathy yelled, the words causing a number of heads to swing in her direction. The bartender, who had no trouble encouraging even the largest of his customers to come to the bar to pick up his drink, smiled at their unspoken thoughts as he carried a glass of whiskey to the table then put it down with meaning in front of a grinning Cal.

Taking advantage of the power which the attractive young lady gave him, Cal said, "Thank yew kindly, barkeep; yew kin go now." His hands gestured dismissal, a move that the bartender accepted with a chuckle.

"I'm Kathy Montari." Kathy extended her hand, bringing a surprised look to the bearded face. But Cal took the proffered hand anyway, shaking it lightly as if afraid it might break in his much larger hand.

Kathy found it difficult to begin. "I understand that you and, uh, some other people like you, uh , what I mean is some friends of yours and yourself had a few cocktails with a friend of mine, and, uh, I was wondering if you could tell me anything about what he might have been planning?"

Kathy inwardly cringed at her clumsy beginning. Cal was staring at her with the same blank face she'd seen earlier, a face that successfully masked his thoughts. She decided to try again. "I mean, I know he went into the woods and all that sort of thing, but I was wondering if you knew which direction he took...or, uh, where he might be...uh...now?"

The enigmatic look on Cal's face did not change as he began a slow reply. "Way-yul, me an ma frens had a couple beers with a guy few days back, but I don't rightly know if'n it'd be right tuh say whut we was a-talkin' about." Kathy waited for more but he resumed his stare and his silence.

"Well," Kathy began again, "he and I are...close friends, and I was just sorta worried about him; you know, going out in wilderness like that alone."

"Way-yul," the man relented, "ah kin tell yew we git a whole lotta people like your boyfren; people comin' from thuh city and a-thinkin' they was Kit Carson or somethin'. Ain't so sure your fren should be out there, leastwise not alone he shouldn't."

Kathy had mixed reactions to the comment: She was uncomfortable with the thought that a presumably experienced local like this would think Mark had bitten off more than he could chew, but she wondered if Cal would say the same thing about any city type who invaded his domain. "Do you think he'll get himself into trouble?" she asked.

"Wan't be s'prised." He softened to a slouched position and talked in a slow, matter-of-fact tone, as if warming to the conversation. "They's big animals out there what he ain't never seen outside a zoo. An they's a lotta woods and mountains what kin tarn even thuh best of um around. He shudda had someun wif him, thet's what ah think!"

"I agree," Kathy said softly, thinking that that "someun" should have been her. "Do you know which way he went?"

Cal's interest heightened, and there was suspicion on his face as he asked, "Way-yul now, yew ain't a fixin' tuh go in after um, air yuh?" His expression said here was another nut from the big city.

"Oh no," Kathy said hastily. "I just want to be ready to help him if he's late getting back." When she saw the continued skepticism on Cal's face, she suddenly felt it important that this man approve of what she was up to. "By help him, I mean being able to tell the police where he went, not going in after him myself."

Cal resumed his laid back posture. "Then yew sure got more sense'n he got." He looked the woman over carefully before continuing. "Way-yul...ah guess it won't hurt none ta tell yuh he headed southeast from here, toward where all them dogs is a-comin' from. Said he wanted tuh head where they warn't no civil-i-zation—them wuz his words. If he foller through on whut he said then he gonna git his wish; could go a hunnert miles in thet direction and not see nobody, leastwise not people." He smiled as he added, "Course, ah cain't say thuh same fer animals. They's big bears there, en mountin' lions, en..."

"I get the idea," Kathy said quickly. "Did he say how long he was going to stay out?"

"Said he was a-gonna walk till he din't wanna walk no more. Din't say nothin' about puttin' no time clock on it." As Cal talked he fingered his empty glass in a rather obvious way.

Kathy took the hint. "Another whisky, please, bartender," she yelled, wanting to keep this man talking a while longer.

"An kin ah have one tew, paleeze, bartender?" said a seedy-looking character sitting across the room.

"Me too, paleeze, bartender?" shouted another, his glass raised and an exaggerated smile on his face. The others in the bar laughed heartily.

The barkeep held his smile while pouring another whiskey for Cal. "You unwashed sons-a-bitches start looking like her, maybe you git some service." He delivered the drink amid catcalls and laughter. Even Kathy smiled, pleased with the attention and amused by the friendly horseplay. She gave the bartender a warm smile as he placed the drink in front of Cal, a move that insured more such service in the future.

Kathy wanted to find out more about Mark's whereabouts but was not certain how much she wanted to confide in the man sitting across from her. She lowered her eyes and began fiddling with her half-empty vodka and ginger ale. "I'll tell you honestly, I'm more than a little worried about him. He and I are more than just...friends."

"Kinda figgered thet," Cal interrupted.

"...and I want to make sure he doesn't get lost or hurt, and I want to do it in such a way that he won't get mad at me for interfering." She looked up to see if he understood. "Is there anything else you can tell me that would help?"

"Ah guess ah done told yew all ah know," Cal said, after pausing to down his whiskey. "If'n it helps, ah don't reckon he'll be out tew long. Ah seen it happen a'fore, some city fella with big plans a tamin' the wilderness, then comin' back early cause'n his feet are sore or he ain't got no more coffee." He stared at the suddenly vulnerable young woman then fell silent. At that moment he wished he had more he could tell her.

Kathy could think of nothing more to ask. Cal's comments had not been particularly reassuring, but the interview had had only a faint chance of success from the start. Mark was out there somewhere and, in all probability, no one except himself knew where. *Maybe by now even he doesn't know,* she thought.

As Cal began to rise from his seat, she suddenly remembered a comment he had made earlier. "What did you mean when you said that my friend left in the same direction the dogs came from?" Thoughts of the shepherds and the unsettling affair at San Francisco airport began to return. She had almost forgotten the supposed reason she was here, to investigate the Kelly-dog story. The man in front of her apparently had knowledge of the matter.

"Way-yul...we done told your boyfren 'bout thet but ah don't reckon he believed us none. Buncha strange dogs been comin' out'a them woods, one or tew at a time. They jus appears one day then disappears thuh next. Nobody knows where they's a-comin' from an nobody knows where they's gone tew."

He told Kathy all he knew about the dogs and even some things that were not so much facts as they were "good tellin'" to strangers. The exaggeration, some of it obvious, defused some of her fears, and made her comfortable with the idea that the whole thing was, as her editor suspected, local lore. But as the story unfolded and the similarities between this and the others she was researching became clear, the discomfort in her stomach grew.

"Cal, is there anything about light-colored dogs that make them act differently—German shepherds, I mean?"

"Ain't nothin' I ever heared' of thet'd make much difference in thar be-havior. I just recon'd these is all frum thuh same bunch, maybe even the same mammy an pappy." He raised his eyebrows as he added, "Don't know whut else cud explain er."

An hour later, back in the hotel room and trying to pass the time by working on her article, Kathy ran the conversation through her mind. In all cases the beasts were the same type, and all acted strangely but strangely in much the same way. *What the hell is going o*n? she thought. It was weird, absolutely weird. *This Kelly-dog crap could prove to be the weirdest yet.* According to Cal hundreds have been seen with one or more arriving every few days. Even if one assumed this is where they all came from, how could they get to Pennsylvania or California or God knows where else?

She blanched as she thought of Mark traveling alone right into the path of those dogs. What would happen if he bumped into one? Would it be as friendly as people claimed?

Writing about them would spice to her article, but she would feel better if she could get to the bottom of it. At least the Kelly-dog part of it. Her article would then entertain without importing a sense of the supernatural. Plus it would give her something meaningful to do while awaiting Mark's return.

She decided to go for it. As a first step, she would get in touch with Cal and get him to help her create a list of townspeople to interview. She could add the inevitable whisky bribes to her expense account.

CHAPTER 9

It was hard to judge how much time had passed since the glow first appeared in the red-tinted, early evening sky. By now it was dark and had been for some time, and Mark's concentration was focused less on the glow than on the shadow to his front, a shadow that seemed always to be running away—how long could it keep up this pace? How long could *he* keep up this pace? The glow filled more of the sky than before, but it still seemed a long way off. When he could do so without missing a step, he lifted his eyes to see, hoping each time to catch something he had not seen before.

The creature in front of him showed no sign of fatigue. Neither did it appear to recognize fatigue in its human charge—it set a pace to its liking and the human could follow or not as he wished. The two of them had not communicated since the pause for water earlier in the evening. They marched in silence, the creature leading and Mark following docilely and without question.

Suddenly they were there. Without warning the forest ended and they were at the apex of a gently sloping hill overlooking acres of glowing buildings, the nearest some three hundred yards ahead. Upon seeing them, the creature paused then, as if on impulse, stepped aside to permit its charge a better view, the expression on its small-featured face a cross between amusement and curiosity. Mark stopped a comfortable distance away then gazed at the scene with all the awe and intensity his overstrained system would permit.

Closer examination proved they were not buildings at all. More a collection of ill-defined shapes, each with a smooth surface and each flowing gently into the next with no obvious seams or connectors. Also not obvious were windows, doors or even corners—there were no sharp edges of any kind. The entire thing was in motion, increasing then decreasing in size and pulsating as would tents under a strong wind. The glow was impressive, and, reflecting off the nearby hills, it presented Mark a reminder of the eerie vegetation that had welcomed him into this nightmare a forgotten number of days ago. It appeared to be nothing more than energy. Or some material that emitted a visible form of radiation. The optical confusion provided by so much glare against so dark a sky added to the difficulty of pinpointing the boundaries of each form, although this was softened by a pinkish outline as glow descended into a dark, red sky.

Crisscrossing between the ill-defined structures were tubes of bright light the number of which added considerably to the area's brilliance. Within them Mark could see fleeting shadows moving with incredible speed from one end to the other, sometimes changing directions at intersections—so quickly did this happen that he was left no time to guess at what they were, or how they could so radically alter course without being destroyed in the process. He watched in fascination, confused by what his mind could not understand but unable to turn away. His guide brought him out of his reverie by summarily turning back toward the lights then walking toward them. Fearing being alone more than what lay before him, Mark fell in behind.

As the complex drew nearer and its cool brilliance began to penetrate his body, Mark felt his heartbeat increase. They were now only yards away; soon they would be close enough to reach out and touch the light's surface. Then what?

The question was still echoing in his mind when the creature disappeared—one moment it had been approaching a tube of light, the next it was gone. At the instance of its disappearance, a shadow had moved rapidly away, finally disappearing altogether within one of the pulsating structures. Mark was alone once again.

Paralyzed by fear, he was unable to imitate what the creature had done: walk blindly into that glowing tube. He could only stand where he was, hoping its now-familiar shape would reemerge and offer guidance. But it did not, and each passing second reminded Mark of how isolated and vulnerable he was.

In time the fear of being alone began to equal the uncertainty of the light. He had to take a chance. Slowly and with caution, he approached the point where the beam began, finding it to be clearly delineated with sharp light at one point and total absence of light the next. It had an opening that was large enough to permit him to walk into it without bending. Fascinating, whatever it was, and in recognition of such, he raised a finger to examine the point at which it so suddenly began. As he was about to make contact a powerful hand landed on his shoulder and gave him whatever additional encouragement he needed; he literally leapt into the beam.

A cry of fear exploded from his throat as his body became momentarily enveloped in brilliant light. The sensation lasted for only a faction of a second, after which he found himself in the middle of a large, faintly glowing room. He had had no feeling of movement, other than the involuntary jump into the glow. No acceleration or deceleration. No pain either; no unpleasant sensation at all. The impression was that the room he now occupied was immediately inside the beam, a mere step from the outside.

The awkward entry, coupled with a cry that did not clear Mark's throat until he was well within the enclosure, gained the immediate attention of the room's occupants. There were three of them, and they looked very much alike, the two strangers almost identical to the one Mark had followed.

All were the same color and all were enveloped in the same thick fur. They did not move, nor did they speak—their undersized mouths were tightly closed.

Mark was struck by the untimely thought that he had never seen the one he called Spot with his mouth open. The creature had not eaten or drank while in his presence and communication had somehow been accomplished with its mouth closed.

All three were staring at him with that same dual expression of pity and annoyance seen earlier on Spot. That and their silence made Mark ill at ease, the feeling akin to having crashed a private party, one at which he could not expect to find a friend. He stared at the only one he recognized and inclined his head in question, "Spot...?" he whispered. There was no time for the question to be answered as an alien hand again appeared on his shoulder.

Mark's yell this time was even louder, as he sped from under its grasp. Then, eyes bulging and heart strained to capacity by unkind surprises, he whirled around to view a fourth such creature, this one too close for comfort. The others, not expecting Mark's sudden move, enveloped themselves in a faint protective haze—it was gone in a second.

"Do not stand by the entrance!" Emerging from the same beam, it was possibly the same creature who had frightened him into the device in the first place. At its command, Mark moved further away, his heart still unable to find an acceptable rhythm. The newcomer stepped over to his colleagues, there to join them in silent observation of the human intruder. Soon four heads were swinging back and forth as if engaged in heavy conversation, conversation without sound—Mark wondered whether the problem was in his hearing.

These were not unpleasant looking creatures. Unusual for sure, but far from monsters. They gave the impression of skinny, baby-faced adolescents dressed up as giant teddy bears. If they had been only half the size of himself rather than half a foot taller, he might have considered them cuddly. The truth beginning to leak through, Mark let his eyes drift around the room to in search of confirmation. The inside walls looked no different than the outside, but the glow was more manageable to the eyes. Also like the outside, there was no clue as to what was holding it together. There was the same absence of seams; try as he may, he could see no clear delineation between ceiling, walls and floor.

On one wall, or more accurately, suspended from a light beam projecting from the soft glow that suggested a wall, was a large panel of illuminated buttons. They were arranged in a hexagon and were thirty or forty in number—Mark attempted to pin down the exact amount but was repeatedly defeated by the relentless, optically-confusing pulsing. Also suspended from thin beams of light, were two long rows of cubicles, some large and some small. It was likely that they themselves were composed of light. Contained within them were assortments of plants and rocks, many of which, to Mark's delight, he recognized—for the first time in a number of days here was something he could relate to. It gave a boost to his tortured spirits. Just below the opening of each unit was a bright button similar to those found on the hexagon. It was noticeable only because its intensity was greater than the glowing material that surrounded it. Mark stared at one such button, wondering what it controlled. He was surprised when it began communicating a detailed explanation of its contents—the suddenness of this was not appreciated.

"Hollyhock (Althaea Rosea), Perennial Chinese herb..."

The description went on for twenty seconds and held Mark's close attention; not because he understood anything more than the basics of what it offered, but because the machine was communicating directly to him—somehow he knew this. It was a form of recorder that would play on command. *But what did I do to "command" it?* he thought.

He listened with the intensity of a child being informed of a basic fact of life. Although still hampered by an emotional short fuse, a sense of curiosity mixed with awe had begun to penetrate the fear and hopelessness of before. His hosts were not figments of an overactive imagination nor players in a macabre nightmare. Nor was he insane. *They're aliens*, he mused, feeling more calm at the thought than he would have imagined possible. *I'm in the middle of a UFO encounter!* But how could all this remain hidden when everything is so incredibly bright?

The machine fell silent after offering the word, "Potential:," and Mark wondered whether this was of his doing. He turned to another such cubicle, one with yet another familiar plant, but this one offered no explanation of what it contained. Why? What had he done to get the first to respond? When his eye focused on the glowing button below the unit's opening, he had his answer—it dutifully began relaying a description of its contents. *Incredible!* He wondered at the sophistication that would enable this machine to respond to such a subtle command.

This recording, like the previous one, ended with "Potential:...." There was nothing beyond that point. *I don't understand*, thought Mark. *If the purpose it serves is included within the description, why is "Potential" blank?*

It came to him then that the four aliens were staring at him with unmistakable expressions of amusement. Occasionally the pupils of one would contract at exactly the same time that a human-like smile appeared on its face—the two actions had to be related. *The bastards are enjoying this*, he thought, noting this only out of the corner of his eye—it was difficult to meet their collective glance directly.

It was equally as difficult to resist continuing his inspection of the room's contents.

There were no animals or other living creatures within any cubicle along the room's extended corridor, only plants and rocks, all of which appeared normal—at least there were no examples of the odd-ball vegetation he'd seen on the way in. Additional cubicles, varying slightly in design, rested against the walls of light. Some were empty, some contained unfamiliar objects and some, flat rather than tall, looked to serve the purpose of shelves—a variety of devices, all unrecognizable, rested on their surfaces.

Everything—shelves, buttons, supports and even walls—was made of light, varying intensities of light. There was nothing solid here except himself, the exhibits, and whatever those creatures now in control of his fate might be. Even the floor on which he stood was light, spongy light that gave way like a soft rug as he shifted from one foot to the other.

He realized with a start that the creatures were becoming more animated in their head movements, staring first at him then at one another, even moving their limbs at times. Then, with alarming suddenness, their appetite for staring at one another gave way to a silent agreement to stare at him. And the amused expressions were no longer there. One of the four, not the one he called Spot, then walked over to the hexagonal panel and began touching lights.

A new cubicle instantly appeared in the room, this one large and rectangular in shape. It, like the others, had a glowing button the function of which, as Mark now knew, was to provide information on the contents within. Although currently empty, he could not resist triggering it with his eyes.

"Earth man (Homo Sapiens); dominant biological species of the planet Earth; chemical composition, unknown; extent and depth of knowledge, unknown; level of emotional stability, unknown but questionable; level of civilization, late primitive; offensive weapon capability, late primitive; disease concerns, unknown—caution suggested; Potential:..." As with the other exhibits, "Potential:" was blank.

Apprehension grew within him, dismay as well, this at the certain knowledge that the description—and the cubicle—was meant for him. He was to become a specimen in some alien laboratory. His earlier moment of confidence was no more, especially as he wondered whether he was to be maintained alive or in some exotic form of taxidermy.

One question, however, had been answered. The "Earth man" and "planet Earth" comments proved he was right about who these creatures were. "You really are from outer space!" he whispered weakly.

There was no hesitation in the response; it came from Spot. "To be precise, there are many light years of space between here and your planet, but no biological beings of which we are aware actually reside in such an inhospitable void. In addition, if anyone is from 'outer space,' as you so incorrectly put it, you are."

"But how did you get here?" Mark asked, in his confusion not understanding what the creature was telling him.

"My dear Earthling, it is not we who are there; it is you who are here. You are on our planet, not the other way around."

"What...?" Mark muttered, his voice just above a whisper.

"I believe you are capable of receiving my projections in a clear and concise manner. It would be helpful if you were to reply in kind."

"But..."

"Good point! But perhaps it would be best if we postponed this engaging discussion until another time."

"We want you to enter this chamber!" It came from the alien who had recently manipulated the hexagonal panel. Receiving from another direction what appeared to be a sound, Mark spun around to confront the source. Gesturing with its three-fingered hand, the creature was indicating the recently constructed cubicle, the one with no "Potential:."

Mark stared at the uninviting container of light, its presence now a threat rather than a curiosity. "No way!" he said warily, wondering anew whether they intend to keep him alive. He jumped as Spot picked up the conversation once again.

"From our brief observation of your species, we feel certain you are capable of more understanding than you have thus far demonstrated. We would appreciate your assisting us in our dilemma by communicating in a more succinct fashion."

In his growing apprehension over what might be about to happen, Mark could think of no appropriate response. After a moment of silence, the creature, Spot, continued. "As was previously communicated to you, please enter the chamber!"

Things were happening too fast—"I want to know what's going to happen! What are you... things ...going to do to me?" He was beginning to lose control once again, this time because he saw his mortality suspended from a light beam a few steps away. "I can't enter that ridiculous box!"

"Essentially incorrect," Spot replied, "the process is quite simple. Indeed, strictly speaking, you cannot fail to enter. It will do you no harm and will help us to provide a chemical and gravitational environment which we have every reason to expect will be more suitable to your biological needs. Our environment is even now weakening you, to what eventual result we cannot yet predict."

Mark stared for a long moment, his head turning back and forth from one creature to another. But then, weakened by hunger and fatigue and faced with logic he could not find the energy to refute, he let out a sigh of surrender and began walking toward the cubicle. He paused only a moment before stepping into it. One of the creatures then touched a series of buttons on the hexagonal panel.

The effect on Mark was immediate. Body weight appeared to increase, which was not of itself welcome, but the action permitted a feeling of normalcy. At the same time his breathing became easier and the overwhelming fatigue he had felt fell from his body like discarded clothing. Gone also was his hunger and that nagging state of fear and uncertainty. It was as if he had just emerged from a good night's sleep then concluded a satisfying meal.

"What *is* this thing?" Mark asked, his hands searching the periphery of the chamber—he could not fail to note as he did so that something was blocking the entrance.

"A rest and rejuvenation chamber...with a containment module," said Spot. "If we are correct, it will provide exactly what your body requires."

Mark considered his "chamber" in relation to others within the same room, then was reminded of the glowing button which served to identify the contents of each, "A goddamn exhibit!" he exclaimed in indignation, adding as an afterthought, "Why don't I have a 'potential?'"

The creature's eyes contracted slightly as he smiled. "We do appreciate the irony of your comments while being quite certain that you do not. However, your 'potential,' is what we would determine to be the use of you, both to your species and to your environment. I cannot pretend that we do not attempt to determine what each exhibit's potential is to *us* as well, but that is not the reason for our research."

Mark was not reassured. "And the 'containment module;' is that to keep me prisoner?"

"For the present it is considered best that your activities be curtailed. Surely you would agree that we are in a better position to judge what is currently best for you."

Mark's immediate reaction was to strongly disagree, but his new-found tranquillity seemed to make the creature's statements more acceptable, even logical. Anyway, he accepted them as such, recognizing as he did so how much easier it was to become indignant than to remain so—this machine was acting to block emotions it considered counterproductive. Not that this was unwelcome; he had suffered too much emotional discomfort in the last few days. It was just that it was...annoying...to know he could be so easily manipulated.

Then he remembered something the creature had said earlier. "What did you mean when you said help you out of this dilemma?"

"I believe what I actually said was 'appreciate your assisting us in our dilemma,'" Spot responded.

Mark waited for the creature to continue. When it did not, he was forced to ask again. "All right, goddamn it, what did you mean when you said 'appreciate your assisting us in our dilemma?' What dilemma?"

The creature at first seemed pleased, but then took on a frown. "Well, to be frank, you should not be here. We can assure you that no invitation, either subtle or overt, emanated from us, and we have recently concluded the probability that you did not intentionally invite yourself. In any event, you are not welcome; indeed you present us with quite a...dilemma. We are currently analyzing the circumstances which brought you here and what might be done to recover."

Mark hesitated before asking the next question. "Where exactly is 'here?'"

"You are on our planet, the planet Mantz, which, as I have already stated, is many light years from what you refer to as Earth."

A queasy feeling grew in Mark's stomach, an emotion quickly

countered by the chamber. "It's true then, I'm really not on Earth?"

"Change the inflection in your voice and you have your answer. You have traveled aboard our vehicle, so to speak, to a planet which is not really that far from yours, cosmically speaking. Frankly, it is so close that we feel remiss in failing to recognize prior to this point that it contains sophisticated life forms."

"I went for a walk in the woods, for Christ's sake!" Mark yelled. "Are you telling me your planet is within walking distance?" Mark shook his head in disbelief, "This has got to be a dream!"

"It 'has got,' as you so crudely put it, to be nothing more than it really is, and it really is what you see and feel."

"But, how did I get here?"

"My dear Earth man, you already answered that question, you 'walked.'"

Mark looked at the creature in a new light. It was playing with him, enjoying his confusion and only reluctantly providing meaningful answers. With the return to emotional normalcy provided by the chamber, he was able to see this clearly. Not so certain was how he should handle it. After a moment of reflection, he decided to return sarcasm with sarcasm. "Do you suppose there might be something extra here? I mean I've done some long-distance walking in my life, but I never made it as far as Mans before."

"The pupils in the Mantzite's eyes contracted for a brief moment and a slight smile appeared across its pale, small-featured face. "Mantz," it corrected. "Actually you are quite perceptive, there was an additional factor, our transporter."

Mark waited, then realized that the creature was again forcing him to ask the obvious. "All right, I'll play your silly game, what is a 'transporter?'"

Satisfied, the alien responded in much the same manner as had the exhibits earlier. It was as if his own exhibit button had been pressed. "A rather useful little device which you might think of as a space warp between a point on our planet and a point on yours. The laboratory in which you now find yourself has been located as close to our end as is considered wise. Space, as you may or may not be aware, does not travel in a straight line. With sufficient knowledge, in this case proper application of the warping concept, one can take advantage of this, effectively skipping across great distances in no time at all. We have long known that space warps exist, although it was originally deemed necessary to enter the proximity of a collapsed star, or black hole, to take advantage of one. This is no longer true; we have discovered a way to expand on the concept. Using the substantial gravitational forces of the black hole, we can focus its properties elsewhere, effectively producing a warp when we wish and almost precisely where we wish. The result, which we refer to as our transporter, you might think of as a long tunnel—sometimes depressingly long, in fact. I could explain why this is necessary although I strongly suspect that would prove to be a waste of my time."

Mark noted the abrupt return to sarcasm from what had been a professorial lecture. He suspected the creature had momentarily forgotten itself and now felt the necessity to restore a more appropriate image. It did not, however, last. Spot resumed his explanation, adding hand movements that could almost have been human.

"From this laboratory we walk in a certain direction until fully transported to the place of our destination; in this case your planet, Earth. As I already stated, it is analogous to a tunnel through which we must travel if we wish to avail ourselves of a magnificent shortcut to anywhere in the galaxy. The alternative, as even you are capable of understanding, is light years of tedious travel. I must confess it would be much easier if we could transport ourselves instantaneously, thus obviating the need for the long walk, but that must wait for a...later stage." He hesitated as if not certain how much more he wanted to say.

Mark was incredulous. He was having a conversation with an extraterrestrial, even joking with him. At the moment, it would not seem out of place for the creature to offer cocktails and hors d'oeuvres. And with the up-lifting atmosphere provided by the rest and rejuvenation chamber, he could accept it all as easily as he might accept an introduction to a new neighbor. Finally it all made sense, the changing scenery, the red sky, the oddly-shaped animals, even the breathing difficulty he'd experienced earlier.

Well, maybe not all of it. There were still birds that acted like zombies. And the ability of Spot and the others to speak without opening their mouths—and speak English at that. "What were those birds we kept seeing?" he asked. "They looked like your regular birds but they sure didn't act like them."

"Our mistake, really—we lack convincing authenticity in some species. Admittedly we have much to learn about Earth creatures. In fairness to us, however, we have only been exploring your planet for slightly over one Earth year; not enough time to become experts on all its species."

"You've been on Earth a year without anyone knowing about it?" Mark asked, his surprise causing him to overlook the fact that his question had not been answered.

"Slightly *over* one Earth year, I believe I said."

"But how can you remain undetected, and why don't you let someone know you're there?"

"Your questions are really not logical when presented in that manner. If we have succeeded in remaining undetected, then it is logical that we do not wish to let anyone know we are there, at least not at the present. We have a time-tested procedure for exploring new worlds, and this does not involve communication with dominant species until well along in our acquired knowledge of that planet. To do so in advance of the most logical point could be disastrous for both the new world and ourselves. We might, for example, discover a civilization more powerful than ourselves. We would be foolish to force an introduction if, in doing so, we invited a conqueror to our planet."

"You would prefer being the conqueror yourself!"

"Not so. We intend no harm to, nor dominance of, any planet. Our explorations are for the good of all creatures."

Mark was skeptical in both look and voice. "I can't believe you'd be doing this if you didn't get something out of it for yourselves."

The creature presented Mark a blank expression and did not attempt to respond to the comment. "Perhaps we can continue this discussion after you have had time to adjust to your situation."

Mark jumped at the words. "What exactly is my 'situation?'" he asked.

The creature paused before answering with, "It should be obvious from what I said that we cannot have premature contact with dominant Earth creatures. You are, in a sense, a violation of this strict rule. We have yet to decide how to reconcile such an unsettling dilemma."

This was not what Mark wanted to hear. "What are you going to do to me?"

"For the present," the creature answered, "we will take advantage of your presence and analyze your psyche and physiology."

"My what!"

"We will attempt to learn more about you," the creature said, turning as he did so in an obvious attempt to terminate the conversation.

"Wait," said Mark, not wanting him to go, "you still didn't explain about the birds in the woods, why they acted so weird."

The creature hesitated for a moment then reluctantly turned back toward the Earth man. "As I have already intimated, they were our representatives. And I believe that also answers your question in regard to how we have remained undetected." Then he turned back to his colleagues and gestured toward the nearest beam tunnel. Obediently, each vanished into it. The creature, Spot, entered last, throwing one last glance at his captive before disappearing.

"What do you mean, 'your representatives?'" Mark yelled, Spot's cryptic comment only adding to his confusion. "They were birds, for Christ's sake!" There was no response.

Mark's sigh had no real punch to it. He was alone and on a planet purported to be "many light years from Earth," and about to be experimented upon by alien creatures, yet he was not upset. True, he was experiencing a mercurial pattern of emotions, but only in his mind—as quickly as they threatened to become more than that, they were swept away; the cubicle would not let him feel anything for long. He ran his hands over all sides of it—the "chamber," as Spot had referred to it—but all he could discover was different intensities of light. In some places the glow was thick, as if additional light were needed there to support the structure. In other places it was so thin that he could see through. Touching the entrance again proved that the invisible something was still there, a fact that did not surprise him even though its crystal clarity suggested it could not be that strong. *Maybe it isn't.* He attempted to push through but was greeted by a gentle force, like a water-filled balloon, surrendering at first but firming up as pressure is increased. Pushing harder produced the same result: Except for a slight give to prevent its occupant from being jarred, it was unyielding.

No matter. The chamber permitted him to easily accept this and his confinement in general. *Great gadget*, he thought. It had appeared out of nowhere at the touch of a series of buttons—Mark wished he had paid attention to which buttons had been touched. And the result was tremendous relief. He did not even feel the fatigue one might expect of having to stand in one spot for an extended period of time. Nor did he have an urge to periodically switch weight from one leg to the other. The machine thought of it all. It compensated for anything and everything that even hinted of discomfort, even before that discomfort began.

But it was discomforting, at least intellectually, to know that there was no easy way out of the chamber—later he would have to give that more thought. For the moment, however, he was comfortable, very comfortable, and very happy to be relieved of the agony he'd felt on the "walk" in. He chuckled at what Spot had said about that, then let it fade as if too taxing to keep going. Enveloped in ever-increasing physical and emotional comfort, he closed his eyes then fell immediately into a deep sleep. He had no awareness of being in an upright position.

CHAPTER 10

He awoke in confusion. Spot was standing at the entrance to his cubicle, his eyes deep and intense and his face darkened by a disturbingly-human frown. In his alien hand, held as one would a knife, was a device that projected a thin beam of light out of a glowing handle. A bolt of fear shot through Mark, an emotion that the machine only partially offset. "What's going on, Spot?" he asked hesitatingly.

The frown on the creature's face drifted from anger to annoyance. "Have you a formal identifier?" he asked.

"What do you mean?"

"How are you identified on Earth? Surely your fellow creatures do not yell 'Hey, Earth man' when they wish to gain your attention."

"My name is Mark Carter, if that's what you mean," Mark replied, miffed at the imperious tone in Spot's words.

"Markcarter? You are identified as Markcarter?"

"No, Mark Carter," he corrected, his annoyance rising as the creature continued his curt remarks.

"I believe that is what I said. Well, my dear Markcarter, I am identified as Creson, and I would much prefer that to 'Spot!'"

Mark stared for a moment before responding, and when finally he did it was in anger. "Fuck you, Spot!" he yelled. But his anger slipped away as the machine acted quickly to limit the extent of this emotion.

Creson said nothing for some seconds, but his face had taken on a confused look. Finally he replied. "On analysis I see that your previous comment represents what you would refer to as an expletive, although I cannot understand what it suggests I should do. However, I suppose it is not of critical importance how a marginally civilized creature addresses me. Your hand, please." He held out his own hand in anticipation of

Mark's complying.

"What do you want with it?" Mark questioned, certain that the creature was not interested in shaking hands.

"We must learn more about you, for your own good and for the good of your species."

"Damnit!" yelled Mark, "What do you intend to do?"

Impatient to get on with his experiment, Creson reached through the barrier of the chamber and applied the specialized beam device to casually remove Mark's arm above the elbow. Then, also without resistance, he withdrew the arm from the chamber leaving Mark with a stump and a curious sense of disbelief.

When finally Mark found the means to react it was pitifully inadequate. Held back by the machine, he could only observe his dismemberment with scientific detachment. There was no pain or blood, only a picture-perfect cross-section of his arm.

Creson placed the severed appendage on a light beam that served as a table and began examining it in detail. His face gave no indication of what he thought of this act of mutilation. After a few minutes he said in a matter-of-fact tone, "Move a finger." Although dumbfounded, Mark complied—the index finger attached to the severed hand responded. "Now the one next to it," he indicated the hand's middle finger. Again Mark complied and again a finger moved. Creson watched the series of lights that had appeared above the table when the limb was first placed upon it, then shrugged his shoulders as if unimpressed. Then he went to the room's hexagonal panel and began touching buttons, the effect of which was to produce an intense glow around the severed limb, so intense that its insides were displayed. This lasted for only a second, after which another light appeared just below the others, a light that Mark knew would trigger a summary of information on the human arm—his arm. He diverted his eyes to prevent its grisly information from reaching him.

Creson touched additional buttons and within Mark's chamber the stump of his arm began to glow. It was hard for Mark not to look, and when he did he saw the insides as clearly as he had seen those of its missing partner. It was a sight that did nothing to counter a failing sense of reality. His mind felt as if it were going into overdrive, yet his body, so perfectly controlled by the chamber's machinery, remained calm. The sharp incongruity gave Mark a feeling of controlled insanity.

Creson moved over to the cubicle and, after a quick look at the glowing stump, said, "One more part, if you don't mind." The knife-like beam was once again in his hand.

Mark could not move. He could only watch in horror as Creson reached into the chamber and casually passed the beam of light through his neck. He tried to scream as he felt his head separate from his body, but the only reaction permitted him was to wonder how it was possible that he was still conscious. As the severed head, lifted by the hair, swung out of the chamber, he was able to get a look at what remained in the chamber. His headless body was standing there as if still under his control, and as he continued to stare, it reached out with its remaining arm as if pleading for the return of what it knew was its own.

No amount of tranquilizers could stop the terror that now overwhelmed him, and Mark began a scream that had no lung power to give it voice. And as his eyes widened in response to the trauma, he saw as though through a fog, the body—his body—begin to crumble; it was dying. He struggled to keep it in sight as his head swung back and forth in Creson's hand on its way to the examining table. Then the room began to spin and this, coupled with the horror he had witnessed upon himself, manifested itself in merciful unconsciousness.

Again he awoke with a start, this time experiencing more emotions than the machine had permitted the previous day—was it relenting? He was back in the chamber, his body in one piece. In panic, he reached for his neck then searched for some sign of separation. He found none, but the fact of two hands responding rather than one, proved the restoration was complete. Cautiously, he touched the area on his arm where the break had occurred. Like the neck, no sign of a previous separation could be found.

Creson was standing in front of him, his look one of concern. "Are you feeling well?" he questioned.

"What did you do to me?" Mark said, his voice a salad mix of disgust and horror.

The concerned expression left Creson's face replaced by the more familiar pomposity. "You routinely answer a question by asking one of your own, and frankly many of your questions make no sense at all."

"What the hell did you do with my arm and my head?!" Mark yelled, unwilling to allow the subject to be changed.

Creson pointedly shot a glance at Mark's arms and head then, switching to an exaggerated expression of confusion, raised a three-fingered hand to his chin. "Does your species experience uncontrolled projections while at rest?"

Mark was momentarily taken aback, "You mean dreams?" he asked.

"As you will, dreams?"

"Well...yes, but..."

"Then there you have it. As anyone can clearly see, both of your arms are where they were probably intended to be and are, at least to the casual observer, in perfect working order. The same can be said for your head, allowing of course for the oddity of your species."

Mark was finding it hard to separate fact from fantasy. The experience was too real to have been a dream, but he truly was in one piece and there were no scars that he could see or feel. Resigning himself to the possibility, he carried it a step further in his thoughts, *Is this whole thing a dream?* He stared at Creson, still waiting for a response, an annoyingly smug look on his alien face. "Can you people remove arms and heads?" he asked, the eccentric nature of the question causing him to present it with less force than he'd intended.

Creson's eyes contracted briefly, and a look of amusement appeared on his face. "What purpose would that serve?" he asked. "We have far more sophisticated means of determining the interior of cosmic substance, which certainly includes biological beings. Indeed, we intend to examine you in precisely this manner."

Mark's eyes widened at the comment, and he shrank as far as he could into the chamber. "You stay the hell away from me, Spot!" he yelled.

The alien face softened. "I can assure you that what we intend is quite harmless. In any event you really have no choice in the matter. For your good as well as ours we must learn considerably more about you than is known at the present time."

Creson leaned back against a beam shelf and looked calmly into Mark's eyes, the position and the silence seeming to invite questions. Mark took the bait.

"Who are you people?" he asked tentatively.

Creson responded promptly. "Think of us as scientific observers. We study life, wherever in this galaxy it presents itself. Such efforts have not only enriched our knowledge of life per se, and of its many forms, but have permitted us to assist in the health and longevity of a plethora of alien species."

"Is that what you're doing with me, studying an 'alien species?'"

"Essentially correct, although I would hesitate to present it with the negative inference. We act in behalf of all intelligent species. We have much to offer, and we long ago made a commitment to offer it generously to all."

Mark watched him closely as he spoke. "You're not moving your lips; how can I be hearing you so clearly?"

Creson's eyes contracted briefly as he smiled. "As was explained when you were in an emotional state that might well preclude its understanding, you are not *hearing* at all; nor am I *speaking*."

"You're communicating mentally!" Mark guessed. "Through mental telepathy!"

"Precisely. Regretfully, you seem unable to reciprocate."

"But, how do you know how to speak English?"

"My dear Markcarter, I am not 'speaking' at all. I am merely presenting your mind with ideas which it then converts to forms most easily understood by you. The language of ideas is more practical, and, I should add, more universal. Your own comprehension is testimony to this. Your subconscious converts my ideas to what you refer to as 'English,' that apparently being the only means you have of understanding. I know nothing of your 'English,' nor is it necessary that I do. On your part, I hear sounds coming from your lips but they mean nothing to me. What really matters are the ideas which your mind projects along with the sounds. The process of understanding is, however, by no means easy. That is, as is applied to creatures who have not yet mastered the technique of telepathic thought transference. Since your projected ideas are an unintended by-product of an attempt to communicate by sound, they are inevitably more subtle than we would prefer. Converting such gibberish into meaningful communication takes much skill. Fortunately we have the advantage of considerable practice in this field; you are not the only uncivilized planet with which we have had to communicate."

He continued without giving Mark a chance to respond. "You might appreciate knowing that idea projections coming from you, however inadequate they are at present, demonstrate that your species does have the capacity to communicate through mental projection alone. You either fail to recognize this or are simply lazy. I submit that someday your species will catch on and skip the middle man, so to speak."

Mark was impressed but still not clear on what he was being told. "But you sound so funny, so precise, like someone from another country."

"In a sense I am from another 'country.' I suppose the difference in our 'speech' is due to the manner in which we project the information. Being more civilized than you, we would naturally have a tendency to be more accurate, or as you might put it, 'more better.'" Creson's body quivered in silent appreciation of his own humor.

This pattern of information interspersed with playful insults was becoming familiar to Mark. He smiled before moving the conversation to another subject. "Yesterday you didn't really answer my question about the weird birds we saw in the woods."

"First of all," Creson interrupted, "it was not yesterday; you have been here longer than that—sleeping most of the time, I might add. Secondly, I did answer your question. The answer, if you recall, was that these 'birds' were in reality us. In order to travel about new worlds with a reasonable expectation of remaining anonymous, we routinely disguise ourselves as local creatures, taking into consideration, of course, the characteristics of the planet being explored. For example, where gravity is more intense, converting to a four-legged being permits a better distribution of body weight. The form which appears to work best on your planet, which is a heavier-gravity planet, is the dog—the domesticated variety—although from time to time, depending on the circumstances of the investigation, we have found it convenient to convert to other forms as well. You were unfortunate enough to observe our representatives practicing another promising possibility. On their behalf, I must state that it takes time to become proficient in imitating the behavior of the creatures whose form we elect to assume. Nonetheless, I regret that their incompetence so negatively affected your morale."

Mark remembered the discomfort he'd felt in the woods. "You can disguise yourselves as Earth creatures?" he asked.

"Not disguise so much as convert. With the benefit of centuries of practice, it has become a simple matter for us to alter the genes and chemistry of our bodies to become, in everything except the brain, any creature we wish to imitate. It really is not all that difficult. With respect to the brain, we had to take pains, as you might imagine, to insure that our consciousness remained as it was. Otherwise there would be little purpose in assuming the form of another creature."

"Sounds simple enough," Mark said with a smile, attempting humor but receiving no response. Disappointed, he continued, "But what about the half-dog creature, was that also one of you? And how did he do what he did?" The last question sounded as sheepish as he felt in asking it. He could not believe the creature had actually passed through his body.

Creson understood the Earth man's concern but preferred, as was his habit, to stretch out the answer. "Once again you ask two questions at once, as if you do not desire an answer to the first." He sighed then continued, "I suppose that by answering the second I am, in effect, answering the first." He stared at the ceiling contemplating the wisdom of his words.

"Oh for Christ's sake, will you just answer the question!"

"The first or the second?"

"Your choice!" Mark said, conscious as he belted out the words that the machine was not attempting to counter his frustration.

"Well then, perhaps the second. The 'creature' really did pass through your body; an unnecessary act of truculence to be sure, but you must understand that my colleague was not quite himself at the time, if you'll pardon the pun." Mark's look of surprise caused a deepening of the smile that had already begun to appear on the alien's face. "It is a relatively simple matter to progress from gene manipulation to the rearranging of one's body molecules to avoid coming into contact with those of another creature. Or, for that matter, those of any object, biological or otherwise.

Mark was fascinated in spite of himself. "How are you able to do this? Is it something anyone could learn? Could I do it?"

"Frankly, we have no idea. Preliminary observation suggests limited or atrophied intelligence in your case, although a more thorough study might alter that opinion."

"You mean a study of me!"

"You are the only specimen available at the moment. As alluded to previously, we are not even supposed to have you. But since you are here we might as well take advantage of it."

"If you're not supposed to have me, why am I here?"

"The exploration of Earth has only recently begun and we have obviously not yet perfected the means of getting there and back without introducing contamination into the process."

"What the hell are you talking about? What contamination?" Mark questioned.

"Why you, of course; no offense intended. As I mentioned earlier, we did not invite you, you came on your own, thus presenting us with an embarrassment, a possible health hazard and a legal entanglement. As regards the latter, it is quite forbidden to have you here. Your presence signifies a serious violation of our laws; laws that are highly practical in their assumptions and application. Our investigation at this stage of your planet's exploration must be limited to casual observation and collection of information. How we managed to be so careless as to collect you in the process remains a mystery—a mystery which had better be solved before our Council gets wind of it!"

"How are you going to 'solve' me?" Mark asked, not sure he wanted an honest answer. "And what is this 'Council?'"

"There you go again, two questions at once! This is most disconcerting, you know!" Creson shook his head in mock annoyance, but at the emergence of frustration on Mark's face, he pushed on. "Answering your second question first, our Council is the governing force of this planet, indeed it is influential in the governing of many planets. Its rule is law, not so much because they are who they are, but because their decisions are historically logical and fair. They have our respect and, as a result, they command our obedience. In bringing you here, however accidental that might have been, we violated a very strict rule of procedure governing the exploration of newly targeted planets. A rule that stemmed from past episodes of contamination—many lives were lost, both among our citizens and among certain species of the planets being investigated. In time we progressed to the point where such problems no longer occurred, at least not in a biological sense, but the memory remains so painfully vivid that no one is willing to suggest our precautions be abandoned."

Creson looked sad as he related this to Mark, as if he had experienced it personally. "How old are you?" Mark asked impulsively.

Creson paused for a moment before answering with, "In answer to the question you are really asking, no, I was not alive when all this took place. But due to a very effective teaching process, every Mantzite has a feeling of direct involvement in all aspects of Mantz history." He looked closely at the Earth man as he added, "It is possible that you will be able to share in these teachings."

Mark immediately warmed to the idea. The possibility of being taught alien concepts by the aliens themselves lit a candle of excitement within him. It also reminded him that the rest and rejuvenation chamber really was cutting him loose.

"Regretfully, we know very little about your species, and it is necessary that far more be known before direct contact is attempted. Lest you be unduly concerned about this, we believe we possess enough knowledge to keep you alive. For example, we are aware of your habit of ingesting pieces of plants and animals to obtain sustenance for your body, and we have attempted to synthesize these within the chamber you currently occupy. I trust you no longer feel hunger or thirst?" Mark thought about it for a moment then admitted he did not. "In addition, recognizing the trauma suffered during your introduction to our environment, we have taken the liberty of limiting the extent of your emotions. For the last few days, in Earth terms, we have provided you with complete calm. We are only now returning you to some semblance of emotional normalcy."

Mark shook his head. Countless questions were filling his mind, spurred on by those already answered. He fought to calm his enthusiasm; it was making it difficult to get it all out. But then he remembered something Creson had said earlier. "You called me Mark Carter!" he said accusingly.

"I believe you claim that as your formal identifier," Creson replied, surprised at the outburst.

"But how would you know that unless you were present in my so-called dream; the one where I lost my arm and my head?"

Creson replied abstractly but without hesitation, "In a sense we are always in your dreams. However embryonic your projection capability, it still exists. Even while you rest."

"Then how do I know your name is Creson?" demanded Mark, his level of concern continuing to rise at the thought of the dream being true. "That was also part of my 'dream.'"

Again the answer came without hesitation—Creson was either telling the truth or was impressively fast on his feet. "Cursory examination has been taking place ever since you arrived, even while you slept.

Undoubtedly some of what was projected by us remains a part of your subconscious." With that he turned, walked over to the hexagonal panel and pressed a few buttons. In a flash, Mark's concern was no more.

"Is that the only way you can handle my questions?" he said with a contempt that was less vehement than he wanted it to be.

Creson turned to look at his captive, an expression of compassion on his face. Then, without saying anything more, he walked into a beam and disappeared.

Alone, Mark reflected on his situation. *So I haven't gone nuts*, he thought, *although that might turn out to be the lesser of two evils.* If the head-and-arm incident had also been real, the truth of which he might never know, at least there were no lingering after-effects. But the question of being a legal problem to his captors could have serious implications. The possibilities here were more than unsettling, they were downright scary. He could think of no solution that did not involve either death or enslavement, goulish thoughts that were acknowledged by his mind but not his emotionless body. *Great! Keep me around as a guinea pig, or plow me under to keep their bosses from getting wind of their clumsiness!*

But it certainly wasn't boring. He chuckled at the irony: *If this is the solution to my depression then I do believe I've overdone it.*

Spot had hinted that some form of education process might be offered. At the very least this suggested a breather of sorts before a decision on his life would be made. There was time to come up with something, some logic they would buy. He chuckled again. All he had to do was develop irrefutable human logic then present it to a society which did not, until recently, even know human beings existed.

There was ample room to sit, but Mark had no inclination to do so. He knew he must have been standing for days—exactly how many was still a mystery—yet he felt as comfortable as if he were lying on a soft bed. Why weren't his feet rebelling? They were firmly planted on the chamber's floor, but he felt as if he were floating; there was no clear sensation of weight being supported by those feet. He tried a little jump, careful as he did so to avoid coming in contact with the ceiling. He returned to the surface exactly as he would have on earth—there was even a jarring sensation as legs came in contact with floor. But the feeling of being afloat quickly returned. This was a fascinating machine, able to control gravity, atmosphere and emotions, all at the same time. And provide for his food and water needs—he did not feel hungry at all, although it had been days since he last ate. He tried to tempt himself by focusing his thoughts on a hamburger, but it changed nothing. It was as if he had just finished eating and had no capacity for anything else.

It was while examining the possibilities of his restricted environment that he realized he was still wearing the clothes he'd worn since leaving Kelly. *I must really be putting this machine to the test,* he thought wryly. There was no offensive odor, the chamber was apparently controlling that, but both clothes and body were in need of help. In addition he had, for the first time since arriving, the need to urinate. The thought surprised him. *What have I had to drink lately that would cause me to have to piss?* If he had been here for days, as Creson claimed, how had this been handled previously? For a moment he feared he had let go in his sleep, but a quick check of his pants leg reassured him. Well I haven't been dancing on one leg for the last few days so where did it go?

Thinking about having to urinate added urgency to his need; something had to be done and soon. *I'd love to get out of here and piss into that light beam!* he thought, re-testing the chamber's entrance as he did so. *That would be a neat surprise for anyone standing too close."* As before the entrance failed to yield more than an inch or two. He tried again, this time putting his shoulder into the task. Still nothing. "Jesus, I've got to do something. Hey, somebody, I need help," he shouted to the empty room. There was no response, only the same oppressive silence. "Damnit, I'm going to piss on your panel if somebody doesn't get in here fast!" But the room remained as still and as silent as before.

He decided to urinate through the chamber entrance and take his chances. Preparing himself, he directed a short stream at the opening, then watched as it bounced back to land on the chamber floor. "Shit!" he said, "I'm going to have to swim in the stuff." But as he continued to observe, the unwanted liquid began to vibrate itself out of existence; in seconds all of it was gone. "I'll be damned." He let go again then watched in fascination the process of vibration and evaporation, disappointed as it became obvious that the evaporation could not keep up with the supply. He had to stop then restart a number of times to control it, a process that was not without pain. *Wonder where it's going,* he thought, curious but content to know that it was now the machine's problem and not his.

His feeling of relief was only seconds old when Creson popped into view at a beam entrance—it was like Dracula jumping up in front of a fresh victim. The machine quickly countered the balloon of adrenaline that exploded into Mark's body.

The creature's face was a mask of indignation, his eyes accusatory and unyielding. "We are apparently in error once again," he began, projecting a tone which one would use in disciplining a child. But then his expression weakened from indignation to resignation, and he sighed and began anew. "Earlier forays into alien environments, during which time we attempted to replenish our bodies as routinely as did the creatures whose forms we were assuming, reminded us of the rather disgusting necessity to discharge any substance not fully consumed in the process; 'waste products,' I believe you call them.

"Among other terms," Mark remarked dryly.

"You might imagine how awkward was this discovery considering that we had long since forgotten our own experiences in this regard. As we were not expecting you, we failed to recognize the possibility that you shared the same primitive need. As a result, we did not provide suitable accommodations.

"But perhaps this is now a moot point. Before long you will no longer feel such a need; everything is being provided by the chamber in such form that almost nothing remains. What little bodily waste is created is carried away by the chamber." He paused for a moment then assumed a slim smile before continuing, "In this you may rest assured that we do not get input and outgo confused." His eyes contracted in self-approval. "Until your body has been purged we suspect it will continue to greet us with a surprise or two, and we humbly beseech you to notify us in advance of its approach."

"I tried calling and nobody answered," Mark said sheepishly.

"Ah yes, I see the problem." He pointed to an open beam. "The conveyers through which we travel also permit communication at long distance—this is done on Earth with a telephone, I believe. One must, however, be directing one's thoughts—or in your case one's voice—toward a beam opening in order for the message to be effectively transmitted. Any conveyer beam will do; the message is analyzed and delivered to the correct party automatically."

"Really?" said Mark, staring at the device and awed by its versatility.

Creson resumed his familiar expression of pomposity. "I suspect your question is not so much a challenge to my veracity as a surprise at our impressive achievements. It is 'really' quite simple. Stare at the entrance to a beam and concentrate on what you would like us to know. Present it in voice form, if that makes it easier; I can assure you we are quite capable of translating the thoughts behind your animal utterances."

Mark chuckled at the put-down. It appeared to be some kind of personality trait in this creature, some necessity to provoke others to either anger or laughter. He wondered which Creson had intended this time. "Tell me, why didn't I have to pi..urinate before? I drank water before coming to this odd-ball town; why, days later, am I still getting rid of it?"

"Quite simple: your bodily functions were slowed as part of our efforts to reduce the effects of the trauma you suffered while being introduced to our planet. It took time to get your system to function as we believe it is supposed to, and this was best accomplished while you remained in a form of suspended animation."

At that, Creson turned to leave, his desire to terminate the conversation obvious. Mark stopped him with a change of subject. "Wait. I've been in these clothes for at least a week. How can I get them and me clean?"

Creson paused to consider the new problem, his head nodding his agreement that something indeed had to be done. In time he turned to a nearby beam for what Mark now knew was a communication with someone outside the room. Turning back afterward, he said, "I have arranged to give you a new covering. Kindly hand me that one. Your body will be cleansed within the chamber as you wait." He reached his hand into the cubicle, meeting no opposition from whatever it was that kept Mark in. The action was reminiscent of the earlier dream episode.

"You mean my clothes?"

"As you will, clothes."

Mark began to disrobe, handing the garments one by one to Creson, who easily removed them from the chamber. "How come you're able to get things out of here and I can't?" he asked.

Creson smiled. "Do you really expect me to answer that?" he asked rhetorically. "As you might imagine, the idea is to keep you in, not to provide you with knowledge of how to get out." He continued taking Mark's proffered clothing, handling each item as if it were a long dead animal.

As he got to the final piece of underwear, Mark paused and stared at his captor with a look of suspicion. "Are you a boy creature or a girl creature?" he asked.

"Please explain the relevance of this question," Creson demanded.

"Oh, never mind. Somehow I don't think you'd appreciate the difference." He removed the final article then stood naked in his chamber, sensitive to the fact that it was exposed to all sides.

Creson tossed the underwear into the same beam into which he had tossed the others, causing Mark to wonder how it could know where all those clothes were supposed to go. What kept his dirty socks from flying into the lunchroom?

"I dare say they will be equally as unappreciative of these offerings as they were the last," Creson said, his eyes contracting and his body quivering as he did so. The latter increased as he added, "You really do offer a rich source of humor, you know. Your repeated reference to me as 'Spot' is a good example." He turned and leaned heavily against a beam table, momentarily incapacitated by whatever humor he had visited upon himself. "Arf!" he said, the word bringing an even greater shaking to his alien body.

Mark stared with interest at this inter-terrestrial display of laughter. Creson's behavior was the same as might occur among his friends or even within himself. And it was equally as contagious—with the help of the tranquilizers provided by the chamber, he laughed along with his captor. *I'm breaking this guy up*, he thought, his own laughter increasing at the thought.

CHAPTER 11

Initially untrusting of Kathy's motives, the people of Kelly had responded only reluctantly to her inquiries into the canine-visitor affair, but patience and a generous display of a warm smile and a personality to match quickly melted their resistance. Eleven people had been interviewed thus far and all told essentially the same story. Collectively they verified what Cal had said, adding a few points here and there based on personal experience or their own tendency toward exaggeration.

The stories were similar to those she'd investigated before coming to Kelly, particularly as they involved the same breed and color of dog—she had told no one of the earlier incidents, nor had she mentioned the words, "light-colored shepherds." The fact that everyone talked of that and only that was chilling. There was, however, at least one difference between these and the Pennsylvania and California incidents: The Kelly dogs did not appear to be curious. They showed little interest in their surroundings, only in resting then moving on—to where, no one ever able to find out.

Kathy shook her head. It was not logical to expect that these animals could resurface as far away as Pennsylvania, not without human help they couldn't. It was early afternoon, and she sat in her room searching her notes for a better explanation, chomping as she did so on a slightly stale roll garnered from the previous night's dinner. This thing was not unfolding as she'd expected it would. If it were just the Kelly animals it would not seem so weird; they could be from the same parents, or the same dogs seen again and again. "Is this coincidence or is there really a connection?" she mumbled aloud.

How to work all this into one piece, that was the question. And without tainting what she had with hints of the supernatural—to include anything of what she'd been told in Kelly would shift the focus in that direction. She did not buy the vanishing-dog claims. Those dogs were going somewhere—although probably not as far as Pennsylvania or even

California—and they began their journey in a manner that made sense. She shook her head again. So many people reporting the same thing, at least some of whom had to be considered reliable. The sheriff and the local vet., for example.

Reliable or less reliable, they all swore the dogs could not be held for long. They were always well behaved, surrendering docilely to whomever wanted to take them in tow, but no matter how well tied or how securely confined, they were simply not there when someone later went to look. Equally as odd, while in captivity they accepted little food or water and did not pant or bark. *What kind of dog doesn't bark?* she thought.

Four days had passed since she arrived in Kelly; today began the fifth. Interviewing had occupied most of this time, although lately she found herself passing more and more hours watching the approaches to town. Mark's two weeks were up, if one counted the day it took him to get here, and although he had not sworn by any time limit, Kathy was sure he would soon return. She was, however, uncomfortably aware that he could just as easily bypass Kelly in favor of Jackson. Or emerge somewhere else then hitchhike to Jackson. He could even now be on his way to Pennsylvania, unaware of her growing anguish. Kathy flushed at the thought; how mortifying that would be. "Jerk!" she mumbled unreasonably.

By now, everyone in town knew the real reason she was there and, due to her engaging personality, all were willing to help. If anyone even remotely matching Mark's description entered their community, she would soon know about it. Even Cal had become friendly, and without the inducement of free drinks. From Cal she had gotten more material on the dog mystery—heavily laced with exaggeration, she was sure.

Keeping busy until the end of the two-week period had been tough enough, but each hour beyond that was torture. If only she knew where Mark was now. And where he intended to end his trip—if that were Jackson, she could head on down there to wait. Suddenly she was incapable of further concentration, and in acknowledgment of this she tossed the notes onto the bed then moved to the window to stare out at the vastness of the Wyoming wilderness. "Where are you going to pop up, Mark," she said to the indifferent mountains. "Or are you already back and not telling me?"

Mark had promised he would call as soon as he came out of the woods, but she lacked confidence that he would keep that promise. *Sandy knows I'm here, but would Mark call Sandy if he couldn't get me? Damn, I should've changed the message on my answering machine.* She chuckled at the impact such a message would have on whoever called during her absence, "Surprise, I'm in Kelly waiting for you!" *Actually*, she thought soberly, *it might have been wise to relay calls to Sandy. He'd know how to handle them.*

Hours later she was sitting in front of the room's ancient television still agonizing over her missing lover—she had no idea what was being offered on the screen. Twice during the afternoon she had gotten up to check the calendar, verifying each time that he had indeed been gone two weeks. Twice she had called her apartment to strip messages from the answering device, finding both times that there was nothing there to suggest Mark had even tried to call. "Damn!" She considered again the likelihood of his being on his way home, reluctantly conceding it to be at least a possibility. "Hell with it!" She grabbed the telephone, and with a stern expression that no one was there to appreciate, dialed Mark's home in Pennsylvania.

The unexpected sound of his voice gave a boost to her spirits. "Mark, what are you doing home?" she yelled, her tone combining relief with disappointment, the latter at missing out on what she'd hoped would be a trip home together. But the voice refused to be interrupted—it was a recording. With a sigh bordering on despair, she was about to hang up when she realized that this was a solution to the problem of letting Mark know of her presence in Kelly. She hastened to think of a way to tell him that she had followed him to Wyoming but had a good reason for doing so. The pressure of the moment made it difficult to gather the right words. "Mark," the message began, "uh..., I'm in Kelly, uh...in Wyoming,...here on business—really, its business. But I thought I'd, uh.., wait for you. Maybe we can fly back together. Uh...let me know, will you?"

"Shit!" she cried after slamming the phone back onto its cradle, "I sounded like some kind of geek!" It was an awkward message and the thought of it sitting there for Mark and maybe others to hear did not sit well. She wished she could try again, but she could think of no way to erase what was already there. *Sandy! He could go to Mark's place and erase it.*

Calling Sandy was not a bad idea anyway; maybe Mark *had* called him in search of her. The thought lifted her spirits.

"Hello, this is Sandy Mellon, possibly on a recording and possibly not, depending on whether or not I want to talk to you."

"Cut it out, Sandy, it's Kathy."

"Kathy, honey, where the hell are you?"

"Still in Kelly, where I've been waiting for my jerky boyfriend for five whole days!"

"Mark's not there with you?"

Kathy's heart sank at the question, knowing it meant Mark was not in Pennsylvania either. Her voice diminished noticeably as she answered, "No, he's not, Sandy. I was hoping you knew where he was."

There was a pause at the other end. "Yeah, I guess it has been two weeks. But don't start worrying prematurely, kid, you know he didn't put a definite time limit on it."

"He said two weeks! It's been two weeks!"

"Technically he said 'about two weeks,'" Sandy coaxed.

"Technically, schmectically! He might be in serious trouble!"

"Well, we don't know that. When you go on that long a hike, especially if you're not familiar with the area, it's hard to tell when you're going to get where you're going." Sandy cringed at the awkwardness of his reply; Kathy picked up on it immediately.

"That's exactly my point! He doesn't even know where he is, let alone where he's going! He could be wandering around right now out of food and water and hopelessly lost!"

"And he could be five minutes out of Kelly or Jackson or some other town along the way. Why paint such a bleak picture?"

"Because I'm worried," she replied. "And I think I have a right to be. And as his friend you should be too."

He felt trapped; it would appear callous for him to claim he was not worried—and indeed he really was—but there was no point in adding to her fears. "I'm concerned, but I'm not panicked, nor is there any reason to be." He thought for a moment, then added, "Did you check with the airlines to see if he used his return tickets?"

"No," she said with sudden enthusiasm. That's a good idea; I'll do it. Only problem with that is he's supposed to call me as soon as he gets out of the woods, and that means before he calls any dumb airlines!"

"Well, you know, when you're half eaten by mountain lions you begin to loose it."

"That's not funny, Sandy!"

"Just trying a little levity. Not working, huh?"

"No!"

"Well, just don't get too upset, honey. He really isn't late yet."

"How are we supposed to know when he is late? Do we wait another month and then admit to ourselves that we should have been concerned earlier? Sandy, I think we should let the police know he's out there."

"We can do that. I know someone at the Teton County Sheriff's office I can call."

Kathy was immediately alarmed. "How do you know a Teton County Sheriff? Did somebody call you about Mark?"

"Calm down. I called last week to let them know Mark was in the area and to ask them to keep an eye out for him."

"See, you're worried too!"

"I just thought it'd be wise to let them know he was there," Sandy said defensively. " I didn't want to spread it around because I didn't want it to get back to Mark that I called. He'd probably get pissed if he found out."

"Not if he's really lost! Oh, Sandy, please call them back and tell them to put out a PCP or something."

Sandy chuckled. "That's APB," he said.

"What?"

"That's APB...You said PCP. One is a police dragnet and the other is a chemical."

"Oh for Christ's sake, Sandy, Mark's lost and you're giving me a lecture."

"Now calm down, Mark isn't necessarily lost. He probably knows exactly where he is and is temporarily unable to let us know. I'll get a hold of my contact at the Sheriff's Office and see if they've bumped into anyone roaming around the forest looking for a way out. It won't hurt to make them aware of our concern, but you realize, in a big area like that, they probably have hundreds of campers to worry about."

"And that he's late...or maybe late," Kathy added, ignoring his caveat. "Anyway I've been told this is the off season, between camping and hunting. They shouldn't have too many other campers to worry about."

After promising again to make the call, Sandy worked the conversation onto a lighter subject. He got Kathy talking about her dog, how it was getting along in his apartment where she'd so hastily left it before starting out for California. "Maybe I should send him to Wyoming—you can use him to sniff Mark's trail."

"He has trouble finding his way from the kitchen to the bedroom,"

Kathy offered in response.

"Many of us do, sweetie," Sandy replied.

Immediately after hanging up, Sandy made a search for the number he had obtained almost two weeks before. But his call to the Teton County Sheriff's Office brought only the knowledge that his contact had gone for the day—he left a request to return the call as soon as the officer arrived in the morning. Once the receiver was back in its cradle, he stared at it for a long moment before turning away and saying, "Damnit, Mark, you can really be a pain in the ass at times!"

The next morning he found himself unable to wait for the sheriff's call. As early as was practical, considering the difference in time zones, he called his contact again. This time he got through. The officer was polite but condescending, pointing out Mark's open reservations and the indefinite nature of his venture. "He said it himself," the officer offered. "He said he'd come back when the mood hit him. Think of how silly we'd all feel if we got an army of people roaming over thousands of square miles of rough territory just to find out he's not yet ready to call it quits."

"That's just it," interjected Sandy. It *is* rough territory and a relatively inexperienced guy hasn't been heard from for two weeks—actually two weeks and one day now."

The trooper sighed. "Okay, look, I'll talk to the federal boys, see if they want to begin a search—they help us out when a national forest is involved. I'll give a friend of mine your name and ask him to give you a call to get the details. In the meantime why don't you scrape together a few things so he can get right on it, anything you think might be helpful."

Sandy thanked the officer, alerted his secretary to get the name and number of the Wyoming official when he called, then quickly left the office for Mark's apartment.

The detailed travel itinerary was on the kitchen table where Mark had said it would be, but it told him nothing he did not already know. Shoving it into his pocket, he looked around for something else, disappointed when nothing presented itself. He was almost to the door before he remembered Kathy's plea to erase the message she had left for Mark. A smile appeared on his face; he had been looking forward to finding out why she objected so much to the wording. If it turned out to be something spicy, he would save it for just the right moment.

The device was in the bedroom but it took a few minutes to realize that Mark had squirreled it away in the top drawer of his night table. Extracting it from beneath a stack of typing paper, he pushed the rewind button then, as Kathy knew he would, he played it back. He chuckled but was otherwise disappointed at the awkward lines; not something you would want a lover to hear but not spicy enough to save. He dutifully erased it, reset the unit then headed back to his office.

The call from Wyoming had still not come through. "Crap!" he exclaimed after hearing this from his secretary, surprising her and himself at the same time. *I'm getting as bad as Kathy,* he thought.

He tried concentrating on work, but his eyes kept coming back to the telephone sitting a few inches away, each time willing it to ring. When once such time it did, he was startled into instant movement, grabbing the phone and yelling a breathless hello as if afraid it would change its mind.

"Mr. Mellon, this is Ken Janos in Wyoming. I'm from the U.S. Forest Service, working with the Teton County Sheriff's Office. I understand you have a friend in the area who might be missing."

Sandy breathed a sigh of relief. He had feared a false alarm, where he would have to practice congeniality on some client or business associate when at the moment he felt anything but congenial. "Yes, Mr. Janos, my friend has been out for more than two weeks now and we're afraid he might be lost or hurt." He gave the man Mark's itinerary, admitting the open reservations and Mark's stated intent to keep his return loose. Much to his pleasure, his concern was taken seriously. The disapproval at hearing of Mark's going out alone was obvious, but Janos was genuinely pleased to be warned in advance of a possible problem. Sandy promised to be available to supply anything else he or his colleagues might need.

When he hung up the phone, Sandy felt budding confidence as well as relief. Janos had assured him he would start things going immediately, this on the assumption that Mark was overdue. "At worst, we'll get in a little practice," he had said.

Sandy sat alone and in quiet for some time before his secretary finally brought his mind back to business. Even then, he found it difficult to concentrate for the remainder of that day.

Ken Janos was more concerned than he admitted to the fellow from Pennsylvania. He had seen it happen too many times before. *Why do people do things like this?* he thought, even while recognizing that a quest for adventure, even by the inexperienced, was natural and to be expected.

He had gained his own knowledge by getting out there and facing it first hand, even before qualified to do so. Even now, after years of outdoor activity, both at work and in the pursuit of pleasure, he could scarcely imagine being deprived of the right to roam at will through the wilderness. He could even understand wanting to be out there alone.

Sergeant Ken Janos, now approaching his fiftieth year, most of which had been spent in or near the nation's wilderness areas, was six feet, two inches tall and, when he could manage it, slightly under two hundred pounds. He looked robust and healthy, and this he attributed to a life style that presented on-going mental and physical challenges. For the last ten years he had been assigned to respond to local requests for searches in areas involving federal territory, which in Wyoming meant a good portion of the state. He enjoyed a good rapport with city and county officials and worked well with them during the many times that a search for a luckless traveler had become necessary.

After thinking about how he wanted to go about this, Janos arranged for a man to travel the same path Mark Carter had chosen for himself. "Southeast from Kelly," he said to his colleague over the phone. "Typical pattern: said he wanted to avoid roads and people, anything that reminded him of civilization—could mean he's now in some town trying hard not to be caught by his friends. Put the word out to all points, including local police; have them watch for a lone camper fitting his description. If he's like the others, he'll have a new beard, two weeks of it."

After the last of his calls, he hung up the phone then wondered what he might have forgotten. It was difficult getting started on these things, and this one was starting out worse than most. The target was traveling alone and, after two weeks, he could be anywhere. He could have changed his direction, either intentionally or unintentionally, a dozen times since leaving Kelly. *I wonder how determined a guy he is,* the ranger mused. He wished he had a better understanding of this Mark Carter, including the frame of mind he was in when he entered the woods. It could help them figure out where to go next once his tracks—if they're lucky enough to find any—peter out. "Wanted to lose himself in the woods," he chuckled dryly. "Poor bastard probably did exactly that."

CHAPTER 12

Knowing it was his own fault did not help. And, as Selson also knew, he could expect no solace from his colleagues, no matter how stern and unyielding he set his expression. The incident had been triggered by his interest in an unexplained array of chemicals emanating from the chamber housing the Earth man. The computer was calling it harmless so, as was often the case, his scientific curiosity had coaxed him into using body's senses to expand on what the machine reported. His sudden projection of disgust, followed by his recoil from the tiny opening he was monitoring, had gotten the attention of the other scientists in the room.

They had turned abruptly toward him, their eyes at first questioning but then amused as the disgust on Selson face told them the story. As always when dealing with alien life forms, contamination was a concern, this even though they had long since put in place effective counters against such things. But this was less of a problem at the moment than how to prevent their emotions from bubbling to the surface.

Selson held a high rank, as signified by the "son" in his name. All Mantz citizens had such suffixes such that all one had to do to determine a citizen's rank was to know his name. He, however, unlike his close colleague, Creson, had virtually no sense of humor, a fact which now placed his associates in a difficult position. Wholesale surrender to laughter would not work to their favor.

A number of them swung their heads toward a beam table hoping to hide feelings they could no longer control. The tactic was only partially successful as bulging eyes contracted and relaxed so rapidly, Selson could not fail to know the reason why.

Creson, there at the time, was for once in sympathy with his humorless colleague—more a remembering of similar experiences than a reaction to Selson's humiliation. His expression became one of shared annoyance as he stormed toward the beam leading to the Earth man.

* * * *

When Creson reemerged from the conveyer beam, he was enveloped in laughter, a fact which did nothing to help his lower-ranked colleagues in their attempt at self control. They were further influenced by Selson himself who had created a rejuvenation chamber and was now standing, arms folded across his chest, awaiting the completion of the cleansing process. Reminded of the reason for the quick visit to the Earth man, and always willing to bait his colleague, Creson pointed a finger then increased the contracting of eyes and shaking of body that was the Mantzite way of laughter. It was more than the others could take and a crescendo of such "laughter" burst through like a broken dam. Selson glowered as best he could and for as long as he could, but then, in an action very uncharacteristic of him, he joined the others, eventually contracting and shaking as much as anyone.

Creson, one of the few of his rank to actually explore targeted planets, had visited Earth many times. It was he who had decided that the domesticated canine was the image most readily acceptable to the species understood to be the most dominant on Earth. After bringing a sample animal to Mantz for analysis, he had worked out the details of altering Mantzite genes to match those of the dog creature, a procedure practiced for centuries on their planet. Afterward the captured animal had been returned, no worse the wear—except for a certain nervousness when strangers approached. The success of this particular "disguise" made it the one of choice when on assignment to the third planet from the medium-sized sun recently discovered on an outer spiral of the galaxy.

On his very first field trip, disguised as a six-legged creature, Creson had become aggressive in his quest for direct knowledge of local creatures. On a whim he elected to forsake his standard-issue preparation in favor of local food ingested through his animal mouth. It had been a delightful experience and produced a resolve to stick to alien food for the duration of the trip. Hours later, however, he discovered that this decision would not be without cost. A pressure began to grow in his gut, suggesting something inside was trying to get out. Ignorant of what it might mean, he resisted the pressure. But it would not be silenced, and soon, without decent warning, water began to gush from his body's tail end, continuing with considerable force for what seemed like an eternity. To make matters worse, it brought with it such relief that he was little disposed to turn it off. Afterward he had stood in humiliation, searching his mind for an explanation. It was there, stored along with other bits of historical footnotes for which most Mantzites had little use.

Without a rest and rejuvenation chamber, it had not been easy to cleanse his fur, and even after the passage of hours, there remained an unpleasant smell.

Then, it happened again! This time from a different bodily opening. The humiliation, coupled with a second major cleanup in less than one day, ended his resolve to experience alien sustenance first hand.

Thinking about it now, Creson appreciated the fact that the current surprise involved the less offensive substance, but even so, he would be relieved when his captive's system no longer felt the need to function in such a manner.

He mused over what had become his personal responsibility. Markcarter's behavior was fascinating to observe, and regardless of the prohibition against collecting samples of a planet's dominant species so early in the scheme of things, he looked forward to being able to examine him in depth. It would be foolish and even illogical to rid themselves of such a specimen when to do so would change nothing. Markcarter was an accident, but he was also a fait accompli.

Creson thought about what he would try first. Communicating with the Earth man was tedious, but could he hope to correct this in whatever time he had left? The size and structure of the human cranium appeared to make them capable of thought projections, but they made no attempt to do so. Were they incompetent or simply unaware? And they demonstrate no ability to alter body genes through mental control, even when it is in their best interests to do so, as when this Earth creature became affected by Mantz's alien environment.

Breaking out of his reverie, Creson turned his attention to Selson who by then was in the process of dissolving the no-longer-needed rest and rejuvenation chamber. The customary frown had returned, a sight which tempted one last impulse toward laughter. Creson held it back, his desire now to secure a sedate atmosphere for what he wanted to discuss. In projecting his thoughts to Selson, he took care to keep his thoughts from the others. "I will recommend to Takar that we retain the Earth man for study. It would be senseless at this point to dispose of him simply to remain in technical compliance with Council directives. Returning him to Earth would be even more so."

Both scientists were aware of what could happen should a targeted planet learn of their presence before they had time to pave the way. One such planet had to be summarily abandoned as a result, leaving a once successful society in ruins, its people driven back to a darker age. Although the incident was a millennium old, the experience was still very much a part of everyone's mind.

"You realize," began Selson, "that this is the first violation of this directive in ten point one eight centuries?"

Creson smiled. "I am continually amazed at your ability to remember the most obscure statistic. I submit, however, that it has no relevance to my comment."

"Perhaps it only seems that way because you have given it insufficient thought. There have been only successes connected to our efforts to bring more civilizations into our protection—at least this has been the case for the last ten point one eight centuries." He pointed in the general direction of the contained Earth man before adding, "This episode, if not corrected promptly, has the potential of permitting us another opportunity to observe a catastrophe up close."

"Surely, with the opportunity to study past mistakes," Creson began somewhat testily, "we can prevent their recurrence. I would suggest it is unworthy of us to assume otherwise."

"I submit in return that we will not get the opportunity. The situation is quite clear: we violated the rules when we accepted the Earth man. You should never have led him here."

The comment made Creson defensive, "We did not exactly 'accept him,' he simply appeared!"

"He was led here by you."

"Once within the transporter it would have been irresponsible to allow him to remain there without supervision!" Creson paused to draw a deep breath. The conversation was not proceeding as he would have wished.

"He could have been terminated at that point and returned to the Earth side of the tunnel."

"You fail to take into consideration," projected Creson, "that we do not yet have sufficient knowledge of humans to permit a termination in a manner acceptable to other such creatures. Failure to be precise in such matters would be tantamount to hanging out a sign saying 'extraterrestrials are here!'"

"Perhaps," Selson conceded, not one to prolong an argument solely for argument's sake. "And perhaps this situation was inevitable considering our penchant toward permitting the transporter to remain open for such long periods of time."

"That, I will confess, was and still is a mistake. This has always been a weakness of the early stage of planetary exploration; the responsibility for turning it on and off rests with far too many citizens. But what is a suitable alternative? Until we establish the means for explorers to communicate directly to the laboratory, we must permit them the ability to control the transporter themselves." Creson wondered whether he was getting through to his colleague and, if so, whether he had any hope of gaining his support in his quest to keep the Earth man.

In his reply, Selson gave no indication that he was weakening. "But we have never before suffered a premature invasion by one of the target planet's creatures."

"That it has not happened," Creson countered, "is perhaps more surprising than the fact that it did in this instance. I submit that the lesson to be learned here is that we must devise a method of providing more controlled access to newly targeted planets."

"Which, of course, makes the assumption that both of us will still be employed in our current capacities once this matter becomes known to our illustrious Council."

Creson considered his colleague's words. He had been thinking along the same lines. The Council knew them both and respected their accomplishments, and it surely would not so easily cast them aside. But they were certain to be upset. In addition to concern for the planet being explored, they, and indeed all Mantzites, were security conscious. They had to be in this business. With all the new worlds being visited, each with the possibility of new life forms being discovered, it was feasible, even inevitable, that some of these forms would be capable of doing them harm. Such a fear did not only encompass beings of superior mental or military capability—these might be more easily identified and thus avoided. It included creatures of such physical or mental composition that they could, even without even knowing this, have a harmful effect on Mantz or its society. Some vague combination of destructive body chemicals or brain waves or a new form of pathogen against which Mantzites have no defenses.

"So far the two of you are merely restating the obvious." Takar had entered the laboratory unnoticed by either scientist and had covertly interjected himself into their thought processes, something he knew how to do quite well. Takar was responsible for the entire research facility, reporting directly to the Council. As is perhaps necessary in such a critical position, he was an assertive individual, capable of doing whatever had to be done regardless of how distasteful that task might be. He could make decisions based on cold logic, and the Council had the utmost faith in both his judgment and his willingness to carry out their collective will. Creson and Selson, although less fond of his tough, no-nonsense approach, respected his scientific acumen and brilliant analytical mind.

When first told of the mishap involving the Earth man, Takar had been silent for a long moment, which Creson took as a sign of how intense his displeasure was. When he recovered enough to continue the conversation his manner had changed. Anger and contempt entered his projections, emotions rarely felt by his subordinates. Creson had wondered then whether this reaction was designed to instill a sense of criticality in those who had brought about the breach. He suspected this to be the case, knowing Takar to have reacted to more serious emergencies in the past with less emotion than he offered now.

"I agree," said Creson, skillfully hiding his surprise at being overheard. "It would be wiser to concentrate on the next step."

"You have suggestions?" asked Takar, his face devoid of any hint of his thoughts, a posture to which Creson had become accustomed.

"We could terminate the creature as we would were we to collect too many of a single sample, but I would strongly advise against it. It would be an unnecessary waste of a good subject, an act which would serve no purpose other than to permit symbolic adherence to Council policy."

"Might I suggest that such adherence is not to be taken lightly!" Takar said in irony.

"I quite agree," Creson stated quickly, "but we should guide ourselves in this by what would best serve the Council's true purpose rather than simply act in blind obedience to its laws. Indeed, I might suggest that the latter might be construed by them to be an emotional overreaction, unworthy of our collective genius."

Creson paused to permit Takar to comment. He declined to do so, preferring to stare at his subordinate with that hard expressionless face. Creson felt compelled to continue. "Should we terminate him we would not only lose his value as a specimen, but would risk generating suspicion of our presence among those Earth creatures sufficiently advanced intellectually to understand what they are seeing."

"What do you have that would suggest this to be a problem?" asked Takar.

"For the moment," admitted Creson, "we have nothing specific to indicate that his absence would even be noticed. Further questioning of the creature will be necessary if we are to determine the true extent of the risk we take in this regard. However, I am able to say, from observations conducted thus far, that these creatures are known to raise a fuss when one of their number expires. Thus, a clumsy termination would work to everyone's disadvantage."

"Why would we fare any better if we retained him for experimentation?" Takar asked. "Would a disappearance be any less of a problem than a termination?"

"Possibly not. But in retaining him we might learn enough to permit a decision to terminate more of a chance of success—the specific functions of his body and the circumstances under which other Earth creatures would view a termination as natural. In addition, commenting on your earlier concern, we might discover whether this Markcarter would be missed at all.

"I might add," Creson said after a pause, the pause in itself suggesting he was winning his point, "that it might also prove that no action to terminate need be taken. This creature appears to have fragile emotions; he suffers trauma whenever faced with the atypical. Should he be released on Earth it is quite possible that whatever he reveals of our presence would simply not be believed, that his words reflect an overexposure to the primitive area in which he was found."

Takar mused over what Creson was saying. It was shaping up to be a no-win situation. Releasing the Earth man as is would be foolhardy, yet terminating him without sufficient knowledge to cover their tracks could be worse. And retaining him for study, even on a temporary basis, might coax others of his species to an unacceptable level of suspicion. "Well, we have him and it is clear that we should not," he said, finally. "The Council should be informed and, as of yet, they are not. I must view this as two mistakes. Perhaps a third would pass unnoticed. Retain the Earth creature for study; learn as much as you can about his biology and chemistry—it is likely this information will be needed in the near future. Concurrent to this, conduct a study of the area in which he was discovered, this so we might know whether concern over his disappearance exists—I want to know the depth of this concern should the answer be yes. On my part, I will withhold knowledge of the creature's presence from the Council until I can offer a solution along with the problem." With that he turned and left; the conversation finished as far as he was concerned.

Creson admired Takar's ability to handle such difficult matters with such dispatch, even as he was gratified that the responsibility was Takar's and not his. He was aware that others regarded him as "gentle," a personality trait that guaranteed he would never reach the 'kar' rank, but this was of little consequence. It permitted him the liberty of supporting ideas that were less of a practical approach than a reflection of his personal feelings. He could never, he was sure, vote to terminate the Earth man. He sighed his recognition of the obvious, that his might be the only "no" vote.

The error of the Earth man, for which he had to assume responsibility, would not significantly affect his career. Council members might frown and bluster, but he was too well respected and too valuable a scientist to risk loosing him to poorly-considered discipline. Knowing this had kept him from panicking when it first became apparent that an Earth creature had followed him into the transporter. He had, however, hastened to put into place routine precautions against contamination, this a reflection of an inbred fear that he had trouble dismissing. He, like many of his people, had effectively lived through the time of the troubles, when so many lives had been lost due to careless regard for decontamination.

As part of their formal education, all students were exposed to major events from Mantz's past through the use of an experience scanner, a machine which replayed the past with such clarity and in such depth that the participant was left with the feeling that he or she had been an active participant. Fear, confusion, hatred, prejudice, all emotions felt by the person whose experience had been recorded, were passed on to the student, regardless of how uncomfortable it might make him. The student was thus left with a first-hand knowledge of his planet's history, both factual and emotional; he was an eyewitness to his past.

A recovery period was part of every experience session, this to permit a student time to recover from whatever stress might result. Sometimes it was not enough, and a rest and rejuvenation chamber had to be employed— Creson had been one of those requiring such treatment, and even now he could feel the pain felt by those earlier Mantzites. Sometimes students had trouble accepting the experience at all and had to spend weeks within the protective confines of the chamber before being able to resume their studies. If this happened too often, it was a sign that the individual had reached his or her emotional limit and should not be permitted further sessions. Although more emotional than most, Creson had survived both the basic schooling and the additional sessions required by anyone wishing to achieve the "son" rank.

The chamber currently being used by Markcarter was of the type employed to help troubled students, although here a variance on traditional therapy had been applied, this in deference to his human body. Creson had had to guess at what chemicals to employ, but fortunately it was working. Markcarter no longer showed signs of depression, plus his weight had been restored to what might be expected of his physical and chemical makeup. *There is, however*, he thought, throwing a glance at Selson, *the question of what bodily wastes remain.*

There was still much to learn about the Earth man, both in response to Takar's orders and to satisfy his own curiosity. But he now had the advantage of formal approval. *Takar shows wisdom*, he thought. *It will do little harm to postpone a revelation to the Council until a solution is in hand.* The thought ended with a negative as he realized he might yet be the cause of an intelligent creature's death.

CHAPTER 13

Mark was alone. Creson had left hours ago leaving him to wallow in unsettling thoughts in a chamber that no longer fought so hard to suppress them—Mark was feeling something close to normal emotions, not all of which were appreciated. Principal among the less appreciated was impatience. He was impatient for something to happen and impatient to end the uncertainty that marked his future.

Within minutes of Creson's exit, Mark's body had become clean, the visible dirt evaporating in much the same manner as did the urine—one could actually watch it disappear, although where it exited the chamber was a mystery. But that was some time ago, and nothing had happened in the interim to break the monotony. The least he'd expected was for someone to pop in with a change of clothes, something to cover his nakedness.

Creson's revelations, although believed, left him staring at a glass of water when what he really wanted to see was the ocean. There was so much he hadn't said. About their lives, their capabilities and, of course, their intentions. Perhaps affected by whatever level of chemicals were still permitted by the chamber, he found it difficult to believe that these beings would actually do him harm. Somehow they or he would find an alternative.

An invasion of Earth. If not an invasion, certainly an unauthorized visit. He smiled as he considered the problem of gaining the necessary permission. Hundreds of countries would have to be contacted, and billions in bribes would have to be paid to petty bureaucrats. Even then it would take years to get through the red tape (what country would have the necessary forms on hand?). *I could hire on as their agent,* he thought, enjoying the momentary diversion and seeking to prolong it. *What a fantastic job that would be, beaming from country to country asking if anyone would mind if my buddies, the space creatures, visited awhile.*

When that petered out, he tried moving his thoughts to the shelves and cubicles in the room, and to the many items found on or within them. They contained shapes that made little sense to him—tools, maybe; some were worn or scraped as if used as such. Almost everything was of the ubiquitous glowing material, although some items could have been manufactured in a metal shop on Earth. Still others appeared to be plastic—it was difficult to be sure of any of this from where he stood. Nothing was contained, at least not in a traditional sense; no boxes or other vessels. Nor were there tubes or flasks or whatever else one might expect to see in a scientific laboratory. Nothing to hold any kind of fluid.

But then fluids here grew out of nothing, subtly produced by the mysterious cubicles (or chambers as Spot called them). And the chambers were themselves produced from nothing—a touch of a few lights and they pop into being. *Maybe Spot came from nothing,* he thought, wondering how he could reverse the process and thus free himself.

He stared with longing at the hexagonal panel of lights, aware that it held the key to his escaping the chamber. What he would do when—and if—he managed to get himself out he didn't know, but it would at least be a start. *All I'd have to worry about then is crossing a few thousand light years of space.* He shook his head; the problem was all but insurmountable. Not only were there obstacles and unknowns, but there was also the question of time, how much he had left before a Mantz "solution" was imposed upon him. Even so, he made a mental note to pay attention the next time one of the creatures began playing with the panel of lights.

He was momentarily distracted by one of the exhibits: an Earth plant, a rose with a bright red bud projecting upward from a single stem. It appeared to be not only preserved, but cultivated as well. Whatever the Mantzites had in mind with respect to the collection of alien samples, it did not, at least in this instance, include destroying them in the process. He stared at the familiar sight and wondered whether it sat in a rest and rejuvenation chamber similar to his own—was he also being "cultivated?"

Dashing through light years of space reminded him that he would have to do so naked—Creson had still not provided a clean "covering." Was this some kind of strategy on the alien's part, make his captive focus on embarrassment rather than resistance? If so, he was in for a shock. He'd moon the whole planet if it would get him out of here.

Remembering Creson's instructions, he turned toward a beam entrance, fixed it with a hard stare then yelled, "Are you voyeurs watching me take my bath?"

The promptness of the reply made him jump. "Watching in an awareness sense Markcarter, although as we understand your formulation of the thought 'voyeur,' we have a scientific interest in understanding your species not in becoming participants in your private fantasies."

Mark had not expected a serious reply to what was essentially a rhetorical question. But at least someone was now talking to him, and the words did provoke interesting thoughts. "Don't you guys have sex?" he asked mischievously.

"Further," the projection continued, ignoring Mark's comment, "we have, as you might have surmised, an interest at least equal to yours in seeing to it that any further bodily offerings, with all that entails, is less, shall we say, intense."

Mark chuckled. "Can you people smell?" he asked. For the first time he could believe that what he was "hearing" was not sound. There was no distinctive tone to tell him who it was he was talking to, only a manner of speaking that was similar to Creason's.

"Unfortunately in this instance, yes," came the hidden reply.

Pleased at having someone (*or something*, he thought) to talk to, Mark was reluctant to let it go. "What have you done with my...covering?" he asked.

"The gentleman at the other end voted for immediate destruction, but we were able to persuade him of its possible scientific value. It has been preserved in a separate chamber—air-tight, of course. Your new covering has just been delivered to you."

Mark was confused. His unasked question had been answered, but he was not sure he'd heard it correctly. He searched the nearby tables, thinking a suit of clothing might have spontaneously appeared from the beam. "I don't see it."

"Observe your body my dear Markcarter. A new covering, more presentable than the one you so badly misused, has been provided through the grace of your rest and rejuvenation chamber."

A glance downward proved the alien's point. A coating of smooth fur, thick enough to cover his nakedness, now covered his body in much the same manner as it covered the aliens. There had been no feeling attached to its development; it was simply there when he looked down. Its color was the same light copper beige seen on Spot, and the other aliens in the lab, and the dogs in Kelly. *Popular color in these parts*, he thought. He ran fur-covered fingers over his chest, impressed by the manner in which his body supported it. It was attached to the skin, although the feeling it gave was less that of body hair than of artificial fiber held in place by an inoffensive glue.

Had all this just happened? Had the creature at the other end brought it about while they talked; as a way of further impressing their pet Earth man? "Incredible," he said. "I didn't even know it was there. It feels like part of my body."

"In a sense," came the reply through the beam, "it is part of your body since it was literally grown on your skin. In any event I believe you will find it quite comfortable, more so than your previous covering. You will also find it will prevent a recurrence of the distressing state of sanitation in which you so recently found yourself."

"I'll stay clean?" Mark asked, looking down at his fur once again. "How do you do this?"

"Please direct your thoughts into the beam, Markcarter. Your utterances, always difficult to understand, are doubly so now.

"Sorry," Mark said, turning more toward the conveyer as he spoke. "I said, 'how do you do that?'"

"You would not understand, Markcarter."

"Try me!" The condescending tone was annoying.

There was a pause at the other end followed by a confused, "Try you for what?"

Mark misunderstood the creature's confusion, mistaking it for the banter to which Spot repeatedly exposed him. It hit him the wrong way. "Damnit, I'm an intelligent human being, capable of reasoning, analyzing, planning, creating—you name it. I don't appreciate being toyed with like some dumb laboratory animal."

The creature's tone had an appeal to it as he continued. "We are not insensitive to your feelings, Markcarter, but perhaps you can appreciate ours. You are not our equal in mental achievement. We are scientists and members of a culture far more advanced than yours. We would be pleased to accommodate your intellectual needs but as yet you demonstrate little capability of being able to grasp what has become routine to us. In time this disparity could be reduced, but unfortunately there is no certainty that we will have that time."

Mark was taken aback by the ominous inference in the creature's words. "What do you mean?"

The beam was silent for many seconds, and when finally it resumed, there was a hesitation to it. "As you know, we were not prepared for your visit. It presents certain...problems, some of which you are already aware. There is, as you are also aware, the question of what should be done with you."

"What do you mean, 'done with me?' Why in the hell do you have to *do* anything with me?" No sound came back from the beam. "Are you still there?" The now familiar discomfort in Mark's stomach reappeared, and he wondered whether it would not be easier to let the machine control such emotions for him. "Damnit, why won't you answer me?" But the ominous silence ensued.

He stared at the beam for many minutes, willing it to respond, needing the contact, especially now. *I don't find some way out of here, I'm dead meat!* He leaned back against the rear of the chamber, the despair in his face obvious even through the fur.

CHAPTER 14

"Thar it is. Exactly whut ah been tellin' yew about." Cal indicated the copper-colored dog lying on the lawn across from where he and Kathy stood. Pleased with being able to offer something solid to this skeptical female, he had come to get her immediately after spotting yet another of the unexplained visitors. "He jus come right in an set hisself down fer a nap. Now if we was aim'n tuh fetch um, won't be no problem. He'd come peaceable like."

"You've done it before, you personally, I mean?" asked Kathy.

"Sure as I'm standin' here. Now they's some whut says thet's thuh same dog as befer, but ah ain't one of um. Somebody own a passel a them dogs, and they's gittin' away one-by-one."

"Why would they escape one-by-one? Why not all together?" Kathy asked.

"Don't make no sense tuh me neither, jes statin' fact. Anyway, same's t'others."

Kathy hesitated at Cal's closing comment. "Oh," she said, finally understanding what the mountain man had said, "same as the others?"

"Thet's whut ah said; they all cud be frum thuh same pair. Probably ain't though; they's tew many of um. Likely kill thuh bitch'd had thet many."

"How many have you seen?" Kathy asked.

"Nigh on tuh thutty or forty. Ain't seen um all myself, yew understand; other townsfolk, they seen some."

Kathy was not sure how much of that count was real and how much was exaggeration, but if the number were even half of what Cal claimed, it would be enough to make anyone sit up and take notice. "I don't understand. With that many dogs going through town, why doesn't someone do something about it?"

"Ferinstance?"

"Ferinstance notifying the authorities."

Cal sighed lightly. "Folks hereabouts don't cotton much tuh a-tharities. We'ins kinda figger we kin handle things right fine arself. Sides, ain't no reason tuh fuss none bout a dog er two."

"But this is thirty or forty. And they don't belong around here."

Cal nodded his head thoughtfully. "Yeah, thet dew make us some curious. Ain't thet we ain't done nothin, yew understand. As I done told yew, we tried tuh keep hold of um, tried to foller um, tried to tie um up. Ain't nothing thet'd work. Them dogs jes up an scoot soon's they git a fancy too."

Kathy stared for several minutes, intrigued by this latest addition to the "Kelly-Dogs," as she called them—she had even considered using the phrase in her article. She was far from convinced that Cal was right, that the sightings represented different animals. If there truly had been thirty or more dogs it would challenge the best expert in the world to remember enough idiosyncrasies to tell them apart. At least to some extent, it was the same animals again and again. Claiming otherwise just made good press.

But there obviously were a number of them, perhaps a large number, and that made it interesting. Interesting also was their behavior patterns, such as always choosing Kelly as a resting place before heading elsewhere. And always managing to escape, regardless of the precautions taken.

"I'd love to find out what's really happening to these dogs," she muttered softly.

"Lotta folks done tried. But them dogs is smart; knows tuh wait till thuh right moment fer they does anythin'. Long's yew watch, they gonna watch too."

Kathy thought for a moment. "We could film it," she said, making the assumption that Cal would be a willing co-conspirator. "We could capture this one, set up a video recorder in the room then leave him alone."

"Don't know much about do-dads like thet. Know it'd be easy tuh git hold of um though. Cud do er right now if'n yew want."

The thought excited her. It would be fun to play detective, especially if it proved successful. And the expense of the camera might be recovered from her editor. Logistics could be a problem, though, specifically the video camera itself—who in town would even own one, let alone lend or rent it to her? And what if the mystery is solved and it turns out to be something simple; the effort, and the expense of the camera, would be wasted? *It's a risk I'm willing to take*, she thought. *Besides, however these animals escape, it has to be impressive the way they've got the townspeople buffaloed.*

There was also the problem of where to hide it. Her hotel room would be the most logical place, but would the desk clerk object? Kathy decided to improve her chances by not telling him.

"Let's git er done, Cal!" she said enthusiastically.

The mountain man turned to look at her, a smile of pleasure spreading across his face. "Ah swear, am' gonna git yew talking right purdy a-fer long." Returning his gaze to the animal, he then added, "Where we gonna take um?"

"Up to my room. We can sneak him in."

"Ah hell, they won't care none over at the ho-tell. These here dogs don't never make no noise thet ah ever heared of."

"You never heard one bark? Not even once?"

"Nope. An ain't nobody else ever heard um neither. They's well trained dogs. Wouldn't mind havin' one ma'self."

"You'd think their owner would come after them," Kathy said.

"Maybe ain't got no owner. Maybe thuh guy's dead up'in them woods."

While they spoke they slowly approached the sleeping animal, Kathy more cautious than her newly-recruited partner—resolve was beginning to lose ground to uncertainty. Less obvious but still there, was Cal's wariness. He was more affected by the dog episodes than he cared to admit. There was something unnatural here, something that just wasn't right, even if it was difficult to get this pretty little city gal to understand that. "Ah'll put ma belt round iz neck; yew hold t'other end," he said as he stripped a well-used belt from his faded jeans, made a loop then handed the other end to his nervous partner.

While Cal's hands reached toward the animal's head, Kathy stared at its eyes, knowing she would jump a good ten feet if they opened suddenly. Fortunately they did not, and the capture was as uneventful as it had been so many times in the past. Indeed, the leash was all but secure before the animal so much as raised an eye, and even then, its expression was one of calm, even boredom. Kathy thought she heard a sigh, as if it were resigning itself to having to play yet another silly human game.

"He doesn't seem to care that we've got him," she said.

"More'n likely he knows he got us. He ain't gonna stick round any more'n he wants, en he knows it."

"What do we do now?" Her voice quivered with a combination of excitement and nerves.

"Jes lead um where yuh wants um tuh go."

She moved forward, holding the leash gingerly in one hand, unsure of how the animal would react should too much pressure be applied to its neck. She need not have worried; it got to its feet then docilely followed her lead, the bored look still in its eyes. Anyone who witnessed the procession might have been amused: A women holding a leash as if the animal attached to it had just been rescued from the business end of an outhouse; a man following a few steps behind as if wanting to keep his distance from them both. In this manner they marched the dog down the street, through the lobby of the hotel, up the stairs then into Kathy's room.

After tying the leash to a bed post, Kathy breathed a sigh of relief then fell heavily into a chair. Cal stood awkwardly by the door, unaccustomed to being inside a lady's room—at least this kind of lady. The object of their mutual concern, seeing no further reason not to do so, settled down beside the bed and promptly resumed his sleep.

"Please sit, Cal," she said, amused by his shyness. "Look at that mutt! He couldn't care less that we captured him!"

Cal moved awkwardly to where he could lean against the dresser—there were no other chairs in the room and he was unwilling to sit on the bed. "Like ah done said, he knows he kin leave anytime he gits a mind tuh."

Kathy realized then that she enjoyed Cal's company. Since their shaky introduction, his true personality had leaked out, and it was a personality to which she easily warmed. His presence made the wait for Mark tolerable. Like Cal, she suspected the capture was the easy part. Now she had a video camera to find. "And a couple of cassettes," she exclaimed suddenly, the outburst catching Cal by surprise. She smiled as she tried to explain. "A cassette only lasts six hours. I'll have to get up in the middle of the night to change it." Cal returned her smile but remained silent. "Where can I get all this, Cal?"

Cal scratched his head as he thought about it. "Cain't say they'd be much call fer one in town. Ain't fer tuh Jackson Hole, though. Lotta tourists an ski'n goin on there; probably gotta whole lotta need fer cameras."

"Great, how do I get there?"

Cal looked down at his feet, "Cud take yuh ma'self?"

"Oh thank you, Cal. Can we go now?"

"Don't see why not!" he answered enthusiastically. Since this pretty and personable woman had come all this way just to look for her man, Cal knew he could not be more than a friend, but it felt good just hanging around her—and it wasn't hurting his reputation either. He straightened then turned to lead the way, stopping when his eyes settled on the dog. "Only thing is," he began, disappointed at the thought, "this here dog ain't likely tuh be here when we gits back."

Kathy stared at the sleeping animal for a few seconds then said, "Cal, could you stay with him until I get back. I'd do it but...well, I'm still a little frightened of him." She had considered asking Cal to run the errand for her but decided not to risk the damage to his feelings should he be forced to admit a lack of knowledge of what she needed. Or if he came back with the wrong thing. Anyway, she would have to pay for the rental with a credit card, and that meant being there in person to sign the bill.

Cal accepted her professed fear. He felt it himself, although hearing this little woman say it made him determined she not discover this. "Yew know how tuh drive a pickup?" he asked.

"Hail yes," she said, unsuccessfully imitating Cal's western drawl.

The twenty-seven mile trip to the popular skiing area commonly known as Jackson Hole took almost an hour, this due to her lack of familiarity with a gearshift truck—she hoped Cal had not heard the grinding noises as she and the laboring vehicle took off down the long, bumpy road. As the city of Jackson came into view, she paused, wondering whether it was necessary to go any further; surely there were places in Jackson that rented video cameras. But the logic of this was soon lost to the promise of a romantic resort area never before seen, and she was off again, this time intending to cover the twelve odd miles from Jackson to Jackson Hole.

Jackson Hole is technically a valley, a breathtakingly beautiful valley. Although it was too early for snow to be there, it was easy to imagine how irresistible it could be to anyone who enjoyed winter sports. Or who merely wanted to walk in winter majesty. The resort community itself, Teton Village, was larger than Kathy imagined it would be. Restaurants and shops proliferated the area, arranging themselves in such a way as to be in keeping with the atmosphere of a quaint alpine village. She was tempted to delay long enough to have lunch, but rejected the idea out of consideration for her waiting partner-in-dognapping.

It took a visit to all three ski shops before she found one that would rent a camera on her Mastercard. The first shopkeeper, noting Kathy's exit from a deteriorating pickup, was reluctant to surrender one of his two cameras—he claimed both were in need of repair. Profiting from this experience, she parked the vehicle in a different lot before trying again. This time she was simply unlucky; the shop did not carry such equipment. The third try brought success, and soon woman, video camera, spare cassettes and deteriorating pickup were on their way back to Kelly.

As she pulled away from the town, Kathy was in good spirits. The day was sunny and the high altitude and typically low humidity of that part of Wyoming permitted a deep blue to fill the sky. Against it were brilliantly outlined mountains, all heavily decked with autumn colors. As she watched and admired, a vague feeling of guilt muscled its way into her reverie. Mark was out there somewhere. And he was overdue. "Two weeks and two days!" Surely his food must be getting low by now. And surely he was getting tired of cold nights and sleeping on the ground.

For the remainder of the trip she focused on the options available to her with respect to learning the whereabouts of her tardy lover. There weren't many. "I could call the cops," she mumbled to herself, not at all sure they—or Mark—would appreciate it. "Damnit, he's officially overdue! Well, at least *un*officially overdue."

Thinking of Mark reminded her that Sandy had not called back. Should she interpret this as good news or bad? If Sandy had found out anything, surely he would let her know. But the more she thought about it the more worried she became. Cal noticed the change immediately.

"Somp'in happen?" he asked as she entered the hotel room, his concern as much about the pickup as about Kathy.

"No, everything's fine. I got the camera." She held it up for Cal to see.

"Somp'in eatin at yew then?" Cal persisted, now confused.

Kathy sighed. "Just thinking about my friend. I still don't know where he is and I have no idea how to find him. He might really be lost out there."

Cal was of the opinion that people who went into the wilderness without experience and without a clear idea of where they were going were out of their minds and likely deserved what they got. That, and the feeling that this little lady's guy really was lost, encouraged him to mind what he said. He decided to coax the discussion back to the less painful topic. Pointing to the animal, he said, "How yew fixin' to set up this movie star a yorn?"

After a brief discussion, they decided to tie the dog to a hot water pipe inside the closet, this to fool it into thinking it could not be seen by the woman who slept in the outer room. To start, they moved the camera into position, using a cord from Kathy's bathrobe to lock it in place. The setup was crude but appeared to work. Then they aroused the still sleeping animal, getting the same sluggish but unresisting response as before. It moved without objection to the closet, where it promptly resumed its nap.

To complete the process, Kathy inserted a tape into the machine then turned it on and checked for proper lighting and position. There was just the closet light, but the camera reported enough illumination to capture a good image of the small enclosure. Everything was ready to go. "Should I leave him some water?" Kathy asked.

"Don't need none. Leastwise never did in thuh past."

With nothing more to do here, Kathy suggested they head for the bar to unwind—handling the animal for a second time had brought back the discomfort felt when it was first captured. She did not believe anything would come of what they were planning—at best a smart dog would be caught performing tricks on camera—but even so it was difficult to be nonchalant when everyone in town was so up tight about this.

After a few sips of a marginally recognizable Bloody Mary, her mind drifted from the first mystery to the second—curiously, they both had to do with vanishing acts. "Cal, just how dangerous is it out there?"

Normally the question would trigger in Cal an instinct to boast, to puff what all in town knew were considerable wilderness skills. And if the question came from a pretty girl, especially a pretty girl sitting so close to him, he would be inclined to paint a picture of himself as a conqueror of the jungle. Now, however, seeing the look of hope in her face, he knew he could not add to her misery. "Hail, it ain't thet bad. Some parts is worse'n t'others but your man don't sound like thet'd bother him none."

Kathy knew immediately that the tall, rough-looking woodsman was trying to be gentle, and with this realization came alarm. It was uncharacteristic, too unlike what he'd said in earlier meetings. She leaned forward then began speaking rapidly, "Cal, I've got to let somebody know he's overdue. It's been too long; he might really need help. Who can I call?"

Cal jumped at the unexpected outburst, wondering what had set her off. "Don't rightly know; never had no need," he said defensively. Then he thought for a moment and added, "Went out with thuh rangers on this kind a thing a time or tew though."

"Rangers? How would I get in touch with them?"

"Might try thuh sharf over in Jackson. He'd know, ah reckon."

Kathy completed her drink with more speed than usual, suddenly wanting to be by herself. When the moment was right, she smiled at her friendly companion then, professing a need to lie down for awhile, got up to leave. Cal smiled back, understanding her feelings.

She hesitated at the door to her room, uneasy with what might be waiting for her just inside. Coaxing it opened. she inched her head to where she could see the closet, ready to jump back should a canine Godzilla jump out at her with insane eyes and a bloodthirsty roar. All she saw was a half-opened closet door behind which a sleeping dog lay in quiet repose.

Dinner was crackers and leftover rolls from the night before. It wasn't much but it kept her from having to leave the room. While wrestling with the idea of calling in the police, she got undressed, using the closet only as necessary to pack away her skirt and blouse—more than that was unnerving, especially when there was no one nearby to turn to. On impulse, she rewound the camera, recognizing that the dog's presence attested to the uselessness of whatever had thus far been recorded. She now had a full six hours before she would have to do it again, six hours of not having to go anywhere near that animal. She pulled the door to where it was almost closed, this to reduce her exposure if later it became necessary to pass by on her way to the bathroom.

When finally she decided to put through a call to the Jackson sheriff, it was too late. The reporting of a possible missing person at that hour was not appreciated by the second-shift dispatcher. "Why, at eight o'clock at night is it suddenly an emergency?" the voice had asked.

"Prick!" Kathy mumbled after hanging up. The suggestion had been that she wait until morning. "What difference do they think one night is going to make after all this time?" she said to the empty room. "And do they think he's going to travel around in the dark?" Without examining the logic of it, she decided that, if Mark did pop up during the night, she would not let them know in Jackson.

The ringing of the phone while her hand rested on the receiver caused her to cry out in fright. She had to let it ring once more to give her heart a chance to slow down. "Hello?" she offered tentatively.

"Kathy! I finally got through to you."

The sound of Sandy's voice flooded her with relief. "Is Mark there," she asked quickly.

A conspicuous silence preceded Sandy's answer. "Frankly, honey, I was hoping you were going to tell me he was with you."

"Oh, Sandy," she sighed, fear now beginning to win out over hope.

"I know, kid. Look I've been on the phone to a guy named Ken Janos; nice guy; willing to help. He's been trying to locate Mark for us, but all he knows at this point is that nobody's reported seeing him in Jackson or any of the other nearby towns. He wants to organize a search and I told him we'd cooperate all the way. I gave him all the information I had, but it would help if you'd talk to him as well. He's in Jackson."

"In Jackson!" Kathy exclaimed. "I just got off the phone to Jackson, and they wouldn't give me the time of day!"

"Who'd you talk to?"

"Somebody in the sheriff's office; a smartass dispatcher; an arrogant creep!"

"Sounds like you have something going for the guy. Look, my guy is a ranger; works for the park service; at least I think he does. He seems really nice and, as I say, it would help if you were to give him a call. I've got to tell you though, he's a little leery of having a guy's lady friend this close to the hunt. Thinks you're going to get emotional or something."

"Chauvinist!"

"Not really," Sandy said. "He just wants to concentrate his full attention on finding Mark. He's had cases in the past where he had to spend half his time with, as he put it, 'traumatized loved ones.' Even had to bail one out after she followed them into the woods."

"Did they find him anyway?" Kathy asked, hoping that a happy ending to such searches was routine.

"In this case, yeah. I'm not supposed to tell you this part but it was the wife who actually found him. The rangers might have passed him by if she hadn't gone into the woods to chase a rabbit. He was suffering from hypothermia, but nothing more than that."

"Must've broken his heart to admit that part."

"Not at all. Like I told you he's an all right guy. He just wants to do whatever it takes to bring Mark back in one piece. Now please give him a call; tonight, if you can. He's working on Mark's case at this very moment." Sandy gave her the number.

Although eager to hang up and get in touch with this man, Kathy remained on the phone for another ten minutes. She knew Sandy was deliberately keeping her talking, wanting to make certain she was not overly upset, so she went along with it. They spoke about the latest happenings in the great "Kelly-Dog" caper, including how helpful Cal had been. She also let him know what the betting was in town, how willing everyone was to accept this thing as beyond human understanding.

"Sounds like you're either developing a new religion or using me as a sounding board to see if your story will sell in Peoria."

"How about none of the above," she responded defensively, uncomfortable with the thought that her readers might see it the same way.

I'm only stating facts—weird facts, but facts just the same. And I have yet to find anyone who can come up with a satisfactory explanation!"

"Doesn't mean there isn't one. I don't speak dog myself or I'd corner one at this end and tell him to come out with it. 'What's going on, doggie!' something forceful like that."

"You joke, but don't forget, Mark's out there somewhere. And in the area where the Kelly-dogs are coming from."

"Yeah, but that's not necessarily bad. You said they don't harm anyone; could be they'd lead him back to civilization."

Kathy admitted that she'd had the same thought, that the animals, although still a mystery, probably posed no threat to her wandering lover. She changed the subject before this could be examined in detail.

Sandy sensed a false intensity in what Kathy was doing, but he understood—she was trying to keep busy until Mark was found. He was well aware that she had not come all that way to interview dogs.

Although prolonging the conversation, Kathy felt compelled to ask if Sandy had checked Mark's messages. He had; the embarrassing recording was history. "Don't worry, Kid, I didn't listen to your awkward ramblings."

Kathy chuckled. "Let me know if the inconsiderate jerk shows up in Pennsylvania," she said before hanging up.

Ken Janos was indeed a nice guy. Thorough as well, first asking for her description of Mark then questioning her on discrepancies noted between what she offered and what he had obtained from Sandy. She was embarrassed to admit that on more than one point, Sandy's observations were better than hers. She was even more embarrassed when, after going through a detailed description, she remembered she was carrying a photograph of Mark in her purse.

"I'm going to stay here in Kelly until he's found," she said, careful to heed Sandy's advice and not present that as a challenge. "I want to help however I can, and I promise not to get in the way...and to do whatever you say." She had not expected to be so pleading in tone; Janos's demeanor and apparent competence was tapping into her assertive nature. But it was a relief to know that the search would be led by such a man.

"Actually I'd like to come see you tomorrow morning and get that picture."

"You can have it now, if you want," Kathy said hastily, afraid that the search for Mark was to be a nine-to-five affair.

"Not necessary. We have enough to keep us busy for now. I'll come up about seven, if that's okay with you."

Kathy agreed and the conversation soon ended. Hanging up, she sank onto the bed emotionally drained.

She was at the center of a world of screaming. Thousands of patrol cars dashed through the woods, their sirens going full blast, the combined cacophony bouncing off the deep canyons that surrounded her.

Kathy bolted upright in bed, confused when the ringing did not stop. Nagging in its persistence, it seemed closer. She shook her head then turned on a light. Off to one side, a well-used travel alarm continued its assigned task without regard for its owner's confusion. She sighed then turned it off, remembering as she did so why it had been set—the video tape had to be changed. After a yawn and a quick stretch, she lumbered out of bed then walked with increasing gravity toward the closet; the quiet and the lateness of the hour restoring the uneasy feeling of before. A chill overtook her as she reached for the closet door and pulled it open.

The dog was no longer there. Its jury-rigged leash, still attached to the hot water pipe and still looped at the neck end, lay on the floor. Kathy let out a gasp and frantically searched the rest of the closet with her eyes. Nothing except a few articles of clothing and a video recorder, the latter still on and running. She backed away in haste, fearing the animal had to be somewhere in the room. But she was alone; nothing was lurking in the shadows ready to spring out at her. An examination of the room's only window proved it was closed and locked from the inside. The door to the hallway as well; the night chain was still in place.

Wide-eyed and confused, she settled into a chair and stared at the empty closet. "I don't believe it!" she cried, the sound of her voice striking the quiet air like a percussion instrument. *Cal*! Was he responsible for this, his idea of a practical joke? Another glance at the night chain weakened that thought; Cal could not reset the chain after leaving. "But, hell, neither could anybody else!"

The camera! She jumped up, ran to the closet then, with shaking hands, untied the device and carried it over to the bed. *I got the whole thing on tape*, she thought, the realization bringing with it a feeling of great satisfaction. She hit the rewind button then stared anxiously at the spinning wheels, as if in doing so she could speed them along.

"Shit!" It hit her then that she had no means of reviewing what had been recorded. That would take a VCR or some way of attaching the recorder to the room's TV—the mystery would continue, at least until morning. Disappointed but less frightened than before, she returned the camera to the closet then went back to bed.

Sleep, however, would not come. She lay on her back and stared at the ceiling, unable to keep wild thoughts from running loose in her mind, thoughts about Mark trapped on some mountain ledge, thoughts about dogs walking through walls, thoughts about Ken Janos taming them all. The harder she tried to sleep the more hopeless sleep became. The first hint of daylight was peaking through the curtained window before the effort was finally abandoned.

The introduction of daylight into what had become a collection of gnarled shadows was very welcome. With it came a renewed sense of hope, although she remained in bed with her mind continuing its cruel churning until the travel alarm announced it was time to prepare for the ranger's visit.

It wasn't easy to ignore the closet on the way to the bathroom. There was even a moment when she feared the animal would be there, that it had reappeared as mysteriously as it had disappeared. She could not prevent the sigh of relief when the closet proved to be empty.

She resigned herself to a more immediate worry, the image that bounced back at her from the bathroom mirror. She did not want Janos to think that all Mark had waiting for him was the tired and rumpled creature she was at the moment. With no little effort, she made her repairs.

At precisely seven someone knocked on her door.

"Miss Montari?"

"Yes, but please call me Kathy. Are you Ranger Janos?" His proffered ID made the question an unnecessary one.

"Well, if you Kathy, me Ken," he said in an attempt at humor. Kathy smiled politely.

"Please come in. I have the photograph right here; you're welcome to do with it as you please...I have another," she added awkwardly.

Now it was Janos's turn to smile, "I suspected you might. I want you to know we've been working at this all night. Not myself personally—I cheated a bit and caught myself a nap—but a lot of other guys. And girls," he hastened to add. "We're beginning a preliminary search this morning with a helicopter and some pretty good trackers. What we need is some idea of what direction he took."

"Oh he told me that!" Kathy interjected excitedly. "He said he was going to go southeast. He said he wanted to stay away from people and highways."

"Yes, we're aware of that from Mr. Mellon. What we need now is something specific. Did he have a particular mountain in mind or a specific body of water? Or a likely exit point after he finished the trip? We need to find a campfire or something like it to give us a trail to follow." Kathy thought for a moment then admitted she had nothing else to offer. It was embarrassing to reveal that Mark had confided so little in her.

"While all this is taking place," the ranger continued, understanding the young woman's embarrassment, "the helicopter will make a broad search in the hopes of spotting something obvious. If your man is in trouble maybe he was able to lay something out on the ground, something we can spot from the air. It's worth a try. We'll look southeast from Kelly to start. Thirty miles or so."

"But Mark said he was going to travel for a hundred miles or more," Kathy interrupted.

The ranger smiled. "You'd be surprised how difficult it is to go a hundred miles in this country. Most people find themselves lucky to do a dozen. If we don't find anything, we'll branch out. To the north and south as well as further southeast. It might be he got lost and lit off in another direction. Or maybe he decided the scenery was better somewhere else. What I'm saying is we'll try all approaches and we won't stop until we find him."

Kathy hesitated before asking, "What are the chances he'll be found...I mean...healthy?"

"Excellent! We've had, unfortunately, a whole lot of practice at this sort of thing. We've gotten pretty good at protecting people who visit our state. Be bad for the tourist business if we weren't. I suspect, though, he's not too many miles from where we are right now." His comments and accompanying smile were a routine part of the response to this inevitable question.

"Do you ever lose one?" Kathy asked softly.

This was the second most commonly asked question, and it was always difficult to answer in a manner satisfying to an anxious loved one. "I can only say that anything can happen, but it generally doesn't. We take this kind of thing seriously; we don't like even the thought of failure. Cuts down on our bonuses, you know."

Kathy laughed, notwithstanding her awareness that Janos had answered the question in the affirmative. "With all that wilderness out there, how can you ever hope to find one man traveling alone?"

"Well, there is one good thing about dealing with an inexperienced target...uh, camper, I mean...and that's the fact that he's less likely to wander into the real heavy stuff. They generally stick to trails, or to meadows and clearings when they can't find trails. This makes it easier for us; lets us get a solid fix on where the guy is heading. He'd have to go some to get away from us."

"I'm so glad you're working on this," Kathy said, relief evident in her voice. "I just didn't know what to do next."

"Don't worry. This happens occasionally, but in almost every case we find a tired, red-faced guy who took a wrong turn or misread a map."

She could not help but ask, "'Almost' every case?" "What happens the other times?"

"Please. Don't worry needlessly. We're already hard at work, and we're a lot better at finding him than he is at hiding from us."

The ranger was comforting to talk to. He made her feel that Mark's life was in good hands. Although wanting to prolong the conversation a while longer, she understood when Janos began making noises and movements suggesting he would like to go. "I'll have a talk with Cal Simmons about what your guy might've said to him before he left," he said, standing up. "Incidentally, Cal will eventually be joining us; damn good man to have along on this sort of thing."

As he turned toward the door, Janos noticed the video camera lying on a shelf inside the closet. He smiled then gestured toward it with a angling of his head and questioning eyes.

"Oh, that's just part of a little legwork I've been doing for an article I'm writing. I do that for a living."

"What kind of things do you write about?" he asked out of politeness.

"Articles for magazines, that sort of thing. This one's about dogs. Kelly has a dog mystery going, and it fits with what I'm trying to do. Nobody knows where the mutts come from and nobody can seem to hold onto them for very long." She continued to inform the patient ranger about the Kelly-dog episode, and how she tried to discover the secret of their escapes.

"Did you find out?" Janos asked, noting the absence of any animal.

"I think so. The dog's gone and the recorder was on when he left.

Only problem is I have no way to play back the tape."

Janos looked the video camera over. "You're in luck," he said. "This has a playback capability. I think most of the new ones are that way."

The adrenaline surged in Kathy's body as she realized how close that put her to an answer to the great dog mystery. "How do I use it?" she asked.

With reluctance that was difficult to conceal, Janos extracted the instruction manual from the camera case then quickly determined the specifics of playback. When ready, he showed Kathy how it worked then watched while she got it going. They were immediately rewarded with the picture of a sleeping dog.

"Let me know how it turns out," he said, anxious to get back to the search and unwilling to chance another delay.

"I will. And please let me know if I can help," Kathy said, wishing that Janos would offer to take her along on the search. "I'll be glad to do anything you say."

"Will do." The forest ranger either failed to notice the hint in her voice or declined to acknowledge it. He said his polite good-byes then left.

Alone and vaguely disappointed, Kathy wondered what she would do while awaiting a report from Janos. It could be hours, even days. She sat on the bed and tried to ward off a growing anxiety, in which imagination presented itself as fact. She thought of going to find Cal; he would know what was going on in the woods. And he'd be someone to talk to.

Thinking of Cal reminded her of the escape scene which had yet to be viewed. Pleased at the diversion, she grabbed the recorder then sat herself down on the bed. Ironically, the prospect of concluding the Kelly-dog mystery left her a bit empty, afraid even. Afraid of having too much time on her hands. She shook her head. There was still the story, assuming she could concentrate on it. Hell, writing it would take... She shook her head again. It was mostly written; she could finish the rest in an hour or two. And then what would she do? With a sigh that spoke of the great misery she felt, she turned on the replay then settled back to watch.

For a few seconds the scene was a comforting one, but then she woke to the fact that this "diversion" could last for hours, hours spent watching a dog sleep. She began to fast-forward, less concerned now with finishing than with escaping boredom. Even so, most of the tape had unwound before, after a brief gap, the dog's image disappeared.

She was confused. Even at a rapid speed, the escape should have stood out. And what was that gap? She rewound the tape to a little before the point of change then let it play in regular time—she would bear with the sleeping image until it happened. Within seconds she was greeted by the chilling sight of the dog opening its eyes and staring straight at the camera. It was as if it were staring at her. Its canine face held an expression that, on a human, would be interpreted as studied nonchalance. For a while nothing else happened, but then, with nothing obvious to cause it, the screen went blank. When it reappeared a few seconds later, the dog was no longer there.

"Damn!" She rewound to the break and tried again, hoping it was a mechanical problem. But nothing she did altered what proved to be a stubbornly inactive screen at the moment of truth. No matter how many times she backed and replayed, the screen was always blank for as long as it took for the animal to disappear.

Frustrated, she sat on the bed and thought over the possibilities. Someone could have come into the closet; that would explain the dog's looking up. That someone could also have turned off the machine, then turned it back on again after he removed the animal. But would the result be a gap? And even if this were possible, how would that someone get in?—equally as important, how did he get out? Further, that dog was staring right into the camera, not at the closet entrance where an intruder would first appear.

Determined to get to the bottom of it, she rewound the tape once more then, after a few tries back and forth, stopped the image at the last instant before the screen went blank. The dog was as it was before, still staring calmly at the camera, but a strange light shot out from the lower right side of its body. She focused all her attention on this light but could not figure out what it represented. It looked like a small flashlight but it could have been something the dog was lying on, something that reflected the closet's single bulb.

"Damnit, something's got to explain this!" With anger beginning to overpower frustration, she revisited the closet and there tried to reconstruct the positioning of both camera and animal. When sure she had the picture, she searched the floor where the dog had slept. There was nothing even slightly suspicious in the area where the light originated, at least nothing that was there any longer.

Defeated, she moved to the still unmade bed and lay down. The idea that her privacy had been invaded bothered her, but she had no feeling of being in danger. Somebody was playing games, nothing more than that. *It's for damn sure that animal didn't do this by himself!* She lay on the bed for a long time trying to put the details of the escape into something her mind could accept.

"A secret door!" She rose from the bed and returned to the closet, this time to examine the wall just beyond where the camera had been hung. The plaster was old and heavily painted. If a secret door were there, it was cleverly hidden. Disappointed, she returned to the bed and dropped heavily onto it.

Maybe she didn't know how he did it, but she was sure it was done by someone from town, someone who knew how to get into that room, someone who thought this Kelly-dog thing was one big joke.

Kelpin felt rejuvenated. The stop in Kelly, although interrupted twice, had done the trick. Now on to his final destination, Washington, D.C.

The second half of a trip was less tedious but always more challenging than the first, since here they had humans and their antiquated means of transportation to deal with, necessary unless one preferred walking hundreds if not thousands of miles. In this, one had to await just the right moment before penetrating a cargo hold, either by entering a suitcase of sufficient size then parking one's body between the molecules of whatever other articles shared the invaded space, or entering directly through the skin of the vehicle. The latter required patience; it would not do to be seen walking through the wall of an aircraft.

The female who had attempted to take him in tow, offered more amusement than disruption. But what this did say was the scrutiny of Mantzite movements, at least in Kelly, was increasing. Kelpin made a mental note to inform the dispatcher of this when next he reported back— an adjustment would have to be made if these suspicions were to be curbed. He also mentally noted the identities of his captors, a routine precaution designed to help his superiors keep track of whoever might be too interested in Mantz affairs.

His canine face broke into a smile as he thought about the game he had played in the early hours of the morning. The human recording device had not been a challenge, although he'd had to overcome it in a way that would tease but not arouse. He had fixed the machine with a calm stare while mentally focusing on the canine paw still tucked under his body—

slowly it transposed itself into a three-fingered hand. Then, careful to avoid its being seen, he'd slid his newly formed hand into a pouch, cleverly hidden in the folds of his canine body. Equally as carefully, he'd extracted the tiny beam device carried by all interplanetary travelers, his slowly moving hand arranging the dials before moving it to where it just nudged the edge of his canine fur. After that, it had been a simple matter of aiming and firing.

The beam had had the desired effect; the human recorder continued to spin, but it was no longer capable of recording anything. Satisfied, he'd gotten to his feet, stretched lazily then, after arranging the cells of his body, walked casually out of the impotent leash and into the room where the female human slept. A quick glance had told him his escape had thus far gone unnoticed. He'd considered rewinding the tape to a point just before the artificially created gap, but then thought better of the idea. A gap would appear more normal than a spontaneous disappearance, more likely to be interpreted as a mechanical error. After an additional blast to get the machine rolling again, he'd returned the versatile tool to his pouch, where it would present no problem when he elected to pass through solid objects. The no-longer-needed hand returned to canine form.

The rest had been even easier. A final glance at the sleeping human and he'd headed for the door, no longer interested in her or her video toys. He'd slowed only to check what might be outside, then passed his body through to the hallway. There, free and well rested, he'd begun the long trip east.

CHAPTER 15

One of them was touching buttons on the hexagonal panel but it appeared to have nothing to do with him; at least he felt no change within his cubicle. From time to time, other Mantz creatures had done the same and each time he had waited expectantly for something to happen. Thus far it had not. For what had to be hours, since first awakening from what felt like a long rest, he had been virtually ignored by what was sometimes a dozen scientists milling about the lab. Half that number were there at the moment, each moving as if time were an enemy. They seemed to make a point of ignoring him. *I must be Spot's personal property*, he mused, the idea bringing with it an interesting question.

"Hey," he yelled at the Mantzite nearest the hexagonal panel, "Is Creson male or female?"

Surprised at being addressed, the creature turned and fixed Mark with an inquisitive stare. As understanding took hold, its face softened into what was by now a familiar image of amusement. Then it walked over to Mark's chamber—he had not expected any response—and stood there casually examining him with large, investigating eyes.

"Why are you so interested in the sexual status of Creson?" It was presented in a teasing manner, as if the inquisitor were unconcerned about the answer but found it entertaining to ask. Mark noted the look of amusement and found it offensive; he was too often being caught either acting like a fool or talking like a schoolboy. He toyed with the idea of "projecting" a colorful response, then thought better of it, a decision reversal that puzzled him and made him wonder whether the chamber's chemicals were still affecting his resolve. No matter. At least he finally had someone to talk to.

"Just curious. You know who and what I am; I'd like to know more about you."

"It wouldn't be that you are concerned about the motive behind his close attention to you?" the creature teased.

"Certainly not, I'm just curious!" Mark was annoyed at having trapped himself into this conversation. The Mantzite continued the smile, but its willingness to play told him at least something: sex played a role in the life of the Mantzites. Maybe only as voyeurs of alien creatures, but that he might be able to find out. He shrugged his shoulders and decided to go for broke, "Since we're on the subject, do you people have different sexes, or do you just press a few buttons on that panel of yours and out pops a baby creature."

The amusement deepened on the alien's face. "Strictly speaking the answer to both questions is yes, but that is something which will have deeper meaning to you after you have had experience implants." Alien eyes mimicked Mark as he tried to imagine what "experience implants" might entail—especially as it had to do with sex. "In answer to an earlier question, Creson is indeed what you would refer to as male."

Mark would have preferred to continue the topic of implants, but he had learned that conversations ended abruptly when he touched on something his captors were not yet ready to discuss. Prudently, he elected to wait until the question might have a better chance of being answered.

"What do you mean, 'what I refer to as male?' Is Creson stuck in-between?"

The creatures eyes contracted once again. "He is, in all respects, a male being, although as on many planets, one's sexual proclivity here is of little importance. My qualified response more reflected the lessor weight placed on sexual labels. Procreation is, and has been for some time, divorced from sexual pleasure. This is an arrangement that benefits everyone, permitting emotions to be fully addressed, in whatever manner the participants wish, while eliminating the element of chance from the procreation process."

"You mean you really do get little creatures from test tubes?" Mark said, more of a statement than a question.

"Not exactly how I would put it, but essentially correct," the creature said, thoroughly enjoying this conversation with the amusing Earth man. "We...creatures...are still necessary to get the procedure going...'kick it off,' I think you might say. But selection of the next generation is a complex procedure requiring sophisticated mind-functioning devices to make the actual decisions."

"Mind-functioning devices?" Mark said. "You mean computers?"

"Correct; exponentially advanced beyond anything to which you might be accustomed, however. They deal with such matters as genetic matches and the elimination of all known and/or potential genetic errors. In addition they accommodate the question of necessity—it makes little sense to permit supply to outstrip need."

"What about religious concerns?" Mark asked, unsure whether the subject had meaning to these creatures—and also unsure whether he wanted an answer.

The Mantzite appeared to be reading his mind. "I do not believe you really want to enter into a discussion on the subject of religion. In any event this is one area in which I have no permission to speak. I suggest we stick to discussing your intense curiosity about our bedroom affairs."

Involuntarily, Mark smiled along with the Mantzite. "Why do you creatures always contract the pupils in your eyes when you laugh?" he asked.

"Why do you creatures always bray like a branz when you laugh? It is simply a difference between our species. There is no cosmic necessity for us to be precisely alike, you know. The real similarity here is the fact that we both do laugh. We have found this to be an indication of higher beings, a trait which would be expected of a planet's dominant species, assuming that species is mentally rather than physically oriented, of course. We would not, for example consider the dominant beasts of Krakoran higher beings, regardless of their ability to offer what could be construed as laughter."

"Somehow I think you know you're deliberately throwing conversation zingers in there! I assume a 'branz' is an animal?"

"Correct. From this very planet; it makes an amusing, even obnoxious sound.

"Mark let the insult pass, "And Crackerran; is that another planet you've explored?"

"Krakoran," the creature corrected. "Yes, one of many. It has no intelligent life that we can perceive, however. Although life per se is readily found throughout the galaxy, it is not easy to find intelligence. Indeed, most planets capable of supporting life offer only primitive, single cell creatures, billions of years away from evolving into anything we would consider being introduced to. We have found that only one life-supporting planet in ten has progressed beyond this primitive stage. Krakoran is part of this ten percent, although here the dominant beasts are too large and too powerful to permit more potentially intelligent beings to evolve, somewhat like the situation you faced with your dinosaurs. Even this planet, however, has utility."

Mark was unsure whether he should let the "has utility" remark slip by, but the conversation was getting afield of the original subject, a subject which appeared to be accepted as a legitimate point of discussion. "How do you people 'kick it off,' the bottled babies, I mean?"

The creature hesitated, not clear on the question being asked. Finally it concluded that Mark had returned to his earlier interest. "The procedure is much the same here as on most civilized planets—including yours, if I am not mistaken. The reproductive products of both sexes are donated by those of our species considered suitable and the...computers...take over from there. The new being's environment is strictly controlled—by these machines and certain of ourselves deemed qualified to do so—from conception through preliminary education. We do, of course, occasionally relax such controls to permit new generations to experience serendipitous situations. Were this not part of the educational process, our species might eventually be incapable of handling the problems presented by newly discovered planets.

"I believe, however," the creature continued with a smile, "that your question more reflects a desire to know how we conduct sexual relations with one another?"

Mark smiled without really wanting to and turned a light shade of pink, a situation which his permissive rest and rejuvenation chamber permitted. "Well," he began in a conspiratorial tone, "it has had me kinda curious. What do your women look like; I mean, how do you tell the difference between a girl and a boy?"

"We have no difficulty," the creature said impishly.

"I mean," Mark continued awkwardly, "what does a girl look like without all that fur on?"

"Would you like me to show you?" the creature asked with a wink, pretending at the same time to tug at her fur.

Mark stood wide-eyed and mouth opened and the color in his face deepened. Pointing at the creature, he asked sheepishly, "You mean you're a woman?"

"Can't you tell?" she asked coyly, taking this moment of Mark's greatest embarrassment to walk away.

It took a few seconds before he could react. "But how do you tell?" he yelled after her. The female Mantzite resumed her manipulation of panel dials making no attempt to answer Mark's question. The smile was still on her face as she disappeared into a tube.

"**I** am, as Leipin stated, a male, Markcarter, although I fail to see how such information could be of consequence to you. You are not what we would call a raving beauty, even in the correct covering." Creson had entered the laboratory a few minutes after Leipin left. Obviously the incident had been discussed. Creson was now incorporating it into his special brand of verbal torment.

Reference to his "covering" reminded Mark that he had no concept of how he looked in his head-to-toe fur coat. There were no mirrors available, at least none that he knew of. He tried to imagine himself with fur surrounding much of his human face. It brought a smile to his lips and a further thought. "How do I get out of this suit; I mean if I have to go to the bathroom?"

Creson's expression turned sober at the question. It was not difficult to guess that he was considering the consequences of error as well as the relevant logistics. "It shall be provided for, Markcarter. It would be greatly appreciated, however, if you would give us ample warning, this to permit the chamber time to remove your covering in advance of the blessed event." He shook his head and frowned at the grinning Earth man before adding, "I must say we shall be most pleased when the final consequences of ingested Earth food are behind us, no pun intended in this case."

He continued without permitting Mark a response, "Now to the business at hand. Since it is impossible at the moment for you to leave, it makes sense to take advantage of your presence. As Leipin alluded to earlier, there is a device we utilize frequently called an experience chamber. It can be made to operate in two directions, as it were, to display or collect experiences. The former is employed rather extensively in the education of our younger generation while the latter enables us to view, and thus share, the experiences of those we invite to our planet. This is also how we make the most of understanding what a returning researcher has seen. The process is harmless and, indeed, you might find it quite pleasant."

"And I have little choice in the matter."

"Such are the pitfalls of uninvited guests, Markcarter. To begin the process, you will be released from the chamber in which you temporarily reside. Since you will then be subject to conditions alien to your system, we must first provide protection against trauma—tranquilizers, to you. The chemistry of our air differs from yours. The effect is minimal but you could experience a light-headed feeling, a feeling aggravated by the difference in gravity between our two planets—Mantz is smaller and subsequently has less gravitational pull."

Mark's interest sharpened at the mention of freedom. His mind raced to examine the possibilities it presented. There were many creatures in the room, but they all looked like ninety-eight-pound weaklings, and none carried anything that could be construed as a weapon. If he were to make a mad dash for the beam tunnel, could they stop him? He wondered whether the recognition of this possibility was the real reason they were applying tranquilizers.

Creson smiled as if interpreting Mark's thoughts. "It would be imprudent for you to attempt to resist us once outside this chamber, Markcarter, if for no other reason than you have no place to go. We are thousands of light years from your planet, and unless you have specific knowledge of space warps, returning unaided would be virtually impossible. I suggest you recognize the inevitability of your predicament and make the most of it. Besides, as previously stated, the experiences we intend you to undertake should be fascinating to a primitive being like yourself." His eyes twinkled at the projected insult, but it lasted only a second. Afterward he turned serious. "Although not the preferred approach, I would also caution that there is more to our capabilities than meets your human eye. We are able to control any conceivable situation involving rambunctious alien beings."

The comment sobered Mark's thinking, and he put aside any thought of escape—at least until more could be learned about his captors.

"As we begin to understand you," Creson continued, "you will begin to understand us, both functions occurring simultaneously. The exchange will permit a clearer picture of our relative capabilities."

"You mean where humans fit in the pecking order." Mark said.

It took a moment for Creson to analyze the comment. "As I understand your meaning, certainly not. We find it illogical, and even unnecessary, to exert control over species of other worlds. There is little to be gained that cannot be achieved by less primitive means. We have for eons provided for both the necessary and desired needs of ourselves and those we bless with our contact, and primitive attempts at dominance and power have long been suppressed within us. Our biggest fear, frankly, is others, others who have not yet progressed to a civilized level."

Mark was surprised at the intensity in Creson's speech. About to point out how meaningless such pronouncements sounded when aimed at a prisoner in a cell, he decided it was not the moment to do so.

Creson turned toward the panel of lights and raised his three-fingered hand to begin the series of buttons that would release his captive Earth man. Mark tried to concentrate on which were chosen, even as a feeling of warmth began to flow over him—Creson's actions obviously had to do with the promised tranquilizers. At least in part due to the medication, he lost track before the first series was completed, and this filled him with a disappointment his body would not let him feel. It was the same dichotomy experienced earlier, where he could think and feel while being denied the ability to act. He wondered how long the feeling would last once he was outside the machine.

The suppression of emotions, however, could be made to work to his advantage. It would permit him to reason with logic without the distraction of fear, anger, anxiety or frustration. Maybe he could not translate these thoughts into action, but they would be there in his mind ready to go when the moment was ripe. He halted all resistance to the machine, hoping that in finding no active resistance, it would not try as hard. There was enough success in what he did to permit him to see and remember some of the second series of lights, the series that, temporarily at least, ended his captivity.

He had seen the first two lights of a five-light series—upper left and down two/over one. Now all he had to do was relax enough that the machine would not want to beat that knowledge out of him—not easy when, to remain calm, he had to fight hard. Creson saved the day when he lifted his hand as an invitation to leave the chamber, an invitation that Mark seized upon in both mind and body.

For the first time since his arrival, he was free. He stood in place just outside the chamber while Creson looked him over, the Mantzite giving the appearance of a physician observing a patient who might not survive the day. In his emotionless state, Mark contented himself to wait for direction, and when an apparently satisfied Creson turned and began walking across the room, he followed without question. He also followed when Creson, without touching additional buttons on the panel, walked into the beam and disappeared.

As before, the transition was instant. Also as before, Mark had no feeling of having traveled more than an inch or two. He marveled at the versatility of this device. It was the same tube that had led him into the laboratory an unknown number of days ago, yet passing back through it did not return him to where he'd begun. The conveyer tube was not a hallway; it was not a connection between two points. It was some kind of programmable transporting system. What determined where a traveler was to go, he had no idea, although even in his tranquilized state, he knew it was something he would have to find out—this tunnel of light would play into his escape in some way, of that he was sure.

The new room was smaller than the one he had just left. And it was occupied by only one chamber, this one notably larger than the one that had cared for him thus far. Like the structures in the lab, it too was composed of the versatile glowing material. Recalling how his own chamber had appeared out of nothing, Mark wondered if this larger one was also an impressive illusion.

A Mantzite was standing by a hexagonal panel of lights, and with a tinge of chemically-suppressed embarrassment, Mark realized it was the same creature he had recently trapped into a discussion of Mantz sexual habits. *A female!*—he wondered anew what identified her as such. Returning his attention to the room, he could see no recording or projection devices, but there were numerous glowing tubes of light the functions of which he could not even guess at. They were attached to the hazy ceiling and all were pointing at a table of light suspended in mid air.

"Please arrange yourself in the center of this platform," Creson projected softly, certain he would not be opposed. Mark did as he was told, even as his mind questioned the glowing material that surrounded the table in such a way as to make its edge impossible to define until close enough to touch. Once he was able to orient himself, he lifted himself into the powdery mist then lay back on what was a surprisingly soft surface.

In stark contrast to his docile body, his mind burned with interest. The chemicals prevented any cooperation between the two, but he was acutely aware of the fact that he had willingly entered an alien device designed to invade his innermost thoughts while imposing experiences no human being had every shared. Part of him was afraid, but a greater part looked forward to what was about to happen, looked forward in the way a child looks forward to his first roller coaster ride. For the first time, he was grateful that the tranquilizing chemicals were there. They permitted him to stare at the hazy ceiling and wait with calm expectation for the experience to begin. It was not long before it did.

At first there was only a darkening of the ceiling and surrounding walls, and Mark could not tell whether this was actually happening or simply the effect the machine had on its victim. He could see no one, not even Creson, who he knew was standing just outside the device's enveloping haze. Then without knowing exactly when it began, he found himself reliving parts of his past, reliving them as an objective observer. It was like showing home movies, only these conferred superior clarity and were three dimensional. And here he was able to climb into the picture and observe from all sides the most minute detail. He found himself experiencing more in this replay than he had during the first go-around.

It began with simple extracts from his youth, then switched without warning to a later period in his life. Then back to the earlier period, and so on. There was no pattern to this that Mark could see, only his response to a questioning process that was so subtle he could not be sure it existed at all. It was a gentle probing that could even have come from within himself. At first the experiences unwound slowly, but then the tempo began speeding up until portions of his life were being reviewed with such speed that it challenged the mind's capacity to keep up. But Mark was able to follow regardless of the speed of the extraction.

After a period of this, the scene changed radically, and Mark found himself wandering through experiences that were unfamiliar to him. Some of the scenery was recognizable, although it took a moment to realize that the reason for this was that he had passed through it recently. Flying by at incredible speed, yet presenting Mark no difficulty in following and understanding every detail, were scenes of Mantz vegetation and Mantz creatures. The experiences paralleled his own, although here he was reliving something of which he could not possibly have had previous knowledge. There was still the sense of being an observer, but he was now an observer of himself as an alien, an alien who had actually lived the scenes unfolding before him. He and the alien whose life he was in the process of living were being reminded of something out of "their" past, or so the machine made it seem. It was as much his experience as it was that of the creature who owned it.

The Mantz phase had begun with a scene of a young Mantzite, then switched to a later period in its life, then back to a younger. It followed exactly the pattern initiated during the review of Mark's past, as if comparing Earth creatures and Earth environment to Mantz creatures and Mantz environment—Mark knew this comparison was taking place. He also knew in fine detail how his counterpart felt during those episodes. They were his own hopes, his own fears, his own desires. He was, for as long as this lasted, an alien being, a Mantzite. He lived like one and he understood life from the viewpoint of one.

The process ended with an emotional jolt. One moment he was an alien enjoying the replay of a cherished experience, the next he was a confused Earth man being observed by a concerned Creson. Light had been restored to the room. Mark tried to question the sudden change but found he could not. His body, exhausted to the point of paralysis, would not respond to his command. His breathing had become shallow and rapid, and his eyes stared weakly at the creature standing over him, a creature for whom he had begun to develop an unexplained fondness, a sense of kinship.

He watched as Creson turned and beamed a message at someone standing across the room—for the first time, and even in his weakened state, Mark was able to detect this. A few seconds later Leipin appeared within the haze of the machine, carrying two instruments that looked like small flashlights. Scattered along the sides of each were dials and depressed buttons, and what could have been a bulb projected from a hollow in one end. She selected one of the units, touched a few buttons then, with a sense of urgency, directed it at Mark. From the "bulb" came a soft cone of light, the large end of which enveloped Mark's body—it had no noticeable effect on his paralysis. Both Creson and Leipin then turned toward the hexagonal panel to examine the lights that suddenly appeared above it. When the glow faded they faced one another again then involved themselves in the Mantzite manner of communication—as before, Mark found himself able to detect this, although he could not understand what the images meant. After another long moment, Leipin adjusted the other beam device, aimed it his way then turned it on. This time he did feel something; and the change was profound. His breathing instantly returned to normal and the hopeless fatigue faded to an unpleasant memory. He watched as the two Mantzites breathed a sigh of relief.

"What happened?" he asked, aware that something was not as it was supposed to be. He spoke the words with same warmth he'd felt upon awakening, warmth brought about by having shared experiences with these people. And by the obvious concern they were showing toward him. Did they reciprocate his feelings; had they lived through his experiences as he lived through theirs? Or was their concern only that a choice experiment had gone awry?

Leipin deferred to Creson who answered, "A minor difficulty, aggravated by the relative absence of information on your species. You reacted differently to the experience chamber than we expected you would. After a minute or two we were forced to terminate the process. Not to do so would have been life threatening. I am certain you can appreciate the difficulties that would have given us with the Council."

Only a part of Mark was amused. "So much for kinship," he mumbled.

"I beg your pardon?" Creson said, his eyes wide in innocent inquiry.

"Not important. Did you say I was only in there for a minute?"

"More precisely, I said 'a minute or two,' Earth minutes, of course. But you are essentially correct; due to medical necessity the scan had to be abbreviated. We will be unable to continue until adjustments are made."

Mark stared at his captive, a skeptical look on his face. "But it seemed so much longer than that. I knew everything was passing quickly, but so many episodes of my life flashed by that it's hard to believe it all happened in only a minute."

"Or two," Creson interjected.

"Oh good grief!" Mark responded weakly, realizing that Spot had resumed his private concept of humor.

Attempting to rise, he found himself unable to do so without help, help graciously provided by Leipin—Creson had already moved away. Then he had to sit on the hazy, ill defined table until his strength returned enough to accompany Creson back to the now-desired rest and rejuvenation chamber. As he sat, Leipin continued to monitor his body, first with the diagnostic device then with the one which provided therapy. Each time the soft glow of the former was applied Leipin turned toward the hexagonal panel to monitor the results. Each time the pattern was different than before, which seemed to please the female Mantzite. To Mark, however, it was all an enigma, although it did remind him of the panel which controlled the locking and unlocking of his chamber. He still remembered the two buttons he had observed earlier.

Curiously, the effect of the tranquilizers had worn off. Mark was able to feel normal emotions—that is, normal for an uprooted Earth man planted in the middle of the planet Mantz. Either the machine had stripped the chemicals from his body or Leipin had done so when she applied the beam therapy device. "What do you call that?" he asked, pointing to the tiny machine that had just saved his life.

Leipin looked first at Creson before answering. Apparently no information was to be given to the Earth man without his permission. Creson nodded his assent. "It may be referred to as a dysfunction alleviator," Leipin began, "offering somewhat more restorative properties than those found within your chamber. Its purpose is to restore failing life functions."

Feeling stronger by the minute, Mark had trouble believing that he'd been in any real danger. In any case, the recovery phase was short. "My life functions were failing because of this machine?" he asked, pointing at the glowing unit. Creson did not respond but Leipin nodded. A hint of apology was written into her expression. "Was it a reaction to the weird experiences or the workings of the machine itself?"

"It is difficult to say at this point," Leipin responded, her manner now more clinical. "Additional analysis will have to take place before we can be certain. In all likelihood it is simply the difference between your physiology and that which the machine has been led to expect would be the case. It happens sometimes with alien creatures...no offense intended."

Mark liked this female Mantzite. She appeared to be more sensitive to his feelings than did Creson. He still could not, however, see any meaningful difference between the two. He found his eyes drifting over her body, even as he tried not to let them. If such overt inspection was noticed, she discretely avoided making her awareness known.

After deciding the time was right, Leipin helped him to his feet then over to the single beam that provided access to and from the experience chamber. Again Creson did nothing to help, permitting his subordinate to handle Mark by herself. *Snob*, Mark thought as Creson vanished into the tube.

"I will not be returning with you, but I will be here when you return," Leipin said as they rested near the conveyer.

"There *will* be another session?" asked Mark, pleased with the prospect notwithstanding what had nearly happened.

"Most assuredly; as soon as adjustments are made and your body functions are properly restored." She applied the soft conical beam once again then, satisfied with the results, said, "I will help you into the conveyer now."

Mark permitted her help, pleased with the first example of friendliness thus far shown by his captors. As his arm wrapped around her, he felt an impulse to renew their earlier discussion. "Creson really is a guy, right? Somehow I don't think he'd make it as a girl." At that, Leipin's eyes contracted and her body gave a series of shivers, a reaction that was even more familiar to Mark after the "minute or two" spent within the grasp of the experience chamber.

"Are all Earth people so preoccupied with this subject?" she asked.

Mark chuckled along with her. "Some more than others," he said.

She paused near the conveyer entrance to give meaning to her words. "Creson is believed to be responsible for a long line of new generation replacements—he is a father, so to speak, many times over. He may appear to you to be somewhat limited in compassion, but his psychological and physiological traits are considered on Mantz to be of the highest quality. That, of course, reflects upon his public or official usefulness." Leipin turned her fur-covered head toward him as she continued. "Although one's private affairs are generally held in confidence, Creson makes little attempt to hide his fondness for pretty little things like me. I hope that satisfies your apparently insatiable curiosity." Smiling coyly, she gently coaxed him into the conveyer beam.

* * * *

Back in the laboratory and once again inside his cubicle, Mark watched as Creson touched the panel lights that would ensure his containment. The procedure again started with the upper left button, suggesting to Mark that this controlled both the opening and closing of the chamber. Three more lights were pressed within his view, and, momentarily released from the machine's control, he felt free to burn the sequence into his memory. Only one button was not seen; only one more before he would know the entire series. *Big deal!* he thought. *I'll be able to lock myself in as part of an escape!*

After securing of the Earth man's chamber, Creason delayed at the panel to watch the flickering lights. When satisfied, he returned to his captive, who had once again settled into the comfort provided by the machine. "Apparently the chamber will have no difficulty restoring your bodily functions to normal. You should be feeling its effects even now." He paused to permit a response from Mark, who merely nodded. Then, with brows knitted in thought and alien hand held up to his small-featured face in a human-like manner of concentration, he began to project what was more a conversation with himself than with Mark. "You are truly an interesting species," he began, "intellectual yet in many ways primitive. Your brain is capable of much more than currently challenges it, yet you seem determined to limit its exposure to new worlds of thought. It is as if you feel threatened by the idea of an expanded mental capacity. You prefer the security of narrow reasoning and limited concepts."

"I love you too, Spot," Mark interjected. The sound of the Earth man's voice brought Creson out of his reverie. After a moment Mark added, "What else did you find out from that experience machine?"

Creson stared a moment longer before answering. "I might ask you the same question," he probed. "How would you define the experience?"

A bell of caution rang within Mark. Creson was asking for information which, by the tone of the question, he had been unable to extract from the machine. What was it he wanted to know? And of what value would it be to withhold it from him? Mark considered what he had just learned, that the machine extracted a moment in a subject's life then compared it to an equivalent moment in a Mantzite life—or perhaps to the lives of countless other creatures from all over the galaxy. In doing this the Mantzites could see how Earth creatures and Earth society stacked up to them and theirs. Surely Creson knew he was aware of that much. "I was able to see myself in earlier life, quite vividly as a matter of fact. I could also see some of you creatures in what looked like similar circumstances."

"And how would you describe the Mantz experiences?"

Again Mark was unsure what Creson wanted to know, and again he considered his answer carefully. The episodes had been more than simply vivid; he had actually lived them! What his Mantz partner knew and felt, he knew and felt, at least when the creature mentally focused on something during the episode.

Maybe that was it; maybe they were afraid he had a working knowledge of every device brought to mind by the creature whose consciousness he briefly shared. "It was like I was following the guy around wherever he went."

"You did not feel you were the...guy...himself?"

Bingo! thought Mark. His alien captor was worried about his acquiring technical knowledge. He shook his head slowly as if examining his feelings at the time. "Not particularly. It was fascinating but difficult to understand. Everything was so...different."

Creson stared at Mark with doubting eyes, but he declined to press the issue. Instead, he continued his questioning, each time confirming more of Mark's suspicions. Mark revealed all that he thought was obvious but withheld anything that might lead his captors to consider him dangerous. He did not want them to become less willing to permit him access to what could prove to be a means of escape.

The conversation came to an end as a telepathic projection came out of the conveyer tube. It caught Mark by surprise but reinforced his belief that he was more attuned to such transmissions, in this case even through a conveyer tube. He must have picked up the talent during the experience session. He still had no idea what was being said; it was more like being an eavesdropper on a foreign-language conversation. He wondered what triggered the change, which episode. He could remember none that touched on that particular subject.

Whatever the cause, it was something he had to keep to himself. Maybe he could develop it to the point where he could listen in on what the Mantzites would continue to think were private conversations. Like the memorized buttons, it was at least something.

"Are you up to another session?" Creson asked, turning back to the Mark after intercepting the message. The question was more one of courtesy, since there was little he could say or do about it.

"Am I expected to die in the process?" Mark asked, only partially in humor.

"We will abide by whatever the machine decides," Creson retorted. "For the present, however, the inconsistencies in your frail human structure have been properly accommodated for through the routine application of Mantz genius."

Mark exhaled an amused grunt in appreciation of the game which the creature played so skillfully. "Ready when you are, Spot," he responded, the off-handed manner of his reply intended to conceal his true feelings at being permitted further access to the experience chamber. This machine offered learning far beyond anything available to his fellow humans. And the creatures who forcibly detained him were unknowing of how much of it he got to keep.

My God! I know how to operate that little beam tool they carry around with them! he thought, recalling a experience shared with a Mantzite counterpart. *I even know about this planet and its environment. And about the guy's family life!* The more he reflected on the morning's experience the more he realized how much information had been poured into his memory, ready to be called upon anytime he wished. There was no feeling of having to work at it, to memorize or study. It was simply there; someone else had done the work of learning then implanted the result into his human head. *How to learn without really trying!* He wondered whether he would have the opportunity to share one of Creson's experiences. Or would his playful antagonist consider that too dangerous?

So involved was he in anticipation of the coming session that he neglected to pay attention to the sequence of buttons used to secure his release. He scolded himself for the oversight even as his body took on the familiar tranquilized-yet-mentally-alert state. As before, he docilely followed Creson through the conveyer to the room housing the chamber.

Leipin was there as promised, and she smiled at him as he entered. He returned the smile, then briefly wondered as he climbed onto the misty table whether it was possible to have an involvement with an alien creature, someone light years away from Earth in more ways than one. The idea gave him a momentary feeling of loss. *My god, what must Kathy be thinking now?* he thought, the tranquilizers blocking the intensity of emotions that stirred within his brain. *I might never see her again. And she might never find out what happened; to her I will have simply disappeared—on purpose.* He considered the state of their emotions when last together, and wished he had focused on the deep feelings he had for her rather than spending the evening locked in what now seemed so unimportant.

The process experienced earlier was repeated: lights dimmed seconds before he began reliving a portion of his life. The first thing he realized as that happened was that the picture was even more real than before. *Whatever adjustments Leipin made to this machine, it sure improved the reception,* he thought, wondering at the same time whether the Mantzites were listening in. Just in case, he decided to concentrate on what he was seeing and thus keep random thoughts from entering his mind, thoughts that might be remembered by this cosmic video recorder.

It was wonderful to be so vividly emerged in his own past. It helped him to better understand himself, even as that applied to the restlessness that had driven him to Wyoming. There had always been restlessness connected with his life and, as he now realized, it had not been all bad. Often it forced him to reach out, to search for change, change that then added to the richness of his life. He could see himself doing the same thing with Kathy, although the way he had gone about it could as easily guarantee disaster—the lady might harbor resentment. Eventually, after tiring of his own crankiness he would have applied the same effort and determination to their problem; had he not stumbled into this cosmic spider web, they might already be on their way to nirvana.

Realizing that his mind had drifted, and again concerned that the Mantzites might be listening in, he renewed his determination to concentrate only on the scenes in front of him. But it was already too late. As if it preferred his topics to its own, the machine abruptly switched from a review of a youthful encounter to his last meeting with Kathy.

The shock he felt challenged whatever of the tranquilizers remained in his system. He was back in her apartment, really there! And the pain of that moment was there as well—Mark found himself wanting to turn it off. *How the hell did I get here?!* he thought.

He wondered whether he could direct the device by focusing on something else. Anything else. He ignored what was in front of him and thought of the Mellon and Carter building. Nothing happened; the experience with Kathy continued to fly by, undaunted by this attempt at diversion. He tried harder, but the result was the same. And with failure came resentment, resentment at the rudeness of this machine and the beings who were directing it. They had no business inviting themselves into his private affairs. They were nothing more than voyeurs to his and Kathy's intimacy. "You have no right!" he tried to shout, realizing as he did so that he could not hear the sound of his own voice. Had he really spoken or only thought he had? Did it really matter?

Midway through the scene with Kathy, the unexpected happened again: The picture froze—all was as it should be, but nothing was moving. Kathy was sitting by her typewriter, one half-filled page of her dog article projecting from the machine. He himself, now detached from his status as an observer, was leaning against a wall, a frown on his face and a half finished drink in his hands. Me-too was lying in the middle of the room staring at a spot on the wall. Mark could sense that something was wrong, not in the scene but with his hosts—was he on the road to dying for a second time? But before he could reason further, the scene moved on, forcing him to live again that difficult evening. Eventually the machine moved on to other times in his life, most of which did not involve Kathy. Mark did nothing to try to coax it back.

As had happened during the earlier session, the scene arbitrarily switched from Earth to Mantz, the suddenness of the transition catching Mark off guard. Stories of an alien society, presented at lightening speeds, began flooding his consciousness, each situation mirroring an Earth equivalent, at least mirroring it as closely as the differences between beings and environment permitted. In response to Mark's contribution of a grade-school experience, it produced a Mantzite early-training experience. Where Mark was guided through a problem at work, it produced a Mantzite vocational problem. Collectively, it confirmed what he'd already guessed, that the creatures were comparing their captive to themselves, learning something about Homo Sapiens in the process.

He hoped that the by-product of this, the learning given him, did not show. He had no doubt that he was picking up knowledge the Mantzites would rather he not have. And if his new-found ability to sense telepathic projections was any indication, he was also expanding the capacity of his mind. Most of the information received was innocent enough, but every now and then a casual comparison would permit an absorption of technical knowledge. Photography had triggered one such incident:

Mark was reliving a scene involving a complex shoot at the Mellon and Carter studio in Pennsylvania. It had taken hours and involved himself, his assistant and one other to bring the idea to fruition. When it came time to compare this to a Mantz equivalent, he discovered that his counterpart handled the matter through use of the ubiquitous light beams, in this case one specializing in the esthetic presentation of images. His Mantz counterpart was exceptionally gifted as an artist and not only had the knowledge and talent to put such a device to its highest use, but actually modified it several times to enhance its effectiveness. The Mantzite had concentrated on the instrument during that portion of his life which Mark shared, with the result that Mark now had clear knowledge, not only of how the alien device worked, but how it could be reworked into a newer-generation machine. The creature had other ideas involving the tools of his trade as well, and in every instance and with the same feeling of professionalism and excitement, Mark now shared that knowledge. They were as much his ideas as they had been those of his Mantz counterpart.

Not all of the comparisons were so pleasant. His professional counterpart had a female with whom he battled constantly, and although his reaction was more subdued than Mark imagined his own would be under such circumstances, the domestic squabbling had its effect on the creature's work. Ideas and procedures were interspersed with anger and frustration, and the effect was so vivid to Mark, so much his own experience, that he was certain that should he ever meet the female face to face, he would be well equipped, and more than willing, to pursue the argument. He wondered whether this was how Kathy and he looked to the world—or rather to the universe.

It was fascinating to view the similarities and contrasts in male-female behavior between two separate planets. Fascinating to note the suggested universality of social behavior, as if some cosmic law were at work. Mark made a mental note to discuss the point later with Creson.

As rapidly as he had been mentally transported to Mantz, he was back in Pennsylvania, this time on a camping trip in a remote mountainous area in the western part of the state. At computer speeds he relived the trip, and the feeling of actually being there brought back the emotions of the time.

He walked alone in wilderness, and had been doing so for days; Kathy was not yet a part of his life. He had forgotten about that trip, including what had motivated him to go. Having the opportunity to re-involve himself now, he began to see similarities between it and the present situation. *Except I didn't bump into Martians!* He remembered coming back refreshed and ready to rejoin whatever he thought he was fleeing.

The experience machine prompted him to also remember a disturbing incident that had occurred along the way. He had come upon a newly born fawn so young it could barely get to its feet. Its mother had seen the approaching human and, realizing it was too late to signal her youngster to hide, was frantically encouraging it to join her in flight. Mark could see at a glance that the fawn was too young to comply, and although wanting to stay and observe, he knew it would be cruel to do so. He moved on, pausing to check again only after he was far enough away to be viewed as harmless. No less panicked, the doe continued to nudge her baby unmercifully, insisting it move to where it could no longer be seen. Mark remembered thinking how nice it would be to be a fly at that moment. He could land on a nearby tree and watch two of natures creatures go about their lives. Reluctantly, he turned and walked away, trying as he did so to make it obvious to the badly disturbed animals that, this time, he was really leaving.

The scene switched to an alien one. He was still in wilderness, but the plant life was now the blue, plastic-like trees he'd remembered from his trip through the transporter. He was Wilpin, a young, low-ranking technician from the research laboratory who was vacationing in much the same manner as had Mark—alone and desirous of remaining so. Feeling as if he were riding inside the Mantzite's mind, Mark was equally as involved as Wilpin in what he felt and saw. He and his host were walking without haste under a lovely, red-tinted sky that softly filtered through numerous layers of perfectly-rounded leaves. Both suns were shining brightly, permitting both close and distant objects to be sharply defined. Mark wanted to stay there forever, even as he knew he would soon have to return to work. He had been out for two days, seeing during that time only one sign of civilization: a small structure which he knew immediately was a commonplace dwelling of primarily laser construction controlled in every way that mattered by a mind-functioning device—a computer. Mark knew all this without actually seeing it. He even knew the computer communicated with the home's occupant via an octagonal panel of lights. He did not, however, know how this computer worked, which series of lights controlled which function—since his host did not concentrate on the specifics, Mark was unable to "listen in." For the same reason, and not withstanding Wilpin's employment within the same laboratory that held Mark's captive body, Mark was unable to determine how the panels of the laboratory worked—Wilpin simply did not bring that subject to mind. Mark wondered whether such information could be withheld should the viewer—in this case himself—attempt to force his host to dwell on a desired subject.

There was water, plenty of it, and there were mountains as well. And other topographical features he'd seen many times on Earth. In this instance at least, a cosmic law probably did apply. The causes of geological upheaval might be expected to be the same no matter where in the universe they occurred. His host momentarily considered the same thing, focusing on a distant mountain and recalling a similar setting on a planet he knew as "Mantz-328." Simultaneous with this reflection, Mark became aware that Mantz-328 was not inhabited by dominant creatures, that it was primitive in animal development and had been routinely categorized by Mantz officials as "under their influence." Mark could not determine what that meant.

By the third day of travel—which Mark now knew to be slightly less than three of Earth's days—host and invisible guest were fighting their way through rubbery tentacles of brush and short, reddish-brown trees. It was a formidable barrier that seemed at times to have been deliberately placed in their way. After hours of struggle, during which time Mark felt the familiar pleasure of hard exercise, they entered a clearing that lead some hundred meters beyond to a stream. Standing in the middle of it, casually satisfying its thirst, was a six-legged animal, twice as big as Mark's host and possessing a single horn in the center of its head. Through his host, Mark knew the beast to be a zander, a rare but not unfamiliar occupant of these woods.

Without realizing he was doing it, he tried to assist Wilpin in holding his breath as the animal raised its head to check out its surroundings, its gaze settling on their location for a moment but then moving on. Soon it returned to its drinking, as yet unaware that it was being observed by representatives of two, widely-separated planets. Mark could sense the dichotomy of emotions felt by Wilpin: He wanted to observe the beast up close but was aware of its shyness and respectful of its formidable horn.

A few minutes later he, and thus Mark, got an idea. They would convert his own DNA to that of a flying insect, a flinac. Then, without alarming the animal, they would land on its back, there to observe without being observed in return.

Wilpin was of the class from which most planetary explorers were drawn and he was highly adept, not only at converting his genes to imitate almost any desired creature, but in being able to master that creature's behavior as well. The latter was by no means easy. Since little of the creature's brain was copied, one had to struggle to learn what to the animal came naturally. Many Mantz travelers found themselves unable to do this and were thus not of much use in the business of exploration, at least not where this involved hiding one's presence in the form of a local creature. Wilpin was a notable exception. Whatever the animal could do, he could do. If it were supposed to fly and had the means of doing so, he would soon be bouncing through the air as if born to do so. It was, of course, necessary to have first studied the targeted animal's behavior, including what talents it enjoyed—and, of course, how its genes were arranged within its DNA. But such things came naturally to Wilpin, and as the result of his duties in the lab, and his experiences on other planets (Earth included), he had in-depth knowledge of hundreds of alien creatures.

Having decided on the Mantz insect, Wilpin immediately began the manipulation of his genes to match those of his choice. Mark shared every moment of the process and thus began to understand it. *My God, It's so simple!* he thought as he mentally participated in the conversion, his mind sailing over the ten trillion cells of Wilpin's body, instructing them in the nuances of rearranging themselves. At lightning speeds he "explained" the gene structure of a flinac to each cell, then supervised the conversion of its chromosomes, genes and DNA to not only imitate that structure but properly protect and store within the converted body, a record of whatever DNA units were not needed in the process, in this case those not required for the construction of a flinac—this information would be needed later when it was time to convert back. He also helped Wilpin release unneeded fluids into the air and revise the chemical structure of the converted cells that remained. Since the target was a substantially smaller being, copious quantities of bodily fluids had to be released, all to be recaptured later when the process was reversed.

The conversion took fifteen minutes, and afterward Mark and his host were, to everything close enough to see, a Mantz insect. He was impressed by what he had done but not surprised that it had been accomplished so quickly. As with his Mantz counterpart, he never doubted he could do it. Not exactly child's play but no harder than algebra had been in grade school.

In his new form, he no longer had a feeling of breathing, yet there was no discomfort associated with the lack of it. And his eyes, which he knew now numbered five, took in a picture that, while not what he and

Wilpin were used to, easily reported back the details of his surroundings. Smiling inside if not on the form he had assumed, he flexed his wings then rehearsed the order of his fourteen legs. With Wilpin concentrating on the process so intently, his knowledge of how best to utilize a creature's body to imitate its behavior was first rate. He was now as expert in such matters as was his host, which meant in this he had mastered a skill that few other Mantzites could touch.

Why doesn't everyone learn from this Wilpin experience? Mark thought, feeling good about what he believed the answer to be. *It doesn't work the same way for everyone. That's what Creson's afraid of; he doesn't know how it'll work on me.* Realizing that he was not truly alone, he scolded himself anew for not controlling his thoughts. He resolved to save this for when he was alone in his chamber.

He knew, as did his host, that the conversion was only temporary, like a stretched rubber band that returns to its original form if pressure is not maintained. To keep the imitation going, one had to continually work at it. If the mental "pressure" became lax, the imitator's body would revert back to what it had been after thirty some minutes. Longer if the re conversion was from a smaller to a larger creature where one had to draw moisture from the air for restoration of bodily fluids, and increase the number of cells to satisfy the requirements of a larger body. Fortunately this requirement of constant pressure did not preclude routine periods of sleep—not a problem to a trained subconscious mind.

Mark was flying, and it was as much his effort as Wilpin's, or so it felt. The zander had moved off in the time it took to convert, but it was still within sight; catching up took only a few minutes. While moving through the red-tinted air, Mark was conscious of the need to watch out for anything that might threaten the flinac he had become. He was also conscious that his reasoning in this was that of a Mantzite and not of an insect.

Mark knew exactly what his host had done to avoid losing Mantzite reasoning powers. It was all there in Wilpin's memory to be drawn upon as Mark wished. He saw early discoverers of this talent find out the hard way how necessary it was to be selective in the conversion process. They had converted to alien form only to realize later, after an automatic re conversion had taken place, that their mental capabilities had been no greater than that of the creature they had imitated. It was some time before selectivity was perfected, but it was now routine to preserve one's consciousness in miniaturized form within an alien body. Mark was now a beneficiary of that learning; he was a flinac with the awareness and brain power of an Earth man/Mantzite.

He and his host found the zander and, without difficulty, landed on its back. A long tail immediately swung their way as if in recognition of their presence; it was easily avoided. They sat unmolested, watching a wild and exceptionally shy animal from a vantage point few were able to achieve. *This is one hell of a variation on the Pennsylvania trip,* he thought, thinking again how nice it would have been to have had this capability during the deer incident in Pennsylvania.

Mark realized with a touch of disappointment that he was not as awestruck by the experience as he thought he would be, this because he understood the zander as completely as an Earth man might understand a deer. Still, he felt a thrill as the animal continued on its way, with only an occasional glance behind to see if the creature seen at the stream was following. It had no awareness that it was hosting that same creature in the form of a converted flinac, who was in turn an unwitting host to a converted Earth man.

The zander paused occasionally to sample this or that vegetation. Its muzzle, which looked like a cross between a horse and an anteater, stretched so far downward that it required little effort to pick up the thick-leafed vegetation found in abundance on the ground. The same was true of the larger leaves found in small but well-endowed trees. For that, it would shift weight to its four hind legs then lift its long muzzle and two front legs off the ground.

Mark could feel the pleasure of his host as he observed this behavior from up close. Indeed, Wilpin, and thus himself, was so intent on the zander that he failed to notice a rapidly approaching predator.

It struck without landing and came within a fraction of an inch of what Mark felt was as much his head as Wilpin's. Momentarily confused, he and his host leaped into the air and began flapping their wings as rapidly as they knew how. Then, without knowing what they were fleeing, they flew a twisted route, hoping to dodge the persisting form long enough to reach a nearby tree. They were pressured on the way by the undaunted predator, who swept by again and again, striking out at the elusive flinac body each time.

Mark could feel Wilpin's desperation as he struggled to review his options. He knew he could not revert to his previous form quickly enough to avoid capture by the bird, and to attempt to do so would eliminate any possibility he had of escaping through the air. Further, he would, during the reconversion process, be neither insect nor Mantzite, only an impotent hybrid with a weak possibility of surviving the bird's attack. For the same reason he could not rearrange the cells of his body to permit the flying predator to pass harmlessly through—there was simply not enough time.

Reaching the tree with only the barest margin of safety, host and guest scampered under one of its broad leaves. It was not enough to block the predator's next assault; Mark felt sharp pain as his host's body absorbed a punishing blow from its blunted beak. Falling to the ground, he shared Wilpin's frantic struggle to regain momentum using the one wing and five legs that still responded to his damaged body's commands. They landed on what looked to Mark to be an acre of leaf then quickly fought their way downward to an area of thicker growth. The bird struck again just as they reached the underside of a large blade of Mantz grass—two of Wilpin's legs, both on the same side of his insect body, disappeared. The remainder of that side was struck numb and the other could not sufficiently compensate to permit much in the way of movement. Out of control, they dropped between blades of grass then lay still, unable to decide what to do next and fearing that it was already too late.

Mark had never felt such pain and despair before. It was he who was in trouble, he who felt his mortality within reach. He lay on the ground, a sense of fatalism permeating his spirits, while the bird pecked blindly at the grass, angered by its inability to locate its weakened prey. Recognizing that movement of any kind would be detected, Mark knew it was still the wrong time to attempt the re-conversion process. He fought to remain motionless, even as the life continued to drain out of him. After a while his patience was rewarded; a badly disappointed bird jumped into the air and flew away.

A number of seconds passed before guest and host felt secure enough to begin taking action to save their lives. Their attitude, however, continued to be one of pessimism; the wounds were too traumatic, too extensive. Mark concurred with his host in what he now knew had to be done. Their backpack was approximately two miles away, tucked into the brush close to where the conversion to a flinac had taken place. There was little hope of being able to travel that far but they were close enough to communicate with it via the multipurpose portable beam which Wilpin, in a fashion common to travelers into potentially dangerous territory, had left on.

After a moment of concentration, Wilpin mentally beamed a message to the tiny machine—it responded immediately. He then ordered it to begin recording the just-concluded experience; again it responded without delay. Mark felt the rapid probing of his and Wilpin's shared consciousness and knew exactly what was happening. The machine, in only a fraction of a second, captured everything, from the time Wilpin left his private dwelling until the present. After it signaled completion, Wilpin then ordered it to continue recording while he attempted to save his life. Simultaneously it opened up communication with the distant laboratory, which in turn quickly reviewed Wilpin's experience before initiating steps to assist in his recovery.

Dreading it as much as his host, Mark helped Wilpin begin the re-conversion process. It was immediately unbearable. Their shared body was pierced by darts of agony as damaged parts failed to respond as they should—Wilpin halted the process long enough to catch his breath. The pain was unceasing and soon consciousness began to fade, the thought of which only increased their panic—reconversion would continue at an uncontrolled pace were they to pass out. Mark struggled as hard as his host to keep this from happening.

Mark understood precisely what portions of his alien body were threatened. He understood its physiology: what did what, what was most crucial for survival. He knew that life-sustaining fluids were leaking at a prodigious rate, that reconversion at the current pace, however more bearable that was, was permitting this leakage to continue unchecked. It was a no-win situation: pain and possible death one way vs. certain death the other. With no feasible alternatives, they elected the unbearable; as quickly as the Mantzite's talents permitted, the insect became a Mantzite.

Mark screamed along with his host throughout the entire process, and even as his mind cried out for the mercy of oblivion, he fought as hard as Wilpin to remain conscious. It was an eternity before restoration was complete, and even then they could only lie on the ground gasp for breath and struggle to endure an intense and unyielding pain. In time, as pain was replaced by a body-wide numbing, shared eyes dared to inspect the damaged side of their body. They sighed in mutual recognition of the irreparable destruction which had once been their lower left side. One leg was barely connected and there was now an unnatural entrance to their abdomen. There was little anyone could do. Help from the laboratory could not come in time, and without that help, they stood no chance at all.

Accepting the inevitable, host and invisible guest lowered their shared head to the soft grass and sighed away their last hope.

The numbing sensation grew but was now accepted with appreciation—it replaced pain, unbearable pain. As it moved through their body, they felt a euphoria that only a great relief can bring. Mark realized he was witnessing the approach of his own death, but it was with more calm than he would have thought possible that he greeted the dark abyss when it came.

CHAPTER 16

Cal wondered at the change. The woman sitting across from him was not the same woman he knew from before. She was more reserved, less friendly. A female problem? A hangover? They had shared a few drinks the previous night, but hardly enough to matter. *Maybe city ladies don't take much to drinkin',* he thought.

What else could it be? The thing with the dog wasn't that big a deal; at least she said it wasn't.

"I can't imagine who would do such a thing, can you?" Kathy asked with more than a touch of sarcasm. She had told Cal that the animal's escape was likely engineered by someone in town.

"Don't seem likely anyone did," Cal answered, missing the sarcasm. "Don't see how he kin git through a door whut's got a chain on er. An don't see how he cud put er back on after he lef neither."

"Oh I don't think someone who knew the town would have any trouble. Maybe there's a secret passage, or maybe he took the hinges off the door."

"Taint likely. Man fixin' on gittin' iz head all broke up, he try tuh fool iz frens like thet. Lotta folks hereabouts don't like not knowin' whut them dogs is up tuh; won't take kindly to findin' out some'ns tryin' tuh make a fool of um."

Kathy realized with a start that Cal was looking at her suspiciously. She exhaled an involuntary chuckle. *My god!* she thought, *he's thinks I'm behind it all! He's either a good actor or as much a victim as I am.* She felt a momentary impulse to say something in her own defense.

Cal relaxed his expression as he leaned back in his chair and said, "Ah done told yuh bout ma fren, Turk, lockin' one up in iz shed. Ain't no sea-cret passageways thar; an takin them old hinges off'en thet door without waking up half thuh town jes ain't likely."

A tinge of guilt swept over Kathy. The man sitting across from her seemed so genuine, so believable. She wondered just how clever he was, whether he could pull off such a thing without giving himself away in a face-to-face encounter like this. Unlikely. "But somebody must've done it!" she pleaded, her attitude noticeably changing. "That dog just didn't vanish into thin air!"

"Some folks say thet's jes whut happened."

"What do you say, Cal?" Kathy asked, leaning into the table and staring intently into his eyes.

Cal fidgeted in his chair. He was obviously uncomfortable with the question. "Ain't thet am superstitious or nothin', but they is some things thet'r better left alone. Maybe this iz one of um."

Kathy leaned back again. "I don't believe that, Cal. Somebody is behind this and I'm going to find out who."

"How yew gonna do thet?" Cal asked softly.

Kathy hesitated. She didn't have the foggiest notion what she would do. Her comment more reflected frustration than determination. "Well, the dog's gone so there's nothing we can do about it now."

At hearing the "we," Cal inwardly relaxed; he was once again being included in the pretty outsider's plans. He wasn't sure what had set her off, but, in any case, she seemed to be coming out of it. *Probably wuz female problems,* he concluded to himself. "Ain't no sweat. They's gonna be t'other comin' along right soon. Kin try agin then."

"But what can we do that hasn't already been done?" Kathy asked, thinking aloud. "We had him captured and under video camera surveillance, and he still got away." Her eyes widened slightly as a thought came to mind. "Someone must've known we were photographing that animal!" she stated emphatically. "Who did we tell?"

Cal looked skeptical, there were not many people he knew who would know how to operate a video camera let alone manipulate it as this lady said had been done. Without enthusiasm for the way the conversation had turned he replied, "Turk, but he ain't no problem; couple guys en thuh bar."

"Would any of them be capable of doing something like this?"

He shook his head. "Don't rightly see none of um cause'n somp'in like this. Don't see um wantin' tuh."

"But they could have told someone else?"

"Cudda told thuh whole town if'n they'd a mind tuh. But don't see no one else wantin' tuh neither."

Kathy sighed her surrender. Telling one person in this town was probably tantamount to telling everybody. Thus they were effectively back where they started. She searched her mind for some way of catching the culprit in the act, something he would not expect. And this time she would not tell anyone, perhaps not even Cal.

An hour later she was strolling toward the edge of town engrossed in thoughts of vanishing shepherds and a lost lover. She had a nagging fear that the two could be related. Something was definitely weird out there and Mark had either passed it by or was now caught up in it.

She drifted along with little thought of where she was going, only that she had to sort things out. The pleasant surroundings helped, helped her relax at least. That was one of the many things Mark and she had in common. *And one of the reasons he should've taken me along!* she thought, her resentment at having been left behind undiminished. But how could she enjoy it now, knowing Mark was out there somewhere and that he was overdue, overdue to the point of being the focus of a formal search?

A single glance took in miles of territory, and Kathy searched for movement that would speak of the whereabouts of one lost human being, a human being who belonged to her. But she could see nothing, not even the search party—Janos had said his men were on the job but he didn't say where. Kathy wondered if she should get in touch with the knowledgeable ranger to find out what was going on.

Waiting was not her thing; if it weren't for the Kelly-dog affair, she was sure she would go out of her mind. She chuckled at the irony. The Kelly-dogs were an important part of her article, more so than when she'd decided to use them as a means of justifying the trip to Kelly. And Mark's expected ire at her inviting herself along on his private hike was no longer a concern; he was overdue and that provided all the justification she needed.

She was still not sure she believed Mark to be lost. It was more than just possible that he was out there because he wanted to be out there; that he would come back when he was ready to come back. And also more than possible that he would resent her having sicked the rangers on him. She pictured his reaction as a bunch of "rescuers" burst into his solitude. "Well, the jerk shouldn't have said two weeks if he didn't mean two weeks!"

she mumbled defensively.

Damn! she thought. *It's closer to three weeks! And he still hasn't let anyone know where he is!* She could understand his going off on some macho thrill, and she could understand, or at least accept, his need to go off by himself, but the thought that he would ignore the feelings of people who cared for him—specifically her—was angering.

Without knowing why, she sank to her knees and began to cry. "God how I've messed things up!" she mumbled between sobs, the thought bringing another barrage of tears. "I'm good for you, Mark. You don't want to leave me." The soft sounds of nature continued, unimpressed by her pathetic plea. After a while she rose to her feet, there to contemplate a world that, for her, was changing too fast. There was no point in continuing the walk. Whatever focus she'd had was lost in the flood of tears.

She would feel better if she knew what was going on with the search party. She wondered whether it was too soon to get in touch with Janos— this could be interpreted as the hysterical interference Sandy had warned against. She also wondered whether she would accompany Janos and his crew if offered the chance, as had the woman who accidentally stumbled upon her husband. She thought not, still feeling in the back of her mind that Mark was going to surface in Pennsylvania, or at least at the airport in Jackson. Her real fear, harder than ever to shake, was that her lover had cooled to their relationship, that he was out there right now trying to decide how to break this to her.

"Stop it! Just stop it!" she demanded of herself, pressing her hands against her temples as if to do so would block further thoughts of Mark. "You're only making yourself miserable!" She closed her eyes and tried to force her mind to think only of the mystery dogs. She thought about what had been done so far, both by her and by Cal and his friends. It was a while before the thoughts began to flow.

Cal had mentioned an incident where a friend had stayed with one of the beasts for an entire night, even sleeping on the floor in plain view of the animal. Yet it still managed to escape. And without wakening its captor. It had slipped out of a tight collar then exited through a supposedly locked door—very similar to her case, except here there was the added mystery of the video camera. *So unless there's a practical joker in town, what we've got here is a race of super dogs who know all about video cameras and how to squeeze through keyholes!* An occasional sob testified to the fact that the previous subject had not been forgotten.

It had to be a practical joker, but how he did it she couldn't imagine—trapping him (or her) would not be easy. The video camera was her best bet, but how to use it without either culprit or beast knowing it was there was the question. *The closet's out; they'd expect that.* A quick examination of the room told her it would be just as effective on the side furthest from the closet, hidden under something that had a reason to be there, clothes or a pillow, maybe a suitcase. She could set it all up beforehand.

Not wanting to lose the boost it was giving her spirits, she poured herself into the details, adding what was felt to be a fail-safe touch: a thin layer of dirt sprinkled over the floor. If the camera were again turned off, at least the culprit would leave footprints.

But suppose he sees me putting dirt on the floor? she thought, wondering if any dog could be that smart. She tried to think of a way to spread it around without the animal becoming curious. "Drug him!" The idea seemed farfetched at first but a few minutes of thought led her to believe it could work. And it would have the added advantage of giving her control—she did not want a smart animal like that roaming around the room while she slept. *Animals are tranquilized all the time; it doesn't hurt them.* The only problem was figuring out how to get the drugs.

Hurrying back to her room, she looked up the number of a veterinarian interviewed as part of her project. The man had been friendly to the point of flirting and willing to discuss anything Kathy wanted to discuss, including drug use in controlling overly rambunctious animals. It took several minutes to get him on the phone.

"I want to be able to put him to sleep, so he won't know what's going on around him."

"Why would you want to do that?" the man asked, the doubt evident in his voice.

This was the difficult part. Regardless of how friendly he might be, the veterinarian was not about to approve a prescription for tranquilizers without good reason. "Its just a little experiment. I can't talk much now, but you'll be able to read about it in my article."

As she feared, it was not enough. "Kathy, I'd love to help but it's not that easy. These are controlled substances you're talking about. They're regularly abused by all kinds of people."

"But this is for a dog," Kathy retorted.

"Doesn't matter, it's the same drug. Works on humans just as effectively as it does on dogs."

"But it is feasible? I mean is there something that would put my pet to sleep for a few hours?"

"Oh yes, no problem there." He discussed how it would be done, including which drugs at what dosages would be used. The man had enjoyed the earlier interview with Kathy and his congeniality over the telephone showed it. He did, however, continue to draw the line at phoning in a prescription to a pharmacy in Jackson, Wyoming. "Sorry, can't do it. Could mean my license if I get caught."

"Don't you ever give medication to the dog's owner; to avoid having to give every injection yourself; I mean when it has to be given every few hours?"

"Well, yes," the man admitted, "but generally that's for someone nearby, where I can at least claim to be supervising its use."

"But what if that someone goes on vacation, and they want to tranquilize their animal for the trip?" Kathy was getting desperate. She had to come up with a situation to the veterinarian's liking or it was no-go. "If it were a long trip, say across country, it could take days, and there would be many injections to administer. Naturally you would give the owner sound advice on how to go about it, but wouldn't you also give him what he needed?"

At this the vet. had to pause. What she was asking was not proper, and there was no way he should accommodate her wishes, but the argument she presented might just sell in Peoria—assuming anyone would want to make waves. He sighed in reluctant capitulation. "Look, I'll agree to phone something in, but as far as I'm concerned you officially told me over the phone that you have your dog what-iz-face with you and that you're having trouble getting him to settle down."

"Me-too," Kathy interjected.

"You too what?" the confused man said.

"Me-too; that's the name of my dog. Remember, you laughed when I mentioned that before?"

"Oh yes," he chuckled, recalling the earlier discussion with this personable young woman. "But anyway, I can't guarantee that the guy will accept a phoned-in script from out of state. After all, he won't know me from Adam. Chances are that, at best, he'll approve only a small quantity—will that do you?"

"I guess you would know that better than I. In any case, I really appreciate the effort."

The man was obviously pleased to help notwithstanding continued apprehension about the propriety of what he was doing. "Look, if anybody asks, you be sure to stick to our story, okay?"

"Okay," Kathy said, happy with her success. She searched in the directory for a Jackson pharmacy then cheerfully passed the number on to her friend. The conversation lingered a few minutes longer, with Kathy simultaneously voicing gratitude and encouraging support; the latter to insure that the maximum effort be put into convincing the Jackson pharmacist to go along.

She recruited Cal's truck once again, expressing a need to get to Jackson. When asked why, she produced a coy smile and hinted at "female needs." The shy mountain man could do nothing but hand over the keys and walk away.

By now her mood was firmly positive. This new plan of attack appeared to be foolproof. No one knew what she was up to, not even Cal. With only a tiny bit of luck the unknown would soon become known, with herself established as the great detective. All that was left to be done was to find and capture another of the strange animals.

She felt guilty even thinking that Cal should be excluded from the plan. If he found out, he would be hurt at being left out when the final chapter of the Kelly-dogs was written. She decided to err on the side of kindness; he would be included. *At least in the capture*, she thought, the idea of having the same thing happen again weakening her resolve—after all, how then could she be sure it wasn't him? *No, he must think I'm going to try to stay awake until the animal does his thing—whoever is doing this will figure that's not likely*. She tried to tell herself that the gentle mountain man wasn't being excluded from the entire plan. "Just from the part that counts," she sighed. Cal's keys rattling against the steering column seemed to cry out in accusation.

The Jackson pharmacist proved to be no problem at all, and soon medication, alcohol, cotton and syringes were spread out on Kathy's bed. There she sat, legs folded, leaning against the headboard and rereading the instructions her Pennsylvania contact had passed along over the phone. They looked simple enough but she decided to wait until the need arose before preparing the syringes. Now it was time to find Cal.

Her luck was on a roll; he was one story down in the bar. Greeting him with a smile, she returned his keys then outlined the dummy plan she'd decided on earlier. She asked for his help in capturing another of the canine visitors, presenting the request in a cheerful manner, even as, behind the smile, she harbored a fear that he would sense the deception. If he did, it didn't show; he appeared pleased at the invitation.

In truth, Cal was hiding a deception of his own. His thinking had turned even more toward letting the animals alone, that whatever was happening was not meant for the living. As before, however, he was reluctant to show concern to this young woman—if she could do it, so could he. "Ain't seen none tuh-day, though. Spec one'll come along soon, but cain't say when."

They sat in silence sipping their drinks, the gap in conversation permitting Kathy's mind to slip toward the subject of Mark's tardy reemergence from the woods. With a start she realized that Janos had said Cal would join in the search. "Weren't you supposed to go along with the rangers?" she asked, alarmed in an inexplicable way at his continued presence in town.

Cal flinched inwardly at the words, but kept his face as impassive as he could manage. "Ain't been invited yet. They allas waits till somp'in pops up a'fore call'n on the locals. Ain't no use gittin' lotta folks runnin' round them woods fer they gits an idee where tuh look."

Kathy searched Cal's face for what he might really be thinking. "What do you think they're doing now?" she asked softly.

Cal was visibly uncomfortable with the subject, but he responded nonetheless. "Searchin' fer clews, I reckon. Spec they got thet coptor up lookin' fer campfires; and spec they got some men on thuh ground searchin' likely campin' areas. Fer long they gonna git an idee where tuh start lookin'. Then they likely git more folks involved."

They lapsed again into silence as Kathy tossed over what Cal had said. It gave her a good feeling every time someone in a position to know said something that made sense, something that suggested calm and routine rather than alarm or panic. What Cal said the searchers were doing seemed logical. Still, she was no closer to finding out where Mark was than before. She finished her drink then got up to leave, smiling a good-bye to her friend as she did so. "I'll either be up in my room or walking down the road to the south," Kathy said, inclining her head in the direction she meant to walk.

Cal smiled, "Thet's east," he said.

"Just what I was about to say," she said, adding a wink to her deepening smile.

With little to occupy her mind, the time passed slowly and worries about Mark kept tapping at the door to her consciousness. She needed to be involved in some way, even while understanding why Janos would consider that impractical. After a fruitless struggle to keep from doing so, she decided it was time to contact the man.

It took a half hour and a number of telephone calls before Janos's voice finally appeared on the line. He was in a helicopter on the way to the search site. Thoughtfully, he had left instructions to permit the woman some leeway in her understandable desire for information.

"Ken Janos here." The helicopter transmission gave the words a funny sound.

"Yes, Ken," she began, remembering his request to use first names. "This is Kathy. I tried not to call you but I just couldn't stand it anymore. Is there any news?"

"Don't worry about interrupting me; I understand how you feel." The words were appreciated and a warm feeling came over Kathy as he continued his attempts at reassurance. "There is something interesting, although we don't know yet what to make of it. We found evidence of where he might have camped a week or so ago; a campfire, with footprints of a man about the same weight as your guy."

"How can you tell it's the same weight?" Kathy asked, immediately interested.

"Not too difficult. Tracks are clear enough to tell my boys a whole lot about the target...uh, I mean your friend Carter."

"The word 'target' doesn't offend me, Ken. If I find out he doesn't have at least one broken leg, I'm going to call him more than that."

Janos laughed before reluctantly presenting what else had been found. "We also found pieces of equipment, including a backpack. If this is your guy, it looks as if he might have wandered off without it." Aware of how the words would sound to this frightened woman, Janos hastened to add, "It still doesn't mean he's lost, only that his equipment is lost."

Kathy stared at the blank wall in front of her. She was shocked, this was not what she'd expected at all. Mark was supposed to be hiding, not lost; an inconsiderate pseudo-macho jerk, not a hurt little boy. The words that struggled to emerge made it sound as if she were choking. "If he lost his pack as long as a week ago then he really must be in trouble. How could he eat? How could he get shelter?"

"Well, that depends on how good a woodsman he is. This time of year it's not difficult to find either if you try. I grant you it's not what we'd hoped for but its not the end of the world either. On the plus side, we also think we know where he camped the night before, and this campsite looked perfectly normal, even professional. That's a good sign; your man probably knows what he's doing."

Janos continued without giving the woman time to respond. He wanted to keep negative speculation to a minimum. "There is one other thing, curious but perhaps working to our advantage; he apparently picked up a stray dog."

A cold chill ran down Kathy's back, and she came close to dropping the telephone. This was too unreal; everywhere she turned there were dogs. Now one has intruded upon the search for Mark. She had to force herself to listen as Janos continued.

"...The dog probably knows better than your friend how to find his way, so it's not a bad thing to have around at a time like this. We tried to follow their trail but it petered out after a few miles. No big deal, though; in that area we should be able to pick it up again. We have some pretty good guys involved in this search, and we're going to get a lot more going soon."

"My God," Kathy said softly, still in shock over the dog and not grasping much of anything else the ranger was saying. "He really is lost in a wilderness...in a nightmare."

This part always took its toll on Janos's emotions, even to the point of making him question whether he was the one to lead such a search. "Well, you're partly right," he responded softly, "but I caution once again, this sort of thing happens, and it rarely ends in anything worse than a worn out guy vowing never to go camping again. Our people are real good at returning lost campers to their families."

Kathy lingered on the word "families," realizing with regret that she did not fit into that category. She was only an "interested bystander." Perhaps now that was all she ever would be. She shook her head as she realized the ranger was still talking. "Beg pardon? What did you say?" she asked in response to something he had asked her.

"I said, how'd you do with your big dog mystery; the video tape?"

"Oh," she replied unenthusiastically, "it didn't show anything interesting. The tape ran out before the dog got away. I didn't get his actual escape." Kathy was not sure why she withheld the truth from Janos. Perhaps it was because she was afraid he would think less of her for involving herself so heavily in what could be a local joke. Or maybe it was that the Kelly-dog affair suddenly seemed so unimportant.

Janos hesitated a moment before resuming. "What kind of a dog was it?"

An adrenaline surge accompanied Kathy's reply. "Light colored; a shepherd." She cringed in anticipation of the answer to the logical follow-up question, "Why do you ask?"

"Oh, nothing specific. Just wondering if the dog we're looking for is the same type that's been popping up in Kelly. We'll keep an eye out for a light-colored shepherd just in case."

Janos had been considerate in responding so quickly to her call; he appeared to recognize how difficult the waiting was for her—this side of him impressed her as much as did his thoroughness. When they came to the question of next of kin, Janos had handled it courteously, professionally and, most of all, diplomatically. The only negative was his failure to hide his relief when informed that there was no one but Mark's friends...and her.

Two hours had passed since she said good-bye to the busy ranger, two hours of lying on the bed and staring up at the ceiling. Mark really was lost. Lost without food, sleeping bag and everything else he was carrying in that backpack. She wondered how easy it was to find something to eat out there. And to find protection against the chilly autumn nights. She recalled the case of the woman stumbling across her husband— hypothermia, Sandy had said. *God, that could be Mark right now.* If he were able to move, he would head toward the setting sun or a specific mountain peak until he found someone or someone found him? He was experienced enough to know that.

She lay pinned to the bed by the weight of troubled thoughts, unable to find a reason why she should ease up on her worrying. In only one sense did she consider herself lucky: being here in Kelly put her thousands of miles closer to her lost lover.

It was painful not being able to do anything. By now she had accepted the probability that it would be counter-productive for her to go along with Ken and the others—she did not have the right training; she would only slow things down. But she had to do something! She wondered when Ken would next try to contact her, and whether it was necessary to stay in her room until then. "Screw it!" she muttered aloud. "There's no way I can keep staring at this ceiling." She got up from the bed, threw on a light sweater, and marched down the stairs to the lobby.

"I'm expecting a telephone call from a Sergeant Janos of the National Park Service," she said to the man at the front desk. "I'll either be walking around outside or in the saloon. I'd be grateful if someone would yell for me when it comes."

The sympathy in the clerk's face told Kathy he was as up to date on Mark as she—outside calls went through the switchboard. There was something else there as well: pessimism, or so it appeared in her current mood.

She left the lobby and walked out into the late afternoon sun. It had been some kind of a day, some kind of a *bad* day. First the dog incident then...Kathy paused in thought, suddenly remembering the animal reported to be with Mark. *Same type? God, could it be the same dog?* A chill ran through her as she considered what that would mean. For it to be the same animal it would have first have had to abandon Mark. "This is ridiculous!" she muttered aloud, walking faster and stamping her feet as she subconsciously sought to walk away from unpleasant thoughts.

Her walk about town was without aim or purpose, and all it did was give her more time to think. Think about the animals she'd been studying, how similar they all were, in behavior as well as appearance. And think about Mark—was she getting carried away or could Mark now be a part of this? Had be become one of the "interesting anecdotes" she was writing about? She acknowledged with a sigh that she might never know. Unless man and dog were found together, alive and healthy. *Then he'll be my favorite mutt, even if he still wants to walk through walls and play with video cameras.*

She considered the wisdom of letting Janos in on everything she knew about the dogs. Would he think she was letting her writer's imagination get out of hand? Would it have any effect on the search if he knew? And if he asked her what she was driving at, what would she say? What could anyone say, that a class of super-dogs was roaming around the United States? That they were able to walk through walls and fly faster than a speeding bullet?

Deciding there were more negatives than positives, she vowed to keep it to herself. She would, however, follow through on her original plan to find out how the animals disappeared. That, at least, might prove useful to the searchers, particularly if it lead to the dogs' owner.

She would also keep the Pennsylvania and California incidents to herself; certainly she would not mention them to Cal. She smiled to herself as she thought of this rugged mountain man, and how willing he was to believe in the supernatural. Hearing of similar animals running around the United States unchecked would be the clincher; he would resign from their dog-napping squad.

She found Cal sitting outside the general store. His face had a hint of relief in it as he let her know he had seen no additional animals. "Sometimes they goes days; sometimes tew comes in one day. Ain't no guessin' when thuh next's gonna git here."

"I wish one would show up so we can get on with it," she said mournfully.

The perceptive mountain man was sympathetic to her real concern. "Jes got a call frum thuh crew up in them mountains. Gotta skedaddle on up there right prompt like." Kathy said nothing, hanging on Cal's next words. "Unnerstan yew already knows they found your man's grubstake an pack." She nodded quickly, wanting him to keep talking. "Peers tuh be a might difficult pick'in up iz trail agin; wants thuh rest of us tuh come on up an hep out. Gonna go tonight."

Kathy waited for Cal to continue, but he did not. "Did they find anything else? Any more equipment, or anything that would tell them what happened?" As she talked, her eyes turned sad and her shoulders began to sag. She wanted to talk more about the search but at the same time did not want to hear bad news. Her friend's demeanor only supported her not-so-hidden fears.

Cal declined to tell her about the odd way Mark's tracks disappeared. They faded out as if man and dog had steadily lost weight until not enough remained of either of them to make an impression in the dirt. Cal shuddered at the thought; this was getting spookier by the minute. "Nothin thet ah ken remember," he said, finally. "Gonna git nuff folks out tuh pick up thuh trail agin, so ain't no need tuh worry none. We gonna find um, sure's am standin' here." Cal's manner did nothing to suggest that he expected to find Mark alive. His eyes averted Kathy's and he spoke softly and unconvincingly. Kathy did not want to press the issue, because she did not want him to say what she was convinced he was thinking.

After Cal left to join the search, now underway on a larger scale, Kathy went to the saloon to eat dinner. Within the normally active room, the sparse crowd was unusually subdued. The word on Mark had gotten around, and these people, who must have seen such drama unfold many times before, had come to a universal conclusion. Pity was in everyone's eyes—Kathy would have preferred simple concern, maybe even an occasional look of hope. The bartender, already fond of the friendly young woman, was especially gentle in the serving of her meal. However well intended this was, it only added to her misery. She ate little, needlessly apologizing to the bartender for the inevitable waste.

Leaving the saloon, she went out into the moonlit darkness and, as she had done earlier that day, began walking aimlessly down the street. It was a chilly evening, somehow appropriate to her mood. It fed an inexplicable sense of guilt, a subconscious desire to be punished. She kept walking until the lights of town were well behind her, until there was nothing but silence and wilderness to act as company. By then her eyes had become acclimated to the darkness, and it was easy to make out the distant group of mountains where the search was supposed to be centered. Staring at this large collection of rocks made her feel closer to Mark, and with a sigh of longing, she held her eyes to the dark silhouette and the bright star that hung just above it, bright because it was not one star but two.

The chill of the night had just about convinced her to turn back when she detected a movement on the trail in front of her. There was a shadow, maybe more than one, and it was coming her way. She fixed her eyes on it, needing to know if something were really there, while at the same time, she shot a glance behind her, checking her path of retreat. The latter told her she had come too far, that she could not hope to get back to town in time.

Adrenaline dashed through her body as she steeled herself for whatever it was that moved relentless toward her from out of the darkness. She kept her breath slow and shallow to minimize sound, as if being heard were the only concern she had. She began to consider options: running might be out, but there must be something she could use as a weapon—a stick, a rock, anything. A quick feel of the ground around her turned up only a small stone, but she wrapped her hand around it before regaining her feet.

There was no pause in the unknown that silently approached, but in seconds it would be upon her. Gripping the rock even tighter, she strained her eyes to see what it was. Too small to be a man, it had to be an animal; perhaps a wild animal.

She was sure the shadows—by now she knew there were two—were aware of her presence, but their rate of approach did not change. Apparently the prospect of a human being blocking their way did not faze them. It was not until the distance between them dwindled to only a few steps that it finally became clear to Kathy what they were. Approaching at a casual pace, both of them with their eyes glued to hers, were two medium sized, light-colored, German shepherds.

CHAPTER 17

Mark was floating in a sea of warm water, his body more comfortable than he ever remembered it being before. Every nerve tingled with pleasure, every sense shouted out its contentment with what the world to it had become. He had to fight off the gentle tugs toward consciousness that threatened to pull him away. But the tugs only grew stronger, then stronger still until finally able to overcome his resolve. Then the euphoria he so hated to lose began to shut down, while his body assumed a weight of its own in preparation for a return to the land of the living.

Opening his eyes, he watched a perennially-concerned Leipin take shape above him. She held the beam device from which earlier diagnoses had been made. Ignoring the reasons why this tiny alien machine was once again necessary to his survival, Mark's half-conscious mind wondered how it could possibly be expected to work on someone whose presence in the universe was not even known when it was invented.

Creson was off to one side, permitting Leipin, with her medical skills, unimpeded access to her patient. Mark felt weakened, although not as seriously as after his first encounter with the experience chamber. As his mind cleared, he made a mental note to question whether this latest event resulted from another problem with the machine. *Or was it a reaction to the horror I just lived...or died...through?*

What an unbelievable experience. He had actually died, gone through the experience and the actuality of dying: the pain, the fear, then the act itself. Mark wondered who this Wilpin was, and whether it was wise to ask. Certainly his captors knew who was involved in each experience, even if they might not know all of what their captive Earth man gleaned from the process. Indeed, not asking might be more revealing than asking.

He lay on the table regaining his strength and considering how the experience chamber worked—it was safe to entertain such thoughts since his brain activity was no longer being monitored. He remembered that it began with gentle probes, and that the probes were asking, not telling. They were coaxing him, not dictating which thoughts he should consider. The probe would offer a question to some part of his consciousness, await a response then analyze that response until able to make a choice between uninteresting and suitable for further exploration. But the choice of whether or not to respond to that probe was his. True the machine would seize on desired paths once such thoughts emerged, but it was man and not machine who decided which experiences were to be exposed for review. He lay quietly on the table wondering how to make use of this knowledge.

The machine had seized on topics involving his use of his body; how and why he moved his hands, his arms and every other body part under his conscious command. Once satisfied, it had compared what it learned to equivalent functions of Mantz creatures (and occasionally creatures of other planets), which in turn had enabled Mark to learn how his body differed from that of his captors—he became as schooled in the workings of their bodies as they became schooled in the workings of his. Apparently this comparison was routine, a natural continuation of the first process.

By far, the most fascinating piece of information he'd picked up was how to go about the complicated process of cell transformation. He was not sure how much ability he had, but the mechanics of transformation were incredibly clear to him—even lying there now, outside the machine, it still seemed easy. He ran the procedure over in his mind, feeling, as had his mental host, that it was old-familiar and old-routine. He had to suppress an urge to put it to a quick test.

He turned his head to better observe Creson. The Mantzite was staring at him with the same thoughtful expression witnessed earlier in the lab, and the look was as unsettling now as it was before. It was not clear whether Creson's concern was for his captive's health or from a fear that Mark was learning more than was intended. "Please rise up, Markcarter," he ordered suddenly.

Mark did as he was told, surprised that he could do so and suffer nothing more unpleasant than a mild dizziness. When Creson continued to stare, the unsettling expression still a part of his face, Mark felt a need to disturb his concentration, to get him off whatever commanded so much concern. "Who was Wilpin, and did he actually die?" he asked.

Creson's face relaxed as he momentarily returned to a familiar form. "I do believe you are still possessed of the necessity to ask two questions at once." But the relaxation was only short-lived, and afterward his face bounced back to that look of concern. "In this instance I would prefer that *you* supply the answers—to them both, of course."

Mark took a moment to think before beginning. "Wilpin was one of your people, working here in the laboratory, I mean. He liked to camp, much the same as I do—or did, before I accidentally camped on your doorstep. I followed him around for several days, the last of which was different than any camping trip I've ever been on before. The guy converted himself into some kind of flying insect then got killed by a bug-eating bird. I watched him die; at least I think he died."

"You *watched* him die?"

"I appeared to have no choice," Mark said quickly, ignoring the emphasis on the word "watched." "Your machine held me captive; I had to watch everything. One thing I don't understand, though, is how you got the experience if Wilpin died?"

Creson continued his look of concern, trying to decide how much of what Mark said was to be believed. Surely this Earth man had knowledge of the recorder Wilpin used just before he died. Is it possible that he recognized so easily the implications of such knowledge, that he would in effect be admitting possession of a new talent, an ability to intercept mental projections not directed at him personally? He considered how to test him further. "No, he did not die," he said, his eyes watching Mark closely for a reaction. That there was not one was of itself suspicious.

Mark recovered from the shock of Creson's words then struggled to respond in some appropriate way. "I'm pleased to hear that," he said. "He did not look so good when the experience stopped." He thought for a moment then asked, "Would it be possible to meet him?"

"Certainly. I will arrange it."

Mark did not expect such an answer; the creature *had* died, he was sure of it. Was Creson just carrying the game a step further? What if he did produce Wilpin; would this mean the new knowledge he thought was his really wasn't? And if wrong here, was he also wrong in what he thought he knew about gene transformation?

This time it was Creson who accompanied him back to the rest and rejuvenation chamber. And in doing so, he inadvertently revealed one additional light of the "lock up" sequence. Mark tucked the knowledge into his mental safe-deposit box, even while unsure what good it would do him. "These sessions are fascinating, Spot," he said with as much passion as he could muster, his intent to keep the Mantzite with him as long as possible. "I believe I'm beginning to understand your species, enough to know there are a lot of similarities between us—we really aren't all that different."

"What a revolting thought!" Creson projected as he busied himself with additional lights on the panel. "We are as different as you are to a branz...a donkey to you." He paused then turned half-way toward Mark, his expression saying he was in deep thought. "I do hope I have not done an injustice to the branz."

Mark chuckled to himself. "You know, for an arrogant ass, you are one of the best...creatures...I know for one-ups-man-ship."

"I am so incredibly relieved that you think so," Creson conveyed sardonically, busying himself again with the panel.

A few seconds passed before Mark tried again. "I don't think," he said, chagrined in advance of Spot's inevitable reaction to this new train of thought, "that you people are really superior to us, only more advanced—like we are to the Greeks and Romans. Which means we could eventually get to know what you know. Seriously, I'd like to learn more about you, more about your society and more about the things you've discovered."

Creson turned and looked the Earth man in the eye, his expression deliberately non-committal. "It is far too soon to consider that. And if it is ever considered expedient to do so, a period of preparation would have to precede it. Even if you were capable of understanding such teachings, they could very easily do you emotional and perhaps physical harm."

Mark's chagrin increased. "What do you mean, harm?"

"If you give a child a gun and show him how to pull the trigger, have you in truth given that child knowledge of the gun or merely acquainted him with its rudiments? Having acquired only the rudiments, can the child possibly know when and under what circumstances to use that gun? Will it have sufficient knowledge of the long term after-affects of its use?"

"I'm not exactly a child!"

"Relatively speaking, you are," Creson countered. "If I should provide you with first-hand knowledge of our use of light, including how it is employed in the formulation and discharge of weapons, how would you handle this? Would you be inclined to use it on our behalf or yours? And in using it for your own benefit, could you be certain that it is being used properly? Would you have any idea of the long range consequences of something of which you have only a rudimentary technical knowledge? I suggest that you would be no better off than our proverbial child with its proverbial gun. In all likelihood you would wind up shooting yourself and others in the proverbial foot."

Mark smiled. "I admit you have a point," he conceded. "Maybe we can talk about technology later. For now, however, I don't see the harm in taking a look—from a distance, so to speak."

Creson turned toward his charge, then paused in thought. "Perhaps it would indeed do no harm," he said, his attitude suggesting he had received an inspiration. "What I might offer, if Takar approves, is to give you a tour of a previously explored planet. I have one in mind which graphically demonstrates the value of proper preparation."

"You mean I would actually visit another planet?"

"In your mind it would seem so, although you would in reality not leave this facility. Through the experience chamber we would mentally connect you to an actual resident of the planet I have in mind—one of our people. I would accompany you on this journey in much the same manner. Through the hosts' eyes we will travel to anyplace we wish. We will be in control for as long as our consciousness travels in his or her body."

"Her?"

"The gender of the guide is unimportant. What is important is that you and I will be in their minds, 'communicating live,' as you might say, directly to the motor functions of their brains."

Mark was momentarily sidetracked, "How do you know I use the expression 'communicating live?' Did that come out of the experience chamber?"

"Precisely. Communication is infinitely more productive via such a device. Were it not for that, and considering how distressingly slow you Earth creatures are in conversing, it could take an eternity to communicate a simple idea to you."

Mark hesitated before asking the next question, concerned that it might lead to discovery of his emerging skills. "Could you teach me to communicate as you do; mentally, I mean?"

Now it was Creson's turn to hesitate. He stared at the Earth man hoping to catch an expression or body movement that would give him away. He saw nothing, although that was not surprising considering how little they knew of the nuances of the human species. "I am not entirely certain you are capable of learning such a thing," he said after a pause. "Still...It could prove helpful if we were to communicate more efficiently. I will give the matter some thought."

Initially pleased with Creson's response, Mark then wondered whether it would be more to his advantage to continue to gain forbidden knowledge in secret—the creatures would control their projections if they knew he was eavesdropping. The thought reminded him of the uncertainty of his position. "Speaking of communicating more efficiently, when are you going to answer my question about what's going to happen to me? You can't keep me here forever."

"Strictly speaking, we can; at least your carefully preserved form," quipped Creson. Although by now used to such comments, Mark did not appreciate them on this subject. "A more proper question would be, do we want to. Frankly I am not certain. Were it left up to Selson you would have been disposed of shortly after you pissed in his face—another of your quaint ways of putting things I believe. Still, I suppose you do have some usefulness."

"Is that a long-winded way of avoiding the question—again?" asked Mark.

Creson smiled. "I do believe your mind is improving," he responded, his contracting eyes attesting to his amusement. "Probably the result of our education process. Imagine what you might be capable of should we continue to expose you to the experience chamber. You might even reach the level of a Mantz infant."

"Look, somebody has got to be looking for me on Earth. What makes you think one of us can disappear without others getting all riled up over it? By now they'll have hundreds of people out searching; what happens when they find nothing?"

The amusement left Creson's face, replaced by an artificial frown. "I suppose you are right," he said. "They will immediately decide that you have walked through a space warp and are now a prisoner of the notorious Mantzites some ten thousand light years away."

Mark annoyance grew. "Well they're bound to think something! They're not just going to give up."

"What choice do they have? They have no capacity to pursue you this far. As a matter of fact, it is unlikely that they would even think this a reasonable possibility. More likely is that you have been totally consumed by one of the many Earth creatures which inhabit that forest—I understand some of them are even more ghastly than you."

"Nothing is totally consumed! Even if there were such animals in Wyoming, they wouldn't eat a whole human. The remains would be easy to find. All you'd have to do is follow the circling buzzards."

Creson blinked, "Buzzards?"

"Yes. Meat-eating birds. They eat dead flesh. When they spot it, they give its location away by circling overhead. You can see them for miles around."

Creson lowered his head in thought. He had just gotten an idea, although it was not one to his liking. If it came to it, if the search on Earth began to jeopardize their further exploration of that planet, the buzzards mentioned by the Earth man could be used to lead searchers to a carefully arranged body. He considered whether it was necessary to bring this to Takar's attention, then realized it was his duty to do so. That, plus the fact that he had faith in Takar's ability to make the right decision when the time came. The institute head was not an insensitive being and was almost as indisposed to the destruction of intelligent life as was he. "I did not know of these buzzards," he nodded. "The information is appreciated."

"You're welcome! But what about my release? If you don't let me go, sooner or later it'll come back to haunt you. Look, you said you wanted to bring benefits to Earth and share whatever it had to offer. How do you think you're going to be able to do that if they find out you...killed...one of its citizens, or even held him captive?"

"I admit it would be a problem, but there exists only a small possibility that any of our actions will be discovered."

"There was only a small possibility that you would trap a live Earth man in your damn transporter too, but it happened! If that happened then so could this, and where would your grandiose plans be then?"

"I am afraid," Creson began after a moment of thought, "that our discussion is somewhat academic, since neither of us will be making the final decision regarding your disposition. I wish you to know, however, that we do not take such things lightly. Our species is deeply committed to the maintenance of alien life forms, particularly those demonstrating at least a potential for meaningful intelligence. Negative actions against such beings are never done with a sense of pleasure. It always hurts us deeply."

"Not as deeply as it would hurt me!" Mark interjected. "Frankly I don't find it comforting to place my future in the hands of creatures who rationalize so easily."

Mark was alone. Creson, professing Mark's need for rest, had left, something that always seemed to happen when the Mantzite felt himself pressured. The Wilpin experience had challenged Mark's already overworked system, he'd said, and following the medical advice of Leipin, he was postponing further sessions until at least the following morning. Although disappointed, Mark was pleased at this confirmation that the sessions would continue. It meant Creson did not know that his charge was developing new and potentially powerful mental skills. Either that or he was unimpressed.

Mark thought about what he'd learned in the few minutes spent inside the machine, minutes which translated into more than a month of his past life. The chamber was not all-powerful; if he could hold out against its lightning-fast probes and concentrate on things *he* wanted to know, there was a chance he could influence its direction. The panel lights and security systems, for example; if he could focus on them the device might compare this to similar technology on Mantz. It was an exciting thought; it led to knowledge of the hexagonal panel that kept him restrained and tranquilized. This time, however, he would limit his thoughts to what was displayed before him. No dangerous digression or analysis. Later, when no one was around, he could daydream to his heart's content.

My God! he mused, interrupting his own train of thought, *I can think at computer speeds!*

It finally dawned on him that while under the machine's grasp his side thoughts had progressed at the same speed as his review of experiences. His "daydreams" were keeping up with the chamber. He considered this for a long moment, searching his brain for some proof that it had developed a new talent. But he could sense nothing specific, nothing that would instruct him, if the skill were there at all, on its routine use. Perhaps the experience chamber was a necessary part of the process, some kind of trigger.

The concept of mental projection was there, however. He had twice picked up another's thoughts and, with the help of Wilpin, projected one of his own, at least to a recording device—he wondered whether the same skill was used to project thoughts to people. The basics were there but not everything; missing was the knowledge of how to control the span of a projection so only those intended to be included would "hear." Wilpin, as he lay dying, had not concerned himself with such niceties.

Then, of course, there was the knowledge of how to convert to a totally different being. This was the most exciting skill wrestled from the machine but also the most sobering, sobering in the respect that one then faces a whole new set of rules concerning survival. After all, Wilpin did die, regardless of what Creson said. And regardless of what he told Creson in return, he had been more than just a spectator. As with anything that came out of that machine, it was as much his experience as Wilpin's. It was he who had directed the conversion process, and he who had suffered death as a result.

Incredible! He knew the precise DNA makeup of an alien insect; he could become one whenever he wished. The memory of what happened to Wilpin while in that form took some pleasure out of the thought, but it was hard to avoid visiting the possibilities this new talent presented. He glanced down at his finger and toyed with the idea of giving it a try. Was it possible to convert only one part of the body, a fingernail perhaps? And if he did, would he be able to return it to its original form? *No sweat on that*, he thought, remembering that a conversion surrendered its hold if the perpetrator did not keep at it. He ran the procedure over in his mind and found the confidence which comes with assured knowledge. He would give it a try, but only so far as to convert a fingernail to a flinac tentacle. He took a deep breath then focused on the index finger of his right hand.

Nothing happened. And the procedure in practice was not as smooth nor as clear as when Wilpin was helping. He renewed his concentration, staring intensely at the fingernail while reviewing at lightening speeds the details of conversion. His muscles tensed to the point of cramping as they attempted to share the intensity of his thoughts. For a long moment nothing else happened, but then, reluctantly and not without its share of clumsiness, previously unused sections of his brain awoke to the demand now being placed upon them, demand for actions never before considered as within human capability. The nail began to reduce in size. There was a momentary tug then a shrinking to about one tenth of what it was before, and so sudden was the transformation that for a moment Mark could only stare in awe. A part of his human body had become something else by the power of his brain alone.

Success was not without its cost. Mark grimaced at the pain that flared up from the unlikely dividing point between flinac and human. The nail had become an tentacle, as had been intended, but as had definitely not been intended, it was attached to what was now exceptionally tender flesh. His beleaguered mind fought this new agony even as it rushed to remember how to reverse the process.

Before the answer could be found, Selson shot from the conveyer into the room; his eyes were large and filled with anger. Mark leaped a good ten inches at the unexpected intrusion. "Christ! You scared the shit out of me!" he yelled, the pain of an exposed fingernail momentarily forgotten.

Ignoring the comment, Selson stared at the captive Earth man and asked with unconcealed passion, "Who taught you to do that?"

"Do what?" Mark asked, sure that his ability to convert body form had been discovered.

Selson did not respond, but his expression now included doubt. The creature from Earth had just communicated in something bordering on normal speed and with normal clarity of idea. Like Creson, Selson knew the man had the mental capacity to eventually be able to communicate telepathically but he was not supposed to know how to make use of such talent. Perhaps there was a latent capability in humans which flared up from time to time without the creature actually being aware of what he was doing. "Did you not just state that you were angry at having inflicted pain upon yourself?"

Mark did not know how to answer, although he was alert to the fact that whatever happened must be concealed from his Mantzite adversary. "I didn't say anything," he said. "Just banged my finger against the chamber wall—its not so soft when you try to poke through it." He demonstrated, using the undamaged hand. "How did you know?" Mark fought to maintain a look of innocence, not easy as the pain was once again making itself known.

Seeing the frown of suspicion linger on Selson's face, Mark wanted to find something to say to divert his attention. But he did not know Selson well enough to know what it would take. "Where is Spot?" he asked in desperation.

"Spot?" Selson repeated. He analyzed the intent of the Earth creature's use of the word, then, finding nothing amusing in it, retorted with, "I think you are being contaminated by excessive exposure to the less desirable traits of my colleague, specifically his presumption of humor." He sighed but in it was the start of surrender. "Much the worse for Earth kind!" At that he turned as if executing a military maneuver and disappeared into the tube.

Mark was relieved, but he could not resist an impishly good-bye, "Give my best to the boys." *Witless asshole!* he thought, even as he chuckled to himself.

Alone once again, Mark tried to figure out how he had accidentally projected his thoughts. Maybe it was the pain, an involuntary reaction to it. Although his finger had not ceased its throbbing, he put aside its reconstruction in favor of finding the answer; it was important that this not happen again.

As with other newly developed talents, the instructions were there in his brain but in confused form—the details were simply not clear. There was enough, however, to know that projections did not travel far; they required electronic assistance. In Wilpin's case his recorder had been left on, thus it had been a simple matter of aiming his thoughts in the right direction. The device would handle the rest, designed as it was to routinely search out the faint signals which indicated a Mantzite was attempting to communicate. All well and good, but that did not explain what just happened.

Was someone or something watching, monitoring like Wilpin's recorder had done, ready to amplify any stray projected thoughts? As the question formed in his mind, he knew he had the answer: The beam! He must have been facing it at the time. He must have projected an image of pain into it. The thought was a comforting one. If this were true, it would mean his thoughts were his alone as long as he did not aim them in the wrong direction.

How to prove it, though, without blowing the whistle on himself. After a moment of thought, he decided to risk a projection aimed as far from the tube entrance as possible. He turned toward the back of the chamber then projected a mental image of need, one with which Selson was likely to identify. *Hey, somebody, I have to piss!* The image was clumsy but it was constructed as Wilpin's experience suggested it should be constructed. Afterward, he waited anxiously, convinced that it had been a dumb thing to do. Nothing happened, at least nothing he could detect. Being careful to control his thoughts, he turned back to the tube and stared. Had his message gotten through? Was he just being ignored? Unlikely perhaps, considering Selson's earlier reaction, but possible.

As he continued to analyze the test, his fingernail slowly resumed its original form. Without any effort on his part, it rebounded to become once again a normal human fingernail. And with this reconstruction came the end of pain. Mark examined the nail carefully, searching for some evidence of what had happened. He saw nothing, not even the tiny gap where a piece of fingernail had chipped off in that long ago time when he was a resident of Earth. It appeared that the process of conversion and re conversion had worked. And he had accomplished it by himself outside the experience chamber.

It was hard to claim resounding success, however. There was more to this conversion thing than the simple transformation of genes. He had converted some genes without preparing others for the change, and that, as he so painfully learned, was a mistake. He wondered what would have happened if something vital had been touched; would he still be alive? The thought was sobering and reminded him of Creson's analogy, the one about the kid playing with guns.

CHAPTER 18

"I want to know your thoughts on how far he has progressed. It is essential that Takar be kept informed of everything of relevance in regard to the Earth creature." There was a frown on Selson's face as he released the projection. He did not like the effect the Earth man was having on his laboratory, and he particularly did not like this individual specimen. Markcarter was crude and slow thinking and, if truly a representative of Earth's dominant species, Selson would be quite content to bypass the planet entirely. He would only reluctantly admit to himself that part of his resentment stemmed from the manner in which the creature had been taken. That and the still unknown consequences of this act.

Selson preferred order. Order in his life and order in the laboratory. The Earth man symbolized disorder. They were not prepared for him. The orderly investigation of this planet was being threatened by his continued retention. Selson was strongly in favor of correcting the mistake as quickly as possible, before an already messy problem snowballed into something impossible to correct. One Earth man knowing of their presence was manageable; ten would be less so; one hundred would be impossible. The longer this creature's disappearance remained unexplained to others of his species, the more danger there was that the one would become ten, and the ten, one hundred.

Responsibility for monitoring Markcarter's environmental needs had been given to him. It was he who determined precisely what was required to keep the Earth man alive and healthy. The outflow from the creature's chamber he studied carefully, not only to determine how much of the input chemicals were being consumed—and thus how much needed to be replaced—but to satisfy a curiosity that routinely governed his behavior in the study of new species. Each time Markcarter experienced an emotion, Selson was immediately aware of it; the machine would compensate then report exactly which chemicals were used and in what quantity. Through this, he was able to tell what the Earth man was feeling at any point in time, which in turn permitted him a reasonable guess as to his thoughts as well—at least to the extent that any Mantzite could understand the mind of a human. What it told him was that more was taking place within this creature's brain than they were yet aware of—the Earth man was planning something.

"His brain, however inadequately controlled and under-utilized, is not unlike ours," Creson replied. "Still, it is not clear exactly how quickly he is able to assimilate the knowledge to which we inadvertently expose him—one of the unfortunate side effects of the experience chamber, as we both know. He obviously receives more benefit from the sessions than we would prefer, but how much more I cannot say. I can say that it is of such significance to him that he feels the necessity to hide it from us."

"He has acquired some proficiency in telepathy," Selson interjected. "The creature may or may not be aware of it, but he has already demonstrated this to me personally. In addition, he has gained better control of his mind; I can no longer detect scattered thoughts."

Creson paused for a moment to digest what Selson had said. When finally he replied, his manner was subdued. "I really cannot blame Markcarter for attempting to hide such things from us. His existence, after all, is in jeopardy, the fact of which he is well aware. We must, however, be alert for further signs of knowledge assimilation. Should he learn more than his frail emotional system is capable of handling, the result would be a complete mental breakdown."

"He also has some capability within the area of gene transformation," Selson offered. "This too he is attempting to hide. How advanced his knowledge has become is difficult to assess, but I have observed an ability to limit conversion to one area of the body. That shows a greater level of sophistication than I would have thought possible from such a primitive creature. Perhaps less surprising, his confidence outreaches his ability. In attempting gene transformation on himself, he suffered the result one might expect from careless application of so complex a function."

"Was it serious?"

"Unfortunately no," Selson replied. "The creature still lives, and has probably even profited from the experience. I imagine he is now content to await further education before attempting such a thing again. I also imagine he expects us to provide him with that education, and that we will do so in ignorance of the knowledge he has thus far gained."

Creson sighed. "We shall permit the Earth man his little deception," he said, his projected image demonstrating the sadness he felt. "Indeed, permitting a degree of hope will help insure his cooperation. I think, however, that we will soon have to call an end to this; we will have to decide what is to be done with him. Since he is already aware of his predicament, it is unkind to continue to offer only uncertainty."

"The time is not being wasted," Selson protested in seeming contradiction of his well-known views regarding the creature's disposal. "We are acquiring a substantial body of information from him."

"That is not my point," Creson replied. "We are responsible and compassionate beings, and I trust I speak for all of us when I say we do not enjoy watching our subjects suffer."

"As usual, my dear colleague, you are focusing on the wrong point. Naturally we do not enjoy inflicting pain. We are, however, here for a specific purpose, which we all enjoy thinking is for the good of all major life forms in the galaxy, regardless of the planet on which they are found. Having the Earth man present in this laboratory at this time is a threat to that noble goal. All that we are planning for Earth could be thwarted by this single injection of untimely fate. Having said that, however, while we await the inevitable, we could forward that goal by conducting as complete a study of the creature as time will permit."

Creson lessened the intensity of his projections in recognition of the validity of his colleague's thoughts. "Perhaps what we are learning might yet save him," he sighed. "As more information is obtained, more possibilities present themselves. This Earth creature has a natural curiosity, not that dissimilar to our own, and, if sufficiently stimulated, he might be amenable to a long range association with us. Other creatures have done so as you well know."

Takar entered the laboratory just in time to catch Creson's last projection. Without hesitation, he joined the conversation. "Yes, but they have done so only after proper contact had been established with their planet. And then without so much as a hint of coercion."

He was referring to the many intelligent life forms employed by the Mantzites to assist, not only the exploration of their respective planets, but alien planets as well. The Mantzites had faced resentment when this policy was first enacted; resentment by the recruit's fellow creatures, who often treated the chosen individual as a spy or a traitor. Quick to learn from their mistakes, the Mantzites established procedures whereby such individuals were chosen—or at least approved—by representatives of the planet being investigated, and then only after much work had been done to create an aura of trust between the two species. The program now worked well, and now the planetary exploration project was comprised of intelligent life forms from almost all planets within the Mantz federation. Only those considered too primitive were excluded, although even these were handled with such diplomacy that no impediments to employing them in the future were established. Takar's intent was to take the same approach with Earth, although the timing with regard to using the Earth man for this purpose was all wrong.

Forcing a change to the subject, Takar focused his indomitable stare on Creson, then asked, "How have the sessions gone thus far?"

Creson responded without hesitation. "The Earth creature demonstrates much the same pattern of behavior as noticed on other planets of equivalent size and chemistry. The similarities to us are as remarkable as the dissimilarities are amusing. If you require an example, perhaps Selson might be able to provide a description of the dissemination of their waste products."

"I hardly think that is necessary!" Selson interjected, the blush apparent even through the facial fur.

Creson's eyes contracted briefly, both at the memory of his colleague's humiliation and at his predictable reaction at its being brought up before the laboratory head. Receiving no encouragement from Takar to continue this line, he resumed his report, outlining in detail what had been done thus far with the Earth man. He left out nothing that either scientist felt their superior would want to know. "Since he has not chosen to discuss what to him must be astonishing powers, we can only imagine that he feels it to be to his advantage not to do so."

"Why should we not let him know we are aware of these emerging abilities?" asked Takar. "You are familiar with what happened in the past when limited knowledge was too-quickly bestowed upon inadequately prepared creatures. Some turned themselves into even stranger creatures, and some managed to so confuse their forms as to make it difficult to restore them to their proper condition."

"At the moment I would prefer to simply observe what he has in mind. In this, I admit a degree of risk, but this situation—being able to closely monitor a subject so early in the investigation process—is unlike any enjoyed since the early days of planetary exploration. It permits a more rapid assimilation of knowledge, knowledge that might help us overcome what now appears to be a hopeless dilemma."

Takar questioned in more depth the level of skill thus far introduced into the Earth man's brain then agreed that continuing as before was worth the risk. "I am sure you recognize that he could be his own worst enemy should he continue to experiment without supervision."

"Of course," Creson answered. "Although it would help us in this regard if I could expose him to an example of the problem caused by too much use of too little information. I am thinking specifically of escorting him through the chamber to Tanterac." Creson paused to give Takar time to object. The laboratory head gave no indication of disapproval and, secretly pleased, Creson continued. "For the present, at least, it is preferred that we proceed as before, continuing to learn as much as possible while there is still time to do so. In this we must place emphasis on him and his species and not on what he might discover as a result of our probes. Should the decision later be made to keep him alive, there will be adequate time to provide the education necessary to the proper use of such knowledge. We will, of course, take care to avoid awarding him skills that could be employed against us."

The intensity of Takar's glance suggested they had better do more than simply "take care." "Have you received any feedback from the scouts?" He was referring to the two security people sent by Creson to monitor activity on Earth. They were to determine what was being done to discover the whereabouts of the missing Earth man.

"There has been insufficient time, although we have had it reported to us by one of our returning explorers that a search has begun in the area in which the creature disappeared. Our captive is the object of that search."

Takar's frown deepened. "How intense is this effort?"

"Unknown at the present. We do know, however, that it was initiated by a sexual companion to our captive. This female creature is currently residing within the town used by our explorers as a rest stop." Creson paused before continuing, and when finally he continued, he was hesitant. "In addition, we have discovered from the Earth man's latest experience session that this female is investigating Mantz explorers on Earth. Oh, she is not aware of what they represent," he hastened to add, noting the look of surprise which appeared on his superior's face, "only that a certain type of canine is being widely reported as acting in an atypical fashion. Unfortunately she has collected a number of such reports and is now endeavoring to analyze their meaning. From one of our west-coast explorers, we have obtained an excellent idea of her thinking process in this regard. It could not be called innocent, but so far at least, it could not lead her to us. Of greater concern is her emotional attachment to our uninvited guest. Of itself, this could increase the intensity of the search."

Takar was visibly upset. What Creson said, if confirmed, meant something would have to be done with the Earth man soon. "How long before we have a more complete report from the scouts?"

"They are instructed to make available any information they find as they find it. I have taken the precaution of providing them with laser communications which, hopefully, will permit a more timely response. In addition, I have security people stationed in the transporter to relay such messages back to Mantz."

"What ability have the Earth people to detect such communication?" asked Takar, not at all pleased with having to once again step outside the boundaries of prescribed practice.

"Limited, we believe. The area in question is sparse in population and of little concern from a security point of view. We do not believe Earth people feel the need to scan it for unexpected communication. Even if they should, it is unlikely that they possess instruments sensitive enough to detect our transmissions.

Takar sighed. "It would seem we are doing all that we can at the present. The Council still has not been notified, nor will they be until we have sufficient information to suggest an approach to restitution." He hesitated a moment then added in a tone uncharacteristic to him, "I hope we can resolve this matter without negatively affecting our efforts to explore Earth."

For the first time in their long relationship, Creson could detect anxiety in Takar. The head of the research laboratory was worried, and this elevated Creson's fear that precipitous action might be taken against Markcarter. "It is true," he projected with a hint of trepidation, "that damage to the program could occur if the Council discovered our little breech of protocol before you are properly prepared to inform them, but we could do that damage and more should we respond unwisely to the disposition of the Earth man. Beyond that, there is, as I was telling Selson, the question of responsibility to one of the galaxy's intelligent creatures. Disposing of him as we would a tired experiment is not in keeping with our civilized nature."

"Even civilized societies are faced with difficult choices," Takar retorted, not pleased with the implied reprimand. "Being civilized means being inclined to chose that which benefits society as a whole. We must make a decision on the Earth man soon; the clamor involving his disappearance cannot be permitted to become so pronounced that future contact with this planet is made more difficult, perhaps even impossible. At the moment I am inclined to believe the most expedient choice is to return his shell to wherever it is most likely to be discovered by the searchers. I believe you now have sufficient knowledge to make this appear to be a natural expiration. Regrettable choice, but perhaps the only one." At that, Takar turned abruptly and left the laboratory.

Creson exchanged glances with his colleague. Selson was more sympathetic to Takar's view than to Creson's, but he was not insensitive to his friend's known sympathies toward whatever creature was being studied at the moment. Knowing how much a decision to terminate would affect Creson, he refrained from making any comment that might add to his already depressed state. On the plus side, he knew the fear of loosing Markcarter in such a manner would guarantee a burst of creativity from his talented colleague—if a more palatable remedy existed, Creson would come up with it.

Creson shrugged his shoulders and sighed, "I really have nothing more to offer at the moment. I suppose we might as well continue our experiments while the opportunity is still there." But it was one of those things one says rather than believes, and his body language told a story of defeat as he shuffled across the floor toward a conveyer beam.

There was still a sag to his shoulders as he sought out Leipin to begin the next step in the study of the trapped Earth man. He found her in the large hall used for routine rest and rejuvenation by members of the research complex. The walls of the room were plain but its cavity was dotted with chambers, eighty of them, each similar to the one in which Mark now resided—except here there was no need for containment modules. All were suspended from light beams whose upper ends delicately faded into the hazy glow of the ceiling. There were four rows of twenty each, and better than half were occupied by sleeping laboratory workers. There was no particular order to this occupation; everyone simply grabbed whatever available module he or she wished. There was not even a social consideration, to be close to a friend or colleague, since the purpose of the chamber was to render a subject unconscious while the machine brought his body back to peak efficiency. Work hours were staggered such that there was always someone resting and always someone taking his place in the maintenance of laboratory functions. With workers coming and going every few hours, there was rarely a need to create additional chambers, although it was an easy matter to do so when required. The pressing of a few lights and eighty chambers would become eighty-one, or more. Each "extra" would quietly disappear once its occupant completed his period of rejuvenation.

Creson moved over to the panel of lights, touched three, then examined the results. Leipin had only recently entered a chamber, thus there was less of a probability that she was so deeply under the spell of the machine that to disturb her would be painful. Making his decision, he pressed additional lights then watched as the glow within her chamber began to dim. Within seconds she opened her eyes and began a struggle to attain full alertness. Aware that she was being summoned by her superior, she gave no sign of objection.

"My apologies for interrupting your down time," Creson said mechanically, although he rarely believed his demands on others would be considered offensive. He routinely sought out anyone from whom he needed information regardless of where they were or what they might be doing. He had even done this to Takar, and more than once.

Leipin nodded acceptance of the apology. "You are concerned about the Earth man?" she asked, perceiving her superior's train of thought.

"Precisely. We must learn as much as we can about him and as quickly as possible. Have you determined why he is so negatively affected by the experience chamber?"

"His physiology, although not that dissimilar to ours, is difficult for the machine to manage. I believe there is not much more we can do to improve the situation. I suggest short sessions, repeated after a rest of perhaps one to two hours, depending on the degree of physical deterioration after each episode."

Creson lowered his head in thought. "Will the sessions have a lasting effect? Is the deterioration cumulative?"

"We cannot yet be certain. He rebounds quickly after only a short stay in his chamber, with the result that at the start of the next session, his system is back to normal. And he demonstrates a positive attitude toward the sessions, which adds to his restorative powers."

Once again Creson mused. "I will want to continue the process as soon as he is sufficiently recovered. Please let me know when that will be. In the interim please feel free to resume your rest." With that he turned and left the hall.

Leipin sighed then went over to the panel to shut the chamber down; it would no longer be needed, at least not by her. There was insufficient time to gain meaningful rest before the Earth man would once again be ready for a session in the experience chamber.

Leipin liked the Earth man. He was not bad looking for an alien being. Some she had treated were so oddly constructed that she found it difficult to overcome the primitive fear that often accompanies proximity to something so opposed to one's orientation. In addition, the Earth man was amusing, especially as regarded his insatiable interest in Mantz sexual affairs—she enjoyed teasing him about that. Partially in support of the scientific need to know and partially to gain ammunition to continue the game, she intended to orient the machine to probe areas involving human intimacies—sex. Not that she was unaware of the basics of human sexual intercourse; the advance scouts had reported on that subject in great detail. In their canine disguise they had ready access to bedrooms of copulating humans. It seemed this society was unconcerned about the whereabouts of their pets while they involved themselves in intimate pleasures. The Mantz scouts were able to take mental notes without the stars of the show ever seeming to mind.

She wanted, however, to record a direct experience within the laboratory where the machine could gain a clear understanding of how this species replenished itself. Learning about the procreation of alien forms was useful as well as fascinating. Useful if it became necessary to help an endangered species or slow down one that was populating itself into disaster. It was remarkable how planets thousands of light years apart could show such similarities in this area. There was even a running joke about how many light years it has been since the last new sexual position had been discovered.

She turned her thoughts to how the experience sessions were affecting her Earth-man patient. There was something about his system that the machine could not handle, and it was bothersome that the solution still eluded her. Markcarter was in no apparent danger, at least she thought he no longer was, but the process drained his strength more than it did any other creature. Obviously they had a less-than-complete knowledge of the creature's physiology, which in turn suggested it was unwise to continue to force the experience chamber on him. If Markcarter were to expire while under a session—something that came close to happening earlier— it could eliminate the option of returning him to Earth. These Earth creatures, even as primitive as they are, would know that such a death was not due to natural causes.

She had to learn more about his physiology, and it would have to be done while the sessions were taking place—there was no time to do it right. As a physician she resented having to proceed in such an unscientific manner, but as a loyal subordinate to Creson, whom she greatly admired and respected, she would obey without hesitation.

Mark's half-closed eyes were resting on the conveyer beam when Creson popped into view—one moment there was nothing, the next Mark was facing a frowning Mantzite. As had happened earlier with Selson, the unexpected appearance caused lights to blink on the panel as reborn emotions were compensated for.

"Christ! I wish you people would make a little noise before you pop in!" Mark said. "No matter how many times you do that, it still scares the hell out of me!"

Creson took a second to analyze the thought, then assumed that amused expression that was an on-going source of irritation to his captive. "I understand your reaction," he responded. "It had the same effect on us until we learned to project a courtesy warning prior to each appearance."

"I wasn't conscious of any warning," Mark said in confusion.

"Undoubtedly. Since you are incapable of receiving it, I did not send one. In any event it would be too subtle for your primitive mind. If you like I will routinely project a bark before entering." At this, his body began to quiver and his eyes contracted and dilated in rapid succession.

Mark sighed and resigned himself to wait until Creson regained control. It took another few seconds of laughter before the Mantz creature finally announced why he had come. "It is judged that you are capable of continuing the experience sessions. Would it please you to do so now?"

Mark contained the explosive "yes" which nearly left his lips. Instead he merely said, "If you wish."

"Before we begin, I should state that our efforts thus far have reinforced the knowledge gained by observing your species up close. Curious questions remain, however, minor areas on which we are not quite clear. I wonder if you would provide some assistance?"

"Do I have a choice?"

"In this instance, quite honestly, you do. We have no means of compelling such information from you. These are simply matters of curiosity, scarcely of monumental import, and thus the absence of answers would cause us little concern. But if it makes it more palatable, perhaps we might agree to share information with you in return."

"You're on!" Mark said quickly.

"On...?" Creson searched the Earth man's projection for an explanation of the term. "I see. As I understand it, we now have an agreement. To begin kindly explain the process of smoking."

"Smoking?" Mark asked, not sure what Creson was asking.

"Yes. Kindly explain this process."

Mark was as much amused as he was surprised. Was this the first time the Mantzites had encountered people who smoked? If so the tobacco companies would be all for an extraterrestrial invasion; it would open up fantastic new market opportunities. He decided to paraphrase from an old Bob Newhart skit in his answer. "Well, to start with you stick dry leaves in your mouth then set fire to them."

"Yes, we have observed that. You can imagine our reaction when it first occurred in our presence. Our observers thought you might be oriented toward masochism or self destruction. We attempted to learn more about the whys of such action during your sessions but either the experience was too subtle to detect or it was never there to begin with."

Mark was taken aback. He had no recollection of any probes into smoking experiences while under the machine's control. But it reinforced his belief that he had to try harder to control his thoughts; he had to keep the machine from poking its electronic nose into sensitive areas. "I don't smoke," he finally replied.

There was disappointment on Creson's face as he said, "Regrettable. It is a rather interesting idiosyncrasy." He dismissed the subject in favor of other "curiosities," although with some Mark could not tell whether the Mantzite was putting him on or was really confused. Not having studied humans that long, and not having the need to "eat" as such themselves, they claimed difficulty in understanding why humans put so much more into their stomachs than was needed to keep them alive and healthy—a widespread devotion to dieting suggested they did not really want to, that they abhorred the effect this excess had on them even while they continued to encourage it. Although amused by the question, Mark tried his best to take it seriously.

After a while Creson signaled that he had nothing more to ask. "Then it's your turn," Mark challenged. "What can you tell me?"

A smile appeared on the Mantzite's face, and he assumed that now familiar look of superiority. "Much more than you could possibly retain at this stage, but I will nonetheless give it a try. What would you like to know?"

Mark searched his mind and found it unprepared to take advantage of the moment; he could think of nothing meaningful to ask. "How do you people reproduce yourselves?" he asked finally, mildly humiliated at the quality of the question.

"I believe Leipin has a session set up for you which will answer that in graphic detail. Perhaps we can postpone your burning need to know until then?"

"Oh...sure." Mark wondered how Leipin planned to go about this, but he could not risk giving Creson an opening. Instead he began to ask about the people of Mantz, becoming more comfortable in his inquiries as he went along.

True to his word, Creson responded completely and without hesitation. Mark learned how the creatures were raised, how they were educated and the relationships they developed with one another. He hung on every word, fascinated with what was being said and by how similar the Mantzites were to his own people. Creson drew the line when Mark's questions rubbed against sensitive areas, such as security or technology, but he held back nothing concerning his fellow beings.

They lived in organized clusters where conveniences foreign to Mark could be made available to many citizens at once. They were a highly social people, at work and at play, and many opportunities were available in both environments to satisfy this need. They had long since mastered the technology necessary to take advantage of the unlimited energy which poured out of their two suns, the effect being to make more of everything available without resort to excessive physical labor. With most of their physical and psychological needs thus provided for, they had time to devote to other things, such as puzzling over the secrets of the universe. The centuries old planetary exploration project was a consequence of this.

As it turned out, the information gained from their ventures into space did not so much benefit the Mantzites as it did the planets being investigated. They had as yet discovered no planet more advanced than they, although they had a strict contingency plan ready to put in place should one later be found—they would not let their presence be known to that planet until they mastered the secrets which made them superior. Even then, they would remain hidden for as long as they were capable of doing so—no sense tempting fate.

Creson also revealed more about how Mark was brought to Mantz, how the transporter worked, in this case, in error. He explained why everything—animals, sounds, vegetation and colors—slowly metamorphosed from similar to downright frightening.

"But how does it go on and off? Who controls the switch?"

There was a twinkle in Creson's contracting eyes as he responded with, "Two questions again! Answering them in order: It is activated through a switch of sorts, and we do."

"In other words, it's none of my business."

"In a sense, I suppose, it is your business, but that will have no effect on our willingness to answer any questions that even remotely touch on the security of this planet. Surely you can appreciate the wisdom of such caution. I let you follow me through the transporter because you were already too far into it to permit you to return. You were also, if you recall, quite indisposed to rational thinking. In your confused state you would have presented yourself—and possibly us—with serious difficulties had I simply guided you back to your side of the machine."

"No one would have believed me; I didn't believe myself what was happening."

"I could not be certain of that." Then the Mantzite paused as if unsure whether he should reveal what had taken place since Markcarter's capture. A slight shrug let Mark know the decision was being made in his favor. "In any event, your disappearance has caused a bit of a stir. There are other Earth people searching for you, spurred to action by your mate."

Mark's interest took a giant leap upward. A formal search suggested rescue was possible. "How far away are they?" he asked impulsively.

"Roughly ten thousand light years. I shouldn't wait up if I were you."

An Earth posse, looking for him. Pleasing to hear, but what good would it do? Then, remembering something else Creson had said, he asked, "What do you mean by my 'mate?'"

"You are the sexual companion of another of your species; a female identified as 'Kathy.' I believe 'mate' is one of the terms you use to describe such a relationship, is it not?"

"Good enough," Mark said impatiently, "but what do you know about Kathy?"

"From your experience sessions we have quite a good picture of her, and of her relationship with you. She has caused the initiation of a search in the area in which you 'disappeared,' as it were, into our transporter. She, and they, are of the opinion that you are lost."

"How do you know all this?" Mark asked, dumbfounded by the information. Obviously at least one return trip to Earth had occurred since he arrived on Mantz. Was the transporter opened on a routine basis, maybe following a set schedule?

"At this very moment, many of our people are visiting your planet; they are strategically scattered throughout the land mass you refer to as your nation. Soon we will spread ourselves around the globe and thus be in a position to learn everything of consequence concerning your world and the curious species which inhabit it. In light of this, it is not surprising that, if we wished it, we would learn of the search for you. To clarify exactly what was happening in this regard, we sent two scouts to the point where you began your untimely introduction to space travel."

"Kelly?"

"I beg your pardon?"

"Oh, never mind! What else can you tell me?"

"I presume you are referring to the extraterrestrial search. As I started to say the scouts will soon interview your...mate."

"Kathy's in Kelly?" Mark asked.

"Yes," Creson answered, taken aback by the question. "I gather by the elevated decibel level of your voice that she is not supposed to be there. Do you suspect she has come from your part of Earth to...Kelly...just out of concern for you?"

"Of course she did!" Mark yelled. "Did you think she'd sit quietly at home while her MATE was kidnapped and held prisoner on another planet." His voice steadily lost steam as he realized the absurdity of what he was saying.

Creson took up the challenge, and this time there was no hint of amusement. "If someone enters another's home uninvited, is this regarded as 'kidnapping' on your planet? And if he or she is detained by the victim of that invasion do you regard this as unjust?"

"You left the goddamn door open! On anybody's planet that would be REGARDED as negligence!"

Creson pretended to consider the point as he asked, "On how many planets have you studied this situation?" But then he relented. "Well, perhaps you are right. I suppose even on your planet you keep your doors closed to vermin. In any event the 'door,' as you put it, is now tightly shut."

Mark wanted desperately to learn more about that door. "How often is your transporter turned on?" he asked.

Creson smiled at the obvious motive behind Markcarter's question. "It would not be possible for you to operate the transporter," he replied. "It was an astounding set of unfortunate circumstances which permitted your entry in the first place. It is mathematically improbable that they will ever recur. However, in answer to your question, the transporter goes on and off at the command of those who have been authorized to make use of it. I, obviously, am one who has such authorization." Creson paused for a moment, and when he continued, his tone had changed, "It is possible that you might have your chance at the machine, but in all honesty I cannot be certain."

"If I don't, I'm not going back; is that what you're saying?"

Creson was visibly distressed by the continued questioning on this subject. And by his ability to give only partial answers. Even so, he did not feel he could cut it short. He told himself that the effort was necessary if cooperation from Markcarter was to continue. "I am certain you realize that your being here has resulted in monumental problems to us, problems for which we have no immediate solution."

"What will happen if you decide I can't go back?" Mark persisted.

Creson sighed and slowly lifted his eyes to meet those of his captive. "One of our more serious problems, as you now know, is that you are forbidden by the Council to be here. It is entirely within the realm of rational thought that Takar would want to keep this error from being known to them. Should that happen, we will be forced to sweep you under the rug, so to speak. Frankly I do not believe it is Takar's nature to act in such a devious manner, even though he must know that none of us would ever treat the incident other than as he wished. A more likely probability is that the Council will be informed then a decision will be made to remedy the situation in whatever manner is deemed to best suit their long range goals."

"You're still not telling me anything," Mark cried. "What best serves their 'long range goals?'"

"I have promised to take you on a tour of another planet," Creson said, beginning a circuitous approach to the answer. "Its name is Tanterac. It is a planet that was explored by us in much the same manner as we intend for Earth, except this exploration occurred approximately one thousand of your years ago. As with the situation here, mistakes were made early in the exploration phase, resulting in our presence being revealed sooner than we would have wished. We attempted to remedy the situation, and some healing did in fact take place, but as you will soon see, the effect on the dominant life forms of that planet was devastating. I am certain that this will be foremost on the Council's collective mind when your case is reviewed. They will insist that whatever can be done to prevent another Tanterac, be done, whatever that means and regardless of whomever gets hurt in the process."

"Then my life really is in danger," Mark said softly.

"There are a number of possibilities being considered," Creson retorted. "That is merely one of them. I would suggest you help us to concentrate on developing others more suitable to your tastes."

"I have one: send me back!" Mark was both alarmed and angered by Creson's candor and by the casual statement that his demise was "being considered."

"It is, as even you are capable of understanding, not that simple. Your story, and I am certain you would have one, might be believed, and we cannot chance discovery by Earth creatures at this time. To do so would risk a repeat of the Tanterac situation. On the domestic—Mantz—side, allowing your presence to lead to such calamity would be considered by the Council as evidence of gross mismanagement, which in turn might result in the curtailment or elimination of this laboratory's contribution to the planetary exploration program."

"My heart bleeds for you!"

"Please do not misunderstand. It is not personal ambitions that drive us. Too much good has come from this process to permit such a thing to occur. We have, for example, eradicated major diseases on every planet invited to share our friendship. We have little doubt that in time Earth will also be freed of such scourges. We are familiar with the problems of population excess—soon to overwhelm your planet, unless I miss my guess—and of workable methods of prevention and control. These things mean improved quality of life, and, indeed, life itself to countless millions of your people. All this will become moot if initial contact is, shall we say, clumsy?

"As you will see with Tanterac, careful planning and implementation is essential to success. If the schedule with Earth is corrupted, the likely result will be widespread fear followed by chaos and anarchy. You creatures are still at the stage where you react to that which you do not understand with eruptions of emotion and aggression. You will fight each other and possibly us, and should this happen, the Council will be forced to suspend all further contact until matters quiet down. We will be forced to leave you in what might by then be a planet-wide horror. Experience has shown that it could be decades, even centuries before contact again becomes possible.

"Successes abound throughout the galaxy, proving that our program works. It would be criminal to permit such potential to be lost to the people of your planet. Certainly we wish no harm to you as an individual, but under the circumstances, perhaps you might at least appreciate its necessity."

Mark could not believe he was hearing an appeal for acquiescence in his own murder. "No! I don't appreciate anything of the sort! How can you say you're doing good when you kill someone from the society you claim to want to protect. If you're looking for volunteers, buddy, you won't find one here!"

Creson lowered his eyes to the floor but made no attempt to respond. After a moment Mark felt compelled to fill the gap of silence that was becoming, at least to him, ominous. "Look, there are wiser choices than doing me in. The circumstances of my death are bound to be discovered eventually, and when that happens, its going to give you more problems than you can handle. Your future on Earth will be kaput. Nobody will believe you any more."

Creson moved over to the hexagonal panel and began touching lights. Immediately a calm began to flow over Mark, a calm which he fought. "Is that your answer?" he asked. "To use chemicals to shut me up? Is this how you expect me to help you 'concentrate on alternatives?'"

"Frankly, yes," Creson replied, turning back to face his accuser. "I believe you have already discovered that the suppression of emotions has helped you to concentrate during experience-scanning sessions. You needn't reply," he added in response to Mark's widening eyes. "It becomes important for you, recognizing the firmness of our intent as regards contact with your species, that you share responsibility for coming up with an alternative consistent with this objective. In your language, help us to find a way out!" At that he turned back to the panel and stood there staring at its lights. The Earth man was getting to him and he had no idea what he could do about it. At least Markcarter's future was in Takar's hands and not his own.

CHAPTER 19

Mark eased his body into the now-familiar haze of the experience chamber. Already he had his mind focused on areas he wished to explore, this in the hope of getting the jump on the machine's subject-selection process. He needed to share the mind of a Mantzite who had knowledge of rest and rejuvenation chambers, conveyer tunnels, transporters and anything else that might enable an escape to have half a chance of success. So intense was his concentration that he scarcely noticed the preparatory activities performed by Creson and Leipin. He also failed to notice the former's condescending smile as he easily guessed the purpose of Mark's struggle.

For the moment at least, little thought was given to how to make use of whatever information he acquired. The Mantzites were going to "terminate" him, Creson had as much as said so, and to sit and do nothing was to blindly accept this. From deep within his being he understood Creson's concerns, but this in no way meant he was ready to offer himself in sacrifice for a situation not of his making. *I wasn't the one who left the goddamn transporter on!* In any event, he did not see why his retention and possible extermination was necessary to Earth's survival. Indeed, if killing innocent beings was part of the Mantz exploration process, that process and the morality of the creatures conducting it came into serious question.

As Creson had promised, the tranquilizing chemicals supplied earlier permitted him to reason in relative calm. Thoughts flowed with ease and were more carefully constructed, which was what the machine wanted, even needed. Mark appreciated the irony of it also helping him review topics of his own choosing.

As the session began, he focused on each vision as it rose to the surface of his consciousness in response to the machine's subtle probe. At best, he would have only a brief moment to decide whether to suppress it or permit it to blossom into full review. Beating the machine at its own game—vetoing ideas before it grabbed one and ran with it—might not even be possible, but that, at least, he would soon know.

Among his shopping list of subjects, he included gene manipulation and communicating through mental imagery. The former held promise if only he could master it as well as had Wilpin. Wilpin was a real pro; with his skills, he would have at his command a number of disguises, each available through mental effort alone. An improved capacity for telepathic communication would allow him to listen in on the conversations of every Mantzite who entered the lab while he was present. Not knowing he was tuned in, they would be freer in what they said.

Technology was another must. During the Wilpin incident, he had come close to mastering the beam device carried by every Mantzite. He might never gain access to one, but that he knew about it at all proved sensitive information was there for the taking.

None of it would be easy. Even if he could get the experience machine to review subjects of his choice, there was still the problem of coming up with the right triggers. What in his past would lead to a Mantz review of containment chambers or transporters or hexagonal panels?

A smile invaded his concentration as he realized he need no longer worry about the hexagonal panel. A distracted Creson had failed to hide the panel as he freed his captive for the latest session. The five-light sequence which permitted his exit from the cubicle was now firmly entrenched in his mind. *Which leaves the minor problem of how to get out of the chamber to get to the panel to touch the lights that will free me from the chamber!* It was a chicken-before-the-egg situation, a victory but, on the surface, an empty one. Still, it gave him a certain satisfaction to pick up yet another bit of knowledge that his captors did not know he had.

Without warning the image of Kathy appeared in his mind. The sight of this woman he might never see again filled him with such longing that he momentarily lost his focus. He fought to regain control, control that now included battling against himself—part of him wanted to continue the incredibly vivid scene which played before him. Emotion won out over resolve, and he relaxed just long enough to take a closer look, a decision that stripped him of whatever ability he might have had to influence events—Kathy was to be the machine's first subject for this session.

He was back home. The two of them were jogging along the narrow tree-lined paths of Marsh Creek Park, a mini wilderness a short hop from Valley Forge. Near the end of their run and suffering the pleasures of a contrived exhaustion, they collapsed onto a cushion of soft grass by the bank of the gently flowing creek. A smile lit up both their faces as they examined one another in silence. It was a day that Mark had no problem revisiting.

Kathy was so lovely lying there with wisps of moist hair clinging to her face as if arranged by some ancient temptress of love. The clothing too; loose but clinging, it accentuated her body in subtle and sensuous ways. Like that time long ago, his eyes played with that body with calm deliberation as he waited for his breath to return.

"You're getting old, Carter," she said impishly.

Mark smiled. "I can still take you two out of three falls."

"Only because I'd let you win."

Rising to his knees, Mark inched himself closer. Kathy, her expression one of invitation, continued to lie on her side, her head propped up by one arm. The night was dark; the last jogger had long since left the trail; the air was warm and dry. Mark lowered himself to where he lay half on and half off her upper body then touched his lips to hers. It was a gentle kiss that had little chance of remaining so; it became more animated as anticipation swelled within both of their bodies. Mark reached out a hand to caress her hair, then let his hand slip downward, first to the curve of her neck then to where he could trace the inviting outline of her breast. Her nipples hardened as fingertips brushed around then over them. The hand continued downward, past her firm abdomen to her thighs, still moist from the earlier effort and warming to the effort she knew would soon follow. A soft moan escaped her throat and she lowered her head to the ground, allowing Mark to move more of his body over hers. Their breathing by now was as heavy as it had been during their run. The hand slid upward again, this time moving under the loose shirt to the bare breast that offered itself from within. By then neither he nor she was capable of further subtlety. Their hands moved in concert with one another, giving and sharing pleasure and alternately tearing at each other's clothing until the offending cloth no longer stood in the way of their need to possess all they could of the other's body.

"Now, Mark, now!" The invitation was unnecessary. In one continuous movement, Mark rolled their naked bodies over and plunged himself into her inviting warmth, the action bringing a shared gasp of pleasure. Then the coupling which had begun so slowly assumed a state of urgency. A fire was burning within them both, a fire that neither had ever felt so keenly before. Mark immersed himself in his lovely partner, driven by the need to give more with each stroke even as he surrendered to all that she gave him. She urgently sought him, wanting satisfaction yet not wanting it to end. In time it did, and when together that happened they fought hard to deny it, each wanting to continue the coupling forever. Only reluctantly did they admit an end, and then they lay side by side, exhausted and unwilling to disturb the reverie of the moment.

Kathy broke the silence a few minutes later. "Not bad for an old guy." Her voice was a step lighter and out of a dream.

Mark chuckled as he turned his head to face her. She was staring at him with eyes that, although only half open, had not lost their ability to capture his soul. She smiled and took on an impish look as if enjoying the thought of what she next had in store for him. Mark bathed her body with slowly moving eyes, already beginning to consider another encounter. "I think we should rehearse this thing until we get it right," he said.

With a soft chuckle, Kathy raised herself to one elbow, bringing her face to within inches of his. "Lead on, McDuff," she said.

With disturbing suddenness, Mark's world converted to a Mantz scene. He was given no time to say good-bye to Kathy, or at least to apologize for summarily abandoning her. One moment he was enjoying life even more than he had the first go-around, the next he was sharing the mind of a male Mantzite some ten thousand light years away. The machine attempted to counter the worst of his disappointment.

He knew immediately the creature's name (Harset), and also knew where he was and what was expected of him. There was a female creature staring from across a small amphitheater—staring at him as well as at Harset. He felt an attachment to her, as much so as did his mental host. It was a gathering of young Mantzites, the setting and substance intended for educational rather than social purposes—Mark was unable to verify this due to his host's intense concentration on the young female. Out of the corner of their shared eye, he saw someone standing on a platform at the center of the group, and this someone was projecting his thoughts to the audience. Because of his host's diverted attention, what was being said was lost to Mark.

The young female was well aware of Harset's focus on her and, indeed, encouraged it. "You are not paying attention, Harset," she projected coyly, careful to limit the scope of her telepathy to him and to him alone.

"Incorrect, Simtor," he retorted, also taking care to keep the projection within narrow limits. "I *am* paying attention...to you."

She smiled. She enjoyed being with this young Mantzite and, like him, was more interested in their getting together than in completing the lecture. She began projecting a image of sexual invitation, a form of foreplay to this society. Mark could feel the intensity of the projection and the stirring within his host's body in response. It was as if actual touching had occurred.

"Simtor, are you crazy! In front of all these people?"

"They will be unaware if we are careful," she said, smiling and continuing to tease with her special brand of foreplay.

Mark was beset with emotion, most of it familiar. He could feel Harset's embarrassment at being so aroused in front of his peers, but he could also feel intense and demanding desire. The feeling was similar to his own under such circumstances except it was his mind doing the work rather than any other part of his body. The realization of this, however, was of little import at the moment. Mental or physical, what really mattered was keeping it going; Mark tried to will his host toward capitulation.

It was difficult to concentrate on anything except the sexual communication between himself and Simtor, although Mark shared his host's concern for appearing normal to the many students who sat around him. The young female was having the same difficulty. Through eyes clouded by desire, Mark saw how unnaturally straight she sat in her chair, as if called to attention by some military cadre. So obvious was it that he wondered how anyone could remain unaware that something other than a devotion to the speaker was commanding her attention. He wondered whether he and his host were equally as obvious.

The mental foreplay continued until Mark could stand it no longer. Even while a part of him knew it would have no effect, he tried to push his host toward the next step, whatever that might be in this strange new world. Another glance at Simtor proved she shared the same need; a three fingered hand, more natural to Mark than before, covered her face. The other gripped the bottom of her seat as if less than that would see her flying away.

Simtor finally gave in. With shaking hands, he reached into the pocket of the fur that enveloped his body and gripped the beam device he carried there. Pulling it out, he pretended to be seeking a clarification to what the instructor was saying while actually instructing it to key in on Simtor— Mark saw the female Mantzite doing the same. Returning the devices to their respective pockets, the two then grabbed their seats with arms and legs alike, the speed at which they did so attesting to, not only their passion, but the need to prepare for what would soon come. Sharing his host's expectations, Mark mentally did the same.

It came as an overpowering rush of sensual stimulation. Every part of his shared body quivered with erotic stimulation, all of it intense and demanding. Nothing escaped participation not even the fur that belonged as much to him as to his host; it appeared to vibrate as if composed of dormant fibers of nerves now brought to life. He was helpless; he was rocketing to the stars; he was reaching heights never dreamed possible. Gone was any fear of discovery. At that moment he could not care if the whole planet was watching and taking notes. The only important thing was keeping that feeling going. Even when this was no longer possible, he was not disappointed. Coming down slowly, he and his host were left with a rapturous feeling of sensual exhaustion.

Hands and legs still enveloping the seat, Mark and his mental partner fought to keep their eyes open. Along with Harset, he shared the temptation to surrender to the aftermath of feeling, much as he had earlier with Kathy. Gratefully, the lecture went on for a number of additional minutes, enough time for all three to recover. In time he shot a glance at Simtor, who smiled in response. Along with his host, Mark returned the smile.

When the gathering broke up a few minutes later the two young Mantzites, one of whom hosted an exceptionally satisfied Earth man, got to their feet and headed for separate exits. After only a few steps Harset turned and projected a carefully controlled thought at his retreating partner. "I believe we share this class again tomorrow," he said.

Simtor turned and smiled across the short distance that separated them, "I believe you are right," she answered.

In a flash Mark was back in the experience chamber with the device again attempting to select a topic to investigate. But this time the opposition it faced was formidable. Mark's mind refused to let go of the subjects just visited—they were too real; they were too...exhausting. He wondered whether he knew enough to try the Mantz technique on Kathy—was it possible? *I could zap her anywhere, even while we're walking down the street,* he thought.

The Mantz method did, however, leave the details of procreation unanswered. There was no actual touching, and nothing else in the experience provided insight into how procreation was done, or at least how it might have been done before machines took over the process of producing little Mantzites. Obviously a machine was involved in the gathering of Harset's experience as well. Had it considered him unworthy or was a "donation" extracted during the act? Mark made a mental note to wrestle the answer from Leipin later.

There was something else in the Mantz sexual encounter he might be able to make use of. Harset and Simtor had exerted great control over who might be privy to their telepathic projections. Mark reviewed the procedure and discovered that he knew exactly how this was done. Indeed, it was now as routine to him as riding a bicycle—that portion of Harset's consciousness was as solidly entrenched in his mind as if he had studied the methodology for years. Although anxious to experiment, he quickly switched his thoughts to another subject, fearing his captors would learn how interested he was in this one.

The machine continued its relentless probing and, as before, the subtly-suggested topics passed by with lightning speed. Mark continued to be awed by the ability of his mind to keep up with it all. Had the capacity to do this always been there, as Creson himself had suggested? This machine was not supposed to enlarge one's brain; it merely introduced new skills. If his brain were limited to begin with, nothing would come of the sessions.

Obviously his brain was not limited. Maybe under-utilized, but not limited. Even now he could do many of the things his captors could do. And there appeared to be little reason why the human race as a whole could not grow the same way. Little reason that they could not, in time, be mentally equal to the aliens.

So simple! So obvious! Astounding skills, never thought possible on Earth, were, once you shared another's knowledge, child's play. You just did it without thinking about it. He wondered whether it was really that simple. Or was the machine, combined with the chemicals absorbed while in the rest and rejuvenation chamber, making it seem so. He felt a moment of sadness as he realized that a "yes" answer would mean his new powers were not his to keep. Once the chemicals wore off or the machine tired of playing with him, they would evaporate as quickly as they had appeared.

Reflecting on his experience with the converted fingernail, Mark accepted the probability that telepathic communication could not be used effectively without practice. It was there, however, and someday, if he survived the Mantz encounter and found the skill still his to enjoy, he would make good use of it.

"His body seems to have adjusted to the chamber. Perhaps this is the result of the subject matter to which we exposed him." A smile accompanied Leipin's comment.

"Perhaps," Creson replied dryly. "At least he should sleep well tonight." He stared at the Earth man for a moment before adding, "Can you determine how much information he retained?"

"After the second experience, and apparently without intending to, he shared with the machine his elation on having mastered the technique of telepathic communication and mental imagery. He might well have that knowledge; in any event he earnestly believes he has."

Creson paused again, this time longer. When he continued there was a hint of sadness in his projection. "I want you to be certain he remains unaware that we know of this. His morale would suffer needlessly if we poked a hole in his escape bubble."

Leipin stared at her supervisor in confusion. "Escape bubble?" she asked.

Creson smiled. "An Earth man term. I picked it up from his subconscious. Since we are now studying Earth we may as well delve in the vernacular; when in Rome, as they say."

Leipin's stare of uncertainty did not change. *When in Rome?* she thought.

Creson's eyes contracted slightly as he changed the subject. "Where will you direct his thoughts next?"

"I thought it might represent a balance to his emotions if we were to dwell on the creatures of Earth. I am coaxing him toward experiences involving zoos or circuses."

Creson chuckled. "Give him a look at the beasts of Krakoran, up close if you can. That will get his mind off sex in a hurry."

Leipin smiled. "The poor creature will be a vegetable if we expose him to that without preparing him first." She said it lightly, aware that Creson was not serious. "I understand you wish to open him to other planets as well."

"I will want to take him to Tanterac, and I will want to go with him. Is he up to it?"

"There is little to suggest his system would not withstand the experience. I will, of course, monitor him closely and bring him back whenever the signs suggest it wise to do so."

Creson paused before adding to the order. "While we are there, I will want to give him the opportunity to overpower me. Let him find a laser weapon; a simple hand-held one will suffice."

Leipin could not keep the frown from her face. Creson was setting up some kind of test of the Earth man, something she found distasteful, even dangerous. Nonetheless, she obediently began preparations for a transplant of the consciousness of her supervisor and that of the captive Earth creature to the nightmarish planet of Tanterac.

CHAPTER 20

Emerging as they did out of the darkness and looking more like floating ghosts than marching animals, the two shepherds frightened Kathy badly. She struggled to maintain control, even while suspecting the dogs would see through her efforts. An unreasonable but overwhelming feeling of entrapment swelled within her: There was nowhere she could go where they would not follow, no place where they would not already be there lying in wait for her. They were evil; they would be the end of her. And they were now within ten yards of where she stood frozen in fear.

She clamped her teeth together and tightened her hands into fists, this more to convince herself than to frighten them. Regardless, they kept coming, their eyes attached to hers as if this alone would hypnotize her into submission, submission to what she could only imagine. When they closed to within a few short steps, they startled her even more by abruptly sitting down. Then, as if understood by all that this was the time for such things, the world took a time-out. Even the forest participated; nothing moved; nothing made a sound. Kathy let her breath out slowly, aware that, after her rapidly beating heart, it was the greatest source of noise around.

She had expected them to keep coming until they either butted her out of the way or swallowed her up using whatever powers allowed them to do what they did. That they did neither was not of itself calming, and she could do nothing other than stand erect and stare at four canine eyes that now appeared to want nothing more than her attention. Neither human nor canine showed a willingness to break the spell.

In time the paralysis began to loosen its grip. Although too close for comfort, the dogs were in a sitting position and thus less threatening; at least they did not appear to be on the verge of attack. She relaxed further, enough to consider what their presence might mean.

They were the same type of dog: tan German shepherds. Why? And why did they stop in front of her? Why her? Where did they come from? What in God's name did they want?

As with the animal captured earlier, Kathy wondered if these two could recently have been with Mark. The thought made them appear to be less fearsome. Perhaps they were beside her now because of some recognition implanted by Mark. Maybe they intended to lead her to him. "Dumb!" she murmured, jumping slightly at the sound of her own voice. "How would Mark know I was in Kelly?"

It was more and more obvious that the dogs were not intending to do her harm—they had already had plenty of opportunity for that. But then what? Their stance suggested a willingness to obey, but they gave no indication of what else occupied their animal minds. "Okay, dogs!" she said, failing miserably in her attempt to speak with authority. "What gives? You guys want to come home with me, is that it?"

She lowered to a kneeling position but kept herself ready to run should the action provoke something nasty in the animals. She breathed a sigh of relief when they readily accepted the movement. "Nice mutts," she said, reaching out her hands to stroke both animals simultaneously. This they also accepted—the eyes on one contracted slightly but otherwise no unusual movement was noted. Kathy began to pet with more enthusiasm, purging herself of nervousness in the process. They really were friendly animals, odd but friendly. And they were male and female—somehow their being a "couple" made them less threatening. After a few minutes of confidence restoring, she returned to her feet, stared down at the still-sitting dogs and sighed away the last vestige of fear.

"Look, guys, I'm only set up for one dog. One of you has to get lost."

She had no idea how she was going to separate the two, but that problem she could wrestle with later. The important thing was to get at least one of them back to her room. *I sure wish Cal were here*, she thought.

With a less-than-certain stride, she began walking back toward Kelly. She moved slowly and swung her head around after only a few steps to check on the animals—they had risen to their feet and were beginning to follow. "That's the way, boys and girls. Keep it coming."

The walk back was uneventful if one did not count nerves that kept oscillating between fear and reason, the former the case each time she turned her back on her canine entourage. The fear, however, was poorly spent since they seemed interested in nothing other than accompanying her to town. Even the arrival in Kelly did not bring them to alter their behavior. It was as if they had known what they would find and were unimpressed. They followed without hesitation right up to the entrance to the hotel.

Being there gave Kathy a feeling of control. She was back in town; it was less frightening in town; there were people there to call on. As she moved her concern from her own safety to how to separate her new pets, one to take to her room the other to set free to continue whatever mischief he was bred to conduct, she wondered anew why they were so interested in her. They had stopped when she did and were now sitting patiently as if waiting for instructions. There was no sign of hostility in them, but neither was there the reassuring panting or tail wagging one might expect from supposedly friendly dogs. "You guys must really be well trained," she said thoughtfully.

Their only reaction to the human voice was that strange contracting of the eyes she'd noticed earlier. "Well, the rules are still the same: one of you has to go," she said, loosening the cloth belt tied around her waist—

it would make a good-enough leash. She knelt beside the male dog and tied it around its neck. As if trying to be helpful, the animal remained in place until the task was completed. She then rose to a standing position and tugged lightly on one end, pleased when her captive did not resist. She led it to the hotel entrance, stopping at that point only because it was clear the other intended to follow.

"No, girl, you stay put!" she ordered, spreading her hand in front of the animal's face to emphasize the point. It put her close enough to observe its response, and it was far from reassuring. What she saw was a frown, an all-too-human frown. A tug appeared in the pit of her stomach as she wondered how it could do that. She took an uncertain step backward, there to watch the captured animal turn toward its companion and stare at him in ominous silence.

What followed then was another of those eerie time-outs—stillness, silence and staring. Finally the one doing the frowning turned abruptly and began marching up the street—no fanfare, no complaints; it simply left. Kathy watched all this with no inclination to interfere. She had thought the look they were giving each other was the prelude to a fight; she had been ready to drop the leash and dart into the hotel should that prove to be true.

A tug on the leash, more a plea than an order, brought the remaining animal's attention back to its temporary master. It looked briefly into Kathy's eyes then moved without further coaxing through the door, up the stairs and into her room. It showed no concern for what the human female might have in mind. "You're used to houses, huh, boy?" Kathy said, encouraged by its cooperation.

She tied it to a pipe in the same closet from which her previous captive had vanished. Like the earlier animal, it immediately sought out a corner and lay down, its muzzle on its front paws and its friendly eyes looking up at its human companion. "Why are you guys so friendly?" Kathy asked with a tinge of guilt.

She sat on the bed staring at the animal, nervous at the thought of what she was about to do to it. She had a vague knowledgeable of how to handle a syringe, and had even watched her veterinarian give Me-too a shot, but the thought of actually administering one herself gave her pause. Adding to this was the realization that she would be doing so with a strange animal, one that might not be all that appreciative of it. It was friendly now, but that did not mean it would sit idly by while a do-it-yourself veterinarian stabbed it with a sharp instrument.

As the discomforting thoughts bounced around in her mind, the expression on the animal's face turned negative. It was as if it had read her thoughts and now knew what she was up to. Her confidence took another nose-dive, and to combat this she revisited the closet and added the leash that Cal had given her to the animal's neck—there were now two leashes restraining it. Her level of confidence, however, remained at a depressed level.

She decided to involve herself in the preparatory steps. Moving in such a way that the animal could not see, she turned on the video camera carefully hidden on the other side of the room, far enough away to be unheard and unnoticed. It now took in the entire room and would thus catch anyone emerging from a secret passageway regardless of where that secret passageway might be hidden. It seemed silly to hide all this from a dumb animal, but the dog she and Cal had captured earlier had known what a video camera was—the fact that it stared directly into the lens proved that.

With the machine on and the dog apparently taking no notice, Kathy found it easier to breath. Whatever happened now, it would be recorded. Not even Cal knew she was again using a video. In any event Cal was off in the woods with the rangers.

Next was the coating of dirt to be laid on the floor, light to avoid calling attention to it. Kathy picked up the plastic bag in which she had gathered soil from behind the hotel and reached a hand into the opening. The loud ring of a telephone brought it back like a kid's caught in a cookie jar; the timing was suggestive of some playful god unaware or uncaring of how little she appreciated the humor. She stormed over to the instrument and jerked it from its cradle before the offensive ring could be repeated. It was Ken Janos.

She worked on bringing her breathing back to normal as the ranger outlined the situation. Once again he was calling from the woods, this time using a mobile telephone attached to an off-track vehicle. Due to the difficult terrain over which the search had progressed, the vehicle was about to be left behind. Ken wanted to give one last call before that happened.

"We have a good-sized team out here now and searching is going to continue around the clock. I've got to tell you though, we weren't able to pick up his trail again—the tracks just petered out, both Carter's and the dog's. Don't worry though, we'll be fanning out in all directions, anywhere a camper might wander off to. And we still have that helicopter."

"Can you run the helicopter at night, to look for campfires, I mean?" Kathy asked.

"That's exactly what we're doing; its up right now. Maybe we should have you out here advising us."

Kathy paused for a moment before answering, not certain how Janos would feel if she used his comment to invite herself along. "Thanks. Believe me, I'd welcome the chance to come along, but I know you really want me to stay put."

Janos did not evade the issue. "Frankly, I did cringe a little after blurting that out, afraid I'd have to come up with a diplomatic way to back down. It's not that you're a woman; we often have women along with us in a search. It's more that you're too close to the target. And that, we've learned from hard experience, is a disruptive influence. No offense."

"None taken," Kathy answered. "I appreciate your candor." Then she thought about something else that Janos had said, "Your talking about the dog tracks reminds me, I have another of those animals with me; its a light-colored shepherd, just like all the others. In fact, two of them came into town together. I figure there's got to be someone out there who owns a bunch of these dogs, and, if so, maybe Mark bumped into him; he could be there right now."

"Once again our thinking coincides; we've been searching from the air all day. Nothing yet though; if there's somebody out there he knows how to keep himself hidden. Those dogs have to be coming from someplace but I'll be damned if any of us can figure out where."

As Janos talked Kathy observed the captive dog. It was staring intently at the phone, and an uncanny expression of disapproval occupied its canine face. The uncomfortable feeling Kathy was trying so hard to overcome increased at the unlikely sight, one of so many unlikely sights of late. In her study of dogs she could remember nothing that suggested they were even remotely capable of such expressions.

"Kathy, you still there?" Janos was asking.

"Oh, sorry. I was staring at this dog I captured. He certainly doesn't act like any dog I've ever known. Look, if you're having trouble finding out where they're coming from, wouldn't it make sense to use this one? I mean couldn't we put it on a long leash and follow it home?"

"Might not be a bad idea. Why don't you hold onto him until I get back to you. If we don't find anything by tomorrow, say around noon, maybe I'll give you a call. I can always send the coptor to pick him up."

"Okay, Kathy responded. "I'll try to do a better job of holding on to this one than I did the last."

"What about the second one? You said there were two."

"It's wandering around town someplace. I shooed him away when he tried to follow the other up to my room."

"Shows how popular you are," Janos quipped.

"Yeah, I can really attract dogs," Kathy rebutted, wanting to be polite but not in the mood for banter.

"Look, I have to get back to my crew; I'll keep in close touch. You try to relax in the meantime." Kathy acknowledged his concern then said good-bye and hung up the phone.

No sooner did the receiver touch the cradle than it began to ring—the second time in only minutes that it had done that to her. "Shit!" she cried, certain it had rung at that moment just to add to her misery. She snatched it up then blurted out a barely civilized "hello!"

"Kathy, is that you?"

The familiar sound of Sandy's voice added guilt to everything else she was feeling.

"Kathy, what's going on?" he asked.

"Hi Sandy. Sorry to be so emotional. Mark really is lost, I've been talking to the people who are looking for him."

There was a momentary pause at the other end. "Is that the ranger guy I talked to before?" Sandy asked.

"Yeah. Ken Janos, nice guy; seems to know what he's doing. There's a whole crew out there looking for Mark. A helicopter too. Ken said they'd be searching all night."

Sandy's concern came through in his release of breath. "Sounds heavy," he said. "How're you doing, Kid?"

"Well I don't exactly feel like partying, but I'm holding my own. Might even be of help in the search. There's a dog with me right now that might be connected to Mark." She nodded toward the animal as she spoke then nearly dropped the phone when its frown dramatically reappeared—and there was no other word for that very undoglike expression; the furrowed brows were a conscious demonstration of disapproval.

Once again a voice on the phone was asking, "Kathy, you still there?"

"Yes...Sorry. This dog I have with me is giving me the willies." She gathered her composure then began explaining the situation to Sandy. Unsure of who might be listening, she left out the planned tranquilization and video taping.

Sandy listened patiently but was unconvinced that Kathy suspicions were anything other than a subconscious desire to keep herself occupied while the search for Mark continued. Even so, he talked for a long while, wanting to calm Kathy down and, as he admitted to himself later, wanting to be reassured himself. Although anxious to get on with the rest of her plan, Kathy shared his desire to keep the conversation going. In time, after an unspoken recognition that there was little left to be said, they reluctantly said their good-byes. "Call me every day with the latest, okay, sweetie?"

"Sure, Sandy. I really appreciate your call. It's good to hear the voice of someone who really understands."

"Hearing your voice helps take the edge off some of the things I've been thinking too. Mark might be a pain in the ass at times, but I've grown kinda used to him."

Kathy's chuckle was out of politeness. She was too upset to appreciate her friend's perennial attempts to cheer her up through humor. "Goodbye, Sandy; call you tomorrow."

This time she gingerly lowered the phone into its cradle, afraid that it would ring again, provoked by some spirit with a sadistic sense of humor. Gratefully, it remained silent and, taking a deep breath, she turned toward ridding herself of the uneasiness that threatened to flood her already-weakened system. The hard part was about to begin and it would not help if she came at her captive with a shaking hypodermic needle—the way the beast looked at the moment, she was not sure she wanted to come at it at all.

Although its expression now was closer to that of a normal canine, the animal continued to stare, permitting Kathy no time to prepare the syringe let alone administer it. It was a problem, a serious one, considering how intelligent this animal was. Obviously the dog had to be distracted in some way, but what could she do to accomplish that?

She decided to first tackle the problem of loading the syringe, a far easier task. Disguising her movements as best she could, she gathered the materials, wrapped them in a towel, then left the room for the bathroom down the hall. There the animal would not be able to see or hear. The solitude helped, and in minutes she had the syringe filled with the dosage recommended by the pharmacist in Jackson, plus a little extra to make sure it worked quickly. To hedge her bets, she prepared two, thinking the other would come in handy should the animal reacted violently to the first. No way she wanted to come out second on this.

Her reason for being there satisfied, she nonetheless stayed a moment longer, sitting on the edge of the tub and trying to work out best way to go from here. If she could get the dog to turn its head for just a second or two, she could jam the needle into its rump—there would be no time to sterilize the injection site, but that couldn't be helped. Once tranquilized, and there was no doubt in her mind that she would find some way of accomplishing this, she would keep it in that condition until at least the following morning. If someone were rescuing these animals as some kind of local joke, they were sure to try it before then. *That assumes, of course, that somebody knows I have another dog.*

The thought was a disturbing one. If the word didn't get around, she was wasting her time. The culprit would not know she was trying it again and thus would do nothing. She decided to visit the bar, there to casually spread the word of her new attempt to uncover the mystery of the Kelly-dogs, how they were getting away. She would let it slip—subtly, of course—that this time no camera was being used.

First, however, was tranquilizing the animal. That was too traumatic a task to keep hanging. Plus, she wanted it to be there when she returned.

Returning her concentration to the problem of administering the needle, she considered diverting the animal with food. Cal claimed they never ate, but then he was known to exaggerate. The only problem was the hour; where could she get something that a dog would find palatable? And what made her think the mutt would be here when she got back?

She left the bathroom and went down to the lobby, pleased when she got there to see the night clerk in his usual pose: sitting in a chair that leaned backward against a wall, and nodding his head in a loosing battle to stay awake. As she moved to his side, she cleared her throat to get his attention without sending him through the roof, then asked her question in as soothing a voice as she could manage, "Would you by any chance have anything I could feed to a dog?"

The night clerk, after he shook himself of the last vestiges of a disturbed sleep, stared at her with an expression that was half disbelieving and half suspicious. "Would yew run thet by me agin?"

"Something to feed a dog. A bone or something."

Deciding it was better not to ask questions, he stared a few seconds longer then turned his head to one side and assumed what he obviously thought was a shrewd look. "I got a couple dog bones, but my hound don't take kindly ta folks takin' iz food."

Kathy realized the one she would have to make it up to was its master. "Perhaps a bottle of whiskey might help the dog forget its loss," she suggested.

"Might at thet," the man said with a smile, leaving his chair and stepping into his back room to see what he could find. It took longer than Kathy expected, but in time he returned with a crumbled newspaper in his hand. "Found some meat scraps; spec you might prefer these." He apparently considered a bottle of whiskey worth more than a few bones.

The deal set, Kathy returned to her room, opening the door cautiously as she entered, half expecting the animal to be free of his two leashes and walking around the room. But it was exactly where it had been when she left.

A bead of perspiration appeared on her forehead as she realized how close she was to the moment of truth. There was no further reason to put it off; she had to steel herself to jabbing her captive with the loaded syringe. Growling softly and bunching her hands, this to give herself courage, she moved to its side, knelt down, and placed the crumpled newspaper on the side furthest from herself. The idea was to get the dog to look in that direction and away from her. It appeared to work; its eyes followed the parcel, although the look on its canine face as it did so was less than one of anticipation. Nonetheless encouraged, she moved her hand slowly over its head to pry open the paper, noting as she did so that the dog continued to show interest, even as it glanced back once as if doubting her motives. At the same time, she reached a shaky hand into her pocket and grabbed the syringe, arranging it in such a way that her fingers could remove the sterile tip. It popped off without mishap, and the syringe was ready for action.

The paper was now open, and in it she could see an array of fatty and sinuous meat, from what type of creature she did not even want to speculate. "Look at that delicious garbage, doggie!" she said in a quivering voice, hoping the animal would share the enthusiasm that she tried to imbue into her words. She was pleased when, although the suspicious look reappeared, it dutifully sniffed the food. She was less pleased when it followed this with a raising of its muzzle to demonstrate an unmistakable lack of interest.

"Damn you, mutt!" she cried in frustration.

By now her nerves were so aflame, she could barely think straight. She had to do something and fast or the moment would be lost. In desperation she began petting the animal on the near side of its head, applying enough force to cause it to turn away. It permitted this, but she could sense its reluctance. Her jumbled mind barely hers to command, she then pulled the syringe from her pocket, jammed it into a fatty part of the dog's rump and pushed down on the plunger. A cry of surprise left her throat at having actually gone through with it.

The animal sprang to its feet, the suddenness of it knocking Kathy to the ground. Giving her no time to respond, it swung its head around to where it could see her face; its own displaying fading surprise and developing anger. The expression was fearful enough, but it took second place to what followed. In that second of involuntary response to the unexpected, the animal projected a distinctly undoglike message to its assailant, "What have you done!" it said.

Seconds passed before Kathy could regain control of her voice, and by then she was too numb to scream. All she could manage was to lie there shivering in fear while a specter she no longer recognized slowly collapsed on top of her, its muzzle winding up only inches from her face, its exposed teeth suggesting a consequence of its displeasure, a consequence she only narrowly avoided. She pushed it off, struggled to her feet, then stumbled backward toward the bed, her eyes never leaving the inert form on the floor. At any moment it might leap to its feet and start coming her way.

The thing had spoken! Words! Words had come from an animal's mouth. "This isn't real!" she cried, her voice cracked and squeaky. "It's a trick, an elaborate practical joke! This whole Kelly-dog thing is a practical joke, a sick one at that!"

But no amount of rationalization could convince her to approach the animal for a closer look.

She tried to recreate the situation in her mind. She had assumed the words came from its mouth, but she did not remember seeing its lips—muzzle—move. A ventriloquist? Was someone nearby throwing his voice? *But how could he possibly know I was about to give it an injection?*

A disturbing thought hit her, and she stabbed a hand into her pocket, yanked out the other syringe then, as if it were a weapon, pointed it at the sleeping canine. *I have maybe five hours before it wakes up,* she thought, trying not to think of what would happen if that turned out to be a poor estimate.

But what should she do during those five hours, try to sell someone on the notion that she had a talking dog in her hotel room? And what about later when the five hours were up? Should she give it another dose and another after that, keeping it under sedation as long as possible— when would it make sense to permit an angry talking dog, one that vanishes at will, to recover?

"What makes me think he'll just vanish?" she mumbled aloud, remembering how angry it had been at being stuck with a needle.

As she sat there tossing over her limited options, the video recorder came to mind; the event, including the dog's human cry, had been recorded. A chill ran the entire length of her body as she realized it could be replayed to the critical point, the moment of truth. With less than complete enthusiasm—she had been gravitating toward accepting what happened as an overworked imagination—she approached the machine, rewound its tape then pressed play.

It took a number of minutes to get past her early preparatory steps, but she watched every bit of it, partly because she did not want to chance missing anything and partly to delay confirmation of what was clearly impossible. During the time she was out of the room—in the bathroom then down in the lobby scaring up food—the dog made no movement that anyone could call unusual. It just lay with its head on its paws, staring at the wall ahead, its expression suggesting deep thought.

Her heart skipped a beat as the bedroom door opened and in she came carrying the dog scraps. It recovered then beat faster when her image arrived at the point where she administered the syringe. She did not even blink as the animal jumped up, turned around then presented her with that frighteningly human expression of anger—how did it manage that?! At the same time her recorded image jumped as if stung by a wasp— a gasp accompanied this but nothing came out of the dog; it collapsed on top of her in silence. Then, the room still devoid of sound, she lay on the floor, staring with bulging eyes at what looked to all the world like a normal German shepherd.

"Where's the sound?" she cried, her voice a mixture of demand and accusation. The dog's lips had not moved—she was sure of this—and no comment had been picked up on tape.

She could not believe it. Even a ventriloquist off to one side would have been picked up. She replayed the tape, but the result was the same: there was nothing to suggest the dog had spoken, only her reaction when it was supposed to have happened. Maybe she really had imagined it. Doubt swallowed most of her relief as she replayed it yet again, this time stopping the action at precisely the moment when the comment would have occurred. "Goddamnit, the dog's mouth is closed!" she cried to the silent room. "He couldn't have said anything."

She flopped herself on the bed then lay there trying to sort it out. Something had happened, of that she was sure. That animal lying unconscious across the room had said something to her; she could not forget the feeling that cascaded down her body as that happened. "But why isn't it on tape? Everything else is on tape, even my telephone calls." There was enough there to suggest the machine was not at fault, but, if not that then what? It all pointed to her; it as much as said she did not hear what she thought she'd heard.

"No way!" In her heart she knew better. She also knew that now there would be no simple solution to the Kelly-dog mystery. Something was seriously wrong; something that just shouldn't be.

CHAPTER 21

"**I** have already received the necessary permission," said Creson. "Like myself, Takar believes the trip to be appropriate to our goal of mutual discovery."

Creson was explaining the planet Tanterac to a fascinated Mark, this in preparation for their mental transportation to its surface. Mark followed along as would a small child being told of the wonders of a coming visit to an amusement park.

"The final details are being worked out at this very moment. This will be a different procedure than that to which you have become accustomed in that we will be controlling the host bodies ourselves. There will be no witnessed experiences, you will be living in real time, creating your own experiences as it were. While you remain on that planet you will have free use of a Mantzite body; whatever you wish to do, wherever you wish to go, that body will comply. It will seem to you that you are actually there and that the body is yours."

Mark could not keep the smile of anticipation from his face. "I understand the concept of the experience chamber," he said, his voice joining his smile in revealing his feelings, "but how does something like this work. I mean, how can a mind on Mantz control a body on a planet light years away?"

"Actually it is easier than you might imagine. The machine decides what electrical impulses are leaving your brain: where they originate, in what intensity they are projected and what functions they are intended to control. From there it is a simple matter of replicating them within the person acting as the host. Of course the host's consciousness must be temporarily deactivated, but that is easily accomplished by applying essentially the same process in reverse: measuring the host's brain impulses and providing countermeasures to silence them. Except, of course, for visual and other senses which will be redirected to your brain as if they had originated within your own body—this is what gives you the feeling of being present on the targeted planet. You will retain whatever consciousness you currently possess, but do so while encased in another's body, a sensation you might find difficult to live with at first but will soon settle into as readily as we do ourselves. The really difficult part is having to compensate for the variation between Earth creatures and ourselves. It is not easy to take a primitive mind and have it control sophisticated beings."

Mark smiled. "You never stop, do you?"

"But you are such a good subject, Markcarter. So filled with flaws."

"To continue," he said, not giving Mark a chance to retort, "you must remain close to me and do exactly as I say. You, or more accurately, your host's body, is vulnerable to all the dangers of this planet. If you make a mistake, it is he who will suffer for it. And you could be left with problems of your own—psychological mostly, but physical damage is possible as well. Believe me, it is not worth the risk."

"Why physical damage to me? Is the process two-way?" Mark asked.

"It must of necessity be that way. To control a body on Tanterac, you on Mantz must receive and understand what that body is feeling. If you touch something hot on Tanterac, your mind on Mantz must command the host's hand to instantly withdraw. That would not occur were the system to be one way only."

Mark was facing a dichotomy of feelings. He was anxious to get back to the routine experience sessions, there to continue gathering the means of escape, but a diversion such as Creson was offering was a never-in-a-lifetime thing. He only hoped he would live long enough to share it with Kathy. "If it's that realistic, what about the air? Can I breathe it?"

"I suppose you could exist for a short time, but remember you will not be in your own body. We must only compensate for our needs; that is Mantzite needs, and this has already been accomplished with the two bodies we will occupy. You will find a device attached to your host's neck. Please refrain from touching it. It supplies the proper chemicals through the skin to what you would refer to as lungs. Anticipating your next question, gravity is less of a concern. Because of the insignificant difference in size between Mantz and Tanterac and the relative similarity of planet geology, we will not provide for gravitational variation. You should feel no worse there than you do here. And, as you probably are aware, you are less burdened by weight now then you were when you first invaded our planet."

Mark remembered the dizziness he felt early on. Since then, however, the rest and rejuvenation chamber had been compensating less and less, with the result that he was now fully acclimated to Mantz's weaker gravity. He briefly considered what would happen when he again felt the heavier pull of Earth. "Well, I'm ready when you are," he said, putting the idea aside.

Creson smiled then moved toward the hexagonal panel to press the lights necessary to gain Mark's release. As he did so he permitted the Earth man another glimpse of the five-light escape sequence—Mark matched it against his recall. On his way out of the chamber, he realized with a start that this time no calming chemicals had been applied. Uneasy without knowing why, he wondered what that meant. Was tranquilization considered unnecessary this time, or was this an oversight? The latter, if true, was promising; it showed weakness on the part of his captors. Perhaps they were "human" after all.

Following closely behind Creson, Mark was whisked once again through the beam tunnel to the laboratory containing the experience chamber. By now he was used to this unique method of travel, although how the tunnel was controlled was still a mystery. After plunging blindly into its opening he always reappeared exactly where Creson wanted to reappear, this even though the Mantzite never seemed to do anything beforehand to let the device know their intended destination. This time, with no tranquilizers to discourage him, he put the question to Creson. "How did the conveyer know we wanted to go here?"

Creson turned enough to fix his captive with a skeptical glare. To a Mantzite it was a simple matter to direct any of the planet's ubiquitous conveyers; one only had to project an image of one's destination before entering. But it would be foolish to permit the Earth man to gain such knowledge. Markcarter already had the power to project images, whether he was aware of that or not, and could thus, theoretically at least, control the conveyer. "It is too complicated for your inadequately prepared mind. Perhaps in time you will be better able to appreciate the concept." At that, he turned and continued into the room.

The chamber was as it had been before, except now there were two beams of light acting as tables—the second was obviously for Creson. These gently glowing panels lay side by side under an expanded projection of soft light. Creson pointed toward one then instructed Mark to lie down. Afterward he did the same on the other. When satisfied, he nodded toward Leipin who made final adjustments to each subject's position before moving to the control panel to initiate the procedure. "Now remember what I told you, Markcarter!" Creson said before nodding his final approval to Leipin.

He was standing on a hard surface overlooking what appeared to be buildings in the latter stages of deterioration—the transition was so sudden, he came close to losing his balance. Beneath his softly-cushioned, three-toed feet, he could feel a hard surface. It was like concrete only smoother and offering more of a hue of pink. The buildings, or what was left of them, appeared to be composed of more than one kind of material. There was the hard, rock-like substance on which he and Creson now stood, a softer, more pliant material that probably began life as a plant, and a smooth seamless covering of unknown composition—the latter stretched like rubber across the top of each structure. Roads, similar to many he'd seen on Earth, flowed through what must at one time have been a large city. They, like the structures, were in a bad state of deterioration.

Thin, sharply delineated lines crisscrossed the surface of the ground in all directions, giving the appearance of a giant jigsaw puzzle. Upon closer examination they proved to be deep cuts. The pattern was distinctly geometric, suggesting the influence of intelligent beings, but what purpose they served was not immediately obvious. Between the structures there were plants, not many but some, and these looked more natural to Mark than did the alien vegetation of Mantz. It was not that he could remember seeing identical plants on Earth, just that these flowed more like one expected from something growing out of the ground: more random, less perfectly sculpted. Not so easily accepted was their rich, dark green color, darker than anything seen on either Mantz or Earth. The sky was green as well, a light green, but whether this reflected the chemical composition of the air or unseen mega-forests of rich vegetation, Mark had no way of knowing. Like Mantz, two suns angled their way through the sky. Viewed from the surface, they appeared equal in size, and Mark could sense if not feel their intensity. It was like standing in an air-conditioned room looking out on a hot day. He wondered what it was that kept him from being overheated.

The feeling of being there in person was as vivid as it had been during the experience sessions. All his senses were alive and working. He could see, he could feel. He could detect odors and hear noises, most of which were as yet unidentified. And it was himself, not his host, seeing, hearing and smelling. He lifted one leg then stamped it down, recognizing no difference between the resulting feeling and that which he would expect were it his own leg and his own body. And choosing to lift the leg was more than he had been permitted to do while sharing another's experience. This was, for the moment at least, *his* body; he had it all to himself and could create new experiences which his host could only observe—an ironic reversal of roles.

He looked to his left and saw an unfamiliar Mantzite standing next to him, its eyes focused on his. "You're Spot?" he asked, the doubt obvious in his voice.

"Precisely. And you are the inferior creature from Earth?" Creson asked in return.

"Precisely." Mark issued the reply with a smile and a now natural contraction of his eyes. "I must admit you look better in that body than you did before. You must be considerably older on Mantz than you are here."

"Regrettably it would appear so. No doubt the inevitable result of the creatures to which I must from time to time subject myself." Ending the banter, Creson pointed in the general direction of the structures and began describing what they were. "This was beautiful at one time, somewhat like our own planet although less technically advanced. Those structures you see were where the creatures of Tanterac worked. They were brought here daily by surface craft capable of propelling them rapidly along the ground—primitive compared to my planet but more advanced than Earth."

"We have surface craft," Mark said in defense.

"Yes, but not as progressed as these." He pointed at the cuts in the paved surface. "Those groves had two purposes: to produce an even flow of power and to permit computer control of all vehicles. Creatures from this planet would enter a machine, dial a destination, then release themselves in full confidence to the system. The computer could keep track of everyone at once, thus permitting incredible speeds with no danger to any traveler. It would speed vehicles up or slow them down as it thought necessary to permit what was sometimes only fractional separations between them—can you imagine how unnerving it would be for the uninitiated to watch so many vehicles closing in at such fearful speeds? The groves themselves were covered with a soft transparent substance, this to permit pedestrians to cross over without fear of falling in—naturally, the computer would compensate for their presence. As you can see, the groves, and indeed the entire system, have suffered from neglect."

"What happened?" Mark asked.

"We will get to that in time." It was a firm response that tolerated no objection, and Creson followed it by moving away in the direction of the structures. Although wondering what kind of new game his host was playing, Mark remembered the admonition to stay close. He moved quickly to catch up then positioned himself at Creson's side.

"There are creatures still living within these structures," Creson said, "and we can never be certain what dangers they represent. Should one be seen, please make no movement other than that which I suggest to you." As he spoke he reached into a fold within his fur and produced the small flashlight device that Mark recognized as a multipurpose beam, the same carried by the unfortunate Wilpin. In plain view of his captive, Creson made adjustments to its circular dials then held it up as one would a weapon. "I have put this on burn rather than destroy. It should be enough to discourage the uninvited from approaching too closely. If you check within your fold, I believe you will find one of your own."

Mark was surprised that Creson would give him a weapon, even if it were someone else's hand that held it. Reaching into the area from which Creson had produced his, he felt a thin, pencil-like object which he then, with some difficulty, wrestled free. It made him wonder whether his new "covering" on Mantz came equipped with such a pocket. If so, he doubted it would house anything like this.

With the device in hand, he made the adjustments he had seen Creson make earlier, noting as he did so the frown that appeared on the latter's face. Too late he realized that he had demonstrated how closely he had paid attention to the workings of the weapon, even while appearing not to do so. To lessen the impact of this, he held it up for Creson to see then said, "Is it set correctly?"

Creson merely nodded his head, having already seen what adjustments were made. The weapon was essentially harmless; it was there to gain knowledge of the Earth man's proclivity toward violence not to serve as protection—there was little left in this vicinity to do them harm, at least not serious harm.

They resumed their walk through the city where, after a short period of ominous silence, Creson was again pointing out places of interest and describing what once took place within them. He spoke of the function of each structure, why it was there and why it was shaped as it was. The story he told was of an advanced society with definite ideas about themselves. Everything had to conform to those ideas, even the elaborate stone carvings found around doors and windows. One could liken it to all of Earth being filled with Victorian buildings and nothing else.

"It boils down to custom, I suppose. They simply preferred to present themselves in this manner." As he talked, Creson headed for the entrance to one particularly large structure. When they were close enough to examine its v-shaped portico, he said, "You will note the statues. They are found at the entrance of almost every building, and serve to support the religious needs of these people. The few buildings that do not have statues were tolerated but in a condescending manner. It was their way of accommodating the last remnants of primitive cultures—no one took them seriously. The belief symbolized by these statues permeated the entire planet, a sociological anomaly to be sure, and thus it became easy to maintain a feeling of absolute certainty that what they believed was the one and only truth; their doctrine was irrefutable. This proved to be their undoing, I'm afraid. It permitted little room to explain, let alone accept, beings superior to themselves—us. Our existence was simply not possible; we were in direct conflict with eons of teachings. Whatever we claimed to be was anti-truth in their eyes, a contradiction to what could not be contradicted." He sighed before continuing. "Even if they could have admitted our existence, they had no experience in attempting meaningful accommodation with ideas other than their own."

He paused again, this time looking at Mark as if he feared he was getting ahead of himself. "We will talk more of this later." To ward off unwanted comment, he quickly launched himself back into his narrative. "Suggesting a deity from which they themselves evolved, the statues follow their own image. Thus you get a fair idea of how these beings looked in their heyday. As you can see they are not that biologically different from you or me. They have appendages, two more than either of us, but all serving essentially the same function and all boasting grasping power at the ends. Their cranial capacity was exceptionally large suggesting that, in time, they could have progressed further even than ourselves. Body size is smaller than either your people or mine, but the musculoskeletal structure is what you might expect of that size considering the level of gravity that exists on this planet—similar to Mantz, as I mentioned previously. The smallness of their heavily-lidded eyes was necessary considering the brightness of this world, where both suns shine unmercifully all day long. These suns, by the way, are closer to this planet than ours are to Mantz, and were it not for this protective covering we wear, we would be unbearably warm."

Mark looked downward to note for the first time a thin webbing that covered all of his Mantz fur. It contained so many "holes" that he could not imagine it doing any good, but that he felt comfortable in what he could easily believe was a hot world was undeniable.

"Although you cannot tell this from the statues, their skin was dark— a normal consequence to intense ultra violet radiation."

"You keep referring to them in the past tense," Mark interjected. "What happened, are they all dead?"

Creson stiffened for a moment, but then appeared to relent. "It is obvious that something negative has occurred, but if you will postpone that inquiry a bit longer, I will be in a better position to explain, and you in turn will have the background to understand."

He completed his narrative on the nature and meaning of the large structure—or what remained of it—then moved on, describing as before all that he felt would assist Mark in his need for background. It was a fascinating tour; Mark was actually walking in the place where an alien society, light years from Earth, once conducted its daily business, business not all that different from that of his own world. That societies so far apart from one another—Mantz, Tanterac and Earth—could shared such similar needs, was of itself remarkable. Except for the stone representations of its inhabitants, this could have been an ancient city of Earth.

It was, however, depressing to know, as Mark was now sure he did know, that this society was no more. It had risen to impressive levels then...collapsed. Could this happen to his own people? Could it happen to Earth? It was a haunting thought.

They went on, Creson playing the instructor and Mark willing assuming the role of student, until suddenly the city gave way to a rich, green forest. The only continuity between urban and rural was the continuation of the roadway and its deep surface groves, which crashed into the green void as if unable to stop. An odd transition, unexpected but inoffensive. A drab city richly bordered in a dark, unbroken green.

About where the forest began, a pair of Mantzites stood guard, beam weapons in hand and eyes roaming the trees. Walking toward them, Creson projected a greeting—Mark easily picked this up, the response as well; either his skill was expanding or the Mantzites were projecting a wider beam of thought than before. Creson made no further attempt to communicate and the guards did not try to delay them. "Why are they here?" Mark asked.

Creson kept walking but said over his shoulder, "For us, actually. The city contains little of potential harm, but one never knows. It helps to have assistance within hailing distance."

"What about outside the city? Mark asked. "Is there danger there? Will there be guards to call on if we get in trouble?"

Creson shot him a look of amusement. "I do believe that is three questions at once. Is this a trend? Will you next offer four at a time, then five?"

"You hypocritical smartass, I 'do believe' you just hit me with three questions yourself!"

Creson returned his head to the front then smiled. "I do believe you are right. Must be the corrupting influence. At any rate, there is danger outside the city, from both animals and unfriendly remnants of the society which used to rule this planet. I suggest you keep your beam handy."

They walked for miles along the Tanterac landscape, giving Mark plenty of opportunity to examine the alien vegetation. His questions were many and ranged from the variation of plants—in structure, not in color; they were all that same dark green—to the periodic appearance of land and air creatures. The walk itself, with the rapid pace Creson set for himself, was reminiscent of the time not so long ago when the two walked together from Earth to Mantz. "This body is in good shape," Mark commented after an hour of this. "I'm not in the least bit tired."

"Recognizing your human frailties, we made certain that a good physical specimen was available."

"How about yours?" Mark asked. "You don't seem to be hurting any."

Creson took a deep breath then flexed his muscles as if to remind himself of how comfortable this loner body was. "Although not as critical as in your case, I also have available to me a good physical specimen. I must admit it feels good to be able to do so much with so little effort. It is like being young again."

The comment triggered a thought in Mark. "How old are you anyway?" he asked.

Creson's eyes contracted, which Mark interpreted as the lead-in to another sarcastic evasion. "Out of the cradle but not so old as to be disinterested in the mysticism surrounding procreation. In that respect, it pains me to admit, we might have something in common." He sighed once then continued in a more serious vein. "In truth I was around when the nation in which you reside was first approached by visitors across the sea."

"You mean Columbus? But that was five hundred years ago!"

"I am impressed by your proclivity toward mathematics."

"How long do you people live anyway?" Mark asked, ignoring the jab.

"I am what you might call middle aged. Unless I am forced to dwell extensively in the company of creatures such as yourself, I should arrive at twelve hundred of your years."

"Twelve hundred years!" Mark wondered if such longevity could be passed on. To Earth people in particular.

After walking in silence for another few minutes, Mark, even while uncomfortable with the possibility of an affirmative answer, asked softly, "Are you ever tempted to keep the bodies you occupy?"

Creson immediately understood his companion's concern. "It would work for only a short time at best. After that the host body suffers serious and sometimes irreversible damage."

"What is a 'short time' to someone who lives twelve hundred years?"

"My apologies," Creson said. "I often avoid specifics believing they would have little meaning to you; our day is not your day, our hour is not your hour. If you wish I will, as I believe I have been doing with statements involving years, routinely convert time into Earth terms. I cannot, however, guarantee the accuracy of such rapid conversions."

"Fair enough," Mark said, recognizing that Creson had still not answered his question. Was he being evasive; was there something here that applied to his own situation, perhaps a Mantzite controlling his own body back on Earth? "Does this procedure work on animals?" he asked tentatively.

"Of course," Creson answered. "Slight modifications would obviously be necessary, as was done in your case, but there is no reason why this would not work on any creature."

"Then why don't you use it on Earth? Why convert to a dog when you could just enter a dog's mind and make him go where you wanted to go."

"How I wish we could," Creson said wistfully. The problem here is that, although our consciousness remains fully active throughout the process, we must of necessity rely on the subject's cranium to gather and correctly interpret complex information. In the case of an Earth canine, that is sadly lacking. We would glean little of scientific value."

"But a human can do all that; why don't you jump inside a human's head?" Without realizing he was doing it, Mark slowed his breathing less he miss part of the answer.

"We could do so for only a short time. We estimate a maximum of...one Earth day...before the human system would begin to break down. And to relieve you of the concern that is so easily detected in your voice, we would not use this method on you for the simple reason that the resulting deterioration would be such that your damaged body would reveal to even the most amateur human pathologist that something unusual had caused your expiration. There would be found in your body chemical substances unknown to your planet. On the other hand, were we to use human hosts for a short period, then 'jump,' as you so quaintly put it, to someone else, the original host would retain the memory of everything we did while in his body. Whether believed by his fellow humans or not, he or she would be able to relate to the authorities our entire purpose."

"You mean this guy will remember everything I do?" Mark asked, indicating his host's body.

"Precisely. Although essentially deactivated by the machine, he is sharing this experience with you in much the same manner that you share someone else's."

Mark considered the implications of what Creson was saying. He had acquired knowledge from his hosts during experience chamber sessions; was the creature whose body he now controlled acquiring knowledge from him? Had he, in effect, been found out? It might already be too late, but he had to watch his thoughts.

"In addition to the problems I have already stated," Creson continued, "we would need an incredible number of complicated and highly-expensive machines to be able to support all Earth explorers simultaneously. Not at all sensible and not as efficient as converting to some harmless and readily available animal, taking our minds along with us."

Mark's eyes widened at the implications of Creson's comment. "How many machines would you need; how many explorers do you have on Earth?"

Creson threw Mark another of his skeptical glances, but still answered the question. "Let me just say that we do not yet have enough to be able to launch a full-scale investigation of your planet—and I emphasize that we are discussing investigation not invasion. It takes time to install the necessary supporting equipment, both for communication and for efficient movement around the globe—but we have plenty of time; remember, we live twelve hundred...years. Another few years and we might know enough about your species to begin to move such equipment into place. In short, we are still in a preliminary phase. Ultimately there will be tens of thousands of our representatives on your planet, all of whom will travel in secrecy until the moment is deemed proper to reveal our presence."

Mark was instinctively uncomfortable at the thought of so many uninvited alien invaders sneaking around his planet. "How long will that take?" he asked.

"It depends on what we find. It could take decades, even longer. It is critically important that the timing be correct, so important that we will not even consider announcing ourselves until all those with the power to make such a decision agree."

"The Council?" Mark asked.

"Precisely."

"Suppose the people don't want you?"

"Then we will leave," Creson answered immediately. "We have no desire to impose. Should we be unable to convince your fellow creatures of our good intentions, we will leave a number where we can be reached, then 'cut out'—I do hope you appreciate my attempts to communicate in your own vernacular," he said with a smile and slightly contracting pupils.

"Remarkable," Mark replied. "I almost mistook you for a fellow human."

"Now, now, there is no need to be unkind." Creson faked a frown at the suggested insult.

Preoccupied in banter and conversation, neither of them saw the rock as it flew out of the dense brush bordering the road. It landed close to Mark, took a single bounce, then hit him a glancing blow on the shin. He yelled in pain then grabbed his leg. Creson, realizing what was happening, aimed his weapon at a spot slightly higher than he expected the assailant to be. It made no sound but a crackling noise was heard wherever its rays hit.

"Aim your beam about ten meters off the ground. Do not attempt to hit any moving object, only the vegetation." Cringing in pain, Mark tried to do as he was told. The crackling noise increased.

"Quickly," Creson said, "rearrange your body molecules to permit the rocks to pass through. We do not have much time; they will be back."

Mark began the conversion process without thinking. He was driven by instinct, an instinct born of pain and fear of what might be out there. His mind raced through the process of instructing his body's molecules in the best way to avoid contact with alien objects, and in less than thirty seconds they were as fluid as a cloud of smoke. Then he glanced over at Creson to learn what he should do next.

He was startled to note that Creson had not yet completed the process. How he knew this was not clear, but he knew. He had converted faster than his Mantzite captor.

Not until then did he realize that he had employed a talent he did not even know he had. Where he picked it up, he had no idea. There was no experience session that focused on that, nor could he remember it being considered even vaguely by the hosts whose experiences he had shared. Yet, without really trying, he had done it.

Or had he done it? Had he learned more than he realized, or was it simply that he was using the body of a creature who already knew the process? *But I am this guy's mind,* he thought. *It isn't him thinking, it's me!* Confused but encouraged, he continued staring at Creson while the Mantzite completed his conversion.

Afterward, Creson turned to him with a look of appraisal that made him feel exposed and vulnerable. But the look told him a lot; that the knowledge he had just employed was really his, and that his Mantzite captor was not pleased with the thought. The crisis passed when, after a long moment, Creson lowered his eyes as if tiring of the game. "You will probably not need the beam any longer, but keep it handy in the event it becomes prudent to frighten the creatures away. I suggest you remain alert for rocks as well. This procedure is not infallible; the body adjusts more rapidly if you can see the objects as they head your way." Then he turned and began walking at his normal but hurried pace down the road, his manner as sullen as Mark had ever seen it.

Concerned about what was going through his Mantzite captor's mind, Mark hastened to keep up. He had once again given himself away. At least he thought he had—maybe he was being paranoiac, reading too much into Creson's look. Creson would not have issued the command to convert if he did not think his charge capable of obeying. Unless those were Creson's people throwing rock from the trees, this was too dangerous a situation to risk loosing his prize Earth man on a stupid test!

So which was it, himself or his host. He wondered which he preferred. This would not be a bad skill to have should his captors come at him, but their knowing that he possessed it could make them anxious to do so. And they could come at him when he least expected it, when there was insufficient time to convert.

His train of thought was interrupted when a collection of small buildings abruptly appeared through a break in the vegetation. The transition was so sudden that it caused him to pull up and draw a sharp breath. One moment there was thick forest and the next the start of a fair-sized community, one that looked as if it competed with the forest for living space—if so, it was a loosing battle; buildings and paths alike were overgrown with dark green plants. Unlike the city, here there were indications that it was still in use. A thin plume of smoke snaked its way into the green-tinted sky from one of the smaller structures.

Mark decided they were dwellings of some kind. Circular in shape, they appeared to flow into one another to form clusters of half circles. The building material was probably wood, or some local equivalent of wood, but there were filmy openings surrounding the entire lower portion of each structure, leaving only enough room for supports. Most of the rooftop coverings had either disappeared or were presently in tatters, and indeed, the buildings themselves seemed to be in the last stages of disintegration; their rubble was scattered carelessly about the ground. The village, if that's what it was, stretched well into the forest but, conspicuously, there were no residents in view.

"Are there people here?" Mark asked.

As if in answer, a barrage of stones flew outward from the edge of the forest surrounding the village. Calling on a recently-implanted Mantz instinct, Mark automatically focused on the incoming objects, finding it natural and easy to do so. He had no inclination to duck or to otherwise avoid them. As expected, all passed harmlessly through his body without his being able to detect their substance. Only afterward was he surprised at the casual manner in which he met the alien danger, at how quickly he had become acclimated to the use of alien skills.

"I believe that answers your question," Creson said ironically. "Do not attempt to disperse them with your beam; it is no longer necessary." That said, he continued on toward the structures.

Mark followed, but his eyes, now led by Earth instincts rather than instincts borrowed from his hosts, fixed on the hostile creatures that bled from the woods, rocks in their hands and defeated expressions on their faces. They were identical to the statues he had seen in the city, except their color was darker and they looked on the wrong edge of civilized. The savagery of these people was demonstrated when, after a moment of uncertain staring, they were again encouraged to throw stones at their unwelcome guests. It was impossible to ignore these beings as Creson had instructed, especially with so many rocks flying through the air, and Mark was relieved when he and his Mantzite host moved into one of the structures.

Inside, with the only distraction the thud of hard objects hitting the outer walls, Creson began to explain: "This was a typical home of a type used by most of the creatures of this planet. It is still employed for that purpose to some degree, but its occupants are no longer the same beings they once were. A transition has taken place, a terrible transition as it turned out—these people have virtually destroyed themselves. It took, perhaps two years for this to happen but, as you can plainly see, it did happen." He spread his hands outward to indicate he was talking about the entire community then said, "Regardless of where you might travel on this planet, the sight will be essentially the same: an all-but-deserted city and a once-thriving community reduced to savagery. Where there had once been intelligent and progressive beings, there are now only groups of desperate animals. And there is little that anyone can do about it."

Mark waited for Creson to continue, expecting finally to hear the explanation the Mantzite had promised, the how and why of what happened to these people. But Creson was deep in his own thoughts and kept his silence. In time he sighed as if relenting, then said, "I suppose you can say we did this—I refer to my fellow citizens now. Roughly a thousand of your years ago we were in the same stage of investigation here as we are now on Earth. A significant difference is we were not as strict in regard to how cautiously we should proceed. Mistakes were made, serious mistakes, the most serious of which was to permit the local populace to become suspicious. They sensed something out of the ordinary was happening: devil-like beings were appearing among them. After we became aware of this, we made our second mistake: we dismissed it as harmless, or at least easily correctable. After all, were we not going to soon make our presence known in any event?

"Since, at that time, we chose to assume their form rather than the safer domesticated pet approach we now employ on Earth, it was easier for them to detect our presence. Simply put, we had too little knowledge of the behavior expected of a Tanterac body. At first they kept their fears to themselves, not always able to tell who was real and who was an unknown 'devil,' but this had the effect of preventing us from knowing the depth of their collective concern. Apparently they regarded us in a religious sense; we were representative of either their god or its antithesis. As I alluded to earlier, being essentially a mono-religious society, they had no experience in dealing with alternative possibilities. In their minds, there were none. There was only the one 'truth' and what was true at the present had always been true and would always be true in the future—there was seldom, if ever, a challenge to this way of thinking. Thus, everything had to be explained in that vein: we either existed in accordance with unimpeachable beliefs or we did not exist at all.

"Eventually we accepted the seriousness of the problem and set about finding a way of calming the populace down, of blocking the disastrous path down which their minds were leading them. Plans to introduce ourselves were accelerated—better to know the truth than to continue to invent unsettling stories. It turned out to be precisely the wrong thing to do. They took our sudden emergence as proof positive of a spiritual invasion. They were certain they were being punished, that their god was angry, that She was intent upon ending their civilization. Hopelessness abounded; finger-pointing became rampant, everyone blamed everyone else for invoking Her anger. Widespread civil unrest began, unrest that continued unabated for two years and ended with the reduction of their civilization to what you see now.

"We tried everything to convince them of what we were and what we were not, but nothing we did or said worked. We were, after all, spiritual incantations to them, probably there to punish but not to be trusted in any event. We finally had to essentially abandon the planet, both to protect ourselves and to provide an atmosphere which we hoped would encourage them to revert back to what they once were. That is, what they were before we came.

"Sadly, it was too late. It made no difference; we could not reverse their self-induced decline into savagery. Not then and not now—thousands of additional years and hundreds of generations might pass before this planet is once again as it was; maybe it will never be the same. We visit from time to time, both to look for signs of hope and to remind ourselves of the holocaust which could recur should we again ignore the rules of planetary exploration."

At that, Creson turned to stare pointedly at his human companion, his face a mixture of rigidity and sadness. His last projected thought had deliberately emphasized its latter half. "Perhaps you now understand how important we consider the situation with you. It must be viewed in conjunction to what happened here. If we do less than what we know from experience to be necessary, Earth could very well look like this in time. A very short time."

Mark was at a loss for something to say. Creson's motive for taking him on this trip was now obvious—and he had certainly been effective in making his point. A discomfort grew in his borrowed stomach as he considered the implications of what the Mantzite was saying. The Council could not—and apparently would not—release him if to do so would set the stage for another Tanterac. On the other hand, if they were careless enough to permit their captive to escape, he might bring about the same thing, assuming enough humans believed his story.

An inbred sense of survival made him challenge Creson's argument. It assumed he and his all-wise Council knew what would happen if Earth suddenly discovered that a cosmic Big Brother was watching, that he had been for over a year. But they did *not* know what would happen. Earth was not Tanterac. Their presence, even if that came via a surprise discovery, might be accepted as nothing worse than a real life "E.T." "Is this the only time it happened?" Mark asked softly. "I mean, have you had problems introducing yourselves since then?"

"No. We discontinued the program until more stringent safeguards could be put into place; since their implementation, we have had nothing that even remotely compares to this. As with other moments from our past, however, the pain of this event remains with us—the experience chamber, as you well know, is very effective in that regard. So vividly do we remember what happened that we feel physically incapable of deviating from the more successful program we now employ. I ask you to understand that when considering your own plight. It is not that we are unsympathetic to what you face; it is simply that we place more emphasis on the welfare of your fellow creatures."

Mark was incapable of further comment. The Mantzite, his voice pleading, was obviously sincere in what he said. But he wanted "understanding" from a potential victim. Precisely what was it that he wanted Mark to "understand"?

"Adding to the intensity of our regard for this matter," Creson said softly, "is the salient fact of the Council, one of whose members was directly responsible for the Tanterac disaster."

C H A P T E R   2 2

No matter how many times she replayed the video tape and no matter what action she took to examine the more critical frames in detail, she could glean nothing more. Everything leading up to the time the animal was supposed to have talked was there, including its surprise response to the injection—everything but the sound itself. By now Kathy had rejected the possibility of someone standing in the wings playing tricks. That would not even begin to explain how an animal could act in such a human way. A human sound had come out of that dog, a sound that she heard but the camera did not. As illogical as that might seem, there was just no way she could be mistaken.

With acceptance of this as fact, the scene of her on the telephone, with the dog paying close attention, took on new meaning. The animal had been aware of everything said—Kathy's uneasiness grew each time this segment was replayed.

"Okay, what do I do now?" she said aloud, her voice breaking the stillness of the night and adding to her discomfort. She thought of trying to get him to do it again, after the tranquilizer wore off, but that dog was angry going to asleep and he was sure to be angry coming out. And keeping an alert animal tied to a pipe in her closet, effectively blocking the room's only exit, did not strike her as the best of strategy. "No, I've got to keep him doped up," she mumbled, her tone unconvincing even to herself.

For the moment it was the only thing to do, although what good would come out of it, she had no idea. Sooner of later, she would run out of medication.

She had maybe four more hours to figure it out, four hours before the animal was awake enough to...voice...a protest. If a reasonable alternative did not present itself by then, she would give it another injection. If she guessed wrong and it was already too late, she would say "Nice chatting with you" then run like hell.

She sat on the edge of the bed wringing her hands and fighting her mind. It was so hard to think—why did she find that surprising? *Mark bumped into one of these animals; could this have happened to him? Is that why he's missing?* She could not help the wry smile that broke through at the thought of interrogating a German shepherd for information on her boyfriend's whereabouts. *Ridiculous!* But the smile faded as she considered what had already happened. If she were right, and some kind of speech *had* come out of that dog, then why was it "ridiculous" to try to get him to do it again—assuming he was properly restrained, of course, which meant tied hand and foot? What would she have to lose? No one would see or hear, thus no one would catch her playing the fool.

She got up from the bed, inserted a fresh tape into the video camera then pushed the record button. Now if anything happened—movement, if not scary voices—it would be picked up. As before, she positioned it to take in the entire room then concealed its presence with clothing. When she turned back, she saw a German shepherd still sleeping away a tranquilizer high, its slow breathing suggesting it would continue do so for some time.

As her fear abated, her curiosity became aroused. She wondered whether there was anything else about this dog that was out of the ordinary. Maybe it was a sophisticated robot, made of metal instead of flesh. *Some metal*, she thought, remembering the touch of it--softness and warmth. She moved to its side, slowly and with obvious hesitation, then watched for a moment before kneeling down. When nothing changed, she positioned her hand over the sleeping body then, with a deep intake of air to steel her nerves, brought it down. There was only the soft and warmth felt before. Encouraged, she began to stroke, hesitantly at first, as if at any second she might have to pull back her hand. On impulse she inspected the fur around its neck, thinking there might be a remote-controlled speaker to explain the voice. *But it wouldn't explain why no noise appeared on tape!* she thought in disappointment. In any event, there was nothing but the animal itself.

It did not react to the human touch, and this encouraged Kathy to continue. She roamed her hands over other parts of its body—ribs, paws, neck—but found nothing unusual. This was, in everything she knew to look for, a normal dog. She could not help the relief that inched over her as each additional try proved equally as fruitless. She paused a moment to catch her breath, then leaned forward to try again, this time starting lower down. Eventually she arrived at its lower right side.

Whatever relief had wormed its way into her system disappeared the moment her hand touched it. There was something that shouldn't be there, something hard. Her excitement grew as she examined with her fingertips the object tucked just under the skin. It felt like a thin flashlight. She rolled the dog over and searched the area with her eyes. Whatever it was, it appeared to have been surgically inserted—there was no opening. But a few minutes of additional probing proved her wrong. There was an opening, and it was held closed, not by surgical stitches, but by some kind of springy clamp. By then her hands were shaking so much that prying it open was an onerous chore. She did so just enough to reach inside and grab the thin metallic device that was lodged there. The sight of it did nothing to calm her shaking.

She carried it to the bed as if it were a stick of aging dynamite ready to blow. Sitting herself down, she cradled it in her hands then began a slow examination, rotating it as she did so to get a good look at all sides. This was a complicated device. It had many sections, each of which revolved around the main body. Little markings, peppered with characters that made absolutely no sense to her, appeared in each section. It was obviously not a flashlight but what it was, and what purpose it served she could only imagine. About half way down the side were two depressions that appeared to serve as finger grips. Or maybe a trigger—she stared at them for a number of minutes, trying to decide whether it was wise to find out which; did she dare experiment with this thing without knowledge of what the results might be? Curiosity won out, helped by the conviction that she could not stop now.

Among other things, there was the captured animal, possibly connected to Mark's disappearance, possibly not, but in any event going to wake up sooner or later with what might be a desire for revenge. Determination only barely overpowering fear, she placed two fingers in the depressions, held the "flashlight" so it would shine on a nearby wall, then squeezed. An image of, "Safety is on," implanted itself in her brain.

"Jesus Christ!" She threw the instrument across the room, rolled off the bed then pressed herself against the wall. That little device had talked. It had said something; and the voice was identical to that heard earlier from the dog. Her eyes widened in sudden understanding; maybe *this* was the voice she had heard—the device was doing the talking, not the dog.

At least this was more a more acceptable explanation; it made sense. *Or did it?* It would still not explain the dog's expression or how the recording fit the animal's reaction so well. The same objection would apply to someone controlling the voice from outside the room: coordination between animal reaction and sound was too perfect, too unlikely.

Recovering her composure, she revisited the device then, with two shaking fingers, picked it up. It took a moment to drum up the courage, but soon she again had her fingers over the depressions and was ready to squeeze. She steeled herself to suffer the recorded announcement.

"Safety is on."

Although this time it was expected, she still jumped at the words and had difficulty holding on to the instrument. But at least the response was consistent; the same message had appeared; apparently it could be made to recur whenever she wished. Further, it really did sound like a simple recording.

Recording! Dashing over to the video recorder, she rewound the last few minutes then set it to play. As she watched and listened, she occasionally saw and heard her image mumbling, thus assuring that sounds were being picked up. At the proper time, but with only a loud curse as a preamble, her image thrust the small metallic device across the room then fled to a distant wall.

"Where's the damn sound!"

The video continued, with her image cautiously approaching the offending device then again making it 'talk.' As before, the camera picked up no sounds other than those made by her.

"Damn!" she exclaimed as she reset the video, intent on trying once again. This time she sat only a foot from the camera and under the direct scrutiny of it's eye. It also put her within a few inches of the audio pickup. Five times in a row she squeezed the enigmatic impressions, and five times in a row the same caution came back at her from the tiny instrument. Satisfied, she rewound the camera then played it back. Nothing. No words of caution had been detected by the video recorder.

"Crap!" She did not understand. Whatever this device was, it was saying something; she could make it happen anytime she wished. But the sound it made was being ignored by the recorder. The same thing had happened with the dog. It had spoken but in such a way that its voice could not be recorded. How was that possible?

As if out of a dream, she set the camera yet again, then returned to the bed. As she sat there hoping that out of the quiet of the night would come answers, her eyes rested on the sleeping animal, its form now taking on a new dimension. What was it she had here? Was it real, or was she enveloped in some kind of delirium, induced by fears of loosing Mark?

She let her eyes rest again on the talking flashlight in her hand. With so many dials and so many sections on each dial, the possibilities it offered were considerable, more than she could immediately calculate. But did she dare try any of them? The machine kept saying, "Safety is on," which suggested some kind of weapon. If so, and if it had been left on "safe," didn't common sense dictate that she leave it that way?

But this was not the time for common sense. Common sense was not believing in talking dogs and sounds that perfectly good video recorders could not hear!

With as much self-righteousness as she could muster, she pointed the instrument at a window and turned the topmost dial one position. Nothing happened. She let out the breath she had not realized was being held then looked down at the depressions she'd squeezed earlier. Were they the trigger? Did they have to be squeezed to activate each new setting?

She sat there trying to justify what she knew she would do anyway. In time she got up from the bed, moved to the window, opened it wide then pointed the device in the direction of the forest. Without allowing herself time to think, she pressed downward on the depressions.

A thin beam of light appeared, illuminating about ten yards of atmosphere outside the window. After a second it vanished.

Nothing else happened, and shaking in nervous expectation, Kathy turned the topmost dial one additional notch then tried again. The same thing: nothing except that thin beam of light. For the entire length of the top dial, it was the same: no visible change in the response. Whatever the purpose of this device, it was not obvious.

She restored the dial to its initial position then pressed the depressions to make sure it was once again crying out "safety." Then she turned the second dial one position and pointed the device out the window for a second round of tests. This time she was less nervous as she squeezed the two indentations on its side.

She could feel the strength of the heavy beam of light that shot a full city block into the dark. It hit a large boulder and converted it instantly into a pile of rubble. There had been no sound attached to the action.

Kathy saw it all in the light's aftermath. One moment there was a rock, the next, a pile of small stones from which a cloud of dust was just beginning to rise.

She continued to squeeze for another few seconds before she could think to let go. Fortunately the destructive beam had terminated after its initial burst—there was not another. When she felt herself capable of doing so, she inched the instrument back through the window then guided it toward a secure place on the old wooden coffee table that sat nearby. Then she backed up to the bed and lowered herself down. "What in the hell is going on here?" she whispered softly. Her eyes moved to the sleeping animal where they probed, without hope of explanation, its inert body.

"What are you?" she asked the unconscious form. "And what in the hell do I do now?"

An hour later she was still sitting on the bed and still staring at her tranquilized captive. Aware finally of the chilly night air, she permitted herself to move as far as the window. Once it was closed, she considered the weapon she had so recently fired through it. It was deceptively innocent-looking, a toy, a flashlight with dials. She picked it up then returned the second row of dials to its original position. Then she forced herself to re-test the safety, almost dropping it again when it announced in its unique way that it was not going to make the hotel vanish.

She was without a clue. Nothing she could think of made sense. She crossed over to the animal and reaffirmed that it was still breathing and that it was still under the effect of the tranquilizing drug. She had another three hours before a decision would have to be made whether or not to administer another dose. Three hours to figure out how to get it to...to respond. Yes, that was it: she had to get it, or whoever controlled it, to...talk. Talk about who and what it was and what it knew about Mark. She considered the weapon lying in her hand. She could threaten the animal with it, assuming it was capable of understanding such an action— the idea was still hard to accept.

There was the danger to herself to consider as well. If she did let it wake up, what was it likely to do—she couldn't see it letting her get close enough to administer another shot? And what if it saw her threat as the bluff it really was—regardless of what that animal might represent, she did not want to see it disintegrate as did the rock. She chuckled at the irony: Here she was sitting in a western town, covering a dog with her "gun." "This town ain't big enough for both of us, doggie!" she whispered, her attempt at humor weak and unconvincing.

To hedge her bets, she prepared two additional syringes then placed them close by on the bed. Then she removed the belt from her bathrobe and another from a pair of slacks and proceeded to tie the dog's front and rear paws—fear made her tie them tightly. When she was sure they would hold regardless of what the animal might try, she returned to the bed to wait. It was just after midnight; it would be close to three in the morning before the tranquilizer wore off and the animal awoke. The problem now, as she saw it, was to stay awake until then. These dogs were known to have escaped bonds in the past—something Kathy could now more easily accept—and she did not want it to surprise her while she slept.

Knowing she had to stay awake, however, made it harder to do so. After only an hour, even while holding the weapon in a ready position all that time, her head began to dip—a momentary surge of fear brought her back. She tried the television. Reception in the mountain-bound valley was not all that good, and the programming options at that late hour were almost nonexistent, but at least it was noise.

The strategy worked, but only for a half hour. Then she was back to the head dipping—it took a monumental effort to keep from giving in to it. She tried standing up, then she tried walking around the room. Again it worked for only a short time. Plus, it was tiring. As a form of compromise, she traded the bed for a plain wooden chair set in the center of the room. Before sitting down on it, she checked to see that her position would permit her to monitor the sleeping animal. She also checked to see that the syringes were within easy reach.

By the middle of the third hour she was nodding every few seconds and there was little she could do to stop it. She tried bouncing her legs up and down, but in no time at all they had slowed to a bare twitch. She tried humming, but could manage nothing more than a pitiful moan after only a few minutes. The battle to stay awake was not going well. "Damnit!" she cried, pleased at the countering effect the sound of her own voice had on her fading consciousness. Inventing a new burst of determination, she stood up beside the chair. As painful as the thought might be, she would have to stay on her feet, perhaps for as long as another hour.

She questioned whether she could. Maybe it made more sense to give the dog the tranquilizer now then hop into bed, there to await a less agonizing hour for their little chat. The thought was tempting, very tempting, but there was no way she could give up now. Besides she had to have this thing resolved before Ken Janos called. One more hour; just one more hour.

But it was more than an hour before her captive finally began to stir.

When she saw it was about to wake up, her fatigue began to fade. It vanished altogether as anticipation of confronting the unknown brought on a rush of adrenaline. After taking a deep breath to calm herself, she sat down on the chair then leaned forward with her elbows on her knees, hoping this might present a more determined appearance. She kept her eyes on the animal, afraid she would miss something should they waver for so much as a second. She had no idea what she was searching for or what she expected to come out of the encounter. She knew only that somewhere inside that enigma in front of her was an answer.

A number of agonizing minutes passed before the animal took a deep breath, let it out, then opened its eyes. For a moment it appeared to be confused, but then its eyes hardened and it began scanning the room, finally stopping at Kathy—her resolve came close to collapse when its head rose from the floor and its eyes latched onto hers. Its expression, accusatory and threatening at the same time, had resumed its all-too-human look. It appeared to be on the verge of taking control—seeing that look, it was easy to accept that it could. Kathy found it difficult to swallow. She had made a mistake letting this beast wake up. And now she was trapped.

Inexplicably, it then relaxed. Only slightly, but to a badly frightened Kathy, it was both obvious and appreciated. It kept its head elevated, but it no longer gave the appearance of impending action.

Neither dog nor woman moved. Each stared in silence, a silence that had no end. Kathy realized that the ball had been tossed to her, but she did not know what to do with it. Should she begin talking? Did she seriously expect the dog to respond?—for a few seconds there, it *had* appeared to be on the verge of making a...comment, although considering what had recently happened to it, some kind of response might be expected; a bark if not the king's English.

However reconciled she was to the possibility, Kathy did not welcome the idea of her worst fears being proven true. She had felt overwhelming relief when the dog appeared to back down. Relief but skepticism; it was as if it still expected her to believe it was a normal dog.

Well, normal or not, there was nothing to be lost by giving it a try. "What are you?" she whispered, her voice hoarse and far from what she wanted it to be. In any event, it had no effect on the animal; it did not move so much as an eyelash—Kathy thought this was of itself unusual; a normal animal would have reacted to the sound; this one seemed determined not to. "I heard you talk before!" she said, this time with more authority. "For your own good, you'd better speak up!"

The animal continued to ignore her attempts at communication. Kathy wondered what she could do to change this, to get it to respond as she knew it could. "Damnit mutt, if you ever want to get out of here, you'd better start talking!"

The dog was notably unimpressed. Its look was almost cocky, as if it knew it would get free in due time, with or without human help. Kathy searched her mind for something that might convince it otherwise.

As ideas flowed in and out of her brain, the animal's eyes, now focused on her lap, suddenly widened. Glancing down, she remembered the weapon. Her captive had just now realized it was in her possession. And the look on its canine face said it was also aware of what it could do.

For a moment Kathy was trapped in disbelief—such a thing could have no value to a dog. How, for example, could it set the gages and squeeze the 'trigger?' But it helped her form an idea. Converting her eyes into what she hoped was a sinister look, she raised the instrument and pointed it at what was becoming an increasingly agitated animal. "I'm not kidding, dog," she said. "You talk or I start blasting!"

But rather than becoming a believer, the animal relaxed once again—clearly, it was not impressed. It took a few minutes before the reason for this became clear: Incredibly, it knew that the weapon was on safety! *No animal is that intelligent!* she thought, her mind unable to accept so unreasonable an explanation—it would have to see and understand the dial settings. Feeling increasingly like an involuntary participant in a macabre dream, she held the weapon where the animal could see what she was doing, then turned the second row of dials to its first position, the same setting she'd used to disintegrate the rock. Her eyes remained fixed on her captive as she did this.

The effect was dramatic: its canine eyes widened even more than before, and its body visibly tensed. *My God*, she thought, *it knows! It really knows!* She tensed herself for what she was now absolutely certain was coming. The impossible was about to become the possible. "You have ten seconds, dog, then I squeeze these indentations." Her voice was wobbly and her composure difficult to maintain, but the animal did not seem to notice.

It continued to stare but moved its eyes from the weapon to the woman then back again. Then it let out a deep sigh and relaxed as if recognizing the futility of going on. When it again met the eyes of its dry-mouthed captor, its expression had softened considerably.

"I assume you are aware of how destructive that particular setting can be?"

Despite her resolve, Kathy jumped at the animal's human response. Even though she knew it was about to happen, that it absolutely *had* to happen, her mind still tried to tell her it was a trick—someone was talking for that animal, the proof of which was that its mouth, or muzzle, had not moved. "How can you talk without moving your...," she swallowed with difficulty then completed the question with, "...muzzle?"

"Quite simply, really, I am not talking at all; I am communicating directly with your brain. But would you mind resetting the beam to safety? If you are uncertain how to do this, I will be pleased to help."

Kathy wanted to comply, but found it difficult to do so with hands that would not stop shaking—the animal cringed as it watched her clumsy reworking of the dials. *What kind of creature communicates with a brain?* she thought as she worked.

"That is so much better," it said once Kathy had snapped the dial back into place. "Now we are both more secure. Tell me, how did you know to choose that particular setting?"

It took Kathy a few seconds and one additional hard swallow to respond. "Uh...I experimented out the window," she said, her voice still hoarse and now cracking.

The dog cringed anew. "My dear woman, you might easily have removed this entire town from your planet. I would heartily recommend you not 'experiment' again."

"Yeah, okay." Although the words were barely audible, her voice strengthened as she realized what the animal had said. "What do you mean, 'my planet'?" There was skepticism in both her expression and her voice. "Are you claiming to be an alien? From outer space!"

She wondered why that surprised her. After all, she was holding a conversation with a talking dog who carried a weapon more powerful than any she had ever known. She supposed she was still expecting somebody to come flying out of a secret passageway yelling "Gotcha!" Right now, she would have welcomed it.

"The definition of 'alien' depends on where you happen to be sitting. I am admittedly not of your planet, but I mean you and your species no harm."

Kathy could do little but stare; her mind was temporarily vacant of thought. The creature, as if in understanding, allowed her the time. When finally she had recovered enough to continue the interrogation, she asked, "All the strange dogs that come through this town, are they from the same place?"

"They are my colleagues. And as you are aware, they pass by peaceably."

"But how are they able to escape leashes and locked rooms?"

The creature surrendered a slight smile at the question, an expression that did not help put Kathy at ease. "Perhaps it is best that some of our little tricks remain a mystery," it said.

Within minutes, the Earth woman was loosing herself in questions, questions which were fragmentary and occasionally nonsensical. But Zarpin patiently answered each one, recognizing as he did so what must be going through this creature's mind. He wanted her as relaxed as possible; the weapon she held in her hand was far too dangerous to risk her playing with it again. And he could not employ a protective haze around his body without her seeing it and taking alarm.

For the same reason, he could not chance rearranging the cells of his body to render himself impervious to whatever harm she might attempt. He shuddered to think what this human might do should she see the ties around his neck and limbs summarily pass through his body on the way to the floor.

Between responses to the Earth creature's questions, he tried to reach his colleague. He took care as he did so that the human in front of him would not catch on. He had been clumsy, he realized, and too trusting. He had known she was up to something, but her mind had been in such a jumble that he had been unable to pinpoint the specifics. However, there was time enough for recriminations after this problem was solved, and for the present it could only be solved by limiting the ability of this human to communicate her new-found knowledge to others. She would have to be immobilized until the proper authorities could be notified and a decision as to her disposition communicated back to Sinot and himself.

Zarpin tried again and again to reach Sinot, finally conceding that she must be out of range. With regret he realized that the beam device held by the human would, were it properly set, automatically increase the range of his communication until it reached its intended recipient. Having no other ideas at the moment, he decided to bide his time and periodically repeat the call to Sinot.

Kathy paused in her questioning, wanting to lead this creature into a discussion of her missing lover but more afraid than ever of the answer. Finally, she just blurted it out. "One of you was in the woods with my friend. What happened to him?"

Zarpin knew exactly what the female human meant but was unsure how he should respond. She had the weapon and, particularly on this subject, might be expected to make use of it. On the other hand, the information would do her little good, and it could serve to further calm her down. He decided to tell the truth. "The person you call Markcarter is unharmed. He is with us now, no more than a few days from here."

Kathy jumped at the mention of Mark's name. *This...alien...knows Mark,* she thought. *But how did he know that's who I meant? How did he know I would recognize the name?* She experienced a combination of lightheadedness and elation as the true meaning of the creature's comments sunk in. The unlikely had turned out to be true; there *was* a connection between these dogs and Mark's disappearance. And best of all, he was not lost; he was safe! *Safe?* she thought. *How safe could he be in the hands of space people?*

"What are you doing with him? Why hasn't he come back?"

The creature hesitated, obviously to consider his answer—the pause appeared ominous to Kathy. "I suppose his situation is similar to yours. You are both in a position to do harm to our peaceful exploration of this planet. For the moment, at least, we are unable to decide what is the best way to proceed under such circumstances."

"You're holding him captive!" It was a statement rather than a question.

"No more than you are a captive," the canine replied.

Confused, Kathy asked, "I'm not the captive here, you are." To demonstrate her point she raised the weapon and pointed it at the bound alien. "You mean Mark is holding all of your space buddies with one of these little flashlights?" she asked sarcastically.

The creature contracted his eyes and accompanied this with another of his unnatural smiles. To Kathy, it served as a reminder of the oddity of her situation. "Without meaning to challenge you, the outcome of this 'capture,' as you put it, depends more on us than it does you."

"I have the gun!" Kathy said, emphasizing the weapon again, this time extending her arm as far as it would go toward her adversary.

"Quite correct," the creature stated confidently, "but I have more knowledge as to its use. In addition I strongly suspect that you would not wish to use it, on me or on anyone else. Considering that, and the fact that I also have a companion nearby, it would appear to make sense for you to end the inferred hostility of this meeting before either of us is accidentally harmed. Perhaps you might begin by loosening these bonds." It was intended as both a test and a diversion, the former to see if the human might succumb voluntarily and the latter to instill in her a false sense of security in regard to the bonds—which Zarpin knew he could cast aside whenever he wished.

Kathy's cynical chuckle was enough of an answer, but still she said, "Nice try, fella!" There was no way she would voluntarily weaken her position; the level of fear she had felt earlier had not even begun to fade. "I want to know where Mark is and I want him returned to Kelly!"

The alien sighed. "It might be you who goes to him," he said cryptically.

Kathy tossed her head, not comprehending the creature's meaning. "Where exactly is he?"

"Within walking distance; southeast of here." Zarpin made another clandestine attempt to reach Sinot but, as before, met with no success.

Weakened by all the wrong emotions, Kathy's thinking became desperate. The dog's companion was close by and probably had the same kind of weapon. Worse, this one was catching on; he knew she would find it difficult to use the weapon still clutched in her blood-drained hands. *Don't tempt me though, mutt!* she thought.

For her own protection she had to find this companion and capture her. If she could do that, she could capture her weapon as well. *Then I'd have two space dogs to worry about instead of one.*

Maybe one could be held hostage; maybe she could keep it drugged while the other went to get Mark. Possible, but then what if it brought back more space dogs instead?

She searched her weary mind for ideas. She had to do something now or Mark, and maybe she as well, would be lost. The hostage idea was the only thing that made sense—at least she already had the hostage and a weapon. There must be something she could do to insure that they kept their side of whatever bargain they decided on, but what? She couldn't tell anyone; they would only laugh; it was difficult enough for her to believe even now. Sandy would think she was overreacting to Mark's disappearance, and Janos? Hell, what could she possibly tell him? "Don't worry officer, I solved the case: Mark was captured by Martian dogs?"

She wondered what proof she had that there were aliens in their midst, convincing proof that could be shown to others. Not the animal itself; it would likely clam up if exposed—she might even be considered insane. The weapon maybe. She could show people that, maybe even demonstrate it. It would at least prove something strange was going on.

But what if she were unable to get anyone to believe that the weapon came from the dog—which any sane person would not? And what good would exposure do if all that came out of it was the aliens going back to wherever it was they came from and taking Mark with them?

Regardless of its value in proving an interstellar invasion, Kathy was convinced that the weapon was the key to gaining Mark's release. She would not have to kill anyone (or any*thing*), only threaten to hold onto it indefinitely. The creature in front of her, and whatever society it represented, would not be pleased at the possibility of such power being made available to police or military authorities. She would agree to keep it hidden unless Mark failed to return safely—and promptly. Then, after a suitable number of additional years, to insure that no harm came to either Mark or herself, she would leave it in an agreed-upon place for collection by them or their space-dog friends. *Maybe I'll bury some soup bones along with it!* she thought.

In order to make her plan work, a hiding place had to found that was secure, some place where the device would not be found but where it would surface automatically in the event she were for any reason incapacitated.

The bad of that was it would no longer be available to encourage the cooperation of her hostage—the thought of being alone and unarmed with this creature was not a pleasant one. She had to find a way of retaining its cooperation even after the weapon was safely tucked away.

The lady dog! She thought. *It would have a weapon too.* This meant, of course, that the other animal would have to be captured as well, but that looked to be more workable than any alternative solution she could think of. She couldn't, for example, be sure that a regular weapon—a gun— even if she were able to get hold of one in Wyoming, would be effective against creatures from outer space. She decided to give the plan a try.

But first, a little extra security.

She made her movements slow and deliberate as she picked up a syringe, tested it, then approached the bound animal. Her eyes were those of a determined woman, one who knew what she had to do and would not be prevented from doing it.

Concern showed on her captive's face. "I would prefer you not do that," it said. "I do not believe you understand the implications of this."

Kathy was undeterred. "For the present you must go back to sleep; I can't have you pulling a disappearing act on me. I want my man back, and if you won't do it voluntarily, then I'll have to figure a way to force you."

"What do you have in mind?"

Before answering, Kathy turned the beam back to a destructive setting, smiling as she did so at the response she received from the alien. "You'll find out soon enough. For now you have only to lie back and relax. I'm going to administer this, and I don't want you to move when I do it." She paused in expectation of a reaction, but none came. The alien did nothing more, nor did anything more come out of its still-closed muzzle. It appeared to be reconciled to what was coming. Hands held as steadily as she could manage, Kathy injected the tranquilizer into the creature's rump then stepped back, relieved that the difficult part was over.

After a few seconds, it closed its eyes and began a long sleep. Kathy waited an additional five minutes to make sure it wasn't faking, then tested the bindings. They had not changed, and with a modicum of confidence that her guest would be there when she returned, she placed the weapon back on safety, inserted it into her pocket then steeled herself for the distasteful task of seeking out and capturing another disguised, and probably armed, creature from outer space.

For more than an hour, she walked the darkened streets of Kelly trying to spot a light-colored German shepherd. She looked into every store window and peered down every dark alley. But the animal was nowhere in sight. It took a second trip around, still looking through windows and down alleys, before she finally spotted it.

A shepherd was inside the office of the man who acted as the local police authority. Somehow it had gained access to the building and was now standing on a chair staring at papers laid out on top of a desk. Kathy ducked down to avoid exposing any more of herself than was necessary, then watched, fascinated by what it was doing. Illuminated by a low-powered night light, it looked to be actually reading, and what it was reading appeared to have come from what was a still-opened desk drawer—how it had managed to get that drawer opened she couldn't imagine. Familiar chills ran through her body as she watched the creature stare with unnatural concern at documents that should be of no interest to the shepherd it purported to be.

How did it get inside? she thought. As silently as she could, she moved to the front door then slowly tried the knob. It was locked. A similar try at the rear door proved it was locked as well. However the alien had gained access to the sheriff's office it was not through either of those doors. *Unless it locked them afterward,* she thought, wondering if space people thought along such lines.

Not knowing what to do next, she retreated to the alleyway and waited. There was just enough light to see the entrance from there. That same light, however, imported a ghostly haze to the structure, an image made even more scary by her knowledge of the cosmic event that was enveloping this town. She slid one hand into her pocket for a reassuring feel of the weapon that rested there.

Sinot was not finding what she was looking for. There was little mention of the search being conducted on behalf of the lost camper, Markcarter. Apparently this official was not part of it. Either that or the search was not as monumental an affair as her superiors had feared. *Inconclusive at best*, she thought.

Realizing there was nothing more to be learned here, she returned the papers to their respective drawers, restored everything else to what it had been a short time before, then prepared to leave the office. As was the case during her entry, she elected to exit from the rear. Although late at night, when most of the inhabitants of this community would be sleeping, she did not want to chance further inflaming an already delicate situation by permitting an inadvertent glimpse of herself walking through walls. Adjusting her body molecules, she cautiously poked her head through the old wooden wall then scanned the area for activity. No one was there. She made her exit swift and smooth then paused afterward just long enough to start the process of returning her body to normal density. It was wiser to travel in this fashion. Should someone try to pet her, it would, to say the least, raise unneeded questions if his hand touched nothing but air.

She circled around the back of the building then began walking up the alley toward the town's main street. It was time to return to the proximity of the hotel, there to await communication with Zarpin. Perhaps her colleague was having better success in uncovering useful information than she.

After only a few steps she stopped. There was a human female standing at the end of the alley, her face turned toward the street. It was Markcarter's mate. She was watching the sheriff's office, the same office she herself had just visited. *She was watching me!* Sinot thought, alarmed and confused. She could not imagine what the woman was doing here; or what this meant in regard to Zarpin. Glancing back toward the hotel, she considered returning to check on her colleague then rejected the idea as unnecessary. Her Mantzite superior was quite capable of freeing himself whenever he wished. *But why is this Earthling monitoring me?* she thought? Is this related to her investigation of disappearing dogs, or is it more?

She could see no harm in indulging the woman. Indeed, since Markcarter's mate was a principal in what she and Zarpin had come to monitor, namely the official search for Markcarter, it could serve the cause to stay close. Making the decision accordingly, she strolled up to where she was right behind the human female then sat down, ready to participate in whatever it was the Earthling had in mind.

It took a few seconds to realize that the Earthling was not yet aware of her presence. Vaguely annoyed, Sinot considered coughing or generating some other noise to make her presence known. She tried to remember what sounds came out of an Earth dog, something that would be accepted as natural.

CHAPTER 23

Kathy screamed at the explosion of sound that flew out of the darkness behind her. Whirling around, and struggling unsuccessfully to get the weapon out of her pocket as she did so, she stared in fear and anger at the sought-after animal that now sat so calmly nearby. "Jesus Christ, you dumb mutt!" she yelled. "How did you get out of that office?" Suddenly realizing where she was and what the animal in front of her represented, she struggled to get hold of herself. The comment, however, served a purpose; it helped convince Sinot that she was still being regarded as a simple Earth canine.

Kathy listened but could hear nothing that would suggest anyone heard either the bark or the closely-following scream; the town remained as it was: still and silent. Looking down, she wondered whether the dog had any idea that she had been watching it. She decided it did not, and that, consequently, her plans did not need to be changed. She took a deep breath to further steady herself then began walking down the street toward the hotel, encouraging the dog to do the same. It followed without complaint, although this time she had the disadvantage of knowing what it was—if it had talked to her at that moment, she would have screamed even louder than before.

As expected, getting into the hotel proved to be no problem. Everyone, including the desk clerk, was asleep. As she nervously tackled the stairs, the dog close behind, Kathy reached into her pocket to feel the reassuring shape of the beam weapon. She kept her hand around it as she pushed open the door, ready to pull it out should her captive be other than where she'd left it.

But it was still sleeping soundly; not even its position had changed. Moving further into the room, she tried to keep the sight of its drugged body from her new guest as it entered without objection behind her. Once they were both inside, she closed and locked the door then moved to the center of the room. There, her body shaking and her mouth as dry as it could be, she pulled the weapon from her pocket and pointed it at the new arrival. The reaction was as expected.

Sinot's eyes all but jumped out of their sockets as she recognized the device so commonly in use on her planet but so alien when held by a human. Confused, she glanced around the room, her eyes quickly finding her tied and apparently sleeping colleague. There was something wrong; Zarpin looked unnatural, his position and his breathing. She projected a question to him but felt no response. Indeed, he appeared incapable of responding.

As she returned her gaze to the threatening human, a look of anger spread over her canine face. What kind of species was this that they would do such a thing? She examined the manner in which the Earthling was holding the weapon. Good enough to be effective, but apparently she did not know how to make it work; it was on safety. That meant there was still time. Deciding to postpone any action until more could be learned about what happened to Zarpin, she backed up to a wall then sat down as she knew a human dog should. Then she removed all expression from her face, this to appear as non-threatening as possible.

It took a moment to realize that the female human was talking to her.

"I know all about you," Kathy said, her voice revealing her agitated state. "Your buddy and I had a long chat about who you are and where you came from." She waited for a response, but none came. "You might as well start talking. I told you I already know! He told me everything!" She pointed to the sleeping animal in case there was any doubt who she meant. The new arrival lowered its eyelids slightly but otherwise did not respond. It was then that Kathy remembered what it took to make a believer of the first.

She could see the alarm grow in her new captive's eyes as she turned the second dial of the beam weapon to the setting which she, and more importantly her visitor, knew was lethal. As before, the strategy worked: Canine eyes widened in response to the smooth and obviously knowledgeable movement. "You ready to talk now, or do I have to squeeze these two indentations?" Kathy asked, holding the weapon up so the alien could see where she had placed her fingers.

* * * *

Sinot glanced again at her colleague. He was immobilized, and apparently in such a way that this Earth creature had been able to find and retrieve his beam. Astonishingly, she even knew how to use it. She wondered what had happened in this room and how much else the human female knew. If only Zarpin were conscious enough to communicate instructions! She did not want to break cover without knowing for certain that it was unavoidable.

"I mean it, Mantzite!"

Sinot watched as the beam was pushed even further in her direction, the action emphasizing the depth of this human's feelings. She was aghast that the Earthling knew what planet she and Zarpin were from—they really had communicated. How did she make him do it? How did she even begin to suspect he was capable of it?

If nothing else, it was the confirmation she was waiting for. She now had little choice but to give in to the inevitable. "Is my colleague damaged in any way?" she projected.

Even though expected this time, it was still a shock to hear, or at least feel, a dog speaking. Kathy gulped more than once before answering, and even then she was barely able to coax the sounds from her from her throat. "He's okay, just tranquilized." It came out as a whisper, and, clearing her throat, she tried again: "He's going to stay that way until you get back here with my friend. I think you know what I mean."

The answer came without hesitation. "Yes, I believe I do. But what specifically do you have in mind?"

Kathy was vaguely disturbed by the easy manner in which the creature was admitting knowledge of Mark. "First of all I want your gun...uh weapon." She held out her hand to emphasize the demand.

Sinot paused to analyze the human's thoughts, both what she said and the scattered ideas that her species were always emitting. Finally, after deciding this Earthling had sufficient knowledge to compel her to do so, she again surrendered to the inevitable. It was a few minutes before the weapon saw daylight, however, since she could not risk converting her canine paw to a more efficient Mantz hand. The sight of such a thing could set this woman off in a new and even more dangerous direction.

Kathy examined the weapon to make sure it was the same as the one she still held in a threatening manner. As far as she could see, it was; a quick squeeze on the indentations, followed by a "Safety is on," was the clincher.

She had watched how ineptly the creature had pulled it from its pocket, and this triggered additional questions, all of them troubling. How could this thing, whatever it was, make use of a weapon it could not even hold? Did it require assistance, another creature lurking in the wings? Or was there another piece to this weapon, something not yet handed over? She considered searching the animal but rejected the idea as too risky.

With a voice that still had a quiver in it—from fatigue as well as from anxiety—she informed the alien what she had in mind: "I want you to go back to wherever Mark is and tell those...people...that you get your dog back when I get Mark back. I'm going to hold him here under sedation until you return, and if you don't get back soon, the whole world is going to find out who you are!"

Sinot took a moment to consider her answer. The human female was making matters infinitely worse, but there was little to be done about it at the present. It would be unwise to take action against her without others knowing what was going on. She continued her attempts to calm her down, even as she realized how much this human creature was misreading Mantzite capabilities. "I am in sympathy with your concern for your mate Markcarter, but the matter cannot be so easily resolved, as I am certain you realize. In addition, it would not be in anyone's interest, including yours, that our presence be discovered. We mean no harm, but harm could result from a careless and premature announcement of our presence." That said, she hastened to add, "To be considered as well is whether or not anyone would believe you."

"They won't have to believe me," Kathy interrupted, more harshly than she'd intended. "They'll believe this!" She held up the weapon. "This will be delivered to someone who will have instructions to give it to the authorities if I pop up missing." She grimaced at the clumsy presentation of what she had hoped would be irrefutable logic. "That someone will know the meaning of a weapon as far-out as this; it'll be obvious without my having to say a thing that it was not produced on Earth."

The frown on creature's face, this at hearing her words, caused Kathy to regret the venom that had accompanied them. When she continued, she made her voice more conciliatory. "Look, I have to do this to keep you from doing something foolish to get your dog back...uh, I mean your friend. Beyond that, you have to consider what problems my disappearance would cause. There are hundreds of people out looking for Mark, and they aren't the type to give up easily. If he doesn't come back, or if I disappear as well, you'll have the whole United States Army involved!" Kathy hoped she was not carrying this too far. She did not want to weaken her case through exaggeration.

Sinot understood exactly what was going through the woman's mind. The primary thrust of her effort was the protection of her mate. What happened afterward was of secondary concern only. It would, of course, be an easy matter to dispose of both her and Markcarter, either sooner or later, but that was for someone else to decide. If people were involved in a formal search—not as many as the woman had suggested but enough to be concerned about—then the situation was already too far advanced to expect it to be easily contained.

Sinot did not envy the Council. Everything done thus far had only added to the increasingly negative situation in which they found themselves. Now they had the ultimate decision to face, the termination of intelligent life, and two rather than one. Yet to be determined, assuming they chose to do so, was whether this would aid their efforts or compound their errors.

To assist the Council in making this decision, Sinot wanted to delay her departure for as long as the human female was willing to let slip information they could use. Concerned that the choice of staying might not be hers much longer, she decided on a direct approach. "It would be in your best interests to tell me exactly what is being done to find your mate."

Kathy was pleased that the prospect of large-scale rescue was of such concern to this creature. In her answer she decided to add embellishments that would add to its worries. "When someone is lost everyone pitches in to try to find him. We have all kinds of police forces for just this sort of thing, and they have at their command all sorts of helpful equipment— like helicopters. On top of that, there are people whose job it is to broadcast anything of interest that's happening anywhere in the world. They have to; they have no choice. If someone is lost and he stays lost for too long a time, it becomes a big story that everyone wants to know about."

As the human female went on to tell of a "Janos" and others like him, Sinot examined the unintended thoughts that occasionally accompanied her speech. There was enough there to indicate that a search was indeed underway, a large search. It was the confirmation she sought; her priority now should be to get the news to Takar.

In the interim there was no necessity to contain this creature. She appeared willing to contain herself, to remain as she was in anticipation of a future "prisoner exchange." Sinot glanced at Zarpin, attempted a final projection, then silently admitted that it was hopeless. There was no indication whatsoever that her colleague was even aware of what was going on. Turning back to Kathy, she frowned just enough to lend gravity to her words, then said, "I will communicate your wishes immediately. It will, however, take some time to obtain a reply. I ask, for myself and for yourself as well, that you allow us that time, that you not take any action until I return."

Kathy felt a rush of adrenaline at what appeared to be an impending victory. "Well, that depends on how long it takes you to get back. I won't wait forever." She knew it was a bluff; she had no choice but to wait...and hope. These beings could do whatever they wanted with Mark, and there was little she would ever be able to do about it. The weapon would prove something but not necessarily that aliens had captured her man. And even if she were believed, it would not get him back. They couldn't just form a posse and ride off to Mantz.

Sinot also knew the human female would wait. Her greater concern was the disposition of hers and Zarpin's weapons. "Once the exchange is made, will you return the beam devices?"

Kathy had been hoping the question would not be asked. She could give up one of the weapons but not both—probably the creature knew that. "I've got to hold on to one to make sure you don't come after us later on." Seeing the expression on the alien's face, she quickly added, "Look, I promise no one will ever see it, I mean unless Mark or I disappear."

Sinot was not reassured. This woman did not understand the seriousness of the game she was playing. The Council would not permit such a positive link to discovery to continue for long. "If there is nothing more, then perhaps I should leave." She waited for some response but the human female did not appear to know what to do next.

For the first time, Sinot thought of how her sex compared to that of the human. They were both female and undoubtedly shared many similarities, although the specifics were not easily revealed. This devotion to a member of the opposite sex, for example, was understandable considering the state of Earth's civilization, but it had difficulty standing up to logic. She felt a feeling for her colleague Zarpin, but it was professional, not sexual. Once this tour was over, perhaps a session or two in the experience chamber would provide the answers. "I suggest that you return that weapon to a safe status as soon as I depart. It is more dangerous than you realize, for you as well as for me."

At that, she turned and headed for the door, triggering an automatic conversion of her body molecules as she did so, this to permit passage through the barrier it represented. She caught herself before the change could be detected—it would not do to add further shock to the human's already-unsteady system. Looking back, she asked, "Would you mind escorting me to the street?"

Aided by the early morning light, Kathy watched from the window as the alien trotted down the street in the direction from which it had appeared the day before. After assisting it through the hotel doors, she had dashed back upstairs to where she could verify that it was really leaving. It was time to address the job of hiding the second weapon, and she did not want this joker peeking from the shadows as she did so. She kept her eyes on it until it disappeared around a bend some distance from the edge of town. By now Kelly had come to life, although no one was showing interest in yet another antisocial German Shepherd.

With both weapons concealed in her purse, Kathy left the room to find a way of packaging one of them for shipment. It was not as difficult as she'd feared. Everyone who knew her and had come to appreciate her warm smile and matching personality was anxious to help, although some were curious about what was in the package—she held them off with a smile that hinted at a lover's secret. Once she had the necessary supplies in hand, she headed back to her room.

She wrote two quick letters to Sandy, one explaining that the package accompanying the letter was only to be opened if she failed to return, and the second revealing exactly what had happened and what the object in the package represented. The second one she wrapped around the weapon then placed into a small box. Along with the first letter, she inserted this into a second, larger box then bound and addressed it. Finally she was satisfied. She checked her captive, found him to still be in deep sleep, then took the package to the post office for mailing.

By the time she sat down for a late breakfast, the combination of lingering disbelief and unrelenting anxiety made it difficult to lift even a fork. To the casual onlooker, she was the image of a woman anticipating a great loss. Throughout the meal, slowly consumed and barely tasted, she rehashed the events of the previous night. The fear was hard to shake even as the rest of it excited her. Here she was in heavy negotiations with aliens. Real life aliens, whose existence no one in the world knew about except Mark and her. And their very lives could depend on how she handled it. It was a dangerous game she was playing, an interstellar war game, yet here she sat calmly eating her breakfast. Unreal!

But at least Mark was not lost! He was being held by God-knows-what, but he was alive!

And well? She wondered how he felt at that moment, what his physical condition was, how he was coping mentally. Why did they grab him? *And what would they have done with him if I hadn't come along?* She ran over the details of her plan once again then wondered whether it was enough, whether it would accomplish what she wanted. Or would it only result in Mark and she being fitted for concrete slippers then tossed into some ocean.

"Or zapped with that weird flashlight," she mumbled into her coffee cup.

Everything she could think of to do she had already done; there was nothing now but to wait. If the creatures wanted to come after her, which was probably a good bet, they could. But if her plan worked.... She let out a tired sigh, resigned to whatever fate awaited her captive lover and herself.

C H A P T E R   2 4

"Heeeeeer's Johnny!" Creson yelled, popping out of the conveyer tube into what had been a silent room. With his arms spread wide and a silly open-mouth smile decorating his face, he looked as if he were ready to burst into song. The suddenness of the interruption brought a rush of adrenaline to Mark's system that caused every muscle in his body to jump—it challenged the chamber's ability to cope. Then, with his eyes stretched as far as they could go, he stared at the unlikely sight of an alien playing an American entertainer.

Creson's pupils contracted as finally he spoke. "I got that from your experience bank; thought it might be more appreciated than barking."

Mark was only slightly amused. "Thank you, but a simple 'here I come' will do!"

Mark had been alone for better than three hours, since shortly after he and Creson were mentally retrieved from Tanterac. During that time he had found it impossible to block thoughts of the experience, what he had seen and heard, what he had felt, what it all meant, not only to Creson and his "Council," but to all kinds of creatures wherever they may be found. He also thoughts about the capabilities of the Mantzites; they had incredible skills, much of which took advantage of already-available mental capacity.

Best of all, at least from his point of view, the knowledge was transferable, at least transferable to human beings, whose brain size and capability were similar to that of the Mantzites.

He had learned so much since inviting himself to Mantz, so much about the power of his own mind. He could do things now that were inconceivable a few short weeks ago. And the funny thing was, the power had always been there—he knew that now, not only in himself but in his fellow humans. It only needed someone or something to stimulate it, to get it going. If that were allowed to happen, mankind would be able to perform the same wonders as the Mantzites. If it didn't happen, if the Mantzites decided not to share their experience-machine concept, thousands of years might go by before humans got the idea on their own. Maybe they never would.

His mental skills did not yet match up to those of the Mantzite's, but what he did know he was able to apply with greater speed than his teachers—this was proven again on Tanterac. It was an advantage he might be able to make use of. He wondered what else the Mantzites could do that would be more effective when performed by a human mind. The answer to that could come from sharing one of Creson's experiences; the highly-placed research scientist had to be familiar with every mental skill developed by, not only his own people, but all the people the Mantzites had targeted for study.

What a machine that experience chamber was! Instantaneous training, so effective that the student became as confident in his knowledge as the teacher. All that remained was the coordination of mind and muscle—practice. His earlier clumsiness showed how necessary practice was; the body had to be brought up to par with the mind.

"I trust you have adjusted to your interplanetary travels by now? We tried to allow you the time to do so, recognizing from long experience what grisly exposure can do to innocents such as yourself."

The comment triggered a side thought in Mark: He could not let Creson think the moral of the Tanterac visit was being quietly accepted. "I think you people are over-reacting to the Tanterac mistake," he said. "It's a different situation entirely; things are not like that on Earth. We're not of one mind like they were on Tanterac; we find more reason to disagree than to agree. What I'm saying is that the introduction of way-out ideas, even if they come from outer space, would not be all that weird to us. At least we wouldn't go off the deep end over it."

What remained of Creson's smile disappeared. "The point is not new to me. We, and I include the Council in this, have already given it some thought. But you must understand, there are other than logical arguments to consider here. As previously stated, the person responsible for the Tanterac disaster now sits on the Council. He is, to say the least, a bit inflexible on this subject."

"But he's got to be open to reason. I mean, this is a scientific project you have going here. Scientists are supposed to be open-minded."

"True," admitted Creson, "but open-mindedness is often a matter of interpretation, and in this case the one doing the interpreting has a rather loud voice. Besides, I am not convinced your argument is all that persuasive. The first encounter with cosmic beings is *expected* to result in trauma—the inhabitants of the visited planet would be unusual indeed if that were not the case. Should we be discovered as a result of your little visit, without being able to adequately prepare for this trauma, many of your fellow humans will suffer deep and lasting discomfort. There will be some, perhaps many, who will feel compelled to restructure their beliefs, beliefs that they have, to this point, doubted only in their subconscious."

"But won't that happen anyway?" Mark asked.

Not if we are prepared to address their concerns in advance—this has been proven again and again. In order to do this, however, we need time, time to discover precisely what those concerns are."

It was difficult to think of the words that would refute what Creson was saying. Mark felt himself on the loosing side of the debate that would decide whether or not he would live. "What if I agree to keep all this quiet; even help you find out what you want to know?"

The sadness in Creson's eyes did nothing to halt the slide in Mark's morale. "Such an agreement is impossible to enforce. The fear that it might not be kept will be foremost in the minds of those who will make the decision."

Saddened himself, but for a different reason, Mark continued to argue—and lose—his point. The Mantzites were simply not willing to chance Earth going the way of Tanterac. Translated: they had no intention of releasing him. "What then are you going to do with me?" he asked softly.

The evasiveness of Creson's answer, which he preceded with a sigh, revealed more than his words. "You are, indeed a problem. There is a sizable effort on Earth to find you. We are attempting to discover what the reaction of your fellow humans will be if this effort goes unrewarded. Will they, as you say, 'go off the deep end'? The answer to that question is still coming, and until we know for certain, you must remain our protected guest."

"Yeah, as we protect a Thanksgiving turkey!"

Creson searched his memory but could find no such species of turkey on Earth. But he let it go. This was not the moment for satisfying his scientific curiosity.

After Creson left, Mark turned his thoughts back to escape; specifically, how to assist it by using recently-acquired knowledge. So far he knew how to rearrange DNA to assume other forms—maybe not as smoothly as the Mantzites, but that would come—and he could orient the molecules of his body in such a way that would allow objects to pass through as if he were invisible. This latest skill would have to be tested, but it looked like a good bet. It had worked perfectly on Tanterac; he still remembered the feeling of the rocks as they passed through his body. Even as he saw them coming he had felt no fear. Or even doubt.

He also knew the sequence of lights necessary to open the chamber, for what good that would do him. And he was aware of the workings of a few machines, Wilpin's communication device, for example.

But nothing learned thus far permitted him even a hint of how to work the transporter that would take him back to Earth. He knew roughly where it was—to find it he had only to follow the trail taken on the way in—but how would he get out of the research complex to where the trail began? And how did he know the transporter would be on when he got there? Or that, if on, it was pointed at Earth? Hell, he could wind up on Tanterac or something worse.

Too many questions without answers. Traveling through a Mantz forest, however, would be the least of his problems. The camping experience with Wilpin provided him all the skills he needed. In that respect, he felt like a native.

Thoughts of Wilpin reminded him of the dangers of converting to another form—there were no guarantees, even among experienced Mantzites. What an irony that would be, plowing through thousands of light years of space only to be eaten by a predator while in the guise of a bug!

Before converting to a flinac, the doomed Mantzite had considered the gene structure of a number of animals and insects, including some from Earth—Mark knew that knowledge now lived inside him. He also knew the mechanics of converting to a chipmunk, a German shepherd, even an elephant. (Why Wilpin had chosen an elephant Mark had no idea, but he was fascinated with the thought of giving it a try some day.) There were also skills picked up without his being aware it was happening. The quick conversion on Tanterac drew entirely from latent knowledge— his own knowledge, not Wilpin's; he was *creating* an experience, not sharing one. Every day he picked up something, and what he picked up yesterday he knew even better today. His ability to receive communications not specifically directed at him was a good example—he was getting everything "said" in the laboratory. The flip side of that was true as well: he was more in control of his own thoughts; he could beam them in such a tight pattern that only the intended recipient could detect what was he was "saying." Yet to be figured out, and it represented a big gap in his escape plans, was how to make use of the variety of beam devices available to these creatures. They used them for everything: travel, communications, weapons, even sex.

Converting to another form was probably the key, converting to something small enough to pass through the walls of the chamber. *Pass through!* he thought. *The rock throwing incident on Tanterac!*

Even as he ran the procedure over in his mind, he worked to arrange his body molecules as he had on Tanterac. It was not as easy as he'd remembered it to be; his human body would not respond in the same way as the Mantzite body he had used then. But soon it began to happen; he could feel it; air began flowing through and around every molecule of his body. A few minutes later, he was ready to give it a test.

He took a deep breath, clamped his teeth together to mark his determination, then pushed against the front opening. It pushed back. Confused, he mentally examined his body from head to toe, searching for the error or the omission. He found nothing he had failed to do. He tried again, reaching only a hand forward this time. It confirmed that, converted or not, the rest and rejuvenation chamber was not about to let go of its prize. It apparently knew about body conversions.

Bitterly disappointed, Mark took out his anger on the hated panel that so zealously robbed him of his freedom. "Damn you!" he cried, stabbing at it with eyes that had no mercy attached to them. The light on which his glance was fixed went on.

The suddenness of it softened his anger. No light on that panel had ever gone on without first being touched by a Mantzite. What caused it to do so now? He stared at the panel, wondering if something was about to happen, some other lights or some action as a result of the one that went on. But a number of minutes went by with the light continuing to glow yet stubbornly refusing to reveal the reason why. Defeated, Mark turned his mind back to thoughts of escape.

If he couldn't get out on his own, he would just have to take a chance during one of the trips to the experience chamber, wait for the right moment then dart into a beam tunnel—not a great plan, but time was getting short. He could, at the same time, further confuse his pursuers by converting to another form. That last part meant practice, practice that could not be put off any longer. It was time for a full-body conversion.

He spent the next few minutes reviewing the knowledge implanted in his mind during the Wilpin session. *A chipmunk,* he thought. *It's small and safe—of sorts. And it's something Wilpin felt comfortable with.* The decision made, he dove into the process of educating the many parts of his body in the mechanics of changing from what it was to what he now intended it to be. He gave no thought of failure, no recognition of what had come out of the earlier attempt—this was not the time for caution. For a while everything went exactly as it had with Wilpin, but then the conversion began to speed up, why, he didn't know. Among other things, it left him no time to double-check each step, something Wilpin, even with his high level of expertise, had considered important. The fingernail incident now flooded his mind, encouraging him toward the caution rejected earlier. He tried to slow things down but found he could not. The conversion was progressing at its own speed.

"Shit!" It finally dawned on Mark that the rest and rejuvenation chamber was assisting in the change. Further, the release of so many bodily fluids, necessary for a conversion to a smaller animal, was creating a great humidity imbalance within the chamber. It would be quickly corrected, of course, but the incident was sure to be reported. Selson might already be analyzing the reason for the change.

Well, there was nothing he could do about any of it now. The damage was done, he was on his way, spinning out of control and at dizzying speeds toward a new animal form.

He was able to tell the exact moment when he arrived, the moment when he was no longer a human being, the moment when the last DNA was in place and there was nothing left to be done. With his mind now free of the exceptional demands placed upon it, he had time to marvel at how large the chamber had become and how difficult it was to move as he had for the last thirty years—standing on two legs was a great hardship. But he had done it! Using only his mind, he had become another creature. Not a simulation, not a shared experience, not a spirit occupying somebody else's body. He was, in everything except his mind, a real chipmunk.

Or so he hoped.

But would he get away with it? He stared at the beam opening—also much larger than before—with an agony that was decidedly human. At any moment it could herald the arrival of an unwanted guest, an indignant Selson, an angry Creson. Even if he could return to human form in time, it would make no difference. The chamber knew the secret and would reveal it to anyone who knew how to ask.

The minutes passed in stillness and in silence, but they also passed without interruption. In time, Mark was able to ease off on the worst of his fears. It was possible that he had gotten away with it, possible that the Mantzites had not picked up on the fact that something highly unusual had occurred within the Earth man's chamber. Possible.

But he had difficulty shaking the feeling that the possible was also the unlikely.

Apprehensive yet oddly excited, Mark struggled to bend his new head to where it could observe the results of his efforts. The conversion had gone well. It had been quick and, as far as he could tell, accurate. He had even avoided the most common pitfall of converting, that of forgetting to take one's consciousness along. As much as he was able to do so, he smiled. He was standing on chipmunk legs, but they were his own legs; he could feel the tiny muscles supporting his weight, feel the chamber floor beneath what were now paws—his own paws. He examined his thoughts for things that chipmunks routinely tossed around in their heads, but there was none of that. He felt and thought as he always had. In that respect, he was still a human being.

A human being in a neat disguise. He had rich, silky fur, and stroking it with a paw brought a very unchipmunk smile to his tiny face. *I wish this damn chamber had a mirror*, he thought, even while wondering what effect that would have on his sanity.

It did not take him long to realize that acting the part of a chipmunk was more difficult than converting to one; knowledge of how the chosen animal behaved did not come along with the conversion. Thanks to Wilpin it was there, but the retention of human consciousness made it difficult to bring out. He tried prancing up and down, then he tried running around the chamber. Both were on the clumsy side of awkward, but soon he began to catch on. On impulse he jumped up at the chamber's opening, hoping the animal's sharp claws might find something to grab onto. They did not, but he enjoyed the feeling of being able to leap many times his own height then fall back without shock to his legs.

His sense of smell was acute, and that made him wonder whether it was human scent he was smelling, maybe his own scent. *Crazy!* he thought, failing in his attempt to say it aloud—the chipmunk noise which accompanied the effort brought an end to his reverie; he was spending too much time in this form; he was needlessly risking discovery. Besides, he had yet to test how fast he could reverse the process.

As the re-conversion unfolded, Mark gave thought to the image his rapidly changing body would present to his captors should they appear at that moment. How would they react? Could they—and would they—stop the process in mid stream, thinking that to do so would teach him a lesson?

Chipmunk to human form occupied only thirty seconds, but the chamber once again shared in the process, supplying in quick-time what it determined to be a critical need for moisture. Mark wondered how long it would take if the chamber were not involved, if he had to rely on himself and what moisture he could grab from the air. There was no way of knowing that, but he had the feeling that Wilpin and others whose minds he had briefly shared could not convert anywhere near as fast. How he wished he could confront Creson with that. How galling it would be to the pompous Mantzite!

With a big success behind him, Mark focused on how he would make use of this skill once he got free of the chamber. The choice, although not an easy one to make, was obvious: he would convert to a Mantz flinac, another favorite of Wilpin's. In that form, so common on Mantz, and assuming he were careful to control random projections of thought, he might then ride out of the research facility and even all the way to Earth on the back of one of his captors. There was irony in that, and he appreciated it.

All this meant nothing if he failed to escape the chamber. He stared again at the lights on the hexagonal panel, the lights that decided whether he was to remain a prisoner or be set free. The one that lit unexpectedly was still on. It was the first light in the escape sequence, as if an invisible Creson had started to cut him loose but then relented. He thought back to when it had occurred. He had cursed while staring directly at it, cursed aloud. *Does it respond to sound?* he thought. *Human sound?*

"Fuck you, light!" Nothing changed. "Go to hell, light!" Still nothing.

Although he hadn't expected it to work, he was still disappointed. He stared at the unresponsive panel and felt the frustration of before return. That light was trying to tell him something. Either that or it was another of Creson's teases. *Prick!* he thought, this time to himself.

The light went out.

He stared in disbelief, even as the adrenaline of hope leaked into his body. The light had reacted to something he did. Not sound; that time he hadn't made any sound. He concentrated on it again, this time imagining himself actually touching it.

It went back on.

Hope now exploded within him. Unless this was another part of the game of torment being played out against him, he had the power to manipulate those lights by his mind alone. And from within his chamber! The containment module was either unaware of this capability or was unable to protect against it. He decided it had to be the former—why have a containment unit if it could so easily be defeated? And if the chamber were unaware, this meant the Mantzites did not possess the same skill. One more thing he could do that his captors could not.

He struggled to contain his excitement as he brought to mind the correct escape sequence then focused on the second of the five-light set. As before, he imagined himself touching it. It went on, this time with less effort on his part. Even easier was the third light—his proficiency was increasing by the second.

Slow down, Man! He resisted the urge to mentally press the final two lights, aware that escaping the chamber was only one battle in what could be a long war. Instead, he took a deep breath to calm himself then tried to think it through. The flinac idea was a good one, but there was still the problem of the conveyer and the transporter; maybe he should stay put until the problem of how to use them was solved. That knowledge was bound to come; the Mantzites were careless; this was proven by how much they had already fed him.

No fucking way! he thought. *Those bastards are too close to pulling the plug?* He had to touch the remaining two lights then take his chances.

They came on with remarkably little effort, although nothing happened to tell him of a change in status. Ignoring the doubt that tugged at his resolve, he moved toward the chamber barrier then steeled himself for the opposition felt earlier. It wasn't there; the button sequence had worked; he was free. Elated, he stepped down to the floor then hastily moved away from the chamber, afraid it might reach out and pull him back if he hesitated.

It was odd being where he was with no Creson to supervise him. He felt like a criminal who had left his cell without permission. How long this freedom might last he had no way of knowing, but he suspected he had a minute at best—his chamber was empty; some alarm bell had to be ringing somewhere. Following his hastily conceived plan, he set his nervous mind to becoming a flinac.

Even without the chamber's help it did not take long—each conversion was easier and faster than the last. But being once again in flinac form brought back the strong feelings he had felt with Wilpin, in particular, the last few minutes of that shared experience. It reminded him how personal such experiences were, how intensely an observer felt the emotions of his host, how much they became his own. It also reminded him how important it was to keep an eye out for predators.

It was time to give the conveyer beam a try and take his chances where it might lead and who—or what—might be waiting at the other end. Taking aim at the beam's entrance, he jumped into the air then spread out his flinac wings.

It was not at all what he expected it to be; apparently not all of Wilpin's skill had rubbed off. He wasted a number of precious seconds trying to nail down the mechanics of making his chosen form do what it was designed to do, then some seconds after that re-gaining his sense of direction. He looked like the insect equivalent of a drunken sailor. *Now or never*, he thought as finally he was able to drive his insect form into the cavernous opening.

A quick flash of light and he was in a room with two Mantzites, neither of whom he could see clearly. A closer look proved his insect eyes were looking at his principle adversaries, Creson and Selson, and this brought on a mid-air backpedaling that equaled in awkwardness that which had taken place earlier. They appeared not to notice, but still he chided himself for his stupidity. He might be more capable than the average flinac, but he first saw images as the insect would, a large number of pictures rather than one. Only then was this translated into something that made sense to his human consciousness. Funny that this was not obvious while he was sharing Wilpin's mind. What other surprises was he yet to discover!?

The two Mantzites were communicating with one another in earnest and, thinking themselves alone, made no attempt to limit the scope of their projections. Mark easily picked it up.

"I tell you, it is empty; the chamber is empty!" Selson said, the panic in his voice difficult to conceal. "First he converted to an Earth creature—unusually rapidly, I might add—then he restored himself, waited a short time, then did something that enabled him to disappear altogether. You must get in there and learn what that something is!"

By then convinced, Creson turned and hurried into a conveyer tube. Aware that he would shortly return with confirmation that Selson's instruments reported correctly, Mark decided to wait and see—there was time enough to jump into a beam should they discover his presence. During the short wait, he could not help wondering whether some kind of insect control existed within the laboratory. He decided the safest place might be attached to his enemy.

With growing confidence in his flying ability, he worked his way through the air to the vicinity of the visibly-worried scientist, where he attached himself to what he hoped was an inconspicuous spot on his back. The normally smooth fur of a Mantzite was now a thick bush, but at least it was cover. A greater concern was that Selson might scratch or even swat. If that happened, he could once again be on his way to a flinac death—this time for real.

Creson reappeared after emitting a customary warning, a warning that Mark easily detected. On his face was an expression of great concern. "Markcarter, is not only out of the chamber but out of the exhibit room as well."

"How is that possible?" Selson's tone was demanding, but more suggestive of surprise than anger.

Creson shook his head, the question as puzzling to him as it was to his colleague. "The chamber was off," he replied. "Somehow he was able to influence the settings. Odd that we were unable to detect this capability in him."

"It might well have been we who stimulated it!" Selson offered, his projection including a hint of reproach.

Creson nodded slowly. "If so I would like very much to know how we did it; it might be possible to apply the procedure to ourselves. Perhaps a reexamination of his experiences." Creson, his scientific curiosity aroused, was loosing himself in thought.

His colleague was unsympathetic. "I submit that this is less important at the moment than finding the Earth creature and returning him to his chamber. I will inform Takar then seal off all tubes." At that, Selson turned toward a beam to communicate the dreaded message to his superior.

The thought of being trapped in a room with his these two brought Mark to the edge of panic. Giving only cursory thought to what he was doing, he leaped into the air then worked his way down to the floor. There, momentarily out of sight of the scientists, he raced to convert once again to the only other form he knew for sure: a chipmunk. Fear and anxiety delayed the process, but he managed to complete the conversion a few seconds before Selson ended his report. Working to his advantage was the length of Takar's questioning, the angry nature of which captured the full attention of the two scientists.

As soon as was structurally possible, Mark darted his tiny body across the floor within sight of the two startled scientists, this to get their attention. Then, without waiting to see if he had it, he turned toward the nearest conveyer tube and jumped into its glowing abyss, again without giving thought to where it might lead. At the other end, he instantly committed his entire mind to reconverting to a flinac.

The move had the effect he was looking for. Both Mantzites saw his entry into the tube and the form he had assumed. Both accepted that he had been in that form since exiting his chamber. Selson began instructing the computers to search for a chipmunk, while Creson sent a quick update to Takar. Both knew it no longer made sense to seal off the conveyer tubes since the Earth creature could now be anywhere within the laboratory complex. Besides, the conveyer tubes would be needed to facilitate the search.

As soon as he was able, Selson alerted all members of the research team of Markcarter's fugitive status and his assumption of Earth-animal form. That done, he and Creson took a moment to search each other's eyes, each knowing he should have been aware of the tiny animal that was in their midst—the necessary instruments had not been turned on; neither had thought it necessary. In addition to personal shame, they felt sympathy, both for themselves and for what was sure to result from their carelessness. With respect to the Earth man, Takar would not be put off any longer.

With sadness in his eyes, Creson turned toward the now silent beam into which Markcarter disappeared. There was no telling where the Earth creature might eventually exit if he kept dashing into these things. He apparently did not know that, in the absence of a clearly-expressed destination, the conveyer would make a "best guess"—he could wind up literally anywhere. He decided to close all tubes exiting the complex, this in the hope that it would place limits on how far Markcarter could travel. He wondered whether it was already too late; perhaps Markcarter had already reached one of the long-distance tubes that offered transport from the laboratory to the cities of Mantz. He smiled at the thought of how the poor, unprepared creature would react to what he found there.

"Perhaps a scan?" Creson said, seeing the indecision in Selson's face, an indecision he felt as well. But Selson only stared at his colleague as if offended by the suggestion. Regarding himself as close to infallible in such matters, he had already initiated a scan of the entire complex in search of an Earth chipmunk. When success was not immediate, he broadened this to include any of Earth's biological species. Although Creson was used to such expressions from his sometimes insufferable colleague, he offered a gesture of apology.

The scan produced nothing. There was no chipmunk within the complex, nor was there any other Earth creature that was not already known to the two scientists. Selson paused in thought; did this mean Markcarter really had reached the outer tubes? Or had he converted to yet another form? Selson remembered the last time he himself had tried a body conversion, how long it had taken. More than an hour, and that for a simple form. Admittedly, conversion was not his forte, but this primitive representative of Earth should not be able to do it better! Wearing a characteristically sour expression, he again communicated with Takar, this time to inform him of his new suspicions.

Takar sat in the cushioned beam that acted as his chair and stared at a patch of pulsating light on the wall, a decoration of sorts that had always pleased him in the past. Now it was simply annoying. He could not shake the sense of dread that had overtaken him since Selson's call. Dread at having to tell the Council, at not having told them before, and at the thought of an alien creature with conversion and telekinetic capabilities wandering around their world unsupervised. And undetected!

At his usual rapid speed, he mentally reviewed the information gleaned thus far from the Earth man, most of which came from scanning sessions. He then reviewed reports of the Mantz scouts regarding the Earth man's mate and the search undertaken on her behalf by Earth's legal authorities. With anguish and concern becoming more visible by the second, he lowered his head and stared for a long moment at the series of monitors that surrounded him on three sides, most of which were still and silent. Finally, his decision made, he turned toward a beam and communicated a series of orders.

CHAPTER 25

There was no obvious route of escape. Conveyer beams were everywhere but there were no road signs to tell him where they went. It was like playing Russian roulette.

He had to find his way to that now mystical place where he and Creson entered the laboratory complex an unknown number of weeks ago. If he could make it that far, even if that meant crazy woods and crazy animals, he could stay in hiding until the transporter went on. Hell, with so many travelers going to and from Earth, it had to be on a lot. Maybe it was never turned off. As far as where it went, all he had to do was wait until a light-colored, German shepherd came out of the woods; that would mean the transporter was not only on but was pointed at Earth. Simple, once he found his way to the jumping-off point.

Shit! His wings felt like they were ready to fall off from excessive use. So did everything else in his alien body. By now, even with his crazy flinac eyes, he knew what a conveyer beam looked like, but it was increasingly unlikely that it would lead to a place where he could take a break—there was always someone or something there that made a return to the beam a smart choice. So he had to keep going, flying into beam after beam, naively hoping that beyond the next one was the promised land!

Most of the rooms he entered, as far as he could tell with his insect eyes, were similar to the one in which his chamber stood, but some were positively frightening, filled with creatures he could not hope to identify even with human eyes. Those rooms he left with more haste than usual.

One in particular he did not want to visit again, accidentally or otherwise. It housed some kind of museum filled with an impressive variety of creatures. They were not enclosed in chambers but simply suspended from a single beam, their forms still and lifeless. Collectively they offered a sea of alien bodies and a diversity of oddly shaped limbs and sensory organs, the specific functions of which were anybody's guess. A surprising number had four or more major appendages, most of the additions seeming to serve as extra hands rather than feet. Although curious, Mark could not bring himself to stay long enough to decide whether these were once living beings or only clever projections. It would do little for his morale if they proved to be earlier guests of the Mantzites.

The tubes, although everywhere, had proved to be a bad bet. They led nowhere, at least nowhere when used by a novice Earth man. It was fruitless to continue even while impossible to stop. Recognizing that the decision would be made for him if he did not get some rest, he made one more gallant but unsuccessful try, then retreated to the corner of yet another unidentified laboratory, this one at least empty of Mantzites and alien bodies.

He used the resting time to think. Maybe something else he had learned during the experience sessions could be summoned from wherever it had been planted to the forefront of his memory. Another form or knowledge of those damn conveyer beams. *Shit*, he said as he remember again the visit to Tanterac. *The hell with the beams; I'll go through the walls.*

Still feeling the effect of overexertion but with his enthusiasm renewed, he made his flinac body as fluid as he knew how then, with only a moment's hesitation, flew at the nearest wall. For a moment, it appeared as if he might actually make it—his body pushed well into the wall. But then, like the chamber earlier, the wall pushed back. He landed heavily on the floor.

He lay there for a long moment, wondering how, after such a good start, things could go so sour. To make it easier on his weary system, he reconverted his flinac body to normal density—maintaining two alien forms at the same time was too much. Just as he completed the process, two Mantzites popped out of one of the room's three beams then began to search the room with their eyes. Mark knew they had to be looking for him, but what he did not know was whether they were aware of his new form. Each carried a pencil-thin beam device, which Mark recognized as the same all-purpose tool carried by Wilpin. The "all-purpose," as he well remembered, included a weapon. *Maybe an insecticide also,* he thought with a wry humor he did not feel. He wondered what they would do if they spotted him. They did not look friendly.

His apprehension increased as the search neared the area where he still lay catching his flinac breath. As their eyes fell on him then paused as if unsure, the apprehension turned into panic. Impulsively, he projected an image toward the tube behind them, hoping it would be perceived as coming from that direction. "He's in here! Come quickly!"

It was a mistake; it only confirmed to the newcomers what he was. They raised their weapons and moved in his direction, bringing him to leap into the air then fly as rapidly as his alien wings could manage toward the nearest tube—whatever unknown was in there, it was better than the known that was out here. One of the Mantzites moved to block his way, its eyes easily following Mark's movement. The other ran toward the hexagonal panel to close off the conveyers. Out of the corner of one of his many eyes, Mark saw the single button the creature touched to accomplish this purpose. Its function was confirmed when his flinac body bounced off the conveyer opening.

He recovered as quickly as he could, then flew in an opposite direction, his aim then just to keep moving. It confused his attackers and gave him a chance to focus on the light that the creature had touched. But it was easier in thought than in practice; it was impossible to imagine himself touching anything while so constantly on the move. He had to take a chance. With desperation temporarily outweighing fear, he alighted on a table then forced himself to think, not of his pursuers, but only of the critical light. It worked; unknown to his would-be captors, the tubes were once again operational.

His sudden stop caught the pursuing Mantzites by surprise, and they momentarily overran their quarry, one bumping heavily into a table beam before finally catching himself. The other recovered quickly and lunged backward just in time to close a hand over the target flinac—the shock of being covered by a giant hand brought Mark to momentary paralysis. Elated, the Mantzite reacted with an image of boastful accomplishment. "I got him! The Earth creature has been recovered!"

Mark, however, was not ready to surrender his newly-found freedom. Having little to lose, he began to convert back to chipmunk form, the speed at which he did so causing air and moisture to suck under the Mantzite's hand as if to satisfy a vacuum inside. Even as his attention was drawn elsewhere, Mark enjoyed the thought of the creature's face as the object under its palm began to grow—into what, it could only imagine.

When the process was complete enough to permit movement, Mark sunk his chipmunk teeth into the nearest piece of flesh he could find. Predictably, the hand withdrew. Then, without waiting to see whether it would return, he jumped off the table, ran over to a beam then literally leaped into its glowing void. He left behind a series of cosmic-level expletives.

At the other end, he immediately began searching for the hexagonal panel that he knew would have to be nearby. It was, and he focused on the same light that had closed off beam travel from the other end—hopefully it meant the same here as it did there. The light went on just as an angry Mantzite began taking shape in front of him. Its exit from the tube interrupted, it became frozen in position, unable to move and almost invisible. One foot, more composed than the rest of his body but not yet where it could be called functional, hung awkwardly from the opening. Mark could not help but smile as he stared at what he had to admit was a million-to-one shot.

Recognizing that he would not be permitted time to savor his tiny victory, he reconverted to flinac form then flew toward another of the conveyer tubes, releasing the light just as he entered it. It stiffened slightly but then gave way. It was the start of another headlong dash through the beams in search of an illusive dream—Mark wondered what the statistical probability was of his hitting it by chance. Something had to change and soon; the fatigue was already beginning to return, fatigue born of too many difficult conversions and too large a drain on his emotions.

But success was as illusory as ever, and before long he was crushed to find himself back in the laboratory usually occupied by Selson and his staff, the room from which he had begun his mad and as yet unsuccessful dash for freedom. The only plus was that it was now empty. Settling back into a corner, using a table beam for cover, he considered what was left of his options. There was no obvious path of escape from the laboratory complex. That required knowledge of the beams, and this he did not have. It was hopeless.

He stayed where he was, alternately resting and sulking for over an hour, being reminded once during that time of the necessity to concentrate on maintaining the flinac shape—after some forty minutes, it began to degrade to human form. No one entered the laboratory during this time, but still he toyed with the idea of turning off the conveyer beam as he had before. He did not when he realized it would only serve to pinpoint his location. *They probably know how to override it anyway*, he thought.

Nothing was going his way. Jumping from beam to beam was a colossal waste of time; maybe Creson had arranged it just to wear him out as one might try to wear out an overactive child. Sooner or later someone was bound to find him, and when they did, the rules of the game would change. What he had done would not make his hosts friendlier.

There was one more thing he could try, although the thought of it left him with mixed feelings: He could convert to the same form used by his captors. He could become a Mantzite and walk among them undetected, maybe even grab one, steal his beam weapon and force him to lead the way to the outside. It was as good a plan as any.

A canvass of his expanded memory proved that the knowledge was there—why, he didn't know. Why would Wilpin, or any other Mantzite, want to convert to what they already were? Maybe the blueprint was incorrect; maybe since they were already there, they never put it to the test. Searching his memory further, he found he also had the blueprint of a human being. It dawned on him then that this was necessary for converting back; he had to know the details of how to get there.

Conversion to a Mantzite turned out to be more difficult than converting to a flinac, but the timing was about the same. Afterward Mark angled his head to admire what he could see of his new form. There were no obvious omissions or "brands" of any kind that would give him away, but he wished he had a mirror to make sure. "It's got to do," he mumbled aloud, the words barely out of his mouth when a more genuine Mantzite popped into the room.

Mark was startled away from his self congratulations as the creature, seeing what looked to be a colleague, projected a routine image of greeting. Emotions barely under control, Mark returned the greeting then worried that his mental voice was quivering—was there a uniqueness to mental projections, similar to that of the human voice? Nervously, he turned to a nearby monitor and pretended to be interested in its lights. As he fussed, with no idea of how to make his actions look authentic, he could feel the creature's eyes burning into his fur on the back of his neck. It made it difficult to keep his breathing to a normal level. At any moment he expected to feel the flash of a weapon—would there be a sensation or would he simply cease to exist?

It ended as abruptly as it had begun. Without another "word," the creature turned and exited the laboratory.

Mark was close to collapse. Only with difficulty was he able to keep himself vertical until the dizziness passed and his Mantz heart slowed to normal. He wondered whether the creature had seen through his disguise. Was he even now going for help? *But if he knew who I was, why wouldn't he try to take me himself? He had a beam weapon; all of them do.*

Remaining in this room, regardless of whether or not his Mantzite form was being accepted, was unwise. In addition to the possibility of help even now being on the way, there was nothing here of value; nothing to help him get to the outside. Even so, he paused long enough to examine a cubicle located just above where he stood; he had been too frightened to notice it before. It contained a living being, a being that stared at him with an expression that betrayed frustration and a touch of sadness.

Obviously contained against its will, the creature appeared to be intelligent, its expression one that suggested deep thought. Except for a Mantzite covering, similar to the one given himself, its body exuded a deep shade of red. It was an appealing color, which only added to Mark's feelings of pity—a thing of beauty being mishandled. It stood upright on two legs, both of which ended in rounded hooves interrupted by a slight split in the front; in this respect it gave the impression of having just stepped out of a chapter in Greek mythology. Two upper appendages, possessing gripper-like endings, were exceptionally thin with no more consistency than whips or loose ropes. Above a tiny neck and rounding out the top of a leathery body, was more of a nodule than a head. But the facial features were obvious and not too dissimilar to those of other creatures Mark had seen on Mantz, on Tanterac, and in the laboratories during his mad dash through the tubes. Sharp black discs were probably eyes, while a cavity in the center of its face had to serve as at least a mouth; possibly a nose as well. There were no indications of ears and Mark wondered if it even had the ability to sense sound.

Aware of the similarity of their plights, Mark stared at it with the same curiosity that it stared at him—neither had any idea what to make of the other. *Probably thinks I'm just another Mantzite,* Mark thought, feeling something like kinship to this creature. "I wonder what's in store for you, friend," he said, lowering his head as he spoke to trigger the description that he knew always accompanied an exhibit. A second of focusing was all it took to get the narrative to begin.

He learned that it had recently been brought from a planet called Simerill and that it was not considered to be a dominant species. It was an exhibit, nothing more, eventually to be stored (Mark wondered if this meant alive) or returned to its planet. He couldn't believe it, the thing seemed so sensitive, so bright. *I wonder who makes these decisions,* he thought.

Turning to leave the laboratory, Mark felt rather than heard a pitiful plea to stay. He turned back then saw the black disks of the creature's eyes cloud over and its mouth reduce to a small oval. Even as he could not hope to understand what that meant, it got to him. "I'm sorry, friend," he projected, the sense of camaraderie again strong. "I'm in the same boat as you." He stared a moment longer and wondered whether it even knew what he was trying to say. Thoughts of the creature weighed heavily upon him long after he entered the nearest conveyer tube and disappeared.

No greater success greeted his increasingly weary soul this time, only the senseless entering and leaving of rooms that held no meaning for him. He even returned once to the room that held the still pathetic creature. In another he came upon two Mantzites, both of whom turned at his entry and briefly stared before acknowledging his projected greeting then returning to their work. Prudently Mark resisted the urge to exit immediately, instead pretending to inspect an object on a beam table until it seemed proper to leave.

The Mantzite form was certainly preferable—and probably safer—to that of an insect, but the result was much the same: He was continuing to wear himself out by traveling in circles. *There's got to be a way to tell he conveyer where you want to go!* he thought. He searched his memory, hoping that, like the other things he'd learned, it was in there someplace. After a while he had to conclude that, if there at all, it sure as hell wasn't obvious!

Depression joined the fatigue. A touch of hunger as well—the rejuvenation chamber usually took care of that for him. But how to get food, and where to rest safely was as illusive as how to get out of the complex. With a sigh and that spoke of little hope for success, he pushed toward the nearest tube and tried again.

The senseless flight continued, although now he remained longer within each failure, hoping that a closer inspection would reveal some clue as to how to break out of the agonizing circle. It never did, and the rooms themselves did not differ that much, except for the nature of the exhibits and the personnel assigned to their care. He had begun to think the pattern would never change when chance bought him to the experience chamber. There the familiar sight of the machine allowed him a brief moment of hope; all the answers he was seeking lay inside. But even if he could figure out how to turn it on, there was still the danger to consider. After all, he had almost died even while under the close supervision of a medical expert. Being here was nothing more than another defeat, and his mind ached with thoughts of rest as he jumped into yet another of the beams.

At the other end was a surprise: a huge room containing scores of chambers, each similar to the one that had once restrained him. Most were unoccupied, but some contained what looked to be slumbering Mantzites. Mark approached an occupied cubicle and examined the closed eyes of the creature within, aware that if they opened at that moment he would soil his Mantz costume. They did not; the creature was unconscious; perhaps they all were.

He decided it was a kind of communal rest and rejuvenation room, its size suggesting the probability of hundreds of workers in the complex, perhaps more considering that they would likely rotate usage of each device, using and reusing them in shifts. Aware of his own body's needs and tired of going nowhere, Mark considered using one of the chambers to rest; in current form, he might go unnoticed. Thanks to Wilpin, there was no need to worry about maintaining Mantzite form during sleep; that knowledge was passed on along with everything else. And it would give him time to think. The thought of being so close to his captors was not a comfortable one, but it appeared to be the best of a bad choice of options. He decided to go for it; fatigue was getting in the way of good judgment.

Having made the decision, the next problem was how to get inside the chamber of his choice then turn it on. He sought out the inevitable hexagonal panel, then noticed it was really two panels side by side. One was the standard, identical to those he'd seen in other rooms, but the other was a puzzle. It probably had something to do with the selection of chambers, but what? What light must be pressed to control what chamber?

He would have to play the dangerous game of experimentation with a roomful of adversaries as possible spectators. A sigh of resignation preceded his entry into one of the units, and he felt a heavy discomfort at voluntarily permitting himself to once again be confined. In the event he pressed the wrong button, he feigned sleep before choosing a light at random from the first panel and mentally forcing it on. Afterward he did the same for those lights on the second panel which he knew would have contained him in his old chamber.

A unit twelve rows down went on; fortunately it was unoccupied.

Mark turned the lights out as fast as he could then glanced nervously around the cavernous room. No one was there to notice; no damage had been done. His mouth turned dry as he considered another guess—another error like that and the game could be over. About to mentally touch his new choice, he suddenly realized it was not necessary; if he already knew how to control the one across the room then he would use the one across the room. He moved toward the chosen unit, stepped inside then turned it on. It made no attempt to stop him, nor did it restrain the shaking hand which nervously thrust back into the room. He could apparently use this chamber without fear that it would restrain him against his will.

He soon began to feel the familiar sense of calm and contentment; as hoped, the machine was providing for his needs, this time Mantzite needs. Although wanting to use the time to think things through, he easily surrendered to the bliss brought on by the rapid relief from fatigue and hunger and by the calming agents produced by the unit. Within seconds he was sleeping soundly.

He remained that way for hours, unaware of the Mantzites who came and went as he slept, all taking no notice of the sleeping alien in their midst.

CHAPTER 26

Sergeant Ken Janos was dumbfounded. The area where Carter had knelt down showed clear evidence of the lost camper and a dog, but both tracks disappeared a short distance beyond that, and no amount of searching on the part of dozens of experienced trackers could turn up a trace of where they resumed. This was more than just confusing; the tracks, including those of the dog, were crystal clear and the condition of the ground should have permitted them to remain visible. In desperation, Ken sent men back to Carter's campsite, where the dog had first been discovered, with instructions to follow its tracks back to their origin. If this was the same kind of dog as those spotted in Kelly, maybe its home was hidden somewhere in these woods; maybe Carter was there at this very moment. But the tracks only went back toward town—not much help at all. The men who reported this did so with obvious reluctance; they did not appreciate deviations from what their mountaineer's knowledge told them was logical.

Ken tried to attach reason to the physical evidence, but found it a loosing game. There was too much here that just didn't make sense. The tracks, for example; they suggested man and dog had grown lighter as they traveled away from the campsite; footprints became more and more shallow as if the two were slowly being lifted into the air. This could not have been due to a change in terrain; the ground was soft and moist and there were no connecting rocks on which they could have stepped or streams they could have walked through, nothing to suggest an alternative to vanishing foot prints.

"I just don't get it, Tom," Ken said to the man on his right. "Is there absolutely nothing further on? No signs at all?"

"We searched a couple of square miles and didn't pick up nothing. The area's clean, Ken. Don't look like nobody's been through for some time." Tom Sloan was smaller than his 6 feet, 2 inch boss and, at 165 pounds, a good thirty pounds lighter. But what he lacked in size he made up for in skill; he and Ken had worked together for years, and neither would want to be doing this without the other. Tom's only negative, as far as Ken could see, was a tendency toward exaggeration. And, unfortunately considering what they were facing now, toward the supernatural.

"It would help if we could find dog droppings. The lab might be able to tell us what kind it is." Ken rubbed his forehead as he talked. "It could be the same as keeps popping up in Kelly."

"Yeah, Cal told me about that; sounded mostly like he was trying to put me on." Then he nodded his head and added, "Could be the same, I guess. Anyways, it seems to've disappeared here same as in Kelly. And took Carter with it." He frowned at what his words suggested.

Janos noted the frown and raced to keep things on an even keel. It wouldn't do to permit his easily-persuaded friend to get carried away. "Well, I think we should keep our eyes on the ground where it'll do some good. Why don't you check around to see if anyone's reported a missing dog. If you get a lead, check with the owner to see if it came back—and when. Oh, and ask him what kind of dog it is."

Tom left to comply, which meant contacting the helicopter which would relay the message to headquarters in Jackson. After he left, Ken stayed where he was, staring at the ground and reflecting on the mystery of the disappearing tracks. "Doesn't make sense," he mumbled aloud, poking the toe of his boot in the dirt as if to do so would help his thinking process. "How could anyone keep from making tracks in this dirt? Even if he wanted to hide them, he'd have problems." He wondered whether this was deliberate, that somebody they didn't know about wanted to hide Carter's trail. That would mean Carter was not lost; he was kidnapped. Didn't make much sense, but at least it fit the facts better. Only problem is, if they were going to do that, why wouldn't they erase all the tracks? What's the point of creating a mystery? *Maybe that is the point: to create a mystery. Somebody with a weird sense of humor. Or maybe a nutcase trying to throw us off the track.* The thought made Ken uneasy. His men were armed, but only to the extent necessary to discourage wild animals from attacking. They were not prepared for real, honest-to-goodness criminals.

"Ah, I'm getting as bad as Tom," he mumbled, leaving his spot in favor of the campfire and the coffee offered nearby.

Ken Janos did not like to be so unsure of his facts. Plus, he was ashamed of the fact that he and his men, with all the skills they possessed, could not scare up the tracks of one inexperienced camper. *Maybe we can't spot signs from the air, but we sure as hell should be able to spot them on the ground!* There were no towns nearby, other than the one that served as the jumping off place for Carter, so it was not reasonable to expect that the man had reached civilization on his own, at least not in the direction he was headed. And they'd picked up no sign of anyone else in the area, no one who might have seen him at one time or another. *Other than a goddamn dog, and we don't even know where it came from or where it disappeared to!*

Tom had little to offer from his call to headquarters. Examination of a plaster cast of the dog's tracks indicated an animal about the size of a shepherd, although the lab was unable to say for sure. They did, however, feel the dog was young; there were few signs of wear on its paws.

"Great," said Ken. "All we have to do is look for a giant puppy who likes to fly!"

Tom shuffled his feet a little before offering, "Ya know, Ken, maybe we should call for help on this. Some of this stuff ain't natural."

Ken let his frown be obvious. "I don't know if that'd do anything but hurt us," he replied. "We're a long way from being able to cry 'flying saucer.' All we got is a weird set of footprints. They'll think we're trying to cop out of doing our job." Then he shook his said and added, "No, I think he's here someplace and, one way or the other, we're gonna find him." He smiled to lessen the impact of the scolding then said, "I tell you though, this thing gets any weirder, I just might take you up on that suggestion."

Tom Sloan was not easily dissuaded. "Some of the other guys are gettin' itchy too. They see what we see and they don't feel bad about speculatin'."

There was no smile on Ken's face as he said, "Damnit, they should know better than that! How many times have we come up against something we can't put our finger on, and how many of those times has it led us to Martians?"

"Hey, I'm just telling you what they're thinkin'," Tom said, raising a hand as if to defend himself. "But I will tell ya this, I ain't so comfortable myself."

Sinot lay motionless in the woods listening to the two Earth men discuss Markcarter's disappearance. She was particularly interested in the flying saucer comment. This type of speculation was exactly what the Council needed to be aware of.

It was obvious that her people had erred in not considering such things as footprints. And, of course, in their use of the same disguise over and over again—it was convenient but failed to acknowledge a human tendency to notice such things. A change would have to be made; the lab would have to vary their choices and colors, maybe even permit the use of other domesticated pets as well. The difficulty in that, as everyone knew, was that each selected animal had to be studied in depth to determine what in its genes made it the way it was. That took time, a goodly amount of time. Based on what was happening here, however, it would appear prudent to make the effort.

There were Earth dogs among the searchers, and to prevent them from reacting to what they could regard as a competitor, Sinot had converted to a chipmunk—another popular disguise among Mantz explorers, although not one that would get them into the homes and business's of Earth's dominant species. Plus the chipmunk form created a problem with the beam weapon—no place to hide it on such a small body.

Sinot was painfully aware that she had no such problem; her beam was still in the possession of Markcarter's mate. Traveling in an alien land without protection was unnerving, but she had no choice. She had to get word to the communication link that was still a number of miles away, and without the beam, it was necessary to carry the message on foot.

How fortunate it was that she happened to bump into Markcarter's searchers on the way. Equally fortunate that they did not bump into her first; discovering another light-colored shepherd would only add to already growing suspicions.

With caution and a minimum of noise, Sinot backed away from the perplexed Earth men then gave them and their sensitive animals a wide berth as she pushed her tiny chipmunk body toward the closest rendezvous point. It would take less time if she could revert back to canine form, but that would give the searchers another set of prints to look at—what might they think then? At the rendezvous, a report would be rushed on to Mantz by beam, and soon thereafter—perhaps very soon thereafter—a new set of orders would be issued. Sinot had little doubt that she would soon be returning to the Earth woman's room to pick up Zarpin.

CHAPTER 27

In his borrowed rest and rejuvenation chamber, Mark was as relaxed as he had ever been, and when he awoke, it was to a feeling of supreme tranquillity. It lasted only long enough for him to remember where he was and what he was attempting to do.

As his eyes took in as much as they could of the room, he wondered how long he had been asleep. And what had changed in the interim. Some creatures, present when he drifted off, were no longer there. Others had taken their place—it was difficult to be sure of any of this; the Mantzites looked so much alike. But at least his disguise had proven itself; he had gone undetected in the den of his enemy.

Well rested or not, he was no closer to a solution now than before. He still did not know how to break the pattern of unending laboratories and recalcitrant conveyer beams. And there was little reason to leave this chamber until that changed. He stared at the closest beam and wondered what he was not seeing, what it was that made it work. When he was tired, really tired, it led him here. Had it read his mind?

He had no time to answer the question as just at that moment Selson popped into the room.

Had he not been so alarmed, Mark would have smiled at the now-familiar surly look Selson sported as he slowly glanced around the room, taking in everything and everyone, including a disguised Earth man. Mark closed his eyes to pretend sleep and hoped that what doubled for a heart within his Mantzite body was not beating as loudly as it seemed. But Selson paid him no attention as he then walked over to the panel, touched a few lights and entered a chamber. Much to Mark's relief, his eyes soon closed and his breathing began to slow.

Mark could not bring himself to move. He remembered how quickly the chamber's chemicals had overcome him, but would the same thing happen to Selson; was the effect on an imitation Mantzite body any different than it was on the real thing? Reluctant to take the chance, he continued to feign sleep for a number of additional minutes before giving serious thought to leaving the chamber.

Selson had made at least one decision for him; he had to get out of this room and quickly. Forgetting that there was no "containment module" to overcome, that he could walk away at any time, he stared at the panel, found what he was looking for, then applied the procedure that had released him in the past. Then he chose the light on the second panel that he thought controlled the chamber he was in. It was a bad guess; the lights dimmed in the chamber occupied by Selson—in his haste he had reached out to the last light seen, the one used by his adversary. *All the units in this room and I pick that one!* he thought.

Under lowered eyelids, he watched as Selson opened his eyes first in confusion then in anger—the surly expression returned to his face. He left the chamber in a huff, banged in instructions for another unit and stormed inside, glaring first at the offending chamber as if to properly reproach it. The lights of his new choice brightened, and Selson responded by closing his eyes. But the surly expression was a long time in disappearing.

Mark knew he would be shaking were it not for the calming effect of the rest and rejuvenation chamber. He felt stupid, especially since he had finally realized how unnecessary the button sequence had been. When enough time had past to permit Selson to succumb to sleep, he stepped gingerly to the floor then felt a farewell blast of tranquilizers from a maternal rest and rejuvenation machine. He was once again free to roam the research complex, whatever good that would do.

But the day, which had already given him one unpleasant surprise, offered another. On his way to the beam, he stopped when a movement caught his eye. A Mantzite, a female as Mark now readily recognized, had opened her eyes and, after displaying something similar to a human yawn, jumped to the floor then turned toward the conveyer intending to walk into it. She slowed when finally she saw the semi-paralyzed colleague that was blocking the way. Mark recovered enough to step aside but could think of nothing more than that to do. He tried to remember the greeting given a day before when surprised in Selson's laboratory, but before he could bring it to mind, the Mantzite brushed by, nodded a curt hello then vanished into the beam. Mark stared at the spot where she disappeared for a long time.

By then the chamber's parting gift of tranquilizers was no more; his overworked emotional system had consumed all of it; he was on his own, forced to brave onslaughts against his sanity by himself. But at least the incident proved his disguise was a good one. It was a boost to his confidence, perhaps the only one he was likely to get.

When another Mantzite began stirring within his chamber, Mark decided it was time to move on to whatever lay on the other side of that conveyer tube. He had a nagging feeling that he was close to understanding the device, but there was no time to think it through now. Instead he gave a sigh of resignation then jumped in.

As usual the transporting was immediate, this time depositing him in a large room, one in which he had not been before. It appeared to be some kind of staging area. A number of Mantzites, a few carrying what looked to be backpacks, were scurrying about with serious expressions on their faces. Mark recognized no one, and no one paid him any attention as he stood there quietly observing.

It looked like some were readying themselves for space travel; this could be assumed by the body conversions they were attempting, all of which were alien to Mark. Watching them confirmed his suspicions that his teachers were unable to convert as fast as he—another boost to a shaky confidence. He watched them carefully, hoping at least one was converting to a German shepherd. If that happened, he would be right behind him in the conveyer tube.

Even with the anxiety he felt, Mark was fascinated by the different shapes taking form in front of him. He realized he was seeing life as it existed on planets he knew nothing about, other worlds with all manner of beings, each with the same desire for life as he. Some of the forms reminded him of creatures seen during scanning sessions.

One Mantzite was struggling to assume the form of a being five times his normal size—it was taking forever. Even while certain that he would not take as long, Mark understood what the fellow was going through; it took time to generate the chemicals and additional cells required by such a large body. Still unknown was whether the Mantzite would possess the strength of the form he was assuming. *If I became an elephant, could I just storm out of here?* he mused?

Not anxious to enter yet another tube, Mark stood to one side, watched the transformations and wondered how many planets were represented by them. So far none looked anything like a shepherd, but he did not lose hope. He could probably get to the outside just by following any one of them into a beam as he had followed Creson. That would put him outside the complex and closer to the tunnel to Earth.

With Mantzites coming and going, it took a number of seconds to realize that one of the newcomers was Creson—his day was getting worse. When he realized who he was staring at, Mark at first stiffened then forced upon himself a calm that was far from what he really felt. Here was the one creature sure to see through his disguise.

He watched as Creson moved his eyes move from one traveler to another, omitting none. When it became Mark's turn and the eyes stopped, Mark tried to feign interest in a conversion taking place across the room. He also tired to keep from meeting Creson's eyes. But it was not to be. Apparently satisfied by what he had seen, Creson began walking in his direction. Mark gave no thought to moving away; it would only draw attention to himself. Instead he waited in agony for whatever his Mantzite antagonist had in mind.

Creson did not keep him in suspense. Approaching to within five feet he asked without hesitation, "Are you Tenite?"

Mark was unsure how to reply. He was aware that the name-suffix used by Creson referred to a rank subservient to Creson's own; was the Mantzite mistaking him for a subordinate?

Creson continued without waiting for an answer. "I believe you have been assigned to me. I appreciate your being early; I would just as soon get going. We have a long trip and we must arrive before he does."

With a flash of emotional stability that Mark did not know he possessed, he responded with, "I am ready." He took care to imitate the Mantzite form of expression, but the stare that followed did nothing for his confidence. *Is this real,* he thought, *or is he putting me on?* Creson had said "long trip" and wanting to "arrive before he does." How likely was it that Creson would go on a long trip while his pet project ran around loose in the complex? *The "he" he wants to get there ahead of must be me. He believes I made it out of the complex.* Mark's eyes contracted slightly as he considered the irony of being part of the party sent to retrieve himself.

Creson turned and entered a tube. Mark, not wanting to chance loosing him, was only a step behind. He did not care at the moment where they were headed. Whatever was taking place, it held more promise than what he faced on his own.

Much to Mark's delight they reappeared outside the research complex, the exact spot he had been trying so hard to reach. A feeling of elation flooded his system, even as he wondered how it had happened. If it were due to how closely he'd followed Creson into the tube, then he was okay. But if it were Creson's doing, it meant his captor felt the need to work the conveyor for him, and that would mean he knew he did not have a fellow Mantzite in tow.

Mark shook his head. Maybe it didn't matter. Maybe all that mattered was that he was a step closer to escape. With his new-found skills—and a little luck—he could defend himself. No matter what, he would not allow himself to be taken back inside the complex.

He shifted his thoughts to where Creson was leading him. And of what role he was supposed to play, how he was expected to behave. His inferior rank would at least give him liberty to remain quiet, but sooner or later this strategy would fall short. For the moment Creson did not seem interested in communicating at all. With head down in apparent thought, he set out at a pace destined to put many miles between them and the research complex in short order.

The time and miles went by quickly. As he followed a respectful distance behind, Mark marveled at how familiar the surroundings were to him. Sharing the experiences of Mantzites had given him a form of local knowledge—he felt like a native. So strong was this feeling that he felt competent to explain the basics of each plant and why the color of the water and the sky was as it was. He knew the types and origins of animals and other forms of life found here. And it was all knowledge he had acquired without effort.

Creson maintained his rapid pace and continued to show no desire to communicate, but Mark, aware of how much he did *not* know about Mantz and its people, was becoming more unsure of himself with each step. At some point he would be discovered for what he was, and before that happened he had to come up with a plan. Creson would likely have a weapon, but could he ever hope to take it away from him? How he would love to turn the tables on his captor, show him how it feels to be stuck in a small box on an alien planet. *I'll toss him a tranquilizer from time to time.*

He stopped in mid-thought as he realized Creson's body was in the process of changing. It was subtle at first, leaving Mark to wonder whether the red-tinted air was affecting his imagination, but as time went by, it became pronounced—Creson was converting, to what Mark did not know. Before he had time to think about it, Creson swung his head around, threw a look of disapproval Mark's way then projected an order to begin converting. Without waiting for a response, he turned back and continued walking.

Convert to what? thought Mark. Creson had apparently expected him to know. He watched the Mantzite's changing body hoping to discover in time what it intended to become. As he watched he felt satisfaction at how slow his captor was compared to himself. In fact, Creson was slower than any of the Mantzites whose experiences he'd shared. Talent apparently played a part in the employment of mental powers.

Knowing he had to come up with something, Mark chose what he hoped for most then began converting to it. Creson was currently responsible for the exploration of Earth; if they were heading in that direction then it figured that the standard Earth form would be used, a German shepherd. Mark hoped he could get away with claiming a lapse of concentration should that prove to be a bad guess.

Not knowing how to convert slowly, Mark completed the transformation in seconds, far more rapidly than Creson or any other

Mantzite could—if Creson looked back for even a second, he would realize his subordinate was not a Mantzite. The minutes drifted by in agony, with Mark watching Creson's slow progress and wishing he could do something to speed it up. Fortunately the necessity to concentrate on what to him was a difficult metamorphosis, kept Creson's eyes to the front. In any event, it was now clear that the Mantzite would become what Mark had hoped for. Mark's sigh of relief was louder than was wise.

The fear of being discovered kept Mark from noticing the slow change in scenery, but as the tension softened his awareness increased. Knowing he had to be well within the transporter brought a smile to his canine face and a momentary contracting of his eyes. He considered the possibility that they were heading for a planet other than Earth but then dismissed it as unlikely. Unless dogs were found all over the universe, he was on his way home.

Even so, he was nagged by the feeling that it was all too convenient, too easy.

As they continued their long march and the Earth destination became more of a certainty, Mark began to relax. Each step was a further assurance of survival, like marching away from the front lines of a long-raging battle. Control was slowly being shifted to himself, and the relief it brought with it made him giddy.

Careless as well. Observing the details of the canine shape Creson had assumed, Mark unintentionally projected what was intended only as an amusing thought: "I guess you really are a male." It was "said" in such a way that Creson could not help but pick it up, but inexplicably the Mantzite merely sighed and kept moving.

It was enough to sober Mark considerably. He had made what had to be recognized as an alien comment yet Creson continued to act as if he were unaware of the imitation walking along behind him. *That was a sigh of disapproval*, Mark thought, having heard it so many times before from Creson. *But what the hell does it mean!?* Mentally kicking himself for jeopardizing his chances so close to freedom, Mark wondered whether it was time to make a break for it—the nature of the trees around him as much as said he was committed to Earth. But something made him continue onward, something about the confident stride of the alien in front of him, a stride that said control was still in his hands. As hard as it was for him to do, Mark recovered the steps he'd lost while making the decision then held himself to only a few steps behind.

The scenery continued its slow transformation; Mark was acutely aware of the differences between what he was seeing now and what had been left behind. It was a reversal of what he had faced in ignorance an untold number of weeks ago. It was close to normal, Earth normal. The sky as well; it offered a light blue haze. There were no recognizable landmarks as yet, but that mattered less than the fact that he had made it back to Wyoming, USA. And, most importantly, Earth.

The pace did not vary, however. It continued at something close to a trot, much faster than on the trip in—Creson was in some kind of hurry. It was tiring, but Mark was not inclined to object. He would just as soon keep going, throughout the night if that's what it took to get to safety. As darkness began to descend, he wondered whether Creson intended to do exactly that.

As if in response, Creson pulled to a stop then turned around, the timing of the action causing Mark to fear that he had again projected his private thoughts. He stood there in silence, afraid to say or do anything that might confirm what Creson probably already knew. Instead he watched the shaded face of his one-time captor and tried to keep the frown of concern off his own.

Mark was concerned but not as much as when the trip began. Being on his own turf made a difference. He could vanish into the bush and Creson could do little to stop him. Of course, he had to figure out where he was first.

The scene they were acting out was filled with irony: two dogs facing off against one another in the middle of the wild west, each ready to defend his honor. Mark suppressed a momentary urge to growl.

Creson's projected words returned him to sober reality. "Your body will need sustenance but we will be unable to obtain any until tomorrow."

Mark was instantly alert. What was supposed to happen tomorrow?

"Until then ingest this capsule. It will provide enough of what you require until something more satisfying becomes available." He handed a red, gelatinous pill to Mark with a three-fingered hand. Unwilling to convert in front of his adversary, Mark received it clumsily in his canine paw.

Creson's orders, which were given in a matter-of-fact manner, gave no indication of what he was thinking. Afterward, he strolled over to a tree then sat down, appearing as he did so to have mastered the role of an Earth canine. Mark glanced at the capsule, wondering how wise it would be to take it—Creson had not taken one himself. As if reading his mind,

Creson produced another for himself, reaching into his back pack to do so. He swallowed it without hesitation then looked over to Mark to do the same. Mark took a chance, trusting that he had not been led this far just to be poisoned. Once he was sure the pill had been swallowed, Creson lowered his eyes and turned away.

They let the night fall without comment. For his part, Mark was content to listen to the familiar sounds that poured out of the woods. They filled him with more pleasure than he thought possible—he still vividly remembered the emotional pain of a woods without sound. Along with the vegetation and the sky, it was enough confirmation of where he was that he decided to strike out on his own during the night, this rather than chance whatever Creson had in mind for the following day. There were searchers out there, Creson had said. Well, the skill of those searchers was about to be tested.

There was always the possibility that he would move back into the transporter, but this at least, would not be fatal. Should he see those trees vary even slightly, he would turn around and head the other way like a flash. More of a fear was the creature sitting across from him, still sitting as he was before and still maintaining his silence. *How safe can I be with him running around loose?* Mark thought.

Fear but not bitterness; notwithstanding the Mantzites' tendency to cover up their clumsiness by murdering him, they were quite likable. They had commendable goals. And they had provided him with a fantastic experience; he had visited other planets, seen other creatures, all thousands of light years from where he now sat. He had talked to distant aliens, shared their lives in considerable detail, had even become those creatures for a short period of time. And he had picked up so many skills, skills that would make him appear to be a superman to the people of Earth. It was going to be difficult to turn this all off, to simply get up and walk away.

Would they come after him? Would he have to reveal everything just to protect himself. If he did, would he risk another Tanterac as Creson and the others thought?

He had to tell Kathy. How could he keep it from her?

Again Mark's reverie was broken as he finally realized Creson was staring. Although it was difficult to know for sure in the enveloping darkness, it appeared he was finally beginning to wonder about his silent companion. In time he sighed heavily, bringing Mark to feel vulnerable once again. "In words I believe your species readily understands, you could fuck up your own funeral!"

"What?" said Mark, startled by this totally unexpected outburst. His projected response was instinctive and too Earth-like for the Mantzite he was pretending to be.

"Oh must we go through the same tedious litany as before? I had hoped you had grown more skilled in linguistic ability!"

Mark stared, first in shock then in disbelief and finally in resignation. "When did you find out?" he asked quietly.

"We knew practically from the start. Various members of our staff were assigned to keep an eye on you. We correctly assumed that you would not fly—if you will excuse the pun—to another form if you felt safe in the one you were using. I must say in your last disguise you stood out like a sore appendage. Whatever possessed you to assume such an unattractive form?"

Mark was not sure how to take that. He had, to the best of his knowledge, become an average Mantzite. Had Wilpin's blueprint been some kind of joke, something he'd intended to use at the Mantz equivalent of a Halloween party? *Or is it simply that Spot thinks of himself as some kind of raving beauty?* he thought.

"Must be my inexperience," Mark offered finally, still harboring a degree of shock. He had not missed the earlier use of the word "funeral;" either a bad choice or a Freudian slip. But Creson did not look dangerous nor was there threat in his voice. And except for what might be contained within the backpack, he carried no obvious weapon. He appeared tired and frustrated, even defeated. "Are you escorting me back to Earth?"

Creson thought for a moment before answering. "Takar had a difficult choice to make in your case. As you know, your presence placed us in a no-win situation; we could do nothing right regardless of what we might attempt. There was no desire on any one's part to terminate you, but on the other hand, we did not want to risk jeopardizing all that we have thus far accomplished during the exploration of Earth—I speak now of creating another Tanterac."

At that he looked deeply into Mark's eyes in search of understanding. Mark could feel this, even in the darkness. "What we have to share will be of colossal benefit to your planet; we can point to numerous other civilizations as proof of this. In your case, I must admit we had been leaning toward rendering you impotent to interfere with these goals, hopefully in a manner which you would not have found too unpleasant, but your rapid assimilation of gene transformation ability changed all that. We knew, of course, that you were attempting such things—this was to be expected. But we had no idea you would master it as quickly as you did nor that you would so greatly surpass us in speed. The latter point, by the way, causes us great concern. It is conceivable that such talent might be applied in a manner detrimental to our people—this we cannot allow.

"We were not unduly worried about detecting your whereabouts within the research complex. Once we collected our wits, we found that relatively easy, regardless of the form you chose. The episode did, in fact, provide amusement to those who watched you jump back and forth from one room to another. At first it appeared your plan might be too sophisticated for our simple minds to fathom." At that, his eyes contracted and his body quivered in humor.

"I didn't know how to direct the beam," Mark admitted softly, smiling himself by now.

"So we ultimately gathered. But to get back to the point, it became obvious to us that you were profiting more than we might have liked by the experience sessions. Understand, this did not catch us totally by surprise; such a thing has happened in the past with creatures from other planets. None, however, have ever managed to master it with as much consummate skill as you, and this made us wonder what other talents would grow within you that might put us at an unacceptable level of disadvantage. These fears are obviously not frivolous since you achieved one level in which we have no capability at all; at least no evidence of it has yet surfaced. I am speaking of your psycho kinetic skills, your ability to control objects remotely."

"I didn't think you knew about that," interjected Mark, less crushed than pleased with himself at the skills he had assimilated. "If you knew, why did you let me get this far?"

"Quite simple: we wanted you to escape; we wanted you in undamaged form back on Earth. In our superior wisdom it was determined that the best way to accomplish this without risking the safety of our people was to let you think you had done it yourself through the utilization of 'secret' skills."

A grunting noise came out of the woods from nearby, halting the conversation and bringing hackles to the back of Mark's neck—Creson appeared not to notice. "I think there's a cat in the woods, Spot," Mark said nervously. He scanned the area where the noise originated but saw nothing.

"More precisely it is a felis concolor," Creson responded calmly.

"Goddamnit, this is no time for one of your lectures! In case you've forgotten, we are Earth dogs and that goddamn Earth CAT eats Earth dogs!"

"Only when exceptionally hungry. Normally they are quite afraid of us; I would have thought you would know that since it is a representative of your planet."

Mark could not believe it. A mountain lion was stalking them, and all Creson could think about was playing smartass.

The lion came into view then began an approach with an unmistakably intent to have at least one of them for dinner. Creson turned his head in its direction but did nothing more than that. His face showed no emotion even though the cat was now only yards away. Far from relaxed, Mark acted in new-found instinct. He began changing himself into the largest animal he could manage in the short time remaining to him, accomplishing a miniature sized version in less than twenty seconds—it was enough. The various stages of conversion, as well as the result itself, brought the lion to a startled halt. It had begun its approach against two dogs and was now facing a dog and a miniature elephant, the latter of which it had never before seen.

Its discomfort increased as the newly-evolved beast lifted an alien trunk and trumpeted. That was the clincher. As the woods reverberated with a sound not heard in that area for thousands of years, it decided to call it a day; it turned on a dime and flew into the woods.

The sound also got the attention of Creson. He jerked his head toward Mark then stared wide-eyed at the elephant disguise his companion had so suddenly assumed. The fur on the back of his canine neck stood straight out. He looked so pompous in that pose that Mark toyed with the idea of letting him have another blast.

Creson said nothing during the reconversion to canine form, but the severe expression remained on his face the whole time. Afterward, his voice showing unmistakable anger, he let Mark have his thoughts. "If you wanted to kill a fly, would you drop a tree on it! Frankly, your solutions to simple problems, if I may use a word you are sure to understand, SUCKS!"

Mark was surprised at the outburst and responded defensively: "I didn't notice *you* doing anything to help."

"He would have done us no harm! I had already rearranged the molecules of my body to permit him to pass through. I had assumed you had done the same. Whatever possessed you to invoke a circus act instead? Is your retention span that short? Have you forgotten the procedure?"

Mark hesitated, now more inclined toward embarrassment. "Frankly, I didn't think of it. But what's the difference, my idea worked!"

"So did mine!" said Creson, still angry, "and with less disruption to the emotional well being of, not only myself, but all creatures within a thousand light years of here!"

Mark was reluctant to give Creson the satisfaction, but he wondered why the more simple approach had not occurred to him. If nothing else, it spoke of how awkward such talents could be when applied by someone unaccustomed to their use.

As rapidly as he had become angry, Creson regained control of himself. There was even a hint of embarrassment in his manner as he resumed the conversation of before. "As I was saying before that Earth creature interrupted us, your continued assimilation of unearthly skills caused us to become concerned for our safety. We could not be certain, for example, that you would not use your psycho kinetic ability to attempt to manipulate us or our technology. There are defenses available to us, of course, which for understandable reasons I would prefer to keep to myself, but we have gotten used to not having to use them, at least not the worst of them. This for the simple reason that they are seldom necessary.

"Takar, upon realizing your capabilities and with full knowledge of the harm that could come from the undisciplined use of newly-acquired powers, decided to return you to Earth. He informed all of us of the manner in which he intended to do this and, as you can see, his ideas worked. You have been returned and no one has been hurt, although I have to tell you you were almost exterminated in your role as a flinac. We have automatic decontamination devices in certain of the transporter tubes, and they are set to exterminate, among other things, Mantz insects—even imitation Mantz insects. We had a close moment there getting the tubes reprogrammed. If you had entered one second before we managed to switch it off, POOF, no Earth man."

Mark felt a slight nausea at the thought of how close he had come to disaster. And foolish at having thought himself so much in control of his "escape." "What about your Council," he said sheepishly. "I thought you people were afraid you'd be canned if they found out."

Creson smiled. "I am growing so fond of your quaint way of putting things, Markcarter. Or should I call you Jumbo?" There was a brief pause while the dog form of Creson contracted its pupils and gently shook its body. "In truth," he said after recovering from his self-induced spasm of laughter, "we were, and still are, concerned about, not only *our* future, but the future of the entire planetary exploration project. Takar, as is his nature, has already 'come clean' as you might say. He informed the Council soon after you began your little jaunt through our conveyer system. Although he does not confide such things to me, I got the distinct impression that the Council was not all that pleased with what happened. Nor with what our response had been. Further, even Takar does not know what they will ultimately decide to do in response—to some extent, you are able to influence this."

He hesitated to make sure Mark was following him, then said, "You do, of course, have the option of telling everything to your fellow Earth creatures. Some will believe you although most will probably not. We cannot stop you in this and, in any event, have no intention of trying. However, you must be aware from Tanterac and from the experience-scanning sessions, that it hurts us deeply to bring harm to intelligent beings. Inwardly and outwardly, we wish to represent only positives—you have seen but a small sample of the things we can make available to your species.

"But it is simply not wise to make our presence known to your fellow creatures at this time. Our experience in your case should help you appreciate why this is so. We must learn and we must make alterations in our thinking each and every time something is discovered that represents either potential harm or potential good. The danger of misused psycho kinetic skills is an example of the former, while the development of previously untapped areas of your human brain—to permit cell transformation and more civilized communication—is an example of the latter. Perhaps you have already surmised that the ability to mentally manipulate your genes has considerable potential in eradicating the diseases which periodically attack all biological beings. That is, if you are properly trained."

Mark had not even guessed at this, but it was certainly something he would examine in detail as soon as he had the chance.

"Thus it is in your best interests and in the best interests of your fellow humans for you to restrain yourself in the relating of this incident to others. I implore you to consider it. Without this, I feel certain that no further attempt will be made to contact Earth, at least not for a century or two."

Mark was sympathetic to Creson's appeal, but his thoughts were dominated by the elation that now surged through his body. Creson was confirming that he was about to be released—unharmed and with no strings attached. He began to think about Pennsylvania and Kathy, getting back to both as quickly as he possibly could. He thought of returning to the familiar where no rest and rejuvenation chambers sought to contain him and no alien beings threatened his existence. Captured by such positive feelings, he felt no burning need to call a press conference to discuss his experiences in outer space. Quite the contrary; he wanted to maintain contact with the Mantzites; wanted to keep them headed in the direction of formal contact with Earth.

Creson continued. "If the Council were to determine that circumstances were such that further exploration of Earth was unwise, they would order us to switch our attention to some other planet until things quieted down."

"A century or two."

"Approximately. I should think it unwise to let it go longer than that, considering that you might be capable of visiting us by then. For security reasons we would want to make certain you are civilized beforehand, that we are not visited by trumpeting elephants, so to speak."

They were silent for a long moment before finally Mark spoke. "In all honesty, I don't know if I can keep something like this quiet. If our scanning sessions have taught you anything about human nature, you know that heavy secrets are the hardest to keep, even when you really want to. It's not that I don't understand, I do—and I want to help; help my people as well as yours. I'm just telling you it might not be practical to assume I'll never slip, that I won't give something away. Unintentionally, of course.

It was obvious that his candor did not sit well with his former captor. Creson's expression was pained; Mark could see this, even in the dark. A minute of silence passed before Creson said, "Well perhaps the problem will not arise at all." He paused for another minute then asked softly, "How do you think your fellow creatures would react to your ... 'slips'?"

"You keep getting it backward, Spot. You guys are the creatures; we're people," Mark said impishly.

"I beg your pardon?"

"Skip it. To be honest I don't know, but I don't see instant acceptance. On the other hand, I don't see a Tanterac either; I meant it when I told you that earlier—you people should get away from that kind of thinking. I think the immediate reaction here would be disbelief. When you think about it, what do I have to prove that this happened? People would find it easy to blame it on being too long in the woods. And you can forget about me changing myself into a monster of some kind. That would be the end of any chance I would have for a normal life. I'd be bugged by kooks and curiosity seekers from all over the world. Maybe I'd be gathered up by the U.S. military or by crazy scientists—no offense meant, Spot. Maybe your best protection is in that. I mean, it would be foolish of me to be careless in what I say or do."

There appeared to be little left to say, and they sat in silence listening to the night and tossing thoughts over in their minds. By now, even with his canine eyes, Mark found it difficult to see much of anything; the faint light of the moon was lost in the thick forest. He could make out Creson's face but he could no longer tell what expression the Mantzite displayed on it.

With Creson no longer interested in conversation, Mark's mind drifted to encompass once again the pleasures of his surroundings—Earth surroundings. He sniffed the Earth smells; he listened to the Earth sounds. He let it all in, far enough to caress his soul. So much did he withdraw that, without meaning to, he drifted off to sleep, failing to notice as he did so the faint sound of dogs barking in the distance.

CHAPTER 28

"Creson will handle the matter notwithstanding his feelings," Selson stated to Takar, his voice uncharacteristically combative. "He has never been known to go against your decisions and will not do so now. The Earth man will be terminated and in a manner deemed natural by local authorities. There will be no investigation."

Takar accepted all this in silence then took the time to think it through. He had asked Selson to join him in his chamber because he was worried about the possibility of failure in the plan to resolve the problem of the Earth man. Unlike any other order issued by the Council, total obedience here could not be assured. What was being asked of his people was repulsive to their collective thinking.

They were scientists, trained to seek out and protect life, not cover up mistakes in so uncivilized a manner. Certainly they were not trained to do so—this alone spoke loudly about the possibility of error. Too much could go wrong, and Takar was beginning to regret sending someone as sensitive as Creson to handle it. If Creson succumbed to his sensitivity, if it prevented him from carrying out his orders, the planet Earth would be the looser. They might even become a permanent enemy.

The Council had not been pleased. Takar had explained his failure to report the human invasion as one of practicality; that without enough knowledge to make a recommendation, informing the Council would have served no purpose other than to raise collective anxiety. It was difficult to tell to what degree they accepted this explanation or when their final judgment would come. The Council never did anything in haste; at least they had not been known to do so prior to this impulsive and even petulant order to dispose of the Earth man, an order which, in Takar's opinion, was born not only of an unreasonable fear of another Tanterac, but of a desire for revenge at having been informed so late in the game.

"He has become an incident," they had said in justification, "one which has the potential of doing us considerable harm. There are already too many Earth creatures involved in his disappearance. All this nervous activity will work to everyone's disadvantage, including, we might point out, that of the planet which stands to benefit most by the continuance of our efforts: Earth.

"Return the human to his native planet then have him expire in such a way as will seem natural to all who wish to examine him. As we understand it, the area in which the search is being conducted is filled with hazards, both animal and environmental. Choose one and apply it as quickly and as expeditiously as possible."

Takar had argued that not enough was known about the search to make such a decision; that his scouts had not yet reported back—he informed the council about Zarpin and Sinot and when they were due to report. "We might choose the wrong methodology out of ignorance of the facts." But the appeal was summarily rejected; Takar was instructed in no uncertain terms to carry out his orders as given.

"How would you evaluate Creson's response to the Council's decision?" Takar asked, wanting to be convinced that Selson was right, that emotions would not get in the way of Creson's sense of duty.

In his answer, Selson, as he was prone to do, stuck to the facts. "He thought this approach was extreme and potentially dangerous; that should other Earth creatures suspect something unnatural in the demise of one of their own, there would be such an uproar that our chances of visiting the planet in any disguise and under any circumstances would be nonexistent."

Takar nodded. "Essentially what I told the Council," he said. "Regretfully, they are acting in uncharacteristic haste."

"Creson has grown quite fond of the Earth creature," Selson continued. "And the creature in turn, in its peculiar way, returns that feeling. This, of course, is not unlike Creson; if you will recall it happened in the past, indeed more than once."

"That is because Creson is civilized! Perhaps his heightened sensitivity to the feelings of others makes him more so than the rest of us!" His tone suggested disapproval of Selson's attitude, though it soften as he continued with, "Indeed, it might not hurt for all of us to remind ourselves from time to time that our purpose here is to discover and proliferate conditions for the betterment of all intelligent species—Earth creatures included. The termination of any innocent being, however justified, should diminish us all."

"And I am certain it does," said Selson, unperturbed, "but there are from time to time difficult decisions which must, of necessity, accompany our actions. Creson knows this as well as anyone, and thus, as I said earlier, he will do what is right: terminate the human and put an end to this crisis."

Takar sighed, and compassion appeared in his normally stony face. "In time we might have come up with a less extreme approach, but I suppose that is now academic. The Council is not disposed to relent, and even if they did, it would be difficult to get word to Creson before the act is consummated." He paused to consider this latter point. "We really must do something to improve our ability to communicate through the transporter to our people on Earth. When Creson returns I want you and he to begin working on this."

Selson was relieved. The change in subjects signaled acceptance of what Selson continued to believe was the only practical solution. As brilliant and forceful as he was, Takar needed guidance from time to time, and Selson was pleased that he was able to provide it for him. Taking Takar's remarks as dismissal, he turned and abruptly exited through the nearest tube.

Takar continued to dwell on the subject long after Selson had gone. He knew that some action was better than none, especially with so much activity taking place on Earth, but the action chosen by the Council was wrong. It was to alien to their most basic principles. The Earth creature was not just another cosmic animal; it was a social being, as important to its fellow creatures as Mantzites were to theirs. What would be so wrong with simply returning him to Earth? Contact with this society is inevitable; why not take a chance and allow part of it to occur now? *Are we so inexperienced with alien contact that we could not make it work, notwithstanding an inauspicious start?* he thought.

He spent more than an hour searching his brain for arguments—he could not leave things as they were. But no new thoughts came to mind, nothing other than those which had already failed to impress the Council. After a while, shoulders sagging in defeat, he left his office to seek the comfort of a rest and rejuvenation chamber.

The anxiety Arkot felt made him reluctant to turn off the chamber and, by doing so, disturb the rest of this boss of bosses. He was not accustomed to having to report to someone of Takar's rank; just the thought of it moved him toward seeking out a chamber himself, this for a confidence boost. Aware that it would be worse for him if he did not do it, he bowed to the inevitable, touched the necessary lights then waited in semi-shock for his superior to respond.

Takar opened his eyes, saw Arkot and immediately understood. He stepped from the chamber then entered a tube, motioning Arkot to do the same. In the privacy of his office, he listened to the scout's report relayed through the hastily constructed communication chain from Sinot, then questioned him on the details. "The female is with Zarpin now?" he asked.

"In all probability, yes," Arkot responded, pleased that the worst of the meeting was over. "It would be a relatively simple matter for him to escape, but we cannot be certain as regards the whereabouts of the beams. She has retained one of these weapons to handle Zarpin, but the other might now be difficult to find."

Warming to the moment, Arkot's projections gained strength with each word. "This female appears to be no more devious than the male we have in captivity, but she seems more capable of providing us with what we are seeking to avoid: exposure. If she were to disappear, even if we were able to recover the weapon, it would only accelerate the concerns of the local authorities. They are already skittish as the result of their examination of the point where Creson and the Earth man were enveloped by our transporter. To them, the footprints simply disappeared."

Arkot noted that the laboratory head was hanging on his every word. It encouraged him to go a step further. "If you will forgive an opinion, our difficulties appear to be increasing geometrically. I submit that some action to defuse this situation must be taken immediately; we may not have much time."

After dismissing the scout and informing the Council of the latest chain of events, Takar sat in the quiet of his office trying to think of a practical way out of the seemingly impossible situation he and his colleagues faced. There were too many mistakes being made and it was causing a bad situation to become appalling. Now, through Creson, they were about to make the biggest mistake of all. Yet he had no alternative to offer. Indeed, the Council might yet suggest the same solution for the Earth man's mate. Takar knew how quickly they could come to regret such a move, but in their current frame of mind there was no way he could get this across to them.

His sigh was an admission that it might already be too late, that he might better spend his time on cleanup.

Whatever they decided for the Earth creatures, the weapon must not be allowed to remain in their keeping. In addition to its being solid evidence of an extraterrestrial invasion, it was like giving children a land mine to play with—disaster would be certain to follow. The young woman would have to be brought to Mantz and her memory interrogated for the disposition of the beam. Afterward ... well, that would be up to the Council. *It would be far less complicated if the weapon were not involved,* he thought.

There was something about the woman that he should remember; he glared at the pulsating light on the wall to improve his chances of concentration. After a few minutes, as if reacting to a bee sting, he jumped forward in his seat and began touching the lights on his monitor. There soon appeared the information he sought: a rundown on the area of Earth called "Pennsylvania." As he watched the three-dimensional presentations of real-life scenes, his spirits began to lift. The weapon would not be a problem. And that meant the woman was less of a problem.

Perhaps the time had come! He turned toward the closest beam and projected an order to an assistant then followed this with a direct message to the Council, something he rarely did himself. Within minutes he was given an audience with the entire group.

As he arrived within the council chamber, Takar noted the look of apprehension on each of the members' faces. They were more concerned than he had ever known them to be in the past.

"We have been debating this whole unfortunate incident," the chairman began as soon as Takar was seated, "and have come to the conclusion that our previous comments and instructions might have been too ... hastily conceived and thus somewhat flawed. By your request for an audience, we suspect you are already aware of this. We would be pleased to entertain further comments on the matter."

Encouraged by this unexpected admission, and by its implied concession, Takar related all his thinking to the Council members, seeing as he did so the relief in their collective eyes as each received his projected thoughts and knew his intent. It took less than twenty minutes, during which time no one interrupted and no one offered an alternative opinion. Awakened by regret over actions they now admitted were precipitous, the pendulum of Council emotions had begun swinging the other way. They were now disposed to concluding a dramatic and highly atypical turnabout, tacitly agreeing to a revision of previously unshakable rules of alien contact. No longer would they be so inflexible; no longer need there be only one correct way to approach the wide variety of species yet to be discovered within this and eventually other galaxies. Each new discovery would be considered separately; each would be evaluated for the most appropriate way of gaining the acceptance and support of the creatures involved. Contingency plans would be set up all along the way, this to permit a prompt response should, as in the case of Earth, the unexpected occur.

In better spirits, the Council began to participate in the formulation of Takar's plan, adding those nuances, improvements and safeguards that individual members felt necessary or appropriate. It seemed to Takar that the group was excited about giving it a try, this notwithstanding the impromptu nature of the idea and the circumstances that brought it about. The era of Tanterac was finally coming to an end.

It remained only to determine the best approach under the current circumstances. And, of course, to save themselves from the budding disaster so recklessly set in motion.

"Can you assure us that the weapon will be recovered?" said the Council head.

"I can," said Takar confidently. "Sinot was able to intercept enough of the female's thoughts to know of her intent to send one beam to the area in which she lives. Assuming the chosen transportation system functions properly, a package containing the beam should arrive there shortly. We have reasoned to better than a ninety-nine point seven percent probability that it can only have been sent to one of three places—all are now being covered. As luck would have it, we have a planetary explorer in close proximity to the suspect areas."

Nodding in approval, the Council head continued, "You recognize that formal contact with Earth is approved only if the two creatures prove unwilling to remain silent about their experiences. They must be closely monitored to make certain we know when that moment of revelation occurs, if indeed it occurs at all. I assume your men Creson and Zarpin are capable of implanting the necessary monitors within the subjects' bodies?"

Takar projected an affirmative response. "And, with regard to monitoring, as I have already stated, chance has presented us with a representative in close proximity to the area in which the subjects live. It will not be difficult to follow them in detail."

"Then for as long they remain silent," the chairman continued, "we should proceed with the exploration of Earth as originally planned. That is to say we should not be over-anxious to reveal ourselves until and if it becomes necessary to do so. Regardless of what could be perceived as shifting inclinations, I believe most of us on the Council agree that it is wiser to proceed at the pace which has proven successful in so many prior instances than be forced to respond to serendipitous events."

"Understood," said Takar. "I must ask, however, for your instructions should we be unable to reach Creson in time; that is if he has already carried out your previous orders."

The tactless reference to what was already admitted to be a mistake was uncharacteristic of Takar, and he regretted it immediately. There was embarrassed silence within the chamber. "Under that set of circumstances," the chairman responded coldly, "we would reluctantly conclude that the original guidelines are still in effect. The timing would then be wrong; we could not appear so soon after the loss of Markcarter without others attaching some significance to this. However regrettable, we can not permit the demise of one human to end the possibility of eventual contact with this planet. Needless to say his mate would have to be dealt with as well."

* * * *

Even as he entered his office chamber, Takar was summoning a special task force. Once they appeared, he instructed them to travel as rapidly as possible through the transporter and get to Creson before he took action to terminate the Earth man. He took time to impress upon each of them the critical nature of their mission, that on them would depend, not only the continuation of the Earth project, but the future of planetary exploration itself.

Karpin was aware that Creson and the Earth man had over a day's head start and that the former would not be expected to stop for a rest. Extraordinary measures would have to be employed if they were to have a chance of overtaking them. He instructed Telot to convert his body to that of an Earth eagle as soon as they entered the transporter.

Hours later they were high above the distorted Mantz/Earth and moving as fast as their newly acquired Earth wings would allow. Both were practiced at quick conversions; difficult ones as well—it was the reason they were chosen. In flight they became progressively more adept, soon moving through the air as capably as any Earth eagle could. Much appreciated during this time was the remarkable sight capabilities of this flying creature; they were able to scan great distances and see tiny movement on the ground.

But they did not see Creson or the Earth man. Twice the two scouts swooped down to earth to assure themselves that the prescribed trail was still being followed, and both times they saw that it was—the tracks proved their quarry to still be well ahead. As time pressed on, Karpin became increasingly unsettled; it was going to be difficult to catch up with the energetic Creson. If only Creson and his charge would slow down, or stop. But then, Creson would only do that if he were on the verge of carrying out his orders.

CHAPTER 29

Zarpin knew it would not be long before the female human fell into a deep sleep. As near as he could figure, she had been awake for close to two days now. Sitting in the room's single chair, the austerity of which was expected to keep her awake, the woman's head had lowered to her chest for the last time almost five minutes ago. And no attempt to raise it had since occurred. In quiet anticipation, he continued to watch, needing to make sure before he took action.

He knew the essentials of what had happened; the Earth woman had given him the gist of it between injections. And although the effects of the tranquilizer had made it difficult to interpret her involuntarily emitted thoughts, he was able to fill in the gaps.

Those same thoughts made him aware of the sense of desperation which governed her behavior. The female human realized how little control she had over what she regarded as her enemy. She was aware that she was playing a dangerous game, and that the steps taken thus far to secure the release of her mate had only a slight chance of succeeding. She even feared for her life. Yet she did not hesitate.

Zarpin felt more pity than anger. These Earth people were like children in many ways, but as with children, they were easy to like. He looked forward to the day when contact and counter-contact between Mantz and Earth was commonplace. It was unfortunate that such a serious negative had developed over the capture of this one's mate. Even more unfortunate that he and his partner had to handle the messy containment procedure.

The Earth woman would not, of course, be the one to control events; that would be decided by the Council alone. The weapons she had taken would be picked up in due time, and she would be dealt with in a manner that they thought best.

He fixed his eyes on her face. Not only likable but resourceful; she had surprised him with her use of chemicals. He had expected the usual: a leash, a locked door—no containment at all, as he well knew. Although aware that she'd had something devious in mind, the suddenness of the injection gave him no time to prepare against it. Even so, he regretted the lapse of control that resulted in the compromise of his disguise and the loss of two weapons. This indiscretion would likely be discussed in depth when he returned to Mantz.

At least he had managed to retain a canine shape throughout the ordeal—not easy, considering how difficult it had been to hold on to his subconscious. He shuddered at the effect it would have had on this already agitated woman had she been forced to observe an Earth canine converting to a being she had never before seen.

It had not been easy to come up with a method of lessening the effect of the tranquilizers; there had been so little time between consciousness and another injection. The beam device would have made it a snap, of course; the chemicals could have been neutralized in advance—such is the price of a moment's carelessness.

Still groggy from the last injection, Zarpin had first considered modifying the area on his rump chosen by the Earth woman as the injection site. He dropped the idea because it would likely be detected; the needle might even break. What he decided on instead was simple though not immediately effective; he would increase his metabolic rate to such levels that the chemical would pass quickly through his body. That plan had worked, and now he was able to feign sleep rather than practice it for real.

The Earth woman had been pacing the room when he regained consciousness; a jumble of fatigue-induced thoughts was pouring from her brain. That same fatigue eventually brought her to drop to a sitting position on the bed, where the mental images became less filled with emotion and thus easier to understand. Through them Zarpin learned of his colleague's release and that Sinot's beam device had been mailed to Pennsylvania—the latter subject was capturing most of her thoughts. He knew specifically where the device had gone and who was intended as its recipient.

Twice during this time, the Earth woman had labored over to his supposedly sleeping body to verify that he was still contained. Each time Zarpin feared she might discover him awake and inject yet another dose of the tranquilizer—that would put a crimp in his plans. He needn't have worried; the actions more bespoke nervousness than purpose.

She had tried force-feeding herself, taking bites from a half-eaten sandwich then walking the floor while chewing, but in no time at all she was sitting on the bed with the sandwich enough to one side to demonstrate her disinterest. Then her head began bouncing off her chest; it happened enough times to get her to move to the hard and less accommodating chair. Now this logic had failed as well.

She looked to be incapable of further movement; it was time to act. Concentrating, Zarpin prepared his body to escape its bonds. It did not go as smoothly as he would have liked, this due to the residual effect of so many induced chemicals, but in time the ties around his legs and the leash around his neck fell gently to the floor. When that happened, he rose on all fours then spent a number of seconds working out the pain and stiffness in his muscles. There was no hurry; his adversary could not escape him now.

In time he approached the sleeping woman and, with paws now converted to Mantzite hands, gently removed the beam weapon which had dropped to her lap. Setting the necessary adjustments, he stepped back, stared briefly at her motionless form and, with an expression which spoke of the sadness he felt, pointed the device and fired. The Earth woman they thought of as Markcarter's mate slid slowly to the floor.

Again the dials were spun and again the weapon was aimed and fired. This time the woman rose into the air, moved across the room then descended onto the bed. Her body now where he wanted it, Zarpin turned the device off and returned it to its proper place inside his fur. He then reconverted to canine paws and checked himself over in the mirror, determined that no further mistakes would be made. After listening at the still-closed bedroom door and finding nothing to cause him concern, he slipped through to the hallway.

One final check for unexpected witnesses and he was on his way— there was no reason to hang around town any longer. Few people could be seen that late at night, and those who were there were not interested in a solitary shepherd slowly ambling his way out of town.

It was not until two hours later that Zarpin was in position to communicate to Mantz. Using his newly recovered beam, he passed along the fact of his escape, the recovery of one of the two lost weapons, and the disposition of Markcarter's mate. He also told them where the second beam weapon could be found. His assignment now completed, he then settled back against a tree and began the long wait for fresh orders. As a precaution, he scanned the area for human activity, aware that those who searched for Markcarter were out there somewhere. He found them, but they were many miles away. Curiously, there was something else there as well, something unexpected but easily recognizable. Two Mantzites in Earth-dog form were camped less than five miles from the main search group— there was no way of knowing whether either party was aware of this. Zarpin toyed with the idea of intercepting his people before they inadvertently walked within sensory range of the searchers, but gave up the idea as impractical; they were simply too far away. He would have to do the best he could with what he had. Grabbing the beam device, he chose another of the versatile instrument's many uses, then set it to communicate on as wide a band as possible before sending his message of warning.

CHAPTER 30

Creson knew what he had to do, even recognized the necessity of doing it, but still he hesitated. It was so ... depressing. He had already waited longer than was wise; the warning from Zarpin made that crystal clear. He and Markcarter were too close to the search party; this increased the possibility of detection before the Council's orders could be carried out. He glanced over at his companion to see if he had picked up the incoming communication. The precaution he had taken earlier, that of limiting the awareness range of relayed messages, had proven wise—the beam device picked up Zarpin's projection but reported this only to him.

It was too much to expect of the Earthling for him to keep quiet about the presence of alien explorers on his home planet. Thus there was no alternative but to do as he had been told. Until now, he had hoped something would come up to make the act unnecessary, something the human himself might suggest, something that would at long last make sense. But Markcarter had effectively put an end to such wishful thinking. Perhaps it had been naive to expect otherwise.

Takar was right. The Council was right. And it was right of him to take their orders seriously.

With sense of duty barely overcoming monumental reluctance, Creson gave thought to the specifics of what he must do. Once decided on the methodology, it would not be difficult to make it happen; there was little the Earth man could do to prevent it.

He reflected on his knowledge of the path ahead. Without making Markcarter suspicious he would lead him to higher ground, close to a precipice with sufficient height to do the job. "We will move on," he said curtly, the projection forceful enough to wake Mark up.

Mark looked up, surprised and even startled at the unexpected communication. "I thought we were going to rest for the night," he mumbled sleepily.

"That would not be wise. It is necessary for me to get you back without being detected in the process. Further delay will jeopardize this goal." With that he moved on, thus cutting off further debate.

It was as dark as it could be, and Mark had to wonder how Creson could see at all. Unwilling to risk getting lost at this stage of his escape, he kept as close as he could without being overly friendly. Even so, it was difficult to keep from walking into brush and low-hanging tree limbs—he did so often. Taking no note of his companion's discomfort, Creson moved on at his usual unrelenting pace, keeping this up for nearly an hour.

When finally he stopped, he remained in place for a number of seconds, not turning around and not attempting to communicate. Mark wondered whether there was something ahead, something Creson had detected but was not yet ready to talk about. It brought to mind the half-converted creature he'd encountered on the way to Mantz, the one that had put him into a tailspin. "We will take a moment to catch our breath," Creson said, the friendly comment not matching his mood; the Mantzite was agitated, more so than Mark had seen in him before.

Creson lowered himself to the base of a tree near a small clearing then signaled Mark to do the same. Mark complied, sitting away but still close enough to see Creson's darkened features. As he watched, still curious about the delay, his former captor began to take on a different look. Mark had to strain his eyes to confirm that Creson was converting his front paws to hands, three-fingered Mantz hands.

Before long, one of the distorted limbs reached into a pocket and pulled out a beam device. The move was clumsy, as if Creson were having trouble concentrating. He had less trouble in his aim, however; it was directly at Mark.

"What do you want with that?" Mark asked, not comfortable with having to ask.

"I believe you are familiar with our prolific use of beam technology. It serves us in many ways, including defense."

"I know as much as you've taught me," Mark asked, "but why are you pointing it at me? I'm no threat to you." His earlier confidence began to take a nose dive.

"I believe you know why. I am afraid I did not relate exactly what the Council decided in regard to you. Regretfully, they are rather insistent that Earth not become aware of our presence, at least not at this time. They remain stubbornly unwilling to chance the consequences."

"What about the consequences to me?" Mark had all he could do to keep the quiver from his projected voice.

"I believe you know the answer to that as well. As I say, it is most regrettable, more so than I can possibly relate."

"Yeah, well I can assure you it's 'most regrettable' to me as well." Emotions raced through Mark's mind and body. In the span of a few seconds he had gone from certain release to certain death. Inwardly the anger was as heavy as the fear, anger at the logic of these people who made others pay for their mistakes. Outwardly he said nothing, part of him loath to leave this misguided alien with the memory of an Earth man begging for his life.

Creson paused to gather his thoughts; after all that had happened, it was important that the Earth man understand his feelings. "I was to have disposed of you by now, being ordered in no uncertain terms to avoid unnecessary risk of exposure. But what I must do is so appalling to me personally that I postponed action until convinced that no practical alternative was possible. In so doing I was clearly going against the Council's wishes."

"Why didn't they give the job to someone else; someone used to this kind of dirty work?"

"None of us are really used to 'this kind of dirty work,' as you put it. We are not a violent species. Although there are times when violence is necessary, such as now, there are no experts as such to be found anywhere on our planet. In strict answer to your question, I was selected because of your familiarity to me; it was thought this would be less complicated than tricking you into following someone you did not know."

"Damnit, Spot...!"

Creson looked pained. It was clear he did not want Mark to continue. "I would like you to revert back to human form then put on your old covering," he said. He reached into his backpack and removed the clothes surrendered weeks earlier. They appeared to be in exactly the same condition as they were when he last saw them. The Mantzites had thought of everything.

"What if I refuse to comply; your plan would fall apart if you had to leave me in the form of a dog."

"In that event I would simply render you unconscious. Without a continuing effort to maintain the dog image, your body would revert to its natural form. I believe I mentioned this phenomenon to you earlier."

After a moment of mental confrontation, Mark gave in. But only to stall for time, time to come up with something that would get to the sensitive Mantzite. In retrospect it was foolish to have been so candid in stating that he could not guarantee to keep his mouth shut. What could be said now to erase that?

In human form for the first time since beginning his escape, Mark began to dress. His skin, now that it was free of Mantz fur, looked unnaturally smooth, and compared to what he was putting on, was out of place—it was too clean. In contrast, the clothes felt cold and clammy, and the odor they produced was so strong Mark wondered how Creson had been able to prevent the smell from escaping his backpack.

Mark tried to slow things down; it was all he could think of to do. Further appeal seemed useless, but so did running away. That beam would get him before he went two feet. In time there were no more items of clothing to put on, and he sighed in defeat and stood up to face his adversary for the last time. He felt as he had so many weeks before, dirty and hopelessly lost. Even his beard, now showing weeks of growth, lent authenticity to the image.

"Why didn't you just keep me on Mantz? Why is it so necessary to kill me?"

The pained look on Creson's face deepened. "As you yourself pointed out to me, your disappearance would cause too much of a fuss."

"What do you think my murder is going to do!? Somebody's going to find out, you know! Then where will your grandiose plans be!?"

"Therein lies the problem in the thinking of the Council. Never before have they issued such a questionable decision. If it is any consolation, I do believe they will reconsider in short order."

"Now why doesn't that make me feel better!" asked Mark, sarcastically. "Damnit Spot! I could work with you people; there's no reason to kill me. I could help you gain more information about Earth. I believe in what you're doing and what it could do for all of us. It doesn't make sense to get rid of me now!"

Creson averted his eyes in embarrassment. "It is odd for me to be talking to an Earth creature in this manner, but I want you to know I have become quite fond of you and will sincerely miss your presence. I believe that, notwithstanding your being of an inferi...a different species, we could have become something along the lines of what you refer to as friends."

"It's nice to know you're not prejudiced," Mark said, no longer able to keep the quiver from his voice. The conversation was about to end.

He was going to die, and at the hands of creatures no one on Earth knew about except him. Kathy, Sandy and all the others would be convinced that he had taken on more than he could chew, that he had tackled wilderness he was not qualified to handle, and that it had killed him.

A beam of light enveloped his body instantly rendering him incapable of movement. Creson had fired; his fall into eternity had begun. For a brief moment all senses were deadened, but then he realized he could still "hear." Everything Creson said got through to him.

"I regret that I cannot tranquilize you for this final step; it would be detected within your body and thus our attempt to make this look natural would be defeated."

Mark wanted to answer, to cry out in fear and protest, but he could not. It was as if his body had suffered an electrical short-circuit. He felt himself being lifted then moved through the air just above the ground. Where he was going, he had no way of knowing; the beam blotted out everything. He knew only that he was being led to his death, a death that could come crashing through that unrelenting curtain of light at any second—each movement suggested the final blow. What terrible thing did Creson have in mind? What was it that the tranquilizers were supposed to protect him against?

The movement stopped and he was held motionless in space, still with no sense of where he was. By now the uncertainty was unbearable. He struggled to break free of the beam's paralyzing grip and to see beyond the light that kept him from being witness to his final moments.

Then, without warning, the light went off and he began to fall.

In that horrible cross-section of time Mark knew exactly how he would die. Already on his way to the bottom of some unseen cliff, he would be mercilessly crushed by rocks and forest debris. His life span could now be measured in seconds. He screamed his fear to an impenetrable and indifferent darkness.

The scream was cut off by a bone-crunching jolt, leaving him in a world of fiery pain. It lasted nor more than a second before a dark and silent void enveloped him.

He had no way of knowing how long he had been unconscious. Awakening in total darkness, he lay in shock, unable to move and barely able to think. Pain raced up and down his left leg.

How can that be? he thought. *How can I feel pain?* With aching slowness, he lifted a hand to explore as much of his body as he could reach without bringing on more of the pain. Everything appeared to be where it was supposed to be. And he could feel the touch of his hand as it passed over his body. He was alive! Hurt but alive! He stared into the black void, unable to fathom what this new twist might mean.

After a while, it became easier for his mind to function, to accept reality. He pushed himself up on one elbow then felt for his throbbing leg. There was no doubt that it was broken, but it was not distorted in any way and there was no bone poking through the skin. He moved it into as comfortable a position as he could managed then waited for the worst of the pain to subside.

It was time to consider where he was. It was too dark to see much of anything, but it was obvious from the wind and the distant sounds that he was far from being out of danger. A rock tossed a few feet into the darkness confirmed his worst suspicion; it took many seconds for the faint sound to return from its origin far below. He was suspended on a ledge, how precariously there was no way of telling.

Sounds of movement trickled down from above—Mark tried to guess how far above, how far he had fallen. It had to be Creson. *He thinks the job is done,* Mark thought in anger, careful to avoid calling attention to himself. Creson was probably staring into the void, trying to verify that his pet Earth man was no longer a burden to him. Mark knew he would have to be still and quiet for as long as it took the Mantzite to satisfy himself and move on. Hopefully that would occur before daylight made it obvious that the job was not yet done.

Would he still be here at daybreak? All it would take was one little slip, one little moment of carelessness. The result would be the same; no one would ever know that his death had come in two stages; Creson and his crowd would still win. He toyed with the idea of leaving some form of message out of spite, words scratched on the rock wall revealing the Mantzites to the world. But it would be a meaningless act, and he knew it. Assuming it were seen at all, it would be interpreted as the rantings of a deranged mind, a mind that knew it was about to die. Besides, despite everything, he really was on their side; he did not want to give them away. Because of the shared experiences, he had a big chunk of Mantzite soul inside him, enough to want to protect them as he would his own people, his human people. The Mantzites were far from being monsters. They were decent, highly motivated beings, convinced that they had much to offer and determined to prove this to everyone.

There was no further sound above or below, except for the wind and the occasional cry of a far-away animal. Still, Mark avoided movement of any kind. Creson was clever; he could be lurking above, waiting for just such a slip. The night was chilly which made the time before sunup seem longer. Mark began to shiver, the fact of which made him worry anew about noise. He gave thought to changing himself into a bear; it had fur; it could keep him warm. *But could it fit on this tiny ledge?* he thought. The notion of converting to something else did remind him, however, that except for a flinac and a chipmunk, he had never worked the arms, legs or wings of another creature—this was not the time or the place to be clumsy. Plus, as had happened in the case of Wilpin, the damage to his leg would be expected to be transferred to the imitated form; the bear would sport a giant broken leg. *Yes, but at least it would be covered in fur,* he thought, tightening his soiled clothes around him in an attempt to ward off the cold.

As the sun began to rise (*only one sun now*, Mark thought with a pleasure that seemed out of place), he became aware of how bad his situation was. Overlooking a vast valley some two thousand feet below, the ledge on which he was lying was only three feet wide and less than twenty-five feet long. It offered no path to safer ground; the rock disappeared into the cliff on both sides. Above him was at least twenty feet of solid rock which, even if his leg were not broken, would have been impossible to climb. Mark felt a budding vertigo as he looked into the valley so far below. It appeared to grow in size as the sun continued its assent and plucked the remaining shadows from the valley floor.

He wondered whether it was time to cry for help. He also wondered who would hear it; he had a pretty good idea what would happen if Creson were lured back. *A simple push with that damn flashlight of his and I go tumbling into the abyss.* The thought renewed his anger as well as his fear.

He lay quietly for another hour, still in pain but less so than during the night. There was still no noise from the plateau above, and by now the sun had beaten back the worst of the cold, making it easier to think. He examined the twenty feet of rock reaching upward from where he lay—his new "containment module." Here and there a jagged edge appeared, perhaps enough to use as hand and foot holds—perhaps. Not much promise, especially in his current condition, but to stay where he was would only insure death by exposure or gangrene.

He glanced around for something to support his broken leg, but found nothing except rocks and a scraggly bush that tenaciously grasped at a spoonful of soil. The bush was too small and too flexible to protect his leg on a trip to the top, even if he could figure some way of strapping it on. Climbing without a splint was out. It would just lead to a earlier death. Mark leaned back against the uncompromising rock and searched for some other possibility, something that would make this "survival" more than a cruel false hope.

Creson could not bring himself to leave. Hours before, crippled by emotional distress, he had retreated to a spot under a tree. There he threw the incriminating beam into his backpack then lowered his sagging body to the ground. He did not even bothered to reset the beam so it could receive messages, something he usually did without thinking. What he had done to the Earth man was the worst thing he had ever done in his long and previously productive life.

Not that he had really gone through with it, at least not completely. When the moment of truth arrived, he had punted; he had dropped Markcarter onto a ledge, hoping that there the problem would be resolved with no further intervention on his part. He could not be the instrument of Markcarter's death, and so strongly did he feel this that he overlooked the prolonged agony that would befall his victim in its place.

No question that this was duty, important duty, critically important. But the horror of the act itself, even so far as he carried it, would severely impact upon what remained of his life. It was possible that he would never be able to work again. In more misery than he ever thought possible, he rested his head on restored paws and stared at the spot where the Earth man had begun his fall.

The sun was well into the morning sky before finally he shifted his position, this in response to the macabre invitation offered by the cliff's edge. It wanted him there; it wanted him to witness the effectiveness of his night's work. He had no choice, of course; sooner or later he had to do it; he had to check. Having gone this far, it would be cowardly to turn away and assume a level of innocence he did not deserve.

Even so, it was another thirty minutes before the physical effort could be made. After agonizing to his feet, he paddled over to the cliff's edge, paused short of the rim to steel himself then peered over the edge.

Mark was lying on his back watching the sky above him when the image of Creson popped into view. At first he thought he was hallucinating, this even after the image persisted. But it's expression began to change. It migrated, slowly at first, from one of sadness to one of shock, then to one of pleasure. "Markcarter, you are alive!"

Mark jumped at the words. This was no hallucination. Accepting the validity of what he saw, his immediate thought was one of irony: how unfair it would have been had he struggled up that wall with a broken leg only to find his killer at the top. "That sounds like something I would say," he said harshly, using his human voice for the first time in ages. "Dare I point out that you're stating the obvious?"

He could not believe Creson was still there. After all that waiting in cold and in pain. He might just as well have called out and gotten it over with. The change of expression on Creson's canine face suggested he had come to the same conclusion—his assignment had yet to be completed. "I guess you're going to have to do it again," Mark said, suddenly weary of the whole thing.

The two near-friends stared at each other for a long moment, during which time Creson unconsciously began converting canine paws to Mantzite hands. Far above him, Mark could see two large birds just beginning to circle the area. *Buzzards*! he thought. *Perfect timing!*

Although miles from the scene, the eagle eyes of Karpin and Telot easily picked up the movement on the distant cliff, two figures: a human and a canine. Certainly the dog was Creson but they had no instructions concerning a man. Was this a new twist or was it the Earth man, Markcarter? And was this an inopportune time to attempt contact with Creson? His canine form was staring over the cliff at the human, the latter obviously in a precarious situation. Creson was either trying to save him or kill him.

But which? If it were the former and the man was not Markcarter, then swooping down to help could result in the blowing of all their covers—while attempting to solve the Markcarter incident, they might well create another. But if it were the latter then the man must be Markcarter, in which case they had to stop Creson before it was too late. Unable to decide, they began to circle, their eyes willing the people on the ground to do something to make the choice obvious.

Karpin tried projecting a thought to the canine, but either the distance was too great or Creson's beam device, which should automatically relay a distant message, was not set properly. The pressure of uncertainty growing within him, he knew he could wait no longer. For better or for worse, he had to get in touch with Creson; they had to descend.

By now highly skilled in the use of an eagle's body, the Mantzites literally dropped out of the sky toward the two figures. They dove straight down, imitating the power dive eagles use when hunting. They got within a hundred yards, close enough to try another message, when Karpin pulled into a glide then shot over the trees toward a distant cliff. Easily spotting the reason for the change, Telot did the same. There was movement in the woods below. Humans and their domesticated animals were emerging from the forest. They had already spotted Creson.

CHAPTER 31

"It sounded like a goddamn elephant," Tom said in disbelief. They had just decided to halt search operations for the day when the unlikely sound, distant and haunting, echoed through the wilderness. It was like nothing they had ever heard before, at least not in these woods. Tom stared into the darkness, unable to see twenty yards ahead but trying, as people often do, to use his eyes to assist his ears. There was nothing other than the familiar sounds of nocturnal creatures—normal creatures. Whatever it was they heard, it did not give an encore.

"It couldn't have been," Ken said without conviction.

"Well what would you call it?

"Ken hesitated before attempting an answer. This he didn't need; there was enough odd about this search without elephants popping up in a Wyoming forest. "Weird," he offered, not knowing what else to say. But then he shook his head and added, "Kind of fits thought, doesn't it?"

As time passed and the sound still did not repeat, it became easier to convince themselves that it was other than what they'd originally thought. Perhaps the sound had been influenced by the wind; perhaps it was the voice of more than one animal, the harmony making it appear unnatural.

But Tom Sloan and Ken Janos were not ordinary observers; this was their business. Both knew they had heard something unusual, something that should not have been. It was the same for most of the men with them. Already skittish from too much that could not be explained, they wanted answers, something more reasonable than what their minds were telling them—nothing came close to fitting the sound just heard.

"Should we collect our gear and try to find out where it came from?" Tom asked. "It wasn't that far; a few miles maybe."

Ken shook his head. "Might lose somebody if we move out now—too dark; too many hazards. Besides, whatever it was, it wouldn't just sit there waiting for us. At first light we'll try to pick up its tracks." Like Tom, he would like to have his curiosity satisfied now rather than later, but he could not risk his men just for that. Reluctantly and with little possibility of meaningful rest, he ordered his men to bed down for the night.

As if responding to an alarm clock, Ken lifted himself out of his bedroll just as the first rays of daylight poured into the morning sky. Others soon joined him, others who'd had similar trouble sleeping. It was better to be up, better to be able to replace thoughts with action. Gear was collected quickly, and soon the men were heading rapidly and without complaint toward the area where the unexplained noise had occurred. No one bothered with breakfast, not feeling the need and not wanting to further delay facing their fears. The two dogs, whose contribution so far had been nil, preceded them on a leash, making no sounds and sensing nothing out of the ordinary.

Ken was counting on the dogs, counting on them to pick up a trail then, assuming that trail did not disappear as did Carter's, follow it long enough to see what had made it—they had nothing else to go on at the moment; Carter was as illusive now as he'd been at the start. Besides, everyone, himself included, felt a need to know. He told himself it was always possible that some creature, new to these woods, had been responsible for Carter's disappearance.

After only three miles, his faith in the animals proved justified. They slackened their pace having sensed something ahead. Sniffing the air, they issued a soft growl then moved forward at a more determined pace, leaving Ken to wonder what they saw in that canine inward eye. The search group was closer and more to the south of the noise heard the previous night. Had the animal that made it moved toward them while they slept? The thought was not a comforting one.

The dogs were leading them toward the edge of a tall cliff, an area that Ken knew to be dotted with caves, caves that could hold wild animals. A lost traveler as well. He signaled the men to keep going but to do so in silence.

Tom could feel the hair rising on the back of his neck as the edge of the cliff drew nearer. "I think it's still there!" he whispered to Ken. "Directly ahead."

"Signal the men to follow about a hundred yards behind," Ken replied in response. "You and I will sneak up on it with the dogs." He gave a signal of quiet to his well-trained animals then, still holding them on a leash, encouraged them forward.

As the minutes trickled by, the dog's interest waned. They knew something was out there, even where it was, but they did not display the expected agitation. To them, at least, there was nothing out of the ordinary.

With breathtaking suddenness, the thick tree line gave way to an exposed plateau, beyond which was a wide expanse of valley a few thousand feet below. The clearing was empty except for a light-colored shepherd standing motionless while staring over the side. A chill ran through Ken's body, a chill that he shook off in disgust. About to move forward again, he stopped and looked upward. There were two large eagles diving on the unsuspecting canine. He stared at them in confusion, even after they broke off their attack and flew away. How could eagles, even two of them, expect to overpower a full-grown dog? And why was a supposedly intelligent animal just standing there letting it all happen? "Use a rope," he whispered to Tom after shooting a final glance at their retreating forms. His partner understood and began eating up the remaining distance to the shepherd, making a loop out of his rope as he walked. Unexpectedly the canine did not pick up his presence, a fact that did nothing for Tom's confidence—it was further evidence that the normal no longer applied. Somewhat nervously, he wondered how it would react once it learned he was there. At the nod of Ken's head he quietly took a breath then slipped the noose over the animal's head.

Creson was not unaccustomed to leashes; he had experienced them before when traveling through Kelly and other towns en route to his area of interest. Nonetheless, he reacted with a start, almost falling off the cliff as a result. It took a number of seconds to figure out what was happening, and when finally he did so, he felt a moment of panic that he was not adequately prepared for these creatures. He chided himself for the oversight, even as he reversed the transforming of canine paws into Mantzite hands—had they been seen? He had become too emotionally involved with his current assignment; he had failed to detect what should be obvious to any interplanetary traveler: approaching aliens. His mind emitted images of fear, confusion and disgust, images that Mark easily picked up—something odd was happening to his usually unflappable captor.

Creson regained control, but it was not easy. Unlike Zarpin, he let no misdirected thoughts reach the aliens, but he did not know what hints he had inadvertently given them that he was not what they thought he was. He mentally reexamined his form; it was in every respect a canine form. He forced his mouth open and his tongue out, then hoped this would be accepted as normal canine behavior, friendly behavior. He even wagged his tail.

"What is it?" Mark yelled, still using his voice rather than a mental projection.

Creson held his silence, embarrassingly aware that he had no more of an answer to that question than did Mark. He allowed himself to take in the scene, a scene filled with Earth men with looks of uncertainty. Others were even now joining them, how many he did not yet know. There were also canines, real canines, two impressively muscular ones sitting not far away and staring intently as if daring him to move—he felt no inclination to do so. He turned back toward Mark, revealing not only a residue of uncertainty but the rope that now circled his neck.

By now Mark was ready to shout out his anxiety and impatience. "What the hell is going on, Spot?"

Before Creson could respond, a human face appeared over the edge and stared in amazement at the injured man some twenty feet down. More stunned than amazed, Mark struggled to consider what this new apparition might be. Another Mantzite, this one in human form?

The face began communicating in sound rather than thought—the first human voice he had heard, other than his own, since leaving Kelly some unknown number of weeks ago. "You Mark Carter?" it asked, the tone suggesting disbelief.

Mark jumped at the sound but could manage no words as he marveled at the movement of the man's mouth. To the trooper he appeared to be reading lips. "You okay?" the officer said, troubled by his inability to gain a response.

Swallowing hard, Mark got over his surprise long enough to respond with, "Who are you?" He spoke and acted with caution even while recognizing how illogical this was. Creson had the ability to dispose of him anytime he wished, and no help would be needed for that. These humans or Mantzites or whatever they were, could not make the situation any worse than it already was.

"Teton County Sheriff's Office. Are you Mark Carter?"

Mark could not believe it. "Hot damn!" he said explosively. "I sure as hell am, and I have to say you guys have a great sense of timing."

The trooper's face broke into a broad grin as he turned his head away from Mark and yelled to his waiting companions. "You won't believe this; it's Carter! We got him!"

After a moment of surprise laced with disbelief, Ken emitted a deep sigh then joined his colleagues in smiles. They stared at one another in shared triumph, Ken raising a clenched fist to head level and waving it with passion. The strangeness of the previous night was temporarily erased from their minds as they realized they had once again succeeded. Their quarry was alive and in survivable condition; the kind of message they loved to send could go out to that concerned little lady in Kelly.

Tom turned back to Mark, the smile still fixed to his face. He made a cursory evaluation of the situation below then said, "Don't move! You don't got much room there. We'll get a rope down to you."

"My leg's broken," Mark yelled to the vanishing trooper.

The man returned, a look of concern now overlaying the smile. "How bad is it?"

"Probably just a simple fracture. Painful though."

Tom thought for a moment before saying, "Stay exactly as you are; don't move a muscle. We'll get a man down to take a look at that leg before hauling you up."

Mark lay back but found it difficult to relax. He could no longer see Creson and had no idea what had happened to him, but it did not seem likely that he would try to get rid of them all—although there was no doubt in Mark's mind that the powerful alien could do so if he wished. A saving grace could be the impact this would have on Creson's all-important Council. *Couldn't be happening to a better group!* he thought.

The trooper returned with one other then began securing ropes and a basket stretcher. When all was ready, the second man dropped to the ledge then stood outside Mark in a gesture of protection. "Jim Hartford," he said, offering a gloved hand.

"Mark Carter, really glad to meet you, Jim!"

"Kind of figured ya might be. How long you been on this ledge?" The officer moved his hands professionally along Mark's leg as he talked, evaluating the extent of the damage. Content with his findings, he attached plastic splints then began to wrap them tightly."

Since last night," Mark said. Then, after thinking about it for a second, he quickly added, "This is what comes of walking around in the dark."

"Hell! Damn crazy to do so in these parts. Lucky you caught this ledge." The officer continued working as he talked. "Must admit, though, it would a been easier on us if you hadn't. Now we gotta carry you down."

Mark was thrilled at being able to talk to another human being. And to do so using sound—the vibration felt good in his throat. He wondered what this man would do if he suddenly threw him a projected thought.

"When'd you eat last?" Hartford asked, mostly to keep the conversation going.

Mark chuckled, "Seems like light years ago."

Hartford looked up, mild confusion on his face. "Well, we'll might have some scraps we can let you have."

It took less than fifteen minutes for Mark to reach the top of the cliff, and afterward he lay in the stretcher relishing the fact of where he was. There were a number of troopers there, about twenty-five as far as he could tell; at least that was how many were standing around his stretcher with big grins on their faces. Mark recognized one as Cal Simmons, one of the Kelly people at the bar that night he drunkenly boasted about how able he was to take care of himself in the wilderness. He acknowledged the man with a sheepish grin, receiving in return a calculating expression, as if Simmons were reserving judgment about something.

Dogs were there as well, hopefully real Earth dogs—Mark felt a familiar fear as the doubt set in. He projected a command at one then watched as it perked up its ears and looked around expectantly, searching for the source of what it clearly interpreted as sound.

"Your concern is unwarranted; they are yours, not ours." Creson was tied to a tree off to one side, away from the other animals. The rapid turning of Mark's head at his projected comment did not go unnoticed by Ken Janos.

"Your dog's okay. Lucky you had him around. Our dogs caught his scent, but since you were over the cliff they never would have caught yours. If he hadn't been looking down, we'd still be searching." Ken paused for a moment before asking, "We know you didn't go into the woods with him; where'd you pick him up?"

Mark looked over at Creson. There was no emotion in his face, but Mark knew he had to be more than a little concerned. *That smartass bastard thinks he's playing it cool*, Mark thought. He was unsure, however, how he should play it now. "Bumped into him about three days out, been with me ever since. Nice dog, but a pain in the ass at times." Mark emphasized the word "dog" but got no reaction from Creson. "When I got lost I tried to get him to lead me out, or at least lead me to his home, but I guess he was too dumb to understand." At that Creson's eyes contracted briefly.

There was much Ken wanted to know about where man and animal traveled, but he sensed a need to approach the subject in a circuitous manner—there was something about these two, something odd. "Damn sure somebody owns him; that dog doesn't look wild or mistreated." He fidgeted for a moment before asking the next question, afraid of the answer. "You ah...you hear a strange noise last night?"

Mark had no idea what he meant. "What kind of noise?" he asked.

Ken rubbed the back of his neck as he answered with, "Well, from a distance, and you know sounds can be pretty tricky in these woods, it kinda sounded like a...well like an elephant." He emitted a dry chuckle as he said it, feeling more than a little stupid.

"It was a mountain lion!" Mark said, in sudden understanding. He blurted it out without thinking, flustered at the realization that his elephant act had had an unintended audience.

Ken frowned at the response. "What we heard didn't sound like a mountain lion."

"No, really, I saw it; it made a loud noise then ran away. Didn't like my dog, I guess."

The expression of doubt remained on Ken's face. "You didn't hear anything else, something you couldn't identify?

"Well, to tell the truth," Mark responded, sorry that he had boxed himself in so tightly, "after the lion episode, the only thing on my mind was hightailing it out of there. I wouldn't have heard anything except the noise I made myself."

Although he could not accept what Mark was saying, Ken declined to press the issue. He broke off the discussion and went over to talk to his colleague, noting as he did so that the look on his colleague's face probably mirrored his own: doubt and budding resentment. "There's no place we can get a coptor in here, Tom," he said. "We'll have to get him down the mountain the hard way, on foot. That leg's not badly broken and he doesn't seem to be in bad shape otherwise, so there's no emergency. Call the coptor and tell him we found Carter; tell him to notify the hospital to get ready for a patient with exhaustion, a broken leg and maybe a little hypothermia. We'll give him a call when we get down, probably tomorrow morning. Tell him to take the coptor in and call it a day. Oh, and tell him to try again to get in touch with Carter's girl friend; she needs to know he's okay." The woman had been strangely inaccessible for the last two days.

He placed his arm around his colleague's shoulder, led him further away from the stretcher then began to speak in a conspiratorial tone. "We'll start down the mountain with Carter. You take the dogs and two men and follow their tracks back as far as you can. I want to know what happened last night. Try to catch up to me by nightfall."

Tom signaled the dogs then took off through the trees with two troopers in tow. The remaining men, heeding Ken's instructions, picked up the stretcher and began the long trip to the valley floor. Creson followed on a leash. The crew, exuberant over the successful conclusion of one of their most baffling rescue missions, carried on an uninterrupted conversation with their recovered target. Ken, even while troubled about the unexplained noise of the previous night and about what he was sure was some kind of cover-up by Carter, could not help but join in. He, like everyone else, was soon in high spirits.

The attention drew Mark's mind away from Creson. The disguised Mantzite was still following meekly behind the column of men, tethered to one of the troopers. There was concern on his canine face, but there was confidence there as well.

"I heard you mention something about telling my girl I was safe," Mark said when Ken was near enough to hear his softened voice. "Did she call you?"

"Only a few times a day. Now we have to tell her you're alive; she'll be devastated." He smiled as he added, "I gotta tell you though, we were about to give up on you. This search wasn't exactly what you'd call average. Weird things have been happening." Reminded of his earlier annoyance, Ken wanted to work the conversation back to the noise of the previous night.

"What did you mean when you told Tom to 'try again.' Isn't...can't you find her?" Mark almost slipped and said "isn't she still in Kelly?" He chuckled inwardly at the reaction that would follow his revealing that he knew Kathy was nearby. And to how he knew, that he was a few thousand light years away and happen to overhear an alien creature mention it.

"Forgot to tell you, your girl's in Kelly." (Mark feigned a look of surprise). "She's been pretty upset about your disappearance, and I've been trying to keep her up-to-date on how we're doing. But for the last two days I haven't been able to get in touch with her. I hope she hasn't come out here looking for you. We'd have to do this all over again."

Mark wondered what this could mean. The Mantzites knew about Kathy, including the fact that she was in Kelly, but there was no reason why they would want to go after her—unless she was considered part of the same problem, requiring the same solution. He twisted his head to where he could look into Creson's eyes. The Mantzite refused to return the stare.

Mark could not stop thinking about Kathy even as he responded again to the men's need for conversation as they carried his stretcher down the mountain. He had never considered that she might be directly involved in this. Had things progressed so far that she was a target as well? And did her current unavailability mean the Mantzites had succeeded?

He was unbelievably tired but new fears for Kathy kept him from succumbing to his body's demand for sleep. For miles he stared with heavily-lidded but alert eyes at the darkened canopy of trees, waiting for the chance to communicate with his alien adversary but afraid of what he might hear.

Tom was baffled. He had expected to follow the tracks of Carter and a dog, but there were only those of two dogs. Try as he may, he could find no evidence of Carter other than what was around the area of the cliff. Nor could he see where the second dog had gone. After a long moment of agonizing he decided to follow the tracks backward and hope something would begin to make sense.

In time he and his two colleagues located the spot where the two dogs had spent at least part of the previous night. The signs showed they had used this place only to rest and, from the looks of things, not for long. Searching further, one of the men found what he had not expected to find: signs of a mountain lion—maybe Carter was telling the truth; maybe that was the sound they'd heard. The tracks showed it had stalked the two dogs then moved swiftly toward them in what had to be a charge. This was followed by a frantic scraping of claws as if it suddenly put itself into reverse.

"Somethin' put thuh fear a God inta this'n," one of the men said. "What would'a done that? It weren't them dogs; thuh lion already knew they was here."

Tom was equally as bothered by what he saw. "Search the area carefully," he said. "Whatever scared him had to be pretty close."

Three pairs of experienced eyes scanned the ground, but they saw only the impressions of two dogs lying in rest, one of which warranted a closer look.

"Don't look natural thuh me," the investigating trooper said to Tom, having noticed the impression of a heavy body—he appreciated the fact that it was too small to be an elephant. The men gathered around and compared one resting spot to the other.

"Yeah, you're right, it don't" Tom said. "The other one shows a normal sized dog; this here's a heap bigger."

They stared at the confusing signs, uneasy with their thought. Finally one felt the need to break the spell. "This is bullshit! We're acting like wet-nosed kids. This here's dog sign; nothin in it says nothing about no giant!"

"Yeah, guess we are a bit jumpy at that," Tom admitted, "what with all the crazy things goin' on. Still..." He did not finish, and no one offered to fill in the gap. In time he shook his lowered head then turned to begin the long walk back to Janos and the crew.

Mark awoke in the dark to a warm fire. He was close enough to it to allow a steady flow of heat to pour over his body. He had no idea how long he had been asleep. Creson was tied to a nearby tree, while off to one side, Ken and the others, which now included Tom, were having a hushed and obviously agitated conversation—Creson was listening to every word they said. Anger grew within Mark as he wondered how far Creson and his colleagues had gone to accommodate their Council's wishes.

"Tell me about Kathy, Spot?" Mark asked, the ice in his projected voice obvious. Where is she now?"

Creson jumped at the unexpected interruption to his concentration but was fully in control as he turned toward Mark. In his expression was something approaching pity. A moment of silence passed before finally he responded with, "She has had an encounter with our people, not quite as profound as that which occurred in your case, but perhaps more than she would have liked. Although unable to communicate at the moment, she is at rest within her hotel room."

Creson's words were not what Mark expected. "How can you know all that?" he asked.

"I know," Creson replied softly.

Mark was greatly relieved but unsure whether he could put stock in what Creson said. He finally decided there would be little reason for the Mantzite to lie. "If she's in her hotel room, why can't these people get hold of her?"

"As I said, she is at rest. To obviate incessant questioning on this matter, I will admit to our having influenced this. Our intent was to render her impotent while weightier matters could be decided."

Mark wanted more details, but Creson had already been drawn back to the rangers, who were still conversing actively. "What are they talking about, Spot?" he asked.

Creson sighed. "They followed our trail back to the place where you did your Jumbo act. They are most disconcerted about what they saw there." He sighed again. "I suppose I should have realized how humans go about measuring such things and done something to obliterate the signs. I do not know how we are going to explain how two dogs became a dog and a man."

Mark relived the foolishness he'd felt the previous night. "How about the elephant tracks?" he asked sheepishly.

"There weren't any; if you recall you did not move. In any event that appears to be less of a problem than I would have imagined. Apparently the human mind can tolerate only so many impossibilities before it begins to bury its uncertainty in rationalization. Such is the case here; they have dismissed the 'elephant' as impossible."

Mark realized the predicament Creson was in. The events of the previous night were weighing heavily upon him. He knew Mark could reveal the truth, including the attempted murder. Maybe he wouldn't cooperate in his own exposure, but it was there. It would be enough to upset the Mantzite's plans.

The thought of exposing him, however, could not have been further from Mark's mind. Seeing these men now, especially how badly they were reacting to the relatively minor things they had thus far come across, he was more convinced than before that he should say nothing. Certainly he should not let them know of the frightening things of which he, a fellow human being, was capable.

Nonetheless, he felt pressured, caught between two unpleasant possibilities. Creson had tried to kill him once and might try to do so again if given the chance. On the other hand, if he opened his mouth, Creson might feel obliged to kill everyone.

The idea of mass extermination did not seem reasonable, however. Even if it were within the Mantzites nature to behave in such a manner, which Mark was convinced it was not, there was no practical way to eliminate so many men and still present it to the world as an accident, especially men heavily experienced in avoiding such pitfalls.

When Creson turned back, he had a look of calm resignation on his face. "You don't look worried," Mark projected.

Creson took pains to hide the smile within him. "There are only two reasons for concern," he replied, careful to avoid projecting to the troopers. "One revolves around my apparent capture, and the other around the possibility of the Mantzite research project being discovered by your fellow creatures. The first is not a real problem, as you well know. I can easily condition this body to permit any rope to pass through. I must admit this would be easier if I had your ability to convert rapidly, but my powers, such as they are, are quite sufficient to permit an escape.

"The second consideration depends not so much upon me as it does upon you, and although I am understandably curious, there is little I wish to do at this point to influence the outcome. Thus I merely wait and see."

"I wonder if you're really as cool as you pretend to be," Mark said with a wry smile. "Well, if it's any consolation, I'm not going to do or say anything without giving it a lot of thought. I'm definitely not going to do anything now, except figure a way to get you out of this mess—for my sake, if not yours. If you just walk away, there'll be talk; these guys are not in the mood to suffer yet another mystery." Mark thought for a moment before adding, "What the hell could I say to them? Somehow I don't think telling them you're an imitation dog and have now returned to your home planet, will do the trick."

"It does appear to present a challenge," Creson said, his eyes contracting briefly.

Another challenge was about to present itself, this time to Creson. One of the dogs, sensing the more relaxed atmosphere of the camp, decided to have a closer look at the new canine. Its approach was cautious but not unfriendly, although it did make Creson nervous. It was a female, and she was interested in the disguised Mantzite as a male. Shy yet determined, she stopped just inches from Creson's canine face then stretched her neck to cover the final distance. Creson could do nothing except respond in kind; too many people were close enough to see. As Mark watched in amusement, dog and Mantzite touched muzzles then the intruder began sniffing Creson's body. In clumsy imitation, Creson did the same—the smile on Mark's face grew. To make matters worse, the other dog, a male, issued a low growl, a sound that did not go unnoticed by Creson.

Creson's head came up sharply. "My heavens," he attempted to project to his unexpected rival, "I had no idea she was yours." The dog, unimpressed by this attempt to placate, raised up on all fours then began to approach the loving couple with something less than friendship in mind. The female pointedly ignored him in favor of continuing her not so subtle investigation, but Creson was anything but unaffected.

Mark was practically laughing. "I think you're about to be in a dogfight, Spot. And over a lady you scarcely know. Would you like me to turn myself into an elephant and kick him in the nuts?"

"Hold it, Otto!" Ken had watched with interest before finally issuing the call. He followed this with a summons to the female—both animals obeyed immediately. Ken had been staring at the new dog, agonizing over what to do with it and puzzled by how unusually quiet it was. All it wanted to do was sit on the ground and stare at Carter. It responded in something close to normalcy when Sarah approached, but was too easily put off by Otto's subsequent challenge. "Doesn't act much like a dog of the wild," he said to Tom. "You'd expect him to be tougher than that. Look at his fur; it's too smooth and too clean for a dog that has to fend for himself."

"I wish I knew what the hell was going on!" Tom exclaimed, "I don't like this, Ken! I don't like it one bit!"

Ken did not like it either. A check with the helicopter earlier had provided no help in clearing things up. Although they searched for hours, they had seen nothing even vaguely resembling a shelter. The men on the ground had no better luck. What little they did discover offered more mystery than answers: more tracks going nowhere.

Ken shot a glance at the guest dog, now staring at the troopers, an expression of concern on its face. So close to human in this expression, the sight did nothing to lessen his uneasiness. "All right, goddamnit," he said to the men around him. "Let's stop acting like a bunch of kids!" He tried to force confidence into his voice, but it came up short. "There's an explanation for all this and it's up to us to figure out what it is."

Ken had not been pleased with Tom's report, it having only confirmed his doubts while increasing his uneasiness. He was sure Carter was holding back, but there seemed little he could do about it—he couldn't *force* the man to come clean. Frustration turned to anger as finally he could stand it no longer. Ignoring the drizzle that had just begun to fall, he rose from the log on which he was sitting then walked in a determined manner over to the man whose life he had just saved. *Damnit, he owes us!* he thought. Rolling another log into position, he sat down with visible determination then fixed his eyes on Mark.

"Now why don't you tell me just what the hell is going on!" he whispered, careful to keep the others out of the conversation.

Mark sensed the trooper's rage and made no attempt to evade the question. "Ken, It's as weird to me as it is to you. I've been confused ever since I found that mutt—and I swear he's the reason I got into this mess." *That, at least, is true,* Mark thought as he glanced over at Creson, noting as he did so that the Mantzite was listening intently to everything he said.

"Bullshit! We have tracks that go nowhere, a noise we can't explain, and your oddball companion over there." He pointed to Creson. "It all involves you. Now damnit, I think the least you owe us is an explanation.

Mark was uncomfortable at the appeal to his rescue, but he knew he could not use this to justify his blowing the whistle on the aliens. "There's really nothing to tell," he replied, the guilt and deception obvious in his voice.

The trooper sighed. "Did you see any other dogs?" he asked patiently, as if talking to a recalcitrant child.

Mark remembered in time that they were already aware of a double set of dog tracks. "Yeah," he answered. "One wondered into our camp last night; didn't stay long though.

"Ken frowned at the explanation, obviously not convinced that he was hearing the truth. "Didn't you think it strange that after all this time another dog just happened to stroll into your camp for a chat?" he asked sarcastically.

The word "chat" caught Mark by surprise; it was too close to the truth. He hoped the ranger did not pick up his reaction. "Ken, this whole damn thing has been strange, even that mountain lion trying to attack an animal he's supposed to be afraid of. I had no control over either dog; I was just glad to have their company. Remember I was lost."

Ken fell silent for a moment, obviously unhappy. "We found two sets of dog tracks but we didn't find yours until later," he said after a while. Then we no sooner find yours when the second set of dog tracks disappears."

Mark was expecting this. "As I said, the stranger didn't stay long. Took a shining to this one here," he nodded toward Creson, "and left with him during the night—I woke up to find them gone. I wasn't too wild about being left alone in the woods, so I took off after them. By the time I caught up, the other one had gone." Mark felt small and dirty at having to fabricate such obvious lies, but the alternative—the truth—was not an option.

Ken shook his head in despair. "You're obviously hiding something, but what I can't understand is why. Are you afraid of something? Is that it? Is there something out there you're afraid to talk about?"

Mark's face hardened. "What are you suggesting?"

"I don't know what I'm suggesting, damnit! I just know there's something vital you're not telling me. If anything's out there, I have to know about it!"

Mark hated the idea of inventing yet more lies. Especially to someone who did not deserve them. Softly and in more of a tone of confidence, he said, "There's nothing out there to be afraid of, Ken. Look, I understand how you feel, but please believe me when I say there's nothing I can tell you that you'd want to hear. It's over, Ken; please believe me, it's over."

Ken stared for a long time trying to read between the lines of what the man on the stretcher was saying. After a while a strange expression appeared on his face, as if he were beginning to wonder whether his charge had suffered mentally as a result of his experience. "You may be right, I might not want to hear it. I do, however, have a responsibility to anyone who visits these forests. I can't simply turn my back on something that spells danger to others regardless of how way-out it might be. I ask you again, is there somebody or something out there that I should know about?"

"No, Ken, there isn't. What happened to me was a mistake; it won't happen again. That's all I can tell you or anyone else—unless you want me to continue making up stories?" The silence returned, this time for a longer period of time. Seeing the anger grown on Ken's face, Mark felt compelled to add, "Ken, I say again, there's nothing out there that you or anybody who visits this place has to worry about. What happened was just a fluke; a screw-up; my screw up. That's it, Ken; that's all of it.

There was another moment of silence before Ken said, "You sure you want to let it go at that."

"I have to, Ken. Nothing else makes as much sense."

The trooper said nothing further, but the harsh look had gone from his face. In time he took a deep breath, then let it out as he raised himself to his feet. There was a moment when he seemed ready to continue the conversation, but then it passed; what more could be said? Mark wondered if he would take the man into his confidence should he persist.

He never found out as Ken turned around then walked without haste back to his colleagues. When they raised expectant looks to him, he merely grumbled, "He doesn't know any more than we do." He was at his bedroll and climbing in before they thought to question further.

The men, each with a pained expression, looked at each other. The subject had been summarily terminated—at least for the moment. Conversation decreased then evaporated altogether as one by one they sought the comfort of their sleeping bags.

It was late. The drizzle had stopped a while back, and three fading campfires were struggling to provide warmth to twenty-three rangers, one rescued camper and three dogs. Of that group only one dog remained awake. It sat royally upright, its paws folded out of sight under its body, out of sight for a reason: they were in the process of changing into Mantzite hands.

As the process unfolded, Creson surveyed the camp for movement. Other than that associated with sleeping, there was none; even the dogs were silent. He had to be silent as well. His plans had to be completed before man or animal was awake enough to respond.

When satisfied that the transformation had been successfully completed, Creson rose and walked out of the makeshift leash that had bound him to the tree. Then he moved over to the backpack, now in the care of the searchers, and began rummaging through it, using Mantzite hands to assist. Fortunately no one had given thought to looking inside—presumed to carry the basics of camping, it held no interest to men who spent most of their life in the outdoors. As he searched, he kept an eye on the two canines, one of which was beginning to move his ears in response to the movement within the camp.

He found then removed the beam device he'd carelessly tossed into the bag after using it to propel Mark off the cliff. Discarding it in that manner had been foolish. Not only was it useless for communication or protection purposes, but had any of the Earth men discovered its presence, drastic action might have been necessary to guard against its misuse. As he worked on the new setting for the beam, one of the dogs raised its head to search out the source of what to it was a suspicious clicking noise. Creson barely had time to aim and fire. The blast was short but it had an immediate effect on the animal: it lay absolutely still, no longer breathing.

The look on Creson's face became one of calm and confidence. There no longer being any doubt about what should be done, he was able execute his business with cold precision. First he fired at the second dog, thus eliminating the threat of its raising an alarm. Then he aimed and fired at each of the sleeping men, sparing only his former charge, Markcarter. In a matter of seconds, it was over, and only he and Mark were still breathing.

CHAPTER 32

When Kathy awoke, she felt an overwhelming sense of comfort and contentment. Her body was completely restored; the fatigue was gone; the trauma as well. Never in her life had she felt so refreshed. She lay in bed, unwilling to move so long as that delicious feeling remained. She even took her time remembering where she was and what she was doing there—such things weren't important, at least not at the moment. Eventually she took notice of the clock. Eight o'clock and dark outside; she must have slept an entire day.

Then she remembered! The feeling vanished in a shot as she bolted upright then fixed her eyes on the floor by the closet. The dog, it was gone! Frantically she searched the bed for the weapon she knew should be there. It was gone as well! Out of bed by now, she raced around the room, hoping she had placed it somewhere else. But it was nowhere to be found; the alien creature had disappeared and taken it with him.

Kathy was beside herself; what did this mean? How would it affect her plan to free Mark?

She cautiously approached the spot where the animal had lain for so long, then noticed the binds and the leash that collectively had held it captive. They were intact, not chewed off or untied but connected exactly as they had been earlier. *What kind of a creature can do that?* she thought, trying to ignore the chill that was creeping up her spine.

Confusion mingled with the fear that was still ruling her emotions. She could not understand why the alien simply went away, why it had not first gotten rid of such a damning witness as herself. Did it think she would hold her tongue, tell no one of its visit? If so it was sadly mistaken; she would say and do anything if it meant getting Mark back. There was, of course, the question of being believed, and as she thought about that, it appeared more and more likely that this was what governed the creature's actions—it probably felt no one would believe her. *They will when I show them the other gun*, she thought, remembering the beam weapon shipped to Sandy.

She picked up the phone and dialed Sandy's home number; the package was still on the way but she wanted him to know it was coming, wanted him to get it to a protected area. What she did not want, at least not yet, was to tell him what it was.

"Sandy? It's Kathy," she said as her friend's familiar bark of hello reached her ears.

"Kathy! Jesus Christ, where the hell have you been? I've been trying to reach you for days!

"Kathy was confused. "What do you mean? We talked not too long ago." She tried to remember exactly when they had last communicated, but last's night's horror had robbed her of all sense of time.

There was a hesitation at the other end. "'Not too long ago'? Kathy, it was two days ago! You been hitting the joy juice or something? No one answered the phone in your room and the desk clerk didn't have any idea where you'd gone. You okay, kid?"

Two days? she thought. Was that possible? "Ah, I guess I've been pushing it a bit hard," she said with great hesitation, "what with worrying about Mark and looking into this Kelly-dog thing. Its possible I was asleep longer than I realized." Not being willing to explain more than that to someone who was like a brother to her made her feel lonely. But revealing too much could torpedo her efforts to bring Mark back.

"Yeah, well take it easy, kid. We don't need you lost too." His voice became subdued as he then asked, "What's new with Mark?"

Kathy was pleased to get off the subject of the missing hours but was disappointed that Sandy had less knowledge of Mark's whereabouts than she. "As I say, I've been asleep," she replied. "I'm a little out of touch. I was hoping you might have something."

"Did you talk to the ranger guy?"

"Not yet, I just woke up. I wanted to give you a call first, mostly to see if you got a package I sent yester ... a little while ago. It was small, sent to your apartment."

"What was in it?"

"In it? Ah, just something I wanted you to hold onto for me." She could almost feel the doubt growing at the other end. "Look, Sandy, some strange things have been happening around here, so strange I don't want to talk about it until I'm sure of my facts. It would just sound too ... weird. The note I sent you will probably sound weird as well, but please just do as it says without asking questions. And please don't open the second box. It could be important in getting Mark back."

"Kathy, what the hell are you talking about? Are you saying Mark was kidnapped or something?"

"No, not exactly."

"What do you mean 'not exactly?' He's either kidnapped or he's not!" Sandy's voice was fast approaching a yell.

"I mean I don't know exactly what happened to him. These crazy disappearing dogs might be tied into it, but I don't know exactly how."

"Kathy, you're not making sense!"

"Well, I don't know how else to put it. Please, Sandy, don't question me on this now. I just got up and my mind's not with it. I might still be living a dream, I don't know!"

Sandy paused for a moment to allow Kathy to calm down. Obviously she was going through some kind of trauma. "Okay, kid, we'll play it your way. But what does Janos think?" He was reluctant to press her, but there was no way he could let it go at that. He had to know what was happening to his friend.

"Last time we talked, he was trying to find more footprints—they apparently lost the ones they were following. But he did say Mark picked up a dog."

"Picked up a dog?"

"Yeah, that's what he said, some dog joined Mark in the woods. Now they're both lost.

"There was another hesitation from Sandy's end. "Is this what set you off about the dogs being part of this?"

Kathy sighed. "Maybe. But I think they might really be connected. I ... I don't think I want to say more than that now, Sandy. As I say, it's a little weird."

Sandy tried to hide his growing concern. Kathy was not making sense. And there was that gap of two days where she'd been completely out of touch. "I'll keep an eye out for that package," he said softly. How long ago did you mail it?"

Kathy looked at her watch. *My God, almost three days*, she thought! "I ... I mailed it three days ago, Sandy."

"Three days? I should've gotten it by now. But from that far away you never know. I'll let you know when it comes. Will you be at your hotel?"

"Or thereabouts. Leave a message at the desk."

They talked a while longer, but the doubt in Sandy's voice remained. Kathy mentally kicked herself for bringing up the subject of the Kelly-dogs. It had only raised questions that she was unable to handle over the telephone, especially now when there was no longer any proof.

As she returned the telephone to its carriage, she thought about the package that had not yet arrived. "Damn!" she said to the empty room. "Suppose it doesn't show up." She wondered whether the aliens had the power to intercept mail. If so, her last edge was gone; she would have nothing to hold over them if they refused to give Mark back. Nothing to keep them from coming after the two of them later on either.

It had all deteriorated so quickly. From a position of power, where she held most if not all of the cards, she now had ... what? She sat on the bed wondering where to go from here. *If I no longer have a prisoner and maybe no longer have a gun, why did they let me live?* The thought was simultaneously encouraging and discouraging. Certainly it was encouraging to still be alive; it might even suggest that the creatures intended no harm—that would speak well for Mark. But it was discouraging to think that they might no longer consider her a threat; that they would permit her to say anything she wished knowing it would not be believed. If that were true, it would follow that they would continue to hold on to Mark, if only to cut down on the number of people telling the same story.

Ken Janos! she thought as she reached for the phone. A few seconds of rapid dialing and she was connected to his office and talking rapidly. "I'm Kathy Montari. Ken Janos said I could call anytime to find out how the search for my friend was going." Even now, she felt awkward at having to say "friend."

"Oh, Ms. Montari!" said a surprised male voice, "we've been trying to get in touch with you for some time!" Kathy sighed at this reminder that she had lost two days of her life. "But maybe it's best we didn't get you. It wasn't good news then; now it is! Your guy's been found! He's all right!" The enthusiasm at the other end was obvious.

The receiver crashed to the bedside table as Kathy's hand opened spasmodically in reaction to the shock—this was not what she'd expected to hear. What was going on? Was this another of the creature's tricks? She grabbed for the fallen phone then asked in a quivering voice, "Are you sure?"

As the confirmation came through, shouted as before, Kathy began to break down. Tears poured onto her checks and raking sobs took over her body. She had feared all was lost, that the call to Janos would only confirmation this. Now Mark was back; he was really back. But why had the aliens let him go?

"Where is he now?" she asked after finding her voice once again.

The patient ranger, delighted with his role as the bearer of good news, understood what she was going through. "Still up the mountains. Has a broken leg—nothing serious, but they have to wait until morning to bring him out; too dangerous to do it in the dark. He'll be taken out by helicopter at first light. Directly to St. John's Hospital in Jackson."

"Can I talk to him now, by radio?"

"Sorry. Too many mountains in the way. We need the helicopter to relay transmissions and it's on the ground for the night. I'll try to set up something first thing in the morning. Will you be in your hotel room?"

"Are you kidding!" Kathy sobbed. "I won't leave my bed!" *Damn!* she thought, aware that the comment could have awkward connotations. Putting it aside, she asked, "When will he arrive at the hospital? I'll want to be there."

There was a pause while the man thought. "Stay in your hotel after you talk to him in the morning. I'll send one of our guys over to give you a lift once we know he's on the way. Hope you don't mind a jeep."

It was many minutes before Kathy stopped crying after hanging up the telephone. She still did not understand what had happened, but it no longer mattered. Mark was alive! And free! She was actually going to see him in the morning; actually going to reach out and touch him. The electricity of anticipation surged through her body at the thought.

But what did the aliens expect of her now? Did they think she would keep quiet? *Probably exactly what they think,* she thought. *After all, a deal's a deal.* But at the moment it was a moot point. In her current mood, she was not in the least interested in crying "Martians" to a disbelieving world. Later she and Mark could discuss what approach, if any, they should take.

She looked forward to the fantastic conversations the two of them would have. It could be that Mark had more to offer than she, but that was far from assured. After all, she knew about and had actually used alien weapons, one of which was still in her possession. *At least I think it's still in my possession,* she thought. She doubted Mark could top that.

It took an inordinate amount of time to contact Sandy, this due to a combination of trembling fingers and an antiquated telephone system, but before long the two friends were crying to one another over a span of some two thousand miles, Kathy unabashedly and Sandy with as much reserve as his masculine pride would permit. Then they talked happily for more than an hour.

Far from being able to sleep, Kathy went to the bar for a badly-needed drink and something to eat. There she took great pleasure in telling everyone of Mark's rescue. She even gave the bartender a big hug, this in appreciation of his unabashed expression of pleasure at hearing of her recovered "friend." Later, in anticipation of a rapid exodus in the morning, she paid her hotel bill then spent the rest of the night packing and re-packing just to keep busy. She chuckled as she picked up the still incomplete article on dog behavior. *What a hell of a story that could be!* she thought.

Suddenly remembering the video recorder, Kathy took the instrument down to the lobby then left it, along with a note, on the unattended hotel desk. The note asked that it be returned to the store in Jackson Hole—a generous bribe was tucked inside. In her excitement, she neglected to remove the tape that had recorded more than four hours of an alien creature's life, including its escape from a small hotel room in the little town of Kelly, Wyoming.

CHAPTER 33

Mark knew immediately that the hand shaking him had only three fingers. As he forced the last vestiges of a troubled sleep from his mind, the picture of Creson presented itself; he was no longer in canine form. For a moment Mark thought he was back in the laboratory on Mantz.

He shook his head to clear away the final dredges of sleep then glanced around the campsite, surprised that Creson would reveal himself with so many witnesses present. Everyone was asleep, the dogs included.

Having succeeded in waking his former captive, Creson turned and walked without haste or concern back to the tree to which he had recently been tied. So blasé was his movement that Mark had to wonder how the Mantzite would handle it if someone awoke at that very moment.

Why weren't the dogs responding to the movement and the noise; Creson was making no attempt to keep it down. Another look at the sleeping figures and Mark had the answer he had refused to consider: the dogs were not moving; they were not even breathing. Frantically he studied the chest of the man closest to him—same thing; no movement; he was no longer alive!

"My God, Spot, how could you!" Mark cried aloud.

Creson turned at the human sound, confused at the vehemence in Markcarter's voice. "I could not take a chance on their coming into consciousness at the wrong moment. I think you might agree that this would be unwise."

"But you didn't have to kill them! What kind of beings are you?"

Creson paused for a second then lowered himself down to where he could lean his back against the tree. The beam weapon he put on his lap within easy reach. For just a moment there, his face had revealed confusion; now there was only a sad smile. "Your comment is justified considering the approach I was obliged to take in your case, but it is essentially untrue. Your fellow Earth creatures have not been harmed in any way. I have merely suspended their life functions."

Mark stared again at the motionless forms, relieved but not altogether convinced. When he turned back to Creson, he wondered what the Mantzite had in mind. Was he picking up where they left off on the cliff? "If you kill me now you'll bring about an investigation that'll never end!"

Creson lowered his head as if to escape the bitterness of the comment. His expression became one of shame, which did nothing to calm Mark's re-emerging fears. "With regard to that incident, there are two things which I deeply regret: the decision of the Council to cover up our error at your expense, and my obvious willingness to follow through on it. In the first instance, as I stated previously, the Council acted in a most atypical manner. Their decision shocked me, as much for that reason as for the horror of the act itself."

As he spoke two other Mantzites, neither of whom Mark knew, came into sight and stood by him, the three of them together suggesting a kangaroo court with the Earth man as the guilty party. Mark's discomfort grew.

"As regards the second instance," Creson continued, a pained expression on his alien face. "I had always considered myself a pacifist, one who could do no serious harm to another intelligent being under any circumstances. Regretfully, recent actions proved I am no better than the worst of us; that I can, and obviously will, rationalize even the most horrible of acts rather than stand by my principles and refuse to execute them. I suffer shame and depression over the realization of this weakness in myself."

At that he fell into silence, bringing Mark to wish he could think of something to say to break his mood—Creson really was likable at times. The two newcomers stood respectfully by on either side of their superior, neither appearing to be interested in the conversation. When Creson felt composed enough to continue, he said, "It is necessary to my well being that you understand something; after the first fiasco, and seeing you in serious injury, injury brought about by me, I made a decision to no longer cooperate in the fulfillment of my orders. I will never again act in such a cruel and uncivilized manner, regardless of how such intractability might affect the remainder of my career."

Mark was not sure what Creson was telling him. Was he calling off the execution or was he only passing the buck to the two newcomers, forcing them to do the job for him?

Seeing the confused look on Mark's face, Creson quickly added, "You will not be harmed in any way. You will be permitted to go with these people in peace."

Mark focused on the patiently-waiting Mantzite, his eyes blinking in uncertainty. "I don't understand," he said after a pause.

"You rarely do, but that seems to be a problem inherent in your species," Creson retorted, pleased to have an opportunity to return to the banter which had been so much a part of his relationship with this human.

Without realizing he was doing it, Mark reverted to mind-to-mind communication. "If you're letting me go, why go through all this?" He spread his hands to indicate the campsite and its temporarily paralyzed occupants.

"I thought it might be nice if we had a farewell chat without the fear of interruption. These humans, and even my fellow canines, will be restored as they were with no idea that anything out of the ordinary occurred—unless you tell them, of course. We will, by that time, be on our way back to our own planet. Undoubtedly the female canine will spend time in depression over the loss of such a magnificent specimen as I, but that cannot be helped."

Mark chuckled. "I'll try to console her," he retorted. "But what about the Council? And your orders?"

"As I predicted, the Council now admits to a serious judgmental error. Accordingly, they have reversed themselves with regard to their previously untouchable idea of when a targeted planet should be contacted. As an incidental side benefit of this, they have also changed their collective minds concerning the disposition of your case. These two gentlemen have come a long way to bring this information to me." Creson lowered his head as he added, "The Council asks that you accept their apology and trusts you have suffered no inconvenience."

"Inconvenience!" shouted Mark, once more converting to voice. "They call trying to kill me 'suffering an inconvenience?'"

"Yes, I know how you feel," conceded Creson, "but you must understand that we are, as a species, more in control of our emotions than you. We are inclined toward practicality, and at the time it seemed the only practical thing to do."

"But you said yourself that they acted out of anger at having been disobeyed."

"Actually more out of disappointment at a serious mistake having happened in the first place—I suspect that they consider this primarily my mistake. But your point is well taken; emotions did enter into that decision."

"What about the cover up," Mark asked.

"They have apparently accepted Takar's explanation that it would have been illogical to alarm Council members prematurely. Better to wait until a solution is ready for recommendation. Unusual in a way; generally they take unforgiving exception to even the best of intentions if it is in conflict with their idea of the order of things. In this case, perhaps due to their embarrassment over what they, in their manner, admit to being a bad decision, they have 'looked the other way,' as you Earth creatures might say. Indeed, so many mistakes have been made, involving so many parties, it is probably the only civilized thing to do."

For a number of seconds, no one spoke, Mark getting used to the idea that the Mantzites were going to let him go in peace—for real this time—and Creson permitting him the privacy of his thoughts. Finally Mark broke the silence by asking, "Did I hear you say you're going to make formal contact with Earth?"

"As usual your comments are wrought with error," Creson retorted. "Firstly, since I am communicating telepathically, you technically 'heard' nothing..."

"Oh, for Christ's sake!"

"...Secondly, I believe I 'said' 'should it become necessary.' That is to say communication is authorized if you bring about the conditions which make it prudent that we act in a timely manner to do so. Actually, we would prefer you do not."

"I don't get it."

Creson deliberately sighed before saying, "Banter with you could cease to be entertaining if you continue to give me so many openings. Do try to be more careful." He moved on quickly to give Mark no room to respond, "We realize that you, and incidentally your mate as well, have the power to cause premature contact between our species. Should either of you choose to reveal what has happened over the last few Earth weeks, practically speaking we would have little choice but to begin some form of contact—our Council to yours, so to speak."

Mark was surprised to hear Kathy mentioned in that vein but elected to hold comment for the moment. "Would that be so bad?" he asked softly.

"Not 'bad' so much as unfortunate; bad timing, as it were. We are not ready, and neither are you, and that, we have found from painful experience, has the potential for disaster. Much understanding is necessary before an introduction of this magnitude—so complicated and so emotion-generating—can be successfully brought about. Decades of dedicated work must first take place, decades in which we study your species in depth and through this gain an understanding of your problems, fears, prejudices, needs, goals, aspirations, capabilities. Deprived of this time, we will be less able to be of service, like a builder of bridges who has not had time to investigate the soundness of the rock on which he intends to place his supports.

"Also to be considered, and as you know, we take this quite seriously, we would risk endangering ourselves. You might have capabilities which, if employed by uncivilized individuals, would cause harm to our planet or to our people. Or, through us, to others in the galaxy."

"I take it you're trying to sell me on the idea of keeping my mouth shut," Mark said, more of a statement than a question.

"And your mind as well. Do not forget you now have the capability of communicating mentally."

Mark thought about it for a moment, then said, "I can tell you this much: I understand the situation—pretty well I think—and that includes your fears as well as your goals. And as you might have noticed by my conduct in front of the troopers, I have no intention of just blurting it all out. It's more than just being afraid nobody will believe me; if I understand you correctly, if I tell all, you'd back me up with formal contact anyway."

"Essentially correct," said Creson.

"But, and you might be surprised to hear this, I've been thinking about how my fellow ... creatures ... might react to a careless mention of you. They'll see, not what I see, but monsters."

"I beg your pardon!"

"That's the first reaction people will have; they'll be scared shitless. Take these troopers, for example. Just the hint of something odd has made them walking goose pimples."

"Goose pimples...?"

"An Earth expression; it means they're scared. Anyway, I recognize how much everyone's life and beliefs will be turned upside down by the fact of your existence—not to mention the existence of all the other creatures out there. I don't want to be the one to do that. On the personal side, I can only imagine the reaction I'd get if I suddenly turned myself into an elephant.

"My point is, I'm a believer. Enough of one that you needn't worry;

I'll be keeping it to myself—or almost to myself; I'll tell Kathy when the time is right. Which reminds me, what did you mean when you said Kathy could also reveal your presence; what does she know about all this?"

An enigmatic smile crossed Creson's face. "I think you will find she has an interesting story to tell. Indeed, I believe your mate is convinced that she forced our hand in granting your release—you might have a problem living that down. However, I leave further explanations to her."

Mark was more confused than informed, but Creson was not willing to explain further. Indeed, he appeared to relish his former captive's dilemma.

"I accept your assurances," the Mantzite said, returning to the previous subject, "although I must confess some apprehension as regards a possible lapse of reticence as time goes on. However, since we cannot, or at least will not, act to prevent it, we must simply learn to live with it. We will, of course, monitor the results carefully and be ready to jump in, so to speak, when the felis catus is let out of the bag."

Mark's interest perked at the possibility of further contact. "How are you going to do that, monitor us, I mean?"

Creson knew of the subtle implants that his scouts had recently placed into the bodies of Mark Carter and his mate, but considering the inevitable objections this would provoke, he could not so much as hint of it. "Not difficult, actually," he said. "We will simply act as we did before; our people will continue to explore and investigate. As you know we have large numbers of such explorers currently mingling with representative of your species—without detection, I might add. Should this situation change, should humans become aware of our presence, we will know about it soon enough."

"Well maybe there won't be a problem," Mark said with sincerity. "I'll do my best to allow you the time you need." As he continued to stare at his Mantzite companion, Mark felt a sense of impending loss. "Will I ever see you again?" he asked softly.

"Perhaps," came the projected reply. "I do not know what the decision of the Council will be in that regard, but if it is at all possible I will be in touch." He paused before adding, "If I do see you again, I promise not to try to kill you."

"It's a deal," Mark said with a smile, realizing not for the first time how much he liked this alien creature.

Creson stood up, retrieved his pack and handed it to Mark. "You may keep this if you wish. Regretfully, I cannot leave you with more than that; certainly you can see how unwise that would be. I suggest, in the event you finally realize you have the power, that you not suddenly heal your broken leg. It would likely cause a stir among your already nervous colleagues."

Mark paused to consider this. He was not aware that he could heal a damaged body. Or that it was even possible. He decided to examine his memory in close detail later on, for this and anything else that might be hidden there.

"I am leaving now," Creson said. After I am safely away, we will remotely revive the troopers and their animals, although they will likely continue their sleep. Profiting from what we now know to be mistakes, I have chewed through my leash to permit your fellow creatures a more acceptable explanation for my escape. We will also erase the better part of our tracks and, of course, revise our policy of selecting a single disguise for all explorers—the Kelly-dog mystery will soon fade into oblivion."

At that, he turned and began walking out of camp, looking as usual as if he were about to begin a marathon. But then, at the outskirts, he hesitated and turned to face Mark once more. "Good-bye, Jumbo," he projected in a soft image.

"Take care, Spot," Mark responded, equally subdued.

They stared at one another for a long moment before Creson turned again and walked into the woods, more slowly this time. His two companions followed closely behind, carefully obliterating their tracks as they walked. Mark watched until he could neither see nor hear them any longer.

An empty feeling began to invade both his mind and his body. True it was all over; true that he was safe and would not have to fear being forcibly silenced at some later date. True that he was a partner of sorts, an accomplice in developing just the right conditions for an Earth/Mantz relationship, whatever that might turn out to be. Yet it was hard to overcome the regret, the sadness, the loss, the yearning for some kind of continuance. Something incredibly vivid had come to an end; the most fantastic experience of his life was fast becoming history. *I wonder if I know how to turn that transporter on,* he thought, lying back with his hands propped on his head, unable to sleep and not caring.

Within minutes, the animals and the sleeping troopers began to breathe. Mark was relieved but not surprised. The dog that had previously appeared close to waking at Creson's movements, raised its head, took a fast look around, saw nothing to excite its curiosity, then willingly returned to its rest. Seeing it all, Mark merely smiled. With the sound of humans sleeping, the gentle crackling of the fire, and the nocturnal mumbling of the forest and its unseen creatures, the camp had returned to normal. It was good to be back in familiar surroundings, Earth surroundings, and he lay awake for hours enjoying it all.

Tom was the first to notice that Mark's dog had escaped. After examining the chewed up leash, he shook his head in disgust, although there was an equal amount of relief in his expression. "Hey, Ken," he yelled, "The dog got away; chewed clean through his leash and lit out."

Ken Janos also felt relief. "I thought the people in Kelly said they walked out of their leashes, that the leashes were still buckled up when they found them?"

"Yeah, that's what I been told too, but ya know how these stories get twisted around. You want me to track um?"

"Fuck no!" Ken yelled. "We might find he turned into an elephant!"

Tom laughed, but it was obvious how little inclined he was to press the matter.

Mark was carried the rest of the way down the mountain to a clearing large enough to permit the helicopter to land—it was there by the time they arrived. After seeing that Mark was safely tucked into the back, Ken ordered the pilot to patch a call to Kathy Montari in her hotel room in Kelly. After only a few minutes the excited young woman was on the phone.

"Kathy? Ken Janos. Thought you might like to know we have a soggy ex-woodsman here who claims he knows you."

Kathy was in tears even before Ken passed the microphone back to Mark. The sound of Mark's voice only increased the flow.

"Sorry I didn't call, babe, but I was sort of busy."

"Oh, Mark, you bastard," she cried in joy. "Are you all right?"

"As they said, just a little soggy."

"I was so worried. Oh, Mark I love you so much!"

"Uh, Kathy, they're a lot of weird characters listening in on this conversation. Keep it clean."

"I don't care Mark. I want you here now."

They talked for a number of minutes, the pilot and Ken both content to permit usage of the radio for this purpose. Everyone was elated, and although pretending a willingness to give Mark privacy, they hung on every word. This was part of the reward of concluding a search successfully.

"I better give up this phone now, babe. We'll talk at the hospital." His voice dropped a bit as he added, "I suspect we both have a lot to talk about." Janos shot him a curious look, but said nothing.

He surrendered the microphone then, as the helicopter fired up, shouted affectionate thanks and good-byes to his rescuers. Seconds later he was in the air and on his way to the hospital in Jackson. Staring at the swiftly-passing woods far below, he tried to imagine where the transporter began and where Spot was at that very moment. The feeling of having lost something of great value regained a foothold in his stomach.

It's as if I've known these creatures for a lifetime, he thought. *Wilpin, I know him; I was him. Those others whose lives I shared, who, without knowing they were doing it, taught me so much, they're part of me too; they're kin. And now they're all gone.*

But the restless feeling that had propelled him into this adventure was gone as well, forced out by the monumental events of the last few weeks. *What a way to cure the blues,* he thought. *And what a hell of a place to spend a vacation!*

He stared at the vanishing woodland until it was only a distant blur. Then he turned from the window, surrendered a big sigh and lay back against the cushions to rest.

E P I L O G U E

Inches from his television set and watching with the usual intensity of the young, the thirteen-year-old boy was entertained but confused—to say that the video recording was unusual was an understatement. But heck, it was a "freebie;" how could he complain.

Whoever had rented the camera earlier had forgotten to recover their tape cartridge. Judging from the text, they had recorded a science fiction movie, although so far, it was the worst one he had ever seen. For the longest time, there was only an across-the-room shot of a sleeping dog and some nice-looking lady walking back and forth like she didn't know what she was supposed to be doing—she was interesting in a way he didn't understand, but she was less important to him at the moment than seeing some kind of action. He had passed through the rest of this section quickly, almost giving it up entirely when it persisted for close to half the tape.

At the last minute, the action he'd been hoping for began. The dog, which was not a dog at all but part human—the human part being limited to three-fingered hands—began walking upright like a man as it moved toward the chair where the female star had fallen asleep.

The boy's slowly emerging hormones awakened again; even with her head dipped down to her chest in sleep, the lady looked pretty—a bit soft for his tastes, but still pretty. More important in his mind, however, was the half-dog/half-human. It grabbed a ray gun from the lady's lap then zapped her in such a way that she floated through the air to the bed—neat! The boy perked up considerably, now anticipating the best of both his young worlds: great action and interstellar sex, something he would be prevented from seeing if his mom or dad knew he had this tape.

Another disappointment! The ray gun disappeared into a secret pouch inside the creatures body and the three-fingered hands changed back into paws, but after that it got down on all fours and went back to pretending it was a regular Earth dog—what happened to the sex!? The way it left was neat though; after taking a quick look around, it walked over to the door then right through it.

He waited for more, but the movie returned to the same jerky stuff he'd suffered at the beginning—what a stupid movie! Sure that nothing more of interest was there, he gave up in disgust, rewound the tape then placed it back into his father's rented camera—enough time had been wasted. Grabbing his ski jacket, he then hurried out to film the more exciting atmosphere of Jackson Hole, Wyoming.

Mark and Kathy worked quietly, content with what each was doing and in the knowledge that the other was nearby. The baby was due shortly and Mark looked forward to its coming. Every now and then he projected an image of contentment to what he hoped was a receiving fetus. Each time Kathy would smile. She easily received these transmissions and had even learned to make herself known, at least partially, in the same manner. She looked forward to learning more, assuming Mark ever figured out how to explain the procedure. It was difficult, and she understood why, but she knew he would make it happen some day. Then the child would participate as well.

The two lovers, now husband and wife, had shared their respective Mantz experiences, holding back nothing. Mark understood and accepted what happened to Kathy, but he had trouble getting her to understand and accept what happened to him. It took time and much patient explaining to make her a believer. Some of it was fun, but even so Mark appreciated the necessity to take it slow. He preceded each demonstration with an exact explanation of what would happen—it was one thing to tell someone you were going to walk through a wall and quite another to actually do it. Even so, he occasionally toyed with the idea of popping his head through a wall and yelling, "I'm home."

Conversion of body genes had been held until last. After doing his best to get Kathy prepared then driving her far enough out in the country to permit the expected reaction to go unseen and unheard, he changed himself into a dog. His precaution proved wise as Kathy turned sheet white then collapsed into a faint. In retrospect, he realized a light-colored, German shepherd was a bad choice.

After that episode, Mark took it even more slowly, explaining everything in detail then waiting until the shock of each demonstration had faded before risking another. In time Kathy not only accepted his new skills but found them enjoyable to watch. It was a game, one in which she might someday be able to participate.

Married shortly before Kathy knew she was pregnant, both were now looking forward to what they could teach the baby. Although lacking the more complicated skills, Kathy was on the verge of conquering the concept of mental communication—she improved by the day. She could also control the release of scattered thoughts. Mark had worked hard with her on that, recognizing the danger one-sided mind-reading could present to his marriage.

Mark never gave up the idea of someday recontacting the Mantzites. And specifically Spot. Although nervous about the idea, Kathy shared his interest. Neither had much hope of its ever happening, or at least of its happening quickly, but they were determined to teach their child enough to make contact with him or her desirable to the Mantzites.

"Me Tarzan, you Jane," Mark projected suddenly.

In return, Kathy communicated not so much a statement as an image. But the result was the same: the couple moved into the bedroom.

* * * *

As they lay beneath covers, spent by love making, Me-too quietly entered the room then lay down in a corner. For a moment he watched the couple with affectionate eyes, but then he lowered his head to his paws and began to daydream. After a while, and for a brief moment only, a broad smile crossed his muzzle and his pupils contracted in pleasure.

End

ALSO BY NOEL CARROLL

CIRCLE OF DISTRUST

The superb, tense and gripping tale of Clay Iverson, a brilliant 27 year old engineer, who takes his company's top secret listening device out for a little fun--a lark that plummets him into the midst of a conspiracy that threatens not only his life but that of his lover, Shelly. Overhearing two men in a blimp testing mind-numbing electronics on an unsuspecting crowd of revelers, he turns to Shelly for help. But their cautious inquiries bring swift and terrible retribution, as Clay and Shelly soon find themselves fleeing from Clay's own mysterious and unscrupulous company, fleeing from the FBI... and on the very wrong side of a murderous Black Moslem group.

ISBN: 1-928781-03-9

Hardcover
Published by Hollis Books